EVERYONE AGREED THAT THE

The rescue blasting had been ab[...]
as the nineteenth-century Krakat[...]
ash and rock were pumped into t[...]

When it came down dry, it was like gray-brown snow, piling obscene drifts on houses and trees and the bodies of small animals. Even the sea had a layer of scum on it.

At the center of this vast lake sat a perfect sphere, the bobble. Glowing orange-red peeked through netted cracks in the scab. Of course, nothing marred its surface. A typical bobble, in an untypical place.

In a few months, the molten lake would freeze over, and an unprotected man could walk right to the side of the Peacer bobble. For a few years there would be brilliant sunsets and unusually cool weather. In a century or two, nature would have forgotten this affront, and the Peacer bobble would reflect forest green.

Yet it would be unknown thousands of years before the bobble burst, and the men and women within could join the colony.

As usual, the Korolevs had a plan.

"*Marooned in Realtime* combines the expansive mode of hard SF with the narrow focus of the detective story, complete with a final orchestrated showdown. The result is exciting; you can hardly turn the pages fast enough."

—*Locus*

Books by Vernor Vinge

Tatja Grimm's World
The Witling
*The Peace War
*Marooned in Realtime
True Names and Other Dangers (collection)
Threats . . . and Other Promises (collection)

Across Realtime
Comprising:
The Peace War
"The Ungoverned"
Marooned in Realtime

*A Fire Upon the Deep
*A Deepness in the Sky
*True Names and the Opening of the Cyberspace Frontier
*The Collected Stories of Vernor Vinge

*Available from Tor Books

VERNOR VINGE

MAROONED
IN REALTIME

TOR®

A TOM DOHERTY ASSOCIATES BOOK
NEW YORK

MAROONED IN REALTIME

Copyright © 1986 by Vernor Vinge

Originally published in 1986 by Bluejay Books, Inc.

Edited by James Frenkel

A Tor Book
Published by Tom Doherty Associates, LLC
175 Fifth Avenue
New York, NY 10010

www.tor.com

Tor® is a registered trademark of Tom Doherty Associates, LLC.

ISBN 0-765-30884-3

EAN 978-0765-30884-9

First Tor Paperback Edition: October 2004

Printed in the United States of America

0 9 8 7 6 5 4 3 2 1

To all those Marooned without hope of rescue

I am grateful to:
Mike Gannis for many super ideas related to this story;
Sara Baase, John L. Carroll, Howard Davidson, Jim
Frenkel, Dipak Gupta, Jay Hill, Sharon Jarvis, and Joan
D. Vinge for all their help and suggestions.

Other people have created zoologies and/or geographies of the future. Though they are different from what is described in this story, they are wonderfully interesting:

Dougal Dixon, *After Man,* St. Martin's Press, New York, 1981.

Christopher Scotese and Alfred Ziegler, as described in "The Shape of Tomorrow," by Dennis Overbye, *Discover,* November, 1982, pp. 20–25.

MAROONED
IN REALTIME

ONE

On the day of the big rescue, Wil Brierson took a walk on the beach. Surely this was one afternoon when it would be totally empty.

The sky was clear, but the usual sea mist kept visibility to a few kilometers. The beach, the low dunes, the sea—all were closed in by faint haze that seemed centered on his viewpoint. Wil moped along just beyond the waves, where the water soaked the sand flat and cool. His ninety-kilo tread left perfect barefoot images trailing behind. Wil ignored the sea birds that skirled about. He walked head down, watching the water ooze up around his toes at every step. A humid breeze carried the smell of seaweed, sharp and pleasant. Every half minute the waves peaked and clear sea water flooded around his ankles. Except during storms, this was all the "surf" one ever saw on the Inland Sea. Walking like this, he could almost imagine that he was back by Lake Michigan, so long ago. Every summer, he and Virginia had camped on the lakeshore. Almost, he could imagine that he was returning from a noontime stroll on some very muggy Michigan day, and that if he walked far enough he would find Virginia and Anne and Billy waiting impatiently around the campfire, teasing him for going off alone.

Almost . . .

1

Wil looked up. Thirty meters further on was the cause of all the seabird clamor. A tribe of fishermonkeys was playing at water's edge. The monkeys must have noticed him by now. In past weeks, they would have disappeared into the sea at the first sight of human or machine. Now they stayed ashore. As he approached, the younger ones waddled toward him. Wil went to one knee and they crowded round, their webbed fingers searching curiously at his pockets. One removed a data card. Wil grinned, tugged the card from the monkey's grasp. "Aha! A pickpocket. You're under arrest!"

"Forever the policeman, eh, Inspector?" The voice was feminine, the tone light. It came from somewhere over his head. Wil leaned back. A remote-controlled flier hung just a few meters above him.

He grinned. "Just keeping in practice. Is that you, Marta? I thought you were preparing for this evening's 'festivities.'"

"I am. And part of the preparation is to get foolish people off the beach. The fireworks won't wait till night."

"What?"

"That Steve Fraley—he's making a big scene, trying to argue Yelén into postponing the rescue. She's decided to do it a little early, just to let Steve know who's boss." Marta laughed. Wil couldn't tell if her amusement was directed at Yelén Korolev's irritation or at Fraley. "So please to move your tail, sir. I have some other people to harass yet. I expect you back in town before this flier."

"Yes, ma'am!" Wil gave a mock salute and turned to jog back the way he had come. He had gone about thirty meters when a banshee shriek erupted behind him. He glanced over his shoulder and saw the flier diving in the other direction, lights flashing, sirens blaring. Against that assault, the new-found sophistication of the fishermonkeys dissolved. They panicked, and with the screaming flier between them and the sea their only choice was to grab the kids and scramble up into the dunes. Marta's flier followed, dropping noise bombs on either side of them. Flier and monkeys disappeared over the top of the sand into the jungle, and the noise faded. Wil wondered briefly how far Marta would have to chase them to get them into a safe area. He knew she was equal parts softheartedness and practicality. She'd never scare the animals away from the beach unless there was some chance they could make it to safe haven. Wil smiled to himself. He wouldn't be surprised if Marta had chosen the season and the day of the blow-off to minimize deaths to wildlife.

Three minutes later, Brierson was near the top of the rickety stairs that led to the monorail. He looked down and saw that he hadn't been the only person on the beach. Someone was strolling toward the base of the stairway. Over half a million centuries, the Korolevs had rescued or recruited quite a collection of weirds, but at least they all *looked* fairly normal. This . . . person . . . was different. The stranger carried a variable parasol, and was naked except for a loincloth and shoulder purse. His skin was pale, pasty. As he started up the stairs, the parasol tilted back to reveal a hairless, egglike head. And Wil saw that the stranger might just as well be a she (or an it). The creature was short and slender, its movements delicate. There were faint swellings around its nipples.

Brierson waved hesitantly; it was good policy to meet all the new neighbors, especially the advanced travelers. But then it looked up at Brierson, and even across twenty meters those dark eyes penetrated with cold indifference. The small mouth twitched, but no words came. Wil swallowed and turned to continue up the plastic stairs. There might be some neighbors it was better to learn of secondhand.

Korolev. That was the official name of the town (as officially named by Yelén Korolev). There were almost as many rival names as there were inhabitants. Wil's Indian friends wanted to call it Newest Delhi. The government (in irrevocable exile) of New Mexico wanted to call it New Albuquerque. Optimists liked Second Chance, pessimists Last Chance. For megalomaniacs it was the Great Urb.

Whatever its name, the town nestled in the foothills of the Indonesian Alps, high enough so that equatorial heat and humidity was moderated to an almost uniform pleasantness. Here the Korolevs and their friends had finally assembled the res-

cued from all the ages. Almost everyone's architectural taste
had been catered to. The New Mexican statists had a main
street lined with large (mostly empty) buildings that Wil
thought epitomized their bureaucracy. Most others from the
twenty-first century—Wil included—lived in small groups of
homes very like those they'd known before. The advanced
travelers lived higher in the mountains.

Town Korolev was built on a scale to accommodate thousands. At the moment the population was less than two hundred, every living human being. They needed more; Yelén
Korolev knew where to get one hundred more. She was determined to rescue them.

Steven Fraley, President of the Republic of New Mexico,
was determined that those hundred remain unrescued. He was
still arguing the case when Brierson arrived. ". . . and you don't
appreciate the history of our era, madam. The Peacers came
near to exterminating the human race. Sure, saving this group
will get you a few more warm bodies, but you risk the survival
of our whole colony, of the entire human race, in doing so."

Yelén Korolev looked calm, but Wil knew her well enough
to recognize the signs of an impending explosion: there were
rosy patches on her cheeks, yet her features were otherwise
even paler than usual. She ran a hand through her blond hair.
"Mr. Fraley, I really do know the history of your era. Remember that almost all of us—no matter what our present age and
experience—have our childhoods within a couple hundred
years of one another. The Peace Authority"—her lips twitched
in a quick smile at the name—"may have started the general
war of 1997. They may even be responsible for the terrible
plagues of the early twenty-first century. But as governments
go, they were relatively benign. This group in Kampuchea"—
she waved toward the north—"went into stasis in 2048, when
the Peacers were overthrown. That was before decent health
care was available. It's entirely possible that none of the original criminals are present."

Fraley opened and closed his mouth, but no words came.
Finally: "Haven't you heard of their 'Renaissance' scheme? In
'48 they were ready to kill by the millions again. Those guys

under Kampuchea probably got more hell-bombs than a dog has fleas. That base was their secret ace in the hole. If they hadn't screwed up their stasis, they'd've come out in 2100 and blown us away. And you probably wouldn't even have been born—"

Yelén cut into the torrent. "Hell-bombs? Popguns. Even you know that. Mr. Fraley, getting another hundred people into our colony will make our settlement just big enough to survive. Marta and I haven't spent our lives setting this up just to see it die like the undermanned attempts of the past. The only reason we postponed the founding of Korolev till megayear fifty was so we could rescue those Peacers when their bobble bursts."

She turned to her partner. "Is everybody accounted for?"

Marta Korolev had sat through the argument in silence, her dark features relaxed, her eyes closed. Her headband put her in communication with the estate's autonomous devices. No doubt she had managed a half dozen fliers during the last half hour, scouring the countryside for any truant colonists the Korolev satellites had spotted. Now she opened her eyes. "Everybody's accounted for and safe. In fact"—she caught sight of Wil standing at the back of the amphitheater and grinned —"almost everyone is here on the castle grounds. I think we can provide you people with quite a show this afternoon." She either hadn't followed or—more likely—had chosen to ignore the dispute between Yelén and Fraley.

"Okay, let's get started." A rustle of anticipation passed through the audience. Many were from the twenty-first century, like Wil. But they'd seen enough of the advanced travelers to know that such a statement was more than enough signal for spectacular events to happen.

From his place at the top of the amphitheater, Wil had a good view to the north. The forests of the higher elevations fell away to a gray-green blur that was the equatorial jungle. Beyond that, haze obscured even the existence of the Inland Sea. Even on the rare, clear day when the sea mists lifted, the Kampuchean Alps were hidden beyond the horizon. Nevertheless, the rescue should be visible; he was a bit surprised that the bluish white of the northern horizon was undisturbed.

"Things will get more exciting, I promise." Yelén's voice brought his eyes back to the stage. Two large displays floated behind her. They made an incongruous contrast with the moss- and gold-encrusted temple that covered the land beyond the stage. Castle Korolev was typical of the flamboyance of the advanced residences. The underlying stonework and statuary— modeled vaguely on Angkor Wat—had been built half a thou- sand years earlier, then left for mountain rains to wear at, for moss to cover, for trees to penetrate. Afterwards, construction robots hid all the subtle machinery of late twenty-second-cen- tury technology within the "ruins." Will respected that tech- nology. Here was a place where no sparrow could fall un- remarked. The owners were as safe from a quiet knife in the back as from a ballistic missile attack.

"As Mr. Fraley says, the Peacer bobble was supposed to be a secret. It was originally underground. It is much further underground now—somebody blundered. What was to be a fifty-year jump became something . . . longer. As near as we can figure, their bobble should burst sometime in the next few thousand years; they've been in stasis fifty million years. During that time, continents drifted and new rifts formed. Parts of Kampuchea slid deep beneath new mountains." The display behind her lit with a multicolored transect of the Kampuchean Alps. The surface crust appeared as blue, shading into yellow and orange at the greater depths. Right at the margin of orange and magma red was a tiny black disk—the Peacer bobble, afloat against the ceiling of hell.

Inside the bobble, time was stopped. Those within were as they'd been at that instant of a near-forgotten war when the losers decided to escape to the future. No force could affect a bobble's contents; no force could affect its duration—not the heart of a star, not the heart of a lover.

But when the bobble burst, when the stasis ended . . . The Peacers were about forty kilometers down. There would be a moment of noise and heat and pain as the magma swallowed them. One hundred men and women would die, and a certain endangered species would move one more step toward final extinction.

The Korolevs proposed to raise the bobble to the surface, where it would be safe for the few remaining millennia of its duration. Yelén waved at the display. "This was taken just before we started the operation. Here's the ongoing view."

The picture flickered. The red magma boundary had risen thousands of meters above the bobble. Pinheads of white light flashed in the orange and yellow that represented the solid crust. In the place of each of those lights, red blossomed and spread, almost—Wil winced at the thought—like blood from a stab wound. "Each of those sparkles is a hundred-megaton bomb. In the last few seconds, we've released more energy than all mankind's wars put together."

The red spread as the wounds coalesced into a vast hemorrhage in the bosom of Kampuchea. The magma was still twenty kilometers below ground level. The bombs were timed so there was a constant sparkling just above the highest level of red, bringing the melt closer and closer to the surface. At the bottom of the display, the Peacer bobble floated, serene and untouched. On this scale, its motion towards the surface was imperceptible.

Wil pulled his attention from the display and looked beyond the amphitheater. There was no change: the northern horizon was still haze and pale blue. The rescue site was fifteen hundred kilometers away, but even so, he'd expected something spectacular. The minutes passed. A cool breeze swept slow around the theater, rustling the almost-jacarandas that bounded the stage, sending the perfume of their large flowers across the audience. A family of spiders in one tree had built a for-show web in its upper branches. The web silk gleamed in rainbow colors against the sky.

The elapsed-time clock on the display showed almost four minutes. The Korolev pattern of bomb bursts was still thousands of meters short of the surface.

President Fraley rose from his seat. "Madame Korolev, please. There is still time to stop this. I know you've rescued all types, cranks, joyriders, criminals, victims. But these are *monsters.*" For once, Wil thought he heard sincerity—perhaps even fear—in the New Mexican's voice. *And he might be right.* If the rumors were true, if the Peacers had created the plagues of the early twenty-first century, then they were responsible for the deaths of billions. If they had succeeded with their Renaissance Project, they would have killed most of the survivors.

Yelén Korolev glanced down at Fraley but didn't reply. The New Mexican stiffened, then waved abruptly to his people. One hundred men and women—most in NM fatigues—came quickly to their feet. It was a dramatic gesture, if nothing else: the amphitheater would be almost empty with them gone.

"Mr. President, I suggest you and the others sit back down." It was Marta Korolev. Her tone was as pleasant as ever, but the insult in the words brought a flush to Steve Fraley's face. He gestured angrily and turned to the stone steps that led from the theater.

Wil was more inclined to take her words literally: Yelén might use sarcasm and imperious authority, but Marta usually meant her advice only to help. He looked again to the north. Over the jungle slopes there was a wavering, a rippling. *Oops.* With sudden understanding, Wil slid onto a nearby bench.

The ground shock arrived an instant later. It was a soundless, rolling motion that took Fraley's feet right out from under him. Steve's lieutenants quickly helped him up, but the man was livid. He glared death at Marta, then stomped quickly—and carefully—up the steps. He didn't notice Wil till he was almost past him. The Republic of New Mexico kept a special place in its fecal pantheon for W. W. Brierson; having Wil witness this humiliation was the last straw. Then the generals hustled their President on. Those who followed glared briefly at Brierson, or avoided looking at him entirely.

Their departing footsteps came clearly from beyond the amphitheater. Seconds later they had fired up the engines on their armored personnel carriers and were rumbling off to their part of town. All through this, the earthquake continued. For someone who had grown up in Michigan, it was uncanny. The rolling, rocking motion was almost silent. But the birds were silent too, and the spiders on the for-show web motionless. From deep within the castle's stonework there was creaking.

On the transect, magma red had nearly reached the surface. The tiny lights that represented bombs flickered just below

8

ground, and the last yellow of solid earth just . . . evaporated.

Still the nuking continued, carving a wide red sea.

And finally there was action on the northern horizon. Finally there was direct evidence of the cataclysm there. The pale blue was lit again and again by something very bright, something that punched through the haze like a sunrise trying to happen. Just above the flashes a band of white, almost like a second horizon, slowly rose. The top had been blown off the northern foothills of the Kampuchean Alps.

A sigh spread through the audience. Wil looked down, saw several people pointing upwards. Faintly purple, barely brighter than the sky, the wraith extended almost straight overhead from north to south. A daytime aurora?

Strange lightning flickered on the slopes below the castle. The air in the amphitheater was charged with static electricity, yet all was unholy silent. The sound of the rescue would come loud even from fifteen hundred kilometers around the earth, but that sound was still an hour away, chugging across the Kampuchean Alps towards the Inland Sea.

And the Peacer bobble, like flotsam loosed from ice by a summer sun, was free to float to the surface.

TWO

Everyone agreed with Marta that the show had been impressive. Many didn't realize that the "show" wouldn't end with one afternoon of fireworks. The curtain calls would go on for some time, much more dismal than impressive.

The rescue blasting had been about a hundred times as energetic as the nineteenth-century Krakatoa blow-off. Billions of tonnes of ash and rock were pumped into the stratosphere that afternoon. The sun was a rare sight in the days that followed, at best a dim reddish disk through the murk. In Korolev, there was a heavy frost on the ground every morning. The almost-jacarandas were wilted and dying. Their spider families were dead or moved to burrows. Even in the jungles along the coast, temperatures rarely got above fourteen degrees now.

It rained most of every day—but not water: the dust was settling out. When it came down dry, it was like gray-brown snow, piling obscene drifts on houses and trees and the bodies of small animals; the New Mexicans ruined the last of their jetcopters learning what rock dust does to turbines. Things were even worse when it came down wet, a black fluid that changed the drifts to mud. It was small consolation that the bombs were clean, and the dust a "natural product."

Korolev robots quickly rebuilt the monorails. Wil and the Dasgupta brothers took a trip down to the sea.

The dunes were gone, blasted inland by the rescue-day tsunamis. The trees south of the dunes were laid out flat, all pointing away from the sea. There was no green; all was covered with ash. Even the sea had a layer of scum on it. Miraculously, some fishermonkeys lived. Wil saw small groups on the beach, grooming the ash from each other's pelts. They spent most of their time in the water, which was still warm.

The rescue itself was an undoubted success. The Peacer bobble now sat on the surface. The third day after the detonation, a Korolev flier visited the blast site. The pictures it sent back were striking. Gale-force winds, still laden with ash, drove across gray scabland. Glowing orange-red peeked through netted cracks in the scab. At the center of this slowly freezing lake of rock sat a perfect sphere, the bobble. It floated two-thirds out of the rock. Of course, no nicks or scour marred its surface. No trace of ash or rock adhered. In fact, it was all but invisible: its mirror surface reflected the scene around it, showing the net of glowing cracks stretching back into the haze.

A typical bobble, in an untypical place.

"All things shall pass." That was Rohan Dasgupta's favorite misquote. In a few months, the molten lake would freeze over, and an unprotected man could walk right to the side of the Peacer bobble. About the same time, the blackout and the mud rains would end. For a few years there would be brilliant sunsets and unusually cool weather. Wounded trees would recover, seedlings would replace those that had died. In a century or two, nature would have forgotten this affront, and the Peacer bobble would reflect forest green.

Yet it would be unknown thousands of years before the bobble burst, and the men and women within could join the colony.

As usual, the Korolevs had a plan. As usual, the low-techs had little choice but to tag along.

"Hey, we're having a party tonight. Want to come?"

Wil and the others looked up from their shoveling. After

three hours mucking around in the ash, they all looked pretty much the same. Black, white, Chinese, Indian, Aztlán—all were covered with gray ash.

The vision that confronted them was dressed in sparkling white. Her flying platform hovered just above the long pile of ash that the low-techs had pushed into the street. She was one of the Robinson daughters. Tammy? In any case, she looked like some twentieth-century fashion plate: blond, tan, seventeen, friendly.

Dilip Dasgupta grinned back at her. "We'd sure like to. But tonight? If we don't get this ash away from the houses before the Korolevs bobble up, we'll be stuck with it forever." Wil's back and arms were one big ache, but he had to agree. They had been doing this for two days, ever since the Korolevs announced tonight's departure. If they could get all the gray stuff pushed back from the houses before they bobbled up, it would be sluiced away by a thousand years of weather when they came back. Everyone on the street had pitched in, though with lots of grumbling—directed mostly at the Korolevs. The New Mexicans had even sent over some enlisted men with wheelbarrows and shovels. Wil wondered about that: he couldn't believe that someone like Fraley was really overcome by a spirit of cooperation. This was either honest helpfulness on the part of lower officers, or else a subtle effort to bring the other low-techs into the NM camp, future allies against the Korolevs and the Peacers.

The Robinson girl leaned on her platform, and it drifted closer to Dasgupta. She looked up and down the street, then spoke with an air of confidentiality. "My folks like Yelén and Marta a lot—*really*. But Daddy thinks they carry some things too far. You Early Birds are going to be at our level of tech in a few decades anyway. Why should you have to slave like this?"

She bit at a fingernail. "I really wish you could come to our party. . . . Hey! Why don't we do this: You keep working, say till about six. Maybe you can get it all cleaned by then, anyway. But if you can't, don't worry. My folks' robots can take care of what's left while you go get ready for the party." She smiled, then continued almost shyly. "Do you think that would be okay? Could you come then?"

Dilip looked at his brother Rohan, then replied, deadpan, "Why, uh, yes. With that backup, I think we could make it."

"Great! Now look. It's at our house starting around eight. So don't work past six, okay? And don't bother eating, either. We've got lots of food. The party'll go till the Witching Hour. That will leave you plenty of time to get home before the Korolevs bobble up."

Her flier drifted sideways and climbed beyond the trees that encircled the houses. "See you!" Twelve sweaty shovel pushers watched her departure in numbed silence.

A smile spread slowly across Dilip's wide face. He looked at his shovel, then rolled his eyes at the others. Finally he shouted, "Screw it!", threw the shovel to the ground, and jumped up and down on it.

This provoked a heartfelt cheer from the others, the NM corporals included. In moments, the newly liberated workers had departed for their homes.

Only Brierson remained on the street, still looking in the direction taken by the Robinson girl. He felt as much curiosity as gratitude. Wil had done his best to know the high-techs: for all their idiosyncrasies, they'd seemed united behind the Korolevs. But no matter how friendly the disagreement, he saw now that they had factions, too. *I wonder what the Robinsons are selling.*

The public area of the Robinsons' place was friendlier than the Korolevs'. Incandescent lamps hung from oaken beams. The teak dance floor opened onto a buffet room, an outdoor terrace, and a darkened theater where the hosts promised some extraordinary home movies later.

While guests were still arriving, the younger Robinson children ran noisily about the dance floor, dodging among the guests in a wild game of tag. They were tolerated, more than tolerated. They were the only children in the world.

In some sense, almost everyone present was an exile. Some had been shanghaied, some had jumped to escape punishment (deserved and otherwise), some (like the Dasguptas) thought that stepping out of time for a couple of centuries while their investments multiplied would make them rich. On the whole, their initial jumps had been short—into the twenty-fourth, twenty-fifth, twenty-sixth centuries.

But somewhere in the twenty-third, the rest of humanity disappeared. The travelers coming out just after the Extinction found ruins. Some—the most frivolous, and the most hurried of the criminals—had brought nothing with them. These starved, or lived a few pitiful years in the decaying mausoleum that was Earth. The better-equipped ones—the New Mexicans, for example—had the means to return to stasis. They bobbled forward through the third millennium, praying to find civilization revived. All they found was a world sinking back to nature, Man's works vanishing beneath jungle and forest and sea.

Even these travelers could survive only a few years in real-time. They had no medical support, no way to maintain their machines or produce food. Their equipment would soon fail, leaving them stranded in the wilderness.

But a few, a very few, had left at the close of the twenty-second century—when technology gave individuals greater wealth than whole twentieth-century nations. These few could maintain and reproduce all but the most advanced of their tools. Most departed civilization with a deliberate spirit of adventure. They had the resources to save the less fortunate scattered through the centuries, the millennia, and finally the megayears that passed.

Except for the Robinsons, no one had children. That was something reserved for the future, when humankind's ghosts made one last try at reclaiming the race's existence. So the kids who played raucous tag across the dance floor were a greater wonder than any high-tech magic. When the Robinson daughters gathered up their younger siblings for bed, there was a moment of strange, sad silence.

Wil drifted through the buffet room, stopping here and there to talk with his new acquaintances. He was determined to know everyone eventually. Quite a goal: if successful, he would know every living member of the human race. The largest group—and for Wil the most difficult to know—were the New Mexicans. Fraley himself was nowhere in sight, but most of his people were here. He spotted the corporals who had helped with the shoveling, and they introduced him to some others. Things were friendly till an NM officer joined the group.

Wil excused himself and moved slowly toward the dance floor. Most of the advanced travelers were at the party, and they were mingling. A crowd surrounded Juan Chanson. The archeologist was arguing his theory of the Extinction. "Invasion. Extermination. That's the beginning and the end of it." He spoke a clipped, rattling dialect of English that made his opinions seem even more impressive.

"But, Professor," someone—Rohan Dasgupta—objected, "my brother and I came out of stasis in 2465. That couldn't have been more than two centuries after the Extinction. Newer Delhi was in ruins. Many of the buildings had completely fallen in. But we saw no evidence of nuking or lasing."

"Sure. I agree. Not around Delhi. But you must realize, my boy, you saw a very small part of the picture, indeed. It's a great misfortune that most of those who returned right after the Extinction didn't have the means to study what they saw. I can show you pictures . . . LA a fifty-kilometer crater, Beijing a large lake. Even now, with the right equipment, you can find evidence of those blasts.

"I've spent centuries tracking down and interviewing the travelers who were alive in the late third millennium. Why, I even interviewed you." Chanson's eyes unfocused for a fraction of a second. Like most of the high-techs, he wore an interface band around his temples. A moment's thought could bring a flood of memory. "You and your brother. That was around 10000 AD, after the Korolevs rescued you—"

Dasgupta nodded eagerly. For him, it had been just weeks before. "Yes, they had moved us to Canada. I still don't know why—"

"Safety, my boy, safety. The Laurentian Shield is a stable place for long-term storage, almost as good as a cometary orbit." He waved his hand dismissingly. "The point is, *I* and a few other investigators have pieced together these separate bits of evidence. It is tricky; twenty-third-century civilization maintained vast databases, but the media had decayed to uselessness within a few decades of the Extinction. We have fewer contemporary records from the era than we do from the Mayans'. But there are enough . . . I can show you: my reconstruction of the Norcross invasion graffiti, the punched vanadium tape that W. W. Sánchez found on Charon. These are the death screams of the human race.

"Looking at the evidence, any reasonable person must agree the Extinction was the result of wholesale violence directed against populations that were somehow defenseless.

"Now, there are *some* who claim the human race simply killed itself, that we finally had the world-ending war people worried about in the twentieth century. . . ." He glanced at Monica Raines. The pinch-faced artist smiled back sourly but didn't rise to the bait. Monica belonged to the "People Are No Damned Good" school of philosophy. The Extinction held no mysteries for her. After a moment, Chanson continued. "But if you really *study* the evidence, you'll see the traces of outside interference, you'll see that our race was murdered by something . . . from outside."

The woman next to Rohan gave a little gasp. "But these . . . these aliens. What became of them? Why, if they return —we're sitting ducks here!"

Wil stepped back from the fringes of the group and continued toward the dance floor. Behind him, he heard Juan Chanson's triumphant "Exactly! That is the practical point of my investigations. We must mount guard on the solar frontiers—" His words were lost in the background chatter. Wil shrugged to himself. Juan was one of the most approachable of the high-techs, and Wil had heard his spiel before. There was no question the Extinction was the central mystery of their lives. But rehashing the issue in casual conversation was like arguing theology—and depressing, to boot.

A dozen couples danced. On the stage, Alice Robinson and daughter Amy were running the music. Amy played something that looked like a guitar. Alice's instrument was a more conventional console. They improvised on a base of automatic music generators. Having two real humans out front, whose voices and hands were making part of the music, made the band exciting and real.

They played everything from Strauss waltzes, to the Beatles, to W. W. Arai. A couple of the Arai pieces Wil had never heard: they must have been written after his . . . departure. Partners changed from dance to dance. The Arai tunes brought more than thirty people onto the floor. Wil stayed at the edge of the floor, for the moment content to observe. On the other side, he saw Marta Korolev; her partner was not in evidence.

Marta stood swaying, snapping her fingers to the music, a faint smile on her face. She looked a little like Virginia: her chocolate skin was almost the shade Wil remembered. No doubt Marta's father or mother came from America. But the other side of her family was clearly Chinese.

Appearance aside, there were other similarities. Marta had Virginia's outgoing good humor. She combined common sense with uncommon sympathy. Wil watched her for many minutes, trying not to seem to watch. Several of the bolder partiers —Dilip was first—asked her to dance. She accepted enthusiastically, and soon was on the floor for almost every tune. She was very good to watch. If only—

A hand touched his shoulder and a feminine voice sounded in his ear. "Hey, Mr. Brierson, is it true you're a policeman?"

Wil looked into blue eyes just centimeters from his. Tammy Robinson stood on tiptoe to shout into his ear. Now that she had his attention, she stood down, which still left her a respectable 180 centimeters tall. She was dressed in the same spotless white as before. Her interface band looked like a bit of jewelry, holding back her long hair. Her grin was bounded by dimples; even her eyes seemed to be smiling.

Brierson grinned back. "Yes. At least, I used to be a cop."

"Oh, wow." She took his arm in hers and edged them away from the loudness. "I never met a policeman before. But I guess that's not saying a lot."

"Oh?"

"Yeah. I was born about ten megayears after the Singularity —the Extinction, Juan calls it. I've read and watched all about

17

cops and criminals and soldiers, but till now I've never actually met any."

Wil laughed. "Well, now you can meet all three."

Tammy was abashed. "I'm sorry. I'm really not that ignorant. I know that police are different from criminals and soldiers. But it's so strange: they're all careers that can't even exist unless lots of people decide to live together."

Lots of people. Like more than a single family. Brierson glimpsed the abyss that separated them.

"I think you'll like having other people around, Tammy."

She smiled and squeezed his arm. "Daddy always says that. Now I'm beginning to understand."

"Just think. Before you're a hundred, Korolev Town will be almost like a city. There could be a couple of thousand people for you to know, people more interesting and worthwhile than criminals."

"Ugh. We're not going to stay for that. I want to be with lots of people—hundreds at least. But how could you stand to be locked in one little corner of time?" She looked at him, seemed suddenly to realize that Brierson's whole life had been stuck in a single century. "Gee. How can I explain it? Look— where you come from, there was air and space travel, right?" Brierson nodded. "You could go anywhere you wanted. Now, suppose instead you had to spend your life in a house in a deep valley. Sometimes you hear stories about other places, but you can never climb out of the valley. Wouldn't that drive you crazy?

"That's how I'd feel about making a permanent stop at Korolev. We've been stopped for six weeks now. That's not long compared to some of our stops, but it's long enough for me to get the feeling: The animals aren't changing. I look out and the mountains just *sit* there." She made a little sound of frustration. "Oh, I can't explain it. But you'll see some of what I mean tonight. Daddy's going to show the video we made. It's beautiful!"

Wil smiled. Bobbles didn't change the fact that time was a one-way trip.

She saw the denial in his eyes. "You must feel like I do. Just a little? I mean, why did you go into stasis in the first place?"

He shook his head. "Tammy, there are lots of people here who never asked to be bobbled. . . . I was shanghaied." A crummy embezzlement case it had been. When he thought back, it was so fresh in his mind, in many ways more real than the world of the last few weeks. The assignment had seemed as safe as houses. The need for an armed investigator had been a formality, required by his company's archaic regs: the amount stolen was just over the ten thousand gAu. But someone had been desperate or careless . . . or just plain vicious. Most jurisdictions of Wil's era counted offensive bobbling of more than a century as manslaughter: Wil's stasis had lasted one thousand centuries. Of course, Wil did not consider the crime to be the murder of one W. W. Brierson. The crime was much more terrible than that. The crime was the destruction of the world he had known, the family he loved.

Tammy's eyes grew wide as he told his story. She tried to understand, but Wil thought there was more wonder than sympathy in her look. He stopped short, embarrassed.

He was trying to think of a suitable change of subject when he noticed the pale figure on the far side of the dance floor. It was the person he'd seen at the beach. "Tammy, who's that?" He nodded in the direction of the stranger.

Tammy pulled her gaze away from his face and looked across the room. "Oh! She's weird, isn't she? She's a spacer. Can you imagine? In fifty million years, she could travel all over the Galaxy. We think she's more than nine thousand years old. And all that time alone." Tammy shivered.

Nine thousand years. That would make her the oldest human Wil had ever seen. She certainly looked more human tonight than on the beach. For one thing, she wore more clothes: a blouse and skirt that were definitely feminine. Now her skull was covered with short black stubble. Her face was smooth and pale. Wil guessed that when her hair grew out, she might look like a normal young woman—Chinese, probably.

A half-meter of emptiness surrounded the spacer; elsewhere the crowd was packed close. Many clapped and sang; there was scarcely a person who could resist tapping a foot or nodding in

time to the music. But the spacer stood quietly, almost motionless, her dark eyes staring impassively into the dancers. Occasionally her arm or leg would twitch, as if in some broken
resonance with the tunes.

She seemed to sense Wil's gaze. She looked back at him, her
eyes expressionless, analytical. This woman had seen more than
the Robinsons, the Korolevs—more than all the high-techs put
together. Was it his imagination that he suddenly felt like a
bug on a slide? The woman's lips moved, the twitching motion
he remembered from the beach. Then it had seemed a coldly
alien, almost insectile gesture. Now Wil had a flash of insight:
After nine thousand years alone, nine thousand years on God
knows how many worlds, would a person still remember the
simple things—like how to smile?

"C'mon, Mr. Brierson, let's dance." Tammy Robinson's
hand was insistent on his elbow.

Wil danced more that night than since he'd been dating
Virginia. The Robinson kid just wouldn't quit. She didn't really
have more stamina than Brierson. He kept in condition and
kept his bio-age around twenty; with his large frame and tendency to overweight he couldn't afford to be fashionably middle-aged. But Tammy had the *enthusiasm* of a seventeen-year-
old. Paint her a different color and she reminded him of his
daughter Anne: cuddly, bright, and just a bit predatory when
it came to the males she wanted.

The music swept them round and round, taking Marta Korolev in and out of his view. Marta danced only a few times with
any one partner and spent considerable time off the floor,
talking. This evening would leave the Korolev reputation substantially mellowed. Later, when he saw her depart for the
theater, he suppressed a sigh of relief. It had been a depressing
little game, watching her and watching her, and all the time
pretending not to.

The lights brightened and the music faded. "It's about an
hour to midnight, folks," came Don Robinson's voice. "You're
welcome to dance till the Witching Hour, but I've got some
pictures and ideas I'd like to share with you. If you're interested, please step down the hall."

"That's the video I was telling you about. You've got to hear what Daddy has to say." Tammy led him off the floor, even though another song was starting. The music had lost some of its vibrancy. Amy and Alice Robinson had left the bandstand. The rest of the evening would be uninterpreted recordings.

Behind them, the crowd around the dance floor was breaking up. There had been hints through the evening that this last entertainment would be the most spectacular. Almost everyone would be in the Robinsons' theater.

As they walked down the hall, the lights above them went dim. The theater itself was awash with blue light. A four-meter globe of Earth hung above the seats. It was an effect Wil had seen before, though never on this scale. Given several satellite views it was possible to construct a holo of the entire planet and hang its blue-green perfection before the viewer. From the entrance to the theater, the world was in quarter phase, morning just touching the Himalayas. Moonlight glinted faintly off the Indian Ocean. The continental outlines were the familiar ones from the Age of Man.

Yet there was something strange about the image. It took Wil a second to realize just what: There were no clouds.

He was about to walk around the globe to the seating when he noticed two shadows beyond the dark side. It looked like Don Robinson and Marta Korolev. Wil paused, resisting Tammy's urging that they hurry to get the best seats. The room was rapidly filling with partygoers, but Wil guessed he was the only one who had noticed Robinson and Korolev. There was something strange here: Korolev's bearing was tense. Every few seconds she chopped at the air between them. The shadow that was Don Robinson stood motionless, even as Korolev became more excited. Wil had the impression of short, unsatisfactory replies being given to impassioned demands. Wil couldn't hear the words; either they were behind a sound screen, or they weren't talking out loud. Finally Robinson turned and walked out of sight behind the globe. Marta followed, still gesturing.

Even Tammy hadn't noticed. She led Brierson to the edge of the audience area and they sat. A minute passed. Wil saw Marta emerge from beyond the sunlit hemisphere and walk behind the audience to sit near the door.

Then there was music, just loud enough to still the audience. Tammy touched Wil's hand. "Oh. Here comes Daddy."

Don Robinson suddenly appeared by the sunside hemisphere. He cast no shadow on the globe, though both shone in the synthetic sunlight. "Good evening, everyone. I thought to end our party with this little light show—and a few ideas I'm hoping you'll think about." He held up his hand and grinned disarmingly. "I promise, mostly pictures!"

His image turned to pat the surface of the globe familiarly. "All but a lucky few of us began our journey down time unprepared. That first bobbling was an accident or was intended as a single jump to what we guessed would be a friendlier future civilization. Unfortunately—as we all discovered—there is no such civilization, and many of us were stranded." Robinson's voice was friendly, smooth, the tone traditionally associated with the selling of breakfast food or religion. It irritated Wil that Robinson said "we" and "us" even when he was speaking specifically of the low-tech travelers.

"Now, there were a few who were well equipped. Some of these have worked to rescue the stranded, to bring us all together where we can freely decide humanity's new course. My family, Juan Chanson, and others did what we could—but it was the Korolevs who had the resources to bring this off. Marta Korolev is here tonight." He waved generously in her direction. "I think Marta and Yelén deserve a big hand." There was polite applause.

He patted the globe again. "Don't worry. I'm getting to our friend here. . . . One problem with all this rescuing is that most of us have spent the last fifty million years in long-term stasis, waiting for all the 'principals' to be gathered for this final debate. Fifty million years is a long time to be gone; a lot has happened.

"That's what I want to share with you tonight. Alice and the kids and I were among the fortunate. We have advanced bobblers and plenty of autonomous devices. We've been out of stasis hundreds of times. We've been able to live and grow along with the Earth. The pictures I'm going to show you tonight are the 'home movies,' if you will, of our trip to the present.

"I'm going to start with the big picture—the Earth from space. The image you see here is really a composite—I've averaged out the cloud cover. It was recorded early in the fourth millennium, just after the Age of Man. This is our starting point.

"Let's begin the journey." Robinson vanished and they had an unobstructed view of the globe. Now Wil noticed a gray haze that seemed to waver around the polar ice cap. "We're moving forward about half a megayear per minute. The camera satellites were programmed to take pictures at the same local time every year. At this rate, even climate cycles are visible only as a softening of picture definition." The gray haze—it must be the edge of the Antarctic ice pack! Wil looked more carefully at Asia. There was a blurring, a fantastically rapid mottling of greens and tans. Droughts and wetness. Forest and jungle battling savanna and desert. In the north, white flickered like lightning. Suddenly the glaring whiteness flashed southwards. It surged and retreated, again, again. In less than a quarter of a minute it was gone back to the northern horizon. Except for shimmering whiteness in the Himalayas, the greens and tans lived once more across Asia. "We had a pretty good ice age there," Robinson explained. "It lasted more than one hundred thousand years. . . . We're beyond the immediate neighborhood of Man now. I'm going to speed us up . . . to five megayears per minute."

Wil glanced at Marta Korolev. She was watching the show, but her face held an uncharacteristic look of displeasure. Her hands were clenched into fists.

Tammy Robinson leaned from her seat to whisper, "This is where it really gets good, Mr. Brierson!"

Wil turned back to the display, but his attention was split between the view and the mystery of Marta's anger.

Five million years every minute. Glacier and desert and forest and jungle blended. One color or another might fleetingly dominate the pastel haze, but the overall impression was stable and soothing. Only now . . . only now the continents themselves were moving! A murmur passed around the room as the audience realized what they were seeing. Australia had

23

moved north, sliding into the eastern islands of the Indonesian archipelago. Mountains puckered along the collision. This part of the world was near the sunrise line. Low sunlight cast the new mountains in relief.

There was sound, too. From the surface of the globe, Wil heard something that reminded him of wood surfaces squeaking wetly across each other. A sound like crumpling paper accompanied the birth of the Indonesian Alps. "Those noises are real, friends," said Don Robinson. "We kept a system of seismophones on the surface. What you're hearing are long-term averages of seismic action. It took thousands of major earthquakes to make every second of those sounds."

As he spoke, Australia and Indonesia merged, the combination continuing its slide northwards, turning slightly as it came. Already the form of the Inland Sea could be discerned. "No one predicted what happened next," continued Robinson's travelogue. "There! Notice the rift spreading through Kampuchea, breaking the Asian plate." A string of narrow lakes appeared across Southeast Asia. "In a moment, we'll see the new platelet reverse direction and ram *back* into China—to build the Kampuchean Alps."

From the corner of his eye, Brierson saw Marta heading for the door. *What is going on here?* He started to get up, found that Tammy's arm was still around his.

"Wait. Why are you going, Mr. Brierson?" she whispered, starting to get up.

"I've got to check on something, Tammy."

"But—" She seemed to realize that extended discussion would detract from her father's show. She sat down, looking puzzled and a little hurt.

"Sorry, Tam," Wil whispered. He headed for the door. Behind him, continents crashed.

The Witching Hour. The time between midnight and the start of the next day. It was more like seventy-five minutes than an hour. Since the Age of Man, the Earth's rotation had slowed. Now, at fifty megayears, the day was a little over twenty-five hours long. Rather than change the definition of the second or the hour, the Korolevs had decreed (just another of their decrees) that the standard day should consist of twenty-four hours plus whatever time it took to complete one rotation. Yelén called the extra time the Fudge Factor. Everyone else called it the Witching Hour.

Wil walked through the Witching Hour, looking for some sign of Marta Korolev. He was still on the Robinson estate, that was obvious: as advanced travelers, the Robinsons had plenty of robots. Rescue-day ash had been meticulously cleaned from the stone seats, the fountains, the trees, even the ground. The scent of almost-jacarandas floated in the cool night breeze.

Even without the tiny lights that floated along the paths, Wil could have found his way without difficulty. For the first time since the blow-off, the night was clear—well, not really *clear*, but he could see the moon. Its wan light was only faintly reddened by stratospheric ash. The old girl looked pretty much as she had in Wil's time, though the stains of industrial pollution were gone. Rohan Dasgupta claimed the moon was a little farther out now, that there would never again be a total eclipse of the sun. The difference was not enough for Wil to see.

The reddish silver light fell bright across the Robinsons' gardens, but Marta was nowhere in sight. Wil stopped, let his breath out, and listened. There were footsteps. He jogged in their direction and caught up with Korolev still inside the estate.

"Marta, wait." She had already stopped and turned to face him. Something dark and massive floated a few meters above her. Wil glanced at it and slowed to a walk. These autonomous devices still made him uneasy. They hadn't existed in his time, and no matter how often he was told they were safe, it was still unnerving to think of the firepower they controlled—independent of the direct commands of their masters. With her protector floating nearby, Marta was almost as safe as back in Castle Korolev.

Now that he'd caught up with her, he didn't know quite what to say. "What's the matter, Marta? I mean, is anything wrong?"

At first, he thought she would not answer. She stood with

balled fists. The moonlight showed tear streaks on her face. She slumped and brought her hands up to her temples. "That b-bastard Robinson. That slimy bastard!" The words were choked.

Wil stepped closer. The protection device moved forward, keeping him in clear view. "What happened?"

"You want to know? I'll tell you . . . but let's sit down. I-I don't think I can stand much longer. I'm s-so *mad.*" She walked to a nearby bench and sat. Wil lowered his bulk beside her, then started. To the hand, the bench felt like stone, but it yielded to main body weight like a cushion.

Marta put a hand on his arm, and for an instant he thought she might touch her head to his shoulder. The world was a very empty place now, and Marta reminded him so much of things lost. . . . But coming between the Korolevs was probably the single most boorish, the single most dangerous, thing he could do. Wil said abruptly, "This may not be the best place to talk." He waved at the fountain and the carefully tended trees. "I'll bet the Robinsons monitor the whole estate."

"Hah! We're screened." Marta moved her hand from his arm. "Besides, Don knows what I think of him.

"All these years, they've pretended to support our plan. We helped them, gave them factory designs that didn't exist when they left civilization. All the time, they were just waiting— taking their pretty pictures—while we did all the work, bringing what was left of the human race to one place and time.

"And now that we have everyone together, now that we need everyone's cooperation, *now* they start sweet-talking people away from us. Well, I'll tell you, Wil. Our settlement is humankind's last chance. I'll do anything, *anything,* to protect it." Marta had always seemed so cheerful, optimistic. That made her fury even more striking. But the one did not make hypocrisy of the other. Marta was like a mother cat, suddenly ferocious and deadly in protecting her kittens.

"So the Robinsons want to break up the town? Do they want their own colony?"

Marta nodded. "But not like you think. Those lunatics want to continue down time, sightseeing their way into eternity. Robinson figures if he can persuade most of us to come along, he'll have a stable system. He calls it a 'timelike urbanization.' For the next few billion years, his colony would spend about a month per megayear outside of stasis. As the sun goes off main sequence, they'll move into space and bobble through longer and longer jumps. He literally wants to follow the evolution of the whole goddamned universe!"

Brierson remembered Tammy Robinson's impatience with living at the same rate as the universe. She'd been campaigning for the scheme her father must now be selling to the audience back in the theater.

Wil shook his head and chuckled. "Sorry. I'm not laughing at you, Marta. It's just that compared to the things you should be worrying about, this is ludicrous.

"Look. Most of the low-techs are like me. It's been only weeks of objective time since I left civilization. Even the New Mexicans spent only a few years in realtime before you rescued them. We haven't lived centuries 'on the road' like you advanced types. We're still hurting. More than anything, we want to stop and rebuild."

"But Robinson is so slick."

"He's so slick you can scrape the grease off. You've been away from that kind for a long, long time. Back in civilization, we were exposed to sales pressure almost every day. . . . There's only one lever he has, and that's something you should be worrying about in any case."

Marta smiled wanly. "Yelén and I worry about so many things, Wil. You have something new for us?"

"Maybe." Wil was silent for a moment. The fountain across from their bench burbled loud. There were soft hooting sounds in trees. He hadn't expected this opportunity. Until now the Korolevs had been approachable enough, but they didn't seem to listen. "We're all grateful to you and Yelén. You saved us from death—or at least from life alone in an empty world. We have a chance to start the human race again. . . . But at the same time, a lot of low-techs resent you advanced travelers in your castles above town. They resent the fact that you make all the decisions, that you decide what you will share and what we will work at."

"I know. We haven't explained things very well. We seem

omnipotent. But don't you see, Wil? We high-techs are a few people from around 2200 who brought our era's version of good-quality camping and survival gear. Sure, we can make most any consumer product of your time. But we *can't* reproduce the most advanced of our own devices. When those finally break, we'll be as helpless as you."

"I thought your autons were good for hundreds of years."

"Sure, if we use them for ourselves alone. Supporting an army of low-techs cuts us down to less than a century. We *need* each other, Wil. Apart, both groups face dead ends. Together, we have a chance. We can supply you with databases, equipment, and a good approximation to a twenty-first-century standard of living—for a few decades. As our support decays, you provide the human hands and minds and ingenuity to fill the gaps. If we can get a high birth rate, and build a twenty-first-century infrastructure, we may pull this out."

"Willing hands? Like the ash shoveling we've had to do?" He didn't mean the question to sound nasty, but it came out that way.

She touched his arm again. "No, Wil. That was dumb of us. Arrogant." She paused, her eyes searching his.

"Have you ever been ramjetting, Wil?"

"Huh? Uh, no." In general, Wil didn't go *looking* for trouble.

"But it was a big sport in your time, wasn't it? Sort of like hang gliding, but a lot more exciting—especially for the purists who didn't carry bobblers. Our situation reminds me of a typical ramjet catastrophe: You're twenty thousand meters up, ramming along. All of a sudden your jet flames out. It's an interesting problem. Those little rigs didn't mass more than a few hundred kilos; they didn't carry turbines. So all you can do is dive hell down. If you can get your airspeed above Mach one, you can usually relight the ram; if not, you make a nice crater.

"Well, we're sitting pretty right now. But the underlying civilization has flamed out. We have a *long* way to fall. Counting the Peacers, there will be almost three hundred low-techs. With your help we ought to be able to relight at some decent level of technology—say twentieth or twenty-first century. If we can, we'll quickly climb back. If we can't, if we fall to a premachine age when our autons fail . . . we'll be just too primitive and too few to survive. So. The ash shoveling was unnecessary. But I can't disguise the fact that there will be hard times, terribly hard work."

She looked down. "I know you've heard most of this before, Wil. It's a hard package to sell, isn't it? But I thought I would have more time. I thought I could convince most of you of our goodwill. . . . I never counted on Don Robinson and his slick promises and good-fellowship."

Marta looked so forlorn. He reached out to pat her shoulder. No doubt Robinson had plans similar to the Korolevs', plans that would remain secret until the low-techs were safely suckered into his family's journey. "I think that most of us low-techs will see through Robinson. If you make it clear where his promises must be lies. If you can come down from the castle. Concentrate on Fraley; if Robinson convinces him, you might lose the New Mexicans. Fraley isn't dumb, but he is rigid and he lets his anger run away with him. He really does hate the Peacers." *Almost as much as he hates me.*

Half a minute passed. Marta gave a short, bitter laugh. "So many enemies. The Korolevs hate the Robinsons, the NMs hate the Peacers, almost everybody hates the Korolevs."

"And Monica Raines hates all mankind."

This time her laugh was lighter. "Yes. Poor Monica." Marta leaned toward him and this time really did rest her head against his shoulder. Wil's arm slipped automatically across her back. She sighed. "We're two hundred people, just about all that's left. And I swear we have more jealousy and scheming than twentieth-century Asia."

They sat in silence, her head against him, his hand resting lightly against her back. He felt the tension slowly leave her body. For Wil it was different. *Oh, Virginia, what to do?* Marta felt so good. It would be so easy to caress that back, to slide his hand down to her waist. Most likely there'd be a moment of embarrassed backing away. But if she responded . . . If she responded, they'd be adding one more set of jealousies to the brew.

So Wil's hand did not move. In later times, he often wondered if things might have gone differently had he not chosen the path of sanity and caution.

He thought wildly for a moment, finally discovered a topic that was sure to break the mood. "You know I'm one of the shanghaied ones, Marta."

"Mm-hmm."

"The crime is a strange one, bobbling someone into the far future. It may be murder, but the court can't know for sure. In my time, most jurisdictions had a special punishment for it."

Silence.

"They'd bobble survival equipment and the trial record next to the victim. Then they'd take the bastard who created the problem and bobble him too—so he'd come out of stasis just *after* the victim. . . ."

The spell was broken. Marta pulled slowly back. She could tell what was coming. "Sometimes the courts couldn't know the duration."

Wil nodded. "In my case, I'll bet the duration was known. *And* I'll bet even more that there was a conviction. There were only three suspects; I was closing in on that damn embezzler. That's why he panicked."

He paused. "Did you rescue him, Marta? Did you rescue the . . . person . . . who did this to me?"

She shook her head. Her openness deserted her when she had to lie.

"You've got to tell me, Marta. I don't need revenge"—perhaps a small lie there—"but I do need to know."

She shook her head again but this time replied. "We can't, Wil. We need everyone. Can't you see that all such crimes are meaningless now?"

"For my own protection—"

She got up, and after a second Wil did, too.

"No. We've given him a new face and a new name. He has no motive for harming you now, and we've warned him what we'll do if he tries."

Brierson shrugged.

"Hey, Wil, have I made myself another enemy?"

"N-no. I could never be your enemy. And I want the settlement to succeed as much as you and Yelén."

"I know." She raised her hand in a half-wave. "G'night, Wil."

"Good night."

She walked into the darkness, her robot protector floating close above her shoulder.

THREE

Things had changed by "next" morning. At first, the changes were what Brierson had expected.

Gone was the drear ash and dirty sky. Dawn splashed sunlight across his bed; he could see a wedge of blue between green-leafed trees. Wil came slowly awake, something deep inside saying it was all a dream. He closed his eyes, opened them again, and stared into the brightness.

They did it. "By God, they really did it." He rolled out of bed and pulled on some clothes. He shouldn't really be surprised. The Korolevs had announced their plan. Sometime in the morning hours, after the Robinson party was over and when their surveillance showed everyone safe at home, they had bobbled every building in the settlement. Through unknown centuries they bobbled forward, coming out of stasis for a few seconds every year, just long enough to check if the Peacer bobble had burst.

Wil rushed down the stairs, past the kitchen. Breakfast could be skipped. Just to see the green and the blue and the clean sunlight made him feel like a kid at Christmas. Then he was outside, standing in the sunlight. The street was nearly gone. Almost-jacarandas had sprouted through its surface. Their lowest flowers floated a meter above his head. Spider

32

families scampered through the leaves. The huge pile of ash that he and the Dasguptas and the others had pushed into the middle of the street was gone, washed away by a hundred— a thousand?—rainy seasons. The only sign of that long-ago pollution was around Wil's house. A circular arc marked where the stasis field had intersected the ground. Outside was green and growing; inside was covered with gray ash, the trees and plants dying.

As Wil wandered through the young forest that the street had become, the wrongness of the scene gradually percolated through: Everything was alive, but there was not another human, not a single robot. Had everyone wakened earlier, say at the moment the bobbles burst?

He walked down to the Dasguptas' place. Half hidden by the brush, he saw someone big and black heading his way—his own reflection. The Dasguptas were still in stasis. The trees grew right up to their bobble. Rainbow webs floated around it, but the surface was untouched. Neither vines nor spiders could find purchase on that mirrored smoothness.

Wil ran through the forest, panic rising in him. Now that he knew what to look for, they were easy to spot: the sun's image glinted off two, three, half a dozen bobbles. Only his had burst. He looked at the trees, the birds, and the spiders. The scene was scarcely pleasing now. How long could he live without civilization? The rest might come out of stasis in moments or a hundred years, or a thousand; he had no way of knowing. In the meantime Wil was alone, perhaps the only living man on Earth.

He left the street and scrambled up a rise into older trees. From the top, he should be able to see some of the estates of the advanced travelers. The fear tightened at his throat. Sun and sky sat in the green of the hills; there were bobbles where the palaces of Juan Chanson and Phil Genet should be. He looked south, towards Castle Korolev.

Spires, gold and green! No bobble there!

And in the air above the castle, he saw three close-set dots: fliers, moving fast and straight towards him, like some old-time fighters on a strafing run. The trio was over him in seconds.

The middle flier descended and invited him into its passenger cabin.

The ground fell slantingly away. He had a moment's vision of the Inland Sea, blue through coastal haze. There were bobbles around the advanced estates, around the NM quarter of town. To the west were several large ones—around the autofactories? Everything was in stasis except the Korolev estate. He was above the castle now, coming down fast. The gardens and towers looked as before, but an enormous circle circumscribed the estate—a subtle yet abrupt change in the tone of the forest's green. Like himself, the Korolevs had been in stasis up to the recent past. For some reason they were leaving the rest bobbled. For some reason they wanted private words with W. W. Brierson.

The Korolev library had no bookcases weighted down with data cartridges or paper-and-ink books. Data could be accessed anywhere; the library was a place to sit and think (with appropriate support devices) or to hold a small conference. The walls were lined with holo windows showing the surrounding countryside. Yelén Korolev sat at the middle of a long marble table. She motioned Wil to sit across from her.

"Where's Marta?" Brierson asked automatically.

"Marta is . . . dead, Inspector Brierson." Yelén's voice was even flatter than usual. "Murdered."

Time seemed to stop. *Marta. Dead?* He had taken bullets with less physical sensation than those words brought. His mouth opened, but the questions wouldn't come. In any case, Yelén had questions of her own. "And I want to know what you had to do with it, Brierson."

Wil shook his head, in confusion more than denial.

She slapped the marble tabletop. "Wake up, mister! I'm talking to you. You're the last person who saw her alive. She rejected your advances. Did that make it worth killing her, Brierson? *Did it?*"

The insanity of the accusation brought Wil back to his senses. He stared at Yelén, realizing that she was in a much worse state than he. Like Marta, Yelén Korolev had been raised in late twenty-second-century Hainan. But Yelén had no trace of Chinese blood. She was descended from the Russians who had filtered out of Central Asia after the 1997 debacle. Her fair Slavic features were normally cool, occasionally showing ironic humor. Those features were as smooth as ever now, but the woman kept running her hand across her chin, her forefinger tracing again and again the edge of her lip. She was in a state of walleyed shock that Wil had seen only a couple of times before—and those times had been filled with sudden death. From the corner of his eye, he saw one of her protection robots float around the far side of the table—keeping her widely separated from its target.

"Yelén," he finally said, trying to keep his voice calm and reasonable, "till this moment I didn't know about Marta. I liked . . . respected . . . her more than anyone in the settlement. I could never harm her."

Korolev stared at him a long moment, then let out a shaky breath. The feeling of deadly tension lessened. "I know what you tried to do that night, Brierson. I know how you thought to repay our charity. I'll always hate your guts because of it. . . . But you're telling the truth about one thing: There's no way you—or any low-tech—could have killed Marta."

She looked through him, remembering her lost partner, or perhaps communicating through her headband. When she spoke again her voice was softer, almost lost. "You were a policeman, in a century where murder was still common. You're even famous. When I was a kid, I read all about you. . . . I'll do anything to get Marta's killer, Inspector."

Wil leaned forward. "What happened, Yelén?" he said quietly.

"She—she was marooned—left outside all our bobbles."

For a moment, Wil didn't understand. Then he remembered walking the deserted street and wondering if he was all alone, wondering how many years would pass before the other bobbles burst. Before, he had thought that being shanghaied into the future was the most terrible bobble crime. Now he saw that being marooned in an empty present could be just as awful.

"How long was she alone, Yelén?"

"Forty years. *Just forty goddamned years.* But she had no health care. She had no robots. She had just the clothes on her back. I'm p-proud of her. She lasted forty years. She survived the wilderness, the loneliness, her own aging. For forty years. And she almost won through. Another ten years—" Her voice broke and she covered her eyes. "Back up, Korolev," she said. "Just the facts.

"You know we have to move down time to when the Peacer bobble bursts. We planned to begin the move the night of the party. After everyone was indoors, we'd bobble forward in three-month steps. Every three months, the bobbles would burst and our sensors would take a few microseconds to check the fast-flicker autons, to see if the Peacers were still in stasis. If they were, we'd automatically bobble up for another three months. Even if we waited a hundred thousand years, all you'd have seen was a second or so of flickering and flashing.

"So. That was the plan. What happened was that the first jump was a century long—for everyone in near-Earth space. The other advanced travelers had agreed to follow our programming on this. They were in stasis, too. The difference between three months and a century was not enough to alarm their controller programs. Marta was alone. Once she figured out that the flicker interval was more than three months, she hiked around the Inland Sea to the Peace Authority bobble."

That was a twenty-five-hundred-kilometer hike.

Yelén noticed the wonder on his face. "We're survivors, Inspector. We didn't last this long by letting difficulties stop us.

"Anyway, the area around the Peace bobble is still a vitrified plain. It took her decades, but she built a sign there." The window behind Yelén suddenly became a view from space. At that distance, the bobble was just a glint of sunlight with a spiky shadow. A jagged black line extended northwards from it. Apparently the picture was taken at local dawn, and the black strip was the shadow of Marta's monument. It must have been several meters high and dozens of kilometers long. The image lasted only seconds, the space of time Yelén imagined it.

"You may not know this, but we have lots of equipment at the Lagrange zones. Some of it is in kiloyear stasis. Some is flickering with a period of decades. None of it is carefully watching the ground . . . but that line structure was enough to trip even a high-threshold monitor. Eventually, the robots sent a lander to investigate. . . . They were just a few years too late."

Wil forced his mind past thinking on what the lander found. Thank God Yelén's imagination didn't flash that on the windows.

For now—method: "How could this be done? I thought an old-time army couldn't match the security of your household automation."

"That's true. No low-tech could break in. At first glance, even the advanced travelers couldn't manage this: it's possible to outfight a high-tech—but the battles are abrupt and obvious. What happened here was sabotage. And I think I have it figured out. Somebody used our external comm to talk to the scheduling programs. Those weren't as secure as they should be. Marta was cut out of the check roster, and a one-century total blackout was substituted for the original flicker scheme. The murderer was lucky: if he had tried for anything longer, it would have tripped all sorts of alarms."

"Could it happen again?"

"No. Whoever did it is good, Brierson. But basically they took advantage of a bug. That bug no longer exists. And I'm being much more careful about how my machines accept outside comm now."

Wil nodded. This was a century beyond him, even if his specialty had been forensic computing. He'd just have to take her word that there was no further danger—of this sort of assassination. Wil's strength was in the human side. For instance:

"Motive. Who would want Marta dead?"

Yelén's laugh was bitter. "My suspects." The windows of the library became a mosaic of the settlement's population. Some had only small pictures—all the New Mexicans fitted on a single panel. Others—Brierson, for instance—rated more space. "Almost everybody conceives some grudge against us.

But you twenty-first-century types just don't have the background to pull this off. No matter how attractive the notion" —she looked at Wil—"you're off the list." The pictures of the low-techs vanished from the windows.

The rest stood like posters against the landscape beyond. These were all the advanced travelers (Yelén excepted): the Robinsons, Juan Chanson, Monica Raines, Philippe Genet, Tunç Blumenthal, Jason Mudge—and the woman Tammy said was a spacer.

"The motive, Inspector Brierson? I can't afford to consider that it was anything less than the destruction of our settlement. One of these people wants humanity permanently extinct, or —more likely—wants to run their own show with the people we've rescued; it would probably come to the same thing."

"But why Marta? Killing her has tipped their hand without—"

"Without stopping the Korolev Plan? You don't understand, Brierson." She ran a hand through her blond hair and stared down at the table. "I don't think any of you understand. You know I'm an engineer. You know I'm a hardheaded type who's made a lot of unpopular decisions. The plan would never have gotten this far without me.

"What you don't know is that Marta was the brains behind it all. Back in civilization, Marta was a project manager. One of the best. She had this figured out even before we left civilization. She could see that technology and people were headed into some sort of singularity in the twenty-third century. She really wanted to help the people who were stranded down time. . . . Now we have the settlement. To make it succeed is going to take the special genius she had. I know how to make the gadgets work, and I can outshoot most anyone in a clean fight. But it could all fall apart now, without Marta. We are so few here; there are so many internal jealousies.

"I think the killer knew this, too."

Wil nodded, a little surprised that Yelén realized her own failings so clearly.

"I'm going to have my hands full, Brierson. I intend to spend many decades of my life preparing for the time when the

Peacers come out and I bring the settlement back. If Marta's dream is to succeed, I can't afford to use my own time hunting the killer. *But I want that killer, Brierson.* Sometimes . . . sometimes I feel a little crazy, I want him so bad. I'll give you any reasonable support in this. Will you take the case?"

Even at fifty megayears, there was still a job for Wil Brierson.

There was one obvious thing he should demand, something he would not hesitate to require if he were back in civilization. He glanced at Yelén's auton, still hovering at the end of the table. Here . . . it might be better to wait for witnesses. Powerful ones. Finally he said, "I'll need personal transportation. Physical protection. Some means of publicly communicating with the entire settlement—I'll want their cooperation on this problem."

"Done."

"I'll also need your databases, at least where they deal with people in the settlement. I want to know where and when everyone originated, and exactly how they got bobbled past the Extinction."

Korolev's eyes narrowed. "Is this for your personal vendetta, Brierson? The past is dead. I'll not have you stirring up trouble with people who were once your enemies. Besides, the low-techs aren't suspects; there's no need for you to be sniffing around them."

Wil shook his head. This was just like old times: the customers deciding what the professional should see. "You're a high-tech, Yelén. But you're using a low-tech person, namely me. What makes you think the enemy doesn't have *his* accomplices?" People like Steve Fraley were the puppets now. They yearned to be the puppeteers. Playing Korolev against her enemy was a game the New Mexican President would love.

"Mph. Okay. You'll get the databases—but with your shanghai case locked out."

"And I want the sort of high-speed interface you have."

"Do you know how to use it?" Her hand brushed absently at her headband.

"Uh, no."

"Then forget it. The modern versions are a lot easier to learn than the kind you had, but I grew up with one and I still can't properly visualize with it. If you don't start as a child, you may spend years and never get the hang of it."

"Look, Yelén. Time is the one thing we've got. It's God knows how many thousands of years till the Peacers come out and you restart the settlement. Even if it took me fifty years to learn, it wouldn't interfere."

"Time is something *you* don't have, mister. If you spend a century tooling up for this job, you'll lose the viewpoint that's your value to me."

She had a point. He remembered how Marta had misunderstood the effect of Robinson's sales pitch.

"Sure," she continued, "there are high-tech angles to the murder. Maybe they're the most important angles. But I've already got expert help in that department."

"Oh? Someone you can trust among the high-techs?" He waved at the mug shots on the walls.

Korolev smiled thinly. "Someone I can *dis*trust less than the others. Never forget, Brierson, my devices will be watching all of you." She thought for a moment. "I was hoping she'd be back in time for this meeting. She's the least likely to have a motive. In all the megayears, she's never been tangled in our little schemes. You two will work together. I think you'll find your skills complementary. She knows technology, but she's a little . . . strange." Yelén was silent again; Wil wondered if he would ever get used to this silent communion between human and machines.

There was movement at the corner of his vision. Wil turned and saw that a third person sat by the table. It was the spacer woman. He hadn't heard a door opening or footsteps. . . . Then he noticed that she sat back from the table, and her seat was angled slightly off true. The holo was better than any he'd seen before.

She nodded solemnly at Yelén. "Ms. Korolev. I'm still in high orbit, but we can talk if you wish."

"Good. I wanted to introduce you to your partner." She smiled at some private joke. "Ms. Lu, this is Wil Brierson. Inspector Brierson, Della Lu."

40

He'd heard that name before but couldn't remember just where. The short Asian looked much as she had at the party. He guessed she hadn't been out of stasis for more than a few days: her hair was the same dark fuzz as before.

Lu stared at Korolev for several seconds after she made the introduction, then turned to look at Brierson. If the delay were not a mannerism, she must be out beyond the moon. "I've read good things about you, Inspector," she said and made a smile that didn't involve her eyes. She spoke carefully, each word an isolated thing, but otherwise her English was much like Wil's North American dialect.

Before Brierson could reply, Korolev said, "What of our prime suspects, Ms. Lu?"

Another four-beat pause. "The Robinsons refused to stop." The library windows showed a view from space. In one direction, Wil could see a bright blue disk and a fainter, gray one —the Earth and the moon. Through the window behind Lu hung a bobble, sun and Earth and moon reflected in its surface. The sphere was surrounded by a spidery metal structure, swollen here and there into more solid structures. Dozens of tiny silver balls moved in slow orbit about the central one. Every few seconds the bobbles vanished, replaced by a much larger one that contained even the spidery superstructure. There was a flash of light, and then the scene returned to its first phase.

"By the time I caught up with them, they were off anti-gravity and using impulse boost. Their flicker rate was constant. It was easy to pace them."

Quack, quack. For a moment, Wil was totally lost. Then he realized he was seeing a nuke drive, *very* close up. The idea was so simple that it had been used even in his time: Just eject a bomb, then go into stasis for a few seconds while it detonates and gives you a big push. When you came out of stasis, drop off another bomb and repeat the process. Of course, it was deadly to bystanders. To get these pictures, Della Lu must have matched the Robinsons' bobble cycle exactly, and used her own bombs to keep up.

"Notice that when the drive bobble bursts, they immediately generate a smaller one just inside their defense frame. A battle would have taken several thousand years of outside time to resolve."

Objects in stasis had absolute protection against the outside world. But bobbles eventually burst: if the duration was short, your enemy would still be waiting, ready to shoot; if the duration was long, your enemy might drop your bobble into the sun —and absolute protection would end in absolute catastrophe. Apparently the advanced travelers used a hierarchy of autonomous fighters, flickering in and out of realtime. While in realtime, their processors decided on the duration of the next embobblement. The shortest-period devices stayed in sync with longer-period ones, relaying conclusions up a chain of command. At the top, the travelers' command bobble might have a relatively long period.

"So they got away?" Hidden by time and interstellar depths. Pause, pause, pause, pause. "Not entirely. They claimed innocence, and left a spokesman to demonstrate their good faith." One of the windows brightened into a picture of Tammy Robinson. She looked even paler than usual. Wil felt a flash of anger at Don Robinson. Clever it might be, but what sort of person leaves his teenage kid to face a murder investigation? Lu continued. "I have her with me. We should be landing in sixty minutes."

"Good. Ms. Lu, I would like you and Brierson to interview her then." Beyond the windows, forests replaced the black and bright of space. "I want you to get her story before you and Brierson leave for the restart of Town Korolev."

Wil glanced at the spacer. She was strange, but apparently capable. And she was as powerful a witness as he could get. He ignored Yelén's auton and tried to put the proper note of peremptory confidence in his voice when he said, "One other thing, Yelén."

"Well?"

"We need a complete copy of the diary."

"How— What diary!"

"The one Marta kept all the years she was marooned."

Yelén's mouth clamped shut as she realized he must be bluffing—and that she had already lost the game. Wil kept his eyes on Yelén, but he noticed the auton rise: there was more than one bluff to play here.

"It's none of your business, Brierson. I've read it: Marta had no idea who marooned her."

"I want it, Yelén."

"Well, you can just stick it!" She half-rose from her seat, then sat. "You're the last person I want pawing through Marta's private—" She turned to Lu. "Maybe I could show parts of it to you."

Wil didn't let the spacer reply. "No. Where I come from, concealment of evidence was usually a crime, Yelén. That's meaningless here, but if you don't give me the diary—all of it, and everything associated with it—I'll drop the case, and I'll ask Lu to drop the case."

Yelén's fists were clenched. She started to speak, stopped. A faint tremor shook her face. Finally: "Okay. You'll have it. *Now get out of my sight!*"

FOUR

Tammy Robinson was a very frightened young woman; Wil didn't need police experience to see that. She paced back and forth across the room, hysteria sparking from the high edge in her voice. "How can you keep me in this cell? It's a dungeon!"

The walls were unadorned, off-white. But Wil could see doors opening onto a bedroom, a kitchen. There were stairs, perhaps to a study. Her quarters covered about 150 square meters—a little cramped by Wil's standards, but scarcely a punishing confinement. He stepped away from Della Lu and put his hand on Tammy's shoulder. "These are ship's quarters, Tam. Della Lu never expected to have passengers." That was only a guess, but it felt right. Lu's holdings were compact, built both vertically and horizontally. All the advanced travelers could take their households into space—but Lu's was designed to stay there, to be a home even in solar systems without planets. "You are in custody, but once we get to Town Korolev, you'll get better housing."

Della Lu tilted her head to one side. "Yes. Yelén Korolev is going to take care of you then. She has much better—"

"*No!*" It was almost a scream. Tammy's eyes showed white all around the irises. "I surrendered to *you*, Della Lu. And in

44

good faith. I won't tell you anything if you . . . Korolev will—" She put her hand over her mouth and collapsed on a nearby sofa.

Wil sat down beside her as Della Lu pulled up a chair to sit facing them. Lu's black pants and high-collared jacket looked military, but she sat on the edge of her chair and watched Tammy's consternation with childlike curiosity. Wil cast a meaningful look in her direction (as if that would do any good) before continuing. "Tammy, there's no way we'll let Yelén get at you."

Tammy was upset, but no fool. She looked past Wil at the spacer. "Is that a promise, Della Lu?"

Lu gave an odd chuckle, but this time she didn't blow it. "Yes. And it's a promise I can keep."

They stared at each other a silent moment. Then the girl shuddered, her whole body relaxing. "Okay. I'll talk. Of course I'll talk. That's the whole reason I stayed behind: to clear my family's name."

"You know what's happened to Marta?"

"I've heard Yelén's accusations. When we came out of that strange, overlong bobblement, she was all over the comm links. She said poor Marta got marooned in the present . . . that she *died* there." Frank horror showed on Tammy's face.

"That's right. Someone sabotaged the Korolev jump program. It lasted a century instead of three months, and left Marta outside of stasis."

"And my dad's the chief suspect?" Incredulously.

Wil nodded. "I saw your father arguing with Marta, Tam. And later she told me how your family wants the people of Town Korolev to join you. . . . Your plans would benefit if the settlement failed."

"Sure. But we're not some gang of twentieth-century thugs, Wil. We *know* we have something more attractive than the Korolevs' rehash of civilization. It'll take the average person a while to see this, but given a fair chance they'll come with us. Instead, Yelén's forced us to run for our lives."

"You don't think Marta's been killed?" said Lu.

Tammy shrugged. "No. That would be hard to fake, especially if you"—she was looking at Della—"insist on studying the remains. I think Marta was murdered—and I think Yelén is the murderer. All the talk about outside sabotage is just short of ridiculous."

This was certainly Wil's biggest worry. In his time, domestic violence was a leading cause of death. Yelén seemed the most powerful of the high-techs. If she were the villain, life might be short for successful investigators. But aloud: "She's truly broken up over losing Marta. If she's faking, she's very good at it."

Tammy's response was quick. "I don't think she's faking it. I think she killed Marta for some crazy personal reason, and terribly regrets the necessity. But now that it's done, she's going to use it to destroy all opposition to the great Korolev plan."

"Um." He, W. W. Brierson, might be the cause of Marta's death. Suppose Yelén conceived that she was losing her love to another. For some disturbed souls, such a loss was logically equivalent to the death of the beloved. They could murder— and then honestly blame the loss on others. . . . Wil remembered the irrational hatred in Yelén's eyes when he walked into her library.

He looked at Tammy with new respect. She'd never seemed this bright before. In fact . . . he felt just a little bit manipulated. For all her terror, the girl was a very cool character. "Tammy," he said quietly, "just how old are you, really?"

"I—" The tear-streaked adolescent face froze for a second. Then: "I've lived ninety years, Wil."

Forty years longer than I. Some daughter figure.

"B-but that's not a secret." New tears filled her eyes. "I'd've told anyone who asked. A-and I'm not faking my personality. I try to keep a fresh, open mind. We're going to live a long time, and Daddy says it helps if we grow up slowly, if we don't freeze into adult mind-sets like they did in the old days."

The Lu creature gave one of her strange little laughs. "That depends on how long you plan to live," she said to no one in particular.

Brierson suddenly realized that it was wishful thinking to

regard himself an expert on human nature. *Once* he had been; now that expertise might be as obsolete as the rest of his knowledge. When he left civilization, life-prolonging medicine had been just a few decades old. At that time, Tammy's deception would have been almost impossible. Yelén Korolev had had about two hundred years to teach herself to lie. Della Lu was so disconnected from humanity, it was hard to make sense of her at all. How could he judge what such people said?

Might as well continue the sympathetic role. He patted Tammy's hand. "Okay, Tam. I'm glad you told us."

She smiled halfheartedly. "Don't you see, Wil? My dad's a suspect because we disagreed with Marta. We left to protect the family; my staying behind shows we're not running from an investigation. . . . But Yelén is. On the way down, Della Lu told me how Yelén wants you back in stasis right away. She'll be left all alone at the scene of the crime. By the time you two come out, the evidence will be tens of thousands years stale—heck, what evidence there is will have been manufactured by her

"Now, I brought the family records for the weeks before our party. You and Della Lu should study them. They may be dull, but at least they're the truth."

Wil nodded. It was obvious the Robinsons had their story together. He let the interview go on another fifteen minutes, until Tammy seemed calm and almost relaxed. Lu spoke occasionally, her interjections sometimes perceptive, more often obscure. It was evident that—in itself—clearing the family name was of little importance to the Robinsons. When they were headed, present opinion would be less than dust. But the family still wanted recruits. Tammy's parents were convinced that the people of Town Korolev would eventually realize that settling in the present was a dead end, and that time itself was the proper place for humanity. It might take a few decades, but if Tammy could survive the murder investigation, she would be free to wait and persuade. And eventually she would catch up with her family. Her parents had set a number of rendezvous in the megayears to come. Their exact locations were something she refused to reveal.

"You want to pace your lives, and live as long as the universe?" asked Lu.

"At least."

The spacer giggled. "And what will you do at the end?"

"That depends on how it ends." Tammy's eyes lit. "Daddy thinks that all the mysteries people have ever wondered on—even the Extinction—may be revealed there. It's the ultimate rendezvous for all thinking beings. If time is cyclic, we'll bobble through to the beginning and Man will be universal."

"And if the universe is open and dies forever?"

"Then perhaps we and the others can change that." Tammy shrugged. "But if we can't—well, we'll still be there. We will have seen it all. Daddy says we'll raise a glass and toast the memory of all of you that went before." She was still smiling.

And Brierson wondered if this might be the craziest of all his new acquaintances.

Afterwards, Wil tried to plan out the investigation with Della Lu. It was not easy.

"Was Ms. Robinson distressed at the beginning of the interview?" asked Lu.

Wil rolled his eyes heavenward. "Yes, I believe she was."

"Ah. I thought so, too."

"Look, uh, Della. What Tammy says about Yelén makes sense. It's absurd for the cops—us—to leave the murder scene like this. Back in Michigan, we would have dropped any customer who demanded such a thing. Now, Yelén is right that my hanging around to investigate the physical evidence would be amateurish. But your equipment is as good as hers—"

"Better."

"—and she should be willing to let you postpone bobbling long enough to gather evidence."

Lu was silent for a moment—talking through her headband? "Ms. Korolev wants to be alone for emotional reasons."

"Hmph. She has thousands of years to be alone before the Peacers come out. You should at least do an autopsy and record the physical evidence."

"Very well. Ms. Korolev is a suspect, then?"

48

Wil spread his hands. "At this stage, she and the Robinsons have to be at the top of our list. Once we start poking around, it may be easy to scratch her. Just now it would be totally unprofessional to have *her* do the field investigation."

"Is Ms. Korolev friendly towards you?"

"Huh? Not especially. What does that have to do with the investigation?"

"Nothing. I'm trying to find a . . ."—she seemed to search for the word—"a role model for talking to you."

Wil smiled faintly, thinking back to Yelén's hostility. "I'd appreciate it if you wouldn't model on her."

"Okay." Unsmiling.

If Lu were as smart with gadgets as she was dumb with people, they would make the best detective team in history. "There is something else, something very important, that I need. Yelén has promised me physical protection and access to her databases. I'd like to have your protection, too—at least till we can clear her."

"Certainly. If you wish, I'll manage your jump forward, too."

"And I'd like access to your databases." Cross-checking Korolev couldn't hurt.

The spacer hesitated. "Okay. But some of the information isn't very accessible."

Wil looked around Della's cabin—command bridge? It was even smaller than Tammy's quarters, and almost as stark. A small cluster of roses grew from Della's desk; their scent filled the air. A watercolor landscape hung on the wall facing the spacer. The life tones and shadows were subtly wrong, as if the artist were clumsy . . . or the scene not of this Earth.

And Brierson was putting his life in this person's hands. In this universe of strangers, he must trust some more than others, but . . . "How old are you, Della?"

"I've lived nine thousand years, Mr. Brierson. I have been away . . . a long time. I have seen much." Her dark eyes took on that cold, far look he remembered from their first encounters. For a moment, she looked past him, perhaps at the watercolor, perhaps beyond. Then the expressionless gaze returned to his face. "I think it's time I rejoined the human race."

FIVE

Some fifty thousand years later, all that was left of the only world empire in history, the Peace Authority, returned to normal time. They were welcomed by Korolev autons, and discouraged from interfering with the bobbles on the south side of the Inland Sea. They had three months to consider their new circumstances before those bobbles burst.

What Marta and Yelén had worked so long for was ready to begin.

Thousands of tonnes of equipment were given to the low-techs, along with farms, factories, mines. The gifts were to individuals, supposedly based on their expertise back in civilization. The Dasgupta brothers received two vanloads of communication equipment. To Wil's amazement, they immediately traded the gear to an NM signal officer—for a thousand-hectare farm. And Korolev didn't object. She did point out which equipment was likely to fail first, and provide databases to those who wanted to plan for the future.

Many of the ungoverned low-techs loved it: survival with profit. Within weeks they had a thousand schemes for combining high-tech equipment with primitive production lines. Both would coexist for decades, with the failing high-tech restricted to a smaller and smaller role. In the end there would be a viable infrastructure.

The governments were not so pleased. Both Peacers and NMs were heavily armed, but as long as Korolev stood guard over the Inland Sea, all that twenty-first-century might was about as persuasive as the brass cannon on a courthouse lawn. Both had had time to understand the situation. They watched each other carefully, and united in their complaints against Korolev and the other high-techs. Their propaganda noted how carefully the high-techs coordinated the giveaway, how restricted it really was: no weapons were given, no bobbler technology, no aircraft, no autons, no medical equipment. "Korolev gives the illusion of freedom, not the reality."

The excitement of the founding came muted to Wil. He went to some of the parties. Sometimes he watched the Peacer or NM news. But he had little time to participate. He had a job, in some ways like his of long ago; he had a murderer to catch. Unless something seemed connected with that goal, it drifted by him, irrelevant.

Marta's murder was a major piece of news. Even with a civilization to build, people still found time to talk about it. Now that she was gone, everyone remembered her friendliness. Every unpopular Korolev policy was greeted with a sigh of "If only Marta were alive, this would be different." At first, Wil was at the center of the parties. But he had little to say. Besides, he was in a unique—and uncomfortable—position: Wil was a low-tech, but with the perks of a high. He could fly anywhere he wanted; the other low-techs were confined to Korolev-supplied "public" transportation. He had his own protection autons, supplied by Della and Yelén; other low-techs watched with ill-concealed nervousness when those floated into view. These advantages were nontransferable, and it wasn't long before Wil was more shunned than sought.

One of the Korolevs' fundamental principles had already been violated: the settlement was physically scattered now. The Peacers had refused to move across the Inland Sea to Town Korolev. With dazzling impudence, they demanded that

Yelén set them up with their own town on the north shore. That put them more than nine hundred kilometers from the rest of humanity—a distance more psychological than real, since it was a fifteen-minute flight on Yelén's new trans-sea shuttle. Nevertheless, it was a surprise that she yielded.

The surviving Korolev was . . . changed. Wil had talked to her only twice since the colony's return to realtime. The first time had been something of a shock. She looked almost the same as before, but there was a moment of nonrecognition in her eyes. "Ah, Brierson," she said mildly. Her only comment about Lu's providing him protection was to say that she would continue to do so also. Her hostility was muted; she'd had a long time to bury her grief.

Yelén had spent a hundred years following Marta's travels around the sea. She and her devices had stored and cataloged and studied everything that might bear on the murder. Marta's was already the most thoroughly investigated murder in the history of the human race. *But only if this investigator is not herself the murderer,* said a little voice in the back of Wil's head.

Yelén had done another thing with the century she stayed behind: She had tried to reeducate herself. "There's only one of us left, Inspector. I've tried to live double. I've learned everything I can about Marta's specialty. I've dreamed through Marta's memories of every project she managed." A shadow of doubt crossed her face. "I hope it's enough." The Yelén he'd known before the murder would not have shown such weakness.

So, armed with Marta's knowledge and trying to imitate Marta's attitudes, Yelén had relented and let the Peacers establish North Shore. She'd set up the trans-sea flier service. She'd encouraged a couple of the high-techs—Genet and Blumenthal—to move their principal estates there.

And the murder investigation had truly been left to Lu and Brierson.

Though he had talked to Korolev only twice, he saw Della Lu almost every day. She had produced a list of suspects. She agreed with Korolev: the crime was completely beyond the low-techs. Of the high-techs, Yelén and the Robinsons were still the best suspects. (Fortunately Lu was cagey enough not to report *all* their suspicions to Yelén.)

At first, Wil thought the manner of the murder was a critical clue. He'd brought it up with Della early on. "If the murderer could bypass Marta's protection, why not kill her outright? This business of marooning her is nicely poetic, but it left a real possibility that she might be rescued."

Della shook her head. "You don't understand." Her face was framed with smooth black hair now. She'd stayed behind for nine months, the longest Yelén would allow. No breakthroughs resulted from the stay, but it had been long enough for her hair to grow out. She looked like a normal young woman now, and she could talk for minutes at a time without producing a jarring inanity, without getting that far, cold look. Lu was still the weirdest of the advanced travelers, but she was no longer in a class by herself. "The Korolev protection system is good. It's fast. It's smart. Whoever killed Marta did it with software. The killer found a chink in the Korolev defensive logic and very cleverly exploited it. Extending the stasis period to one century was not by itself life-threatening. Leaving Marta outside of stasis was not by itself life-threatening."

"Together they were deadly."

"True. And the defense system would have normally noticed that. I'm simplifying. What the killer did was more complicated. My point is, if he had tried anything more direct, there is no amount of clever programming that could have fooled the system. There was no surefire way he could murder Marta. Doing it this way gave the killer the best chance of success."

"Unless the killer is Yelén. I assume she could override all the system safeguards?"

"Yes."

But doing so would clearly show her guilt.

"Hmm. Marooning Marta left her defenseless. Why couldn't the murderer arrange an accident for her then? It doesn't make sense that she was allowed to live forty years."

Della thought a moment. "You're suggesting the killer could

have bobbled everyone else for a century, and delayed bobbling himself?"

"Sure. A few minutes' delay would've been enough. Is that so hard?"

"By itself, it's trivial. But everyone was linked with the Korolev system for that jump. If anyone had delayed, it would show up in everyone's records. I'm an expert on autonomous systems, Wil. Yelén has shown me her system's design. It's a tight job, only a year older than mine. For anyone—except Yelén—to alter those jump records would be . . ."

"Impossible?" These systems people never changed. They could work miracles, but at the same time they claimed perfectly reasonable requests were impossible.

"No, maybe not impossible. If the killer had planned ahead, he might have an auton that didn't appear on his stasis roster. It could have been left outside of stasis without being noticed. But I don't see how the jump records themselves could be altered unless the killer had thoroughly infiltrated the Korolev system."

So they were dealing with a fairly impromptu act. And the queer circumstances of Marta's death were nothing more than a twenty-third-century version of a knife in the back.

SIX

Korolev had delivered Marta's diary soon after the colony returned to realtime. Wil's demand for it was one thing that could still bring a flare of anger to her face. In fact, Wil didn't really want to see the thing. But getting a copy, and getting Della to verify that it was undoctored, was essential. Until then, Yelén was logically the best suspect on his list. Now that he had the diary, it was easier to accept his intuition that Yelén was innocent. He set out to read Yelén's summaries and Della's cross-checking. If nothing showed up there, the diary would be a low-priority item.

Yelén had sent down an enormous amount of material. It included high-resolution holos of all Marta's writing. Yelén supplied a powerful overdoc; Wil could sort the pages by pH if he wanted. A note in the overdoc said the originals were in stasis, available at five days' notice.

The originals. Wil hadn't thought about it: How could you make a diary without even a data pad? Brief messages could be carved on the side of a tree or chiseled in rock, but for a diary you'd need something like paper and pen. Marta had been marooned for forty years, plenty of time to experiment. Her earliest writing was berry-juice ink on the soft insides of tree bark. She left the heavy pages in a rock cairn sealed with mud.

When they were recovered fifty years later, the bark had rotted and the juice stains were invisible. Yelén and her autons had studied the fragile remains. Microanalysis showed where the berry stains had been; the first chapters were not lost. Apparently Marta had recognized the danger: the "paper" in the later cairns was made from reed strips. The dark green ink was scarcely faded.

The first entries were mainly narrative. At the other end of the diary, after she had been decades alone, the pages were filled with drawings, essays, and poems. Forty years is a long time if you have to live it alone, second by second. Not counting recopied material, Marta wrote more than two million words before she died. (Yelén had supplied him with a commercial database, GreenInc. Wil looked at some of the items in it; the diary was as long as twenty noninteractive novels.) Her medium was far bulkier than old-time paper, and she traveled thousands of kilometers in her time. Whenever she moved, she built a new cairn for her writing. The first few pages in each repeated especially important things—directions to the previous cairns, for instance. Later, Yelén found every one. Nothing had been lost, though one cairn had been flooded. Even there, the reconstructions were nearly complete.

Wil spent an afternoon going through Yelén's synopsis and Della's corresponding analysis. There were no surprises.

Afterwards, Wil couldn't resist looking for references to himself. There were four clusters, the most recent listed first. Wil punched it up:

Year 38.137 Cairn #4
Lat 14.36N Long 1.01E [K-meridian]
—ask for heuristic cross-reference—

was the header Yelén's overdoc printed across the top of the display. Below it was cursive green lettering. A blinking red arrow marked the reference:

≪ . . . and if I don't make it, dearest Lelya, please don't spend your time trying to solve this mystery. Live for both of us; live for the project. If you must do anything with it, delegate the responsibility. There was that policeman. A low-tech. I can't remember his name. (Oh, the millionth time I pray for an interface band, or even a data set!) Give him the job, and then concentrate on what is important. . . . >>

Wil sat back and wished the context searcher weren't so damned smart. She didn't even remember his name! He tried to tell himself that she had lived almost forty years beyond their acquaintance when she wrote these words. Would he remember her name forty years from now? *(Yes!)* To think of all his soul-searching, to think how close they seemed that last night, and how noble he had been to back off—when all the time he was just another low-tech to her.

With a quick sweep of his hand, Wil cleared the other references from the display. *Let it lie, Wil. Let it lie.* He stood up, walked to the window of his study. He had important work to do. There was the interview with Monica Raines, and then with Juan Chanson. He should be researching for those.

So after a moment he returned to his desk . . . and jumped the display to the first entry in Marta's diary:

<< The Journal of Marta Qih-hui Qen Korolev

Dearest Lelya, >> it began. Every entry was addressed to "Lelya."

"GreenInc. Question," said Wil. "What is 'Lelya'?" He pointed to the word in the diary. A side display filled with the three most likely possibilities. The first was: "Diminutive of the name Yeléna." Wil nodded to himself; that had been his guess. He continued reading from the central display.

<< Dearest Lelya,

<< It's now 181 days since everyone left—and that's the only thing I'm sure of.

<< Starting this journal is something of an admission of defeat. Till now, I had kept careful track of time, and that seemed all that was necessary; you remember we had planned a flicker cycle of ninety days. Yesterday the second flicker should have happened—yet I saw nothing.

<< So I guess I have to take the longer view. (What a mild way to say it. Yesterday, all I could do was cry.) I've got to have someone to "talk" to.

≪ And I've got a lot to say, Lelya. You know how I like to talk. The hardest thing is the act of writing. I don't know how civilization got started, if literacy involved the effort I've had to make. This bark is easy to find, but I'm afraid it won't age well. Have to think about that. The "ink" is easy, too. But the reed pen I've made leaks and blobs. And if I say something wrong, I can only paint out the errors. (I understand why calligraphy was such a high art.) It takes a long time to write even the simplest things. But I have an advantage now: I have lots and lots of time. All the time in the world. ≫

The reconstruction of the original showed awkward block letters and numerous scratch-outs. Wil wondered how many years it had been before she developed the cursive style he'd seen at the end of her diary.

≪ By the time you read this, you'll probably have all the explanations (hopefully from me direct!), but I want to tell you what I remember.

≪ There was the party at the Robinsons. I left early, so mad at Don that I could spit. They've really done us dirt, you know that? Anyway, it was past the Witching Hour and I was walking the forest path to the house. Fred was about five meters up, in front of me; I remember the moonlight glinting off his hull. ≫

Fred? The diary's overdoc said that was the auton with Marta that night. Wil hadn't realized they were personalized. You never heard them addressed by name. Come to think of it, that wasn't surprising; the high-techs generally talked to their mechanicals via headband.

≪ From Fred I had a good view over three octaves. There was no one close by. There were no autons shadowing me. It's about an hour's walk up to the house. I had taken longer. I wanted to be cool when I talked to you about Don's little game. I was almost to the great steps when it happened. Fred had no hint. There was a cinnamon burst of static and then he crashed to the ground. It's the most startled I've ever been, Lelya. Our whole lives we've had autons giving us extra eyes. This is the first time I can remember not having *any* warning of a problem.

≪ Ahead of me, the great steps were gone. There was my reflection staring back. Fred was lying at the edge of the bobble. He'd been cut in half by the stasis field.

≪ We've had some rough times, Lelya, like when we fought the graverobbers. They were so strong, I thought the battle might carry us past fifty megayears and ruin everything. You remember how I was after that. Well, this was worse. I think I went a little crazy. I kept telling myself it was all a dream. (Even now, six months later, that sometimes seems the best explanation.) I ran along the bobble's edge. Things were as peaceful and silent as before, but now the ground was treacherous beneath my feet and branches clawed at me. I didn't have Fred to be my high eyes. The bobble was hundreds of meters across. It met the ground just beyond the great steps. It didn't cut through any large trees. It was obviously the bobblement we'd planned for the property.

≪ Well, if you're reading this, you already know the rest. The Robinsons' place was bobbled. Genet's was bobbled. It took me three days to hike across all of Korolev Town: everything was bobbled. It looked exactly like the jump we'd programmed except for two things: (1) (obviously) poor little Marta had been left outside, and (2) all automatic equipment was *in* stasis.

≪ Those first weeks, I could still hope that every ninety days the stasis would flicker off while the autons checked the Peacer bobble. I couldn't imagine how all this had happened (I still can't), yet it might turn out to be one of those stupid mistakes one can laugh about afterwards. All I had to do was stay alive for ninety days.

≪ There's damn little outside stasis, Lelya. There was no question of salvaging Fred. Looking at that compact pile of junk, I was surprised how little I could do with it—even if his power supply had been on my side of the bobble. Monica Raines is right about one thing: Without autons, we might as well be savages. They are our hands. And that's not the most horrible part: Without processor and db support, I'm a cripple, my mind stuck in molasses. When a question occurs to me, the only data is what's wedged in my own gray matter. The only eyes I see from are my own, fixed in space and time, seeing only a narrow band of the spectrum. To imagine that before our time people lived their whole lives in this lobotomized state! Maybe it helped that they didn't know anything better.

≪ But Monica is wrong about something else: I didn't just sit down and starve. All my time in survival sports paid off. The Robinsons had left a pile of trash just on our side of the property line. (That figures.) At a glance you might not think there was much worthwhile: a hundred kilos of botched gold fittings, an organic sludge pond that made me want to puke, and—get this—a dozen cutter blades. So what if they've lost their micrometer edge? They're still sharp enough to cut a hair lengthwise. They're about half a kilo each, single diamond crystals. I lashed them onto wood hafts. I also found some shovels on a pile of rock ash in town.

≪ I remembered the large carnivores we spotted coming in. If they're still around, they're lying low. After a couple of weeks, I was beginning to feel safe. My traps worked, though not as well as on a sport trip; the wildlife hasn't recovered from the Peacer rescue. Just as we'd planned, the south gallery of the house was left out of stasis. (Remember how you thought it hadn't aged enough?) It's all naked stone, stairs and towers and halls, but it makes good shelter—and parts are easy to barricade.

≪ I didn't remember how long the lookabout would last, so I decided to hit you over the head with my message. I lashed a frame between the trees at the bottom of the great stairs. I spread bark across the framework and used wet ash to spell HELP in letters three meters high. There's no way it could be missed by the monitor on top of the library. I had the sign done a good week ahead of time.

≪ Day ninety was worse than waiting for the judge's call in arbitration. No day ever seemed so long. I sat right by my sign and watched my reflection in the bobble. Lelya, *nothing happened.* You aren't on a three-month flicker, or the monitor isn't watching. I never hated my own face as much as I did that day, watching it in the side of the bobble. ≫

Of course, Marta had not given up. The next pages described how she had built similar signs near the bobbles of all the advanced travelers.

≪ Day 180 just passed, and the bobbles still sit. I cried a lot. I miss you so. Survival games were fun, but not forever.

≪ I've got to settle down for the long haul. I'm going to make those billboards sturdier. I want them to last at least a hundred years. How long can *I* last? Without health care, people used to live about a century. I've kept my bio-age at twenty-five years, so I should have seventy-five left. Without the databases I can't be sure, but I bet seventy-five is a lower bound. There should be some residual effect from my last medical treatment, and I'm full of panphages. On the other hand, old people were fragile, weren't they? If I have to protect myself and get my own food, that could be a factor.

≪ Okay. Let's be pessimistic. Say I can only last seventy-five years. What's my best chance for getting rescued?

≪ You can bet I've thought about that a lot, Lelya. So much depends on what caused this catastrophe—and all the clues are on your side of the bobble. I've got ideas, but without the databases I can't tell what's plausible. ≫ She went on to list the string of unrelated errors that would be necessary to leave *her* outside and all the autons inside, and to change the flicker period. Sabotage was the only possible explanation; she knew that someone had tried to kill her.

≪ I'm not lying down to die. I can't think technical anymore, but I'll bet you still have a fairly short flicker period. Besides, we have gear lots of other places: at the Lagrange zones, the West End mines, the Peacer bobble. With luck, there will be lookabouts in the next seventy-five years. And didn't we leave autonomous devices in realtime in Canada? I think there's a land bridge to America in this era. If I can get there, maybe I could make my own rescue.

≪ So most of the time, I'm optimistic.

≪ But suppose I don't make it? Then I'm the murder victim, and some kind of witness, too. Even though you'll never get Fred's record of the Robinsons' recruiting party, you'll hear about it elsewhere. That's the only clue I have.

≪ Don't let them break up our settlement, Lelya. ≫

SEVEN

The morning of the Monica Raines interview did not begin well. Wil was still asleep when the house announced that Della Lu was waiting outside.

Wil groaned, slowly rising from the unpleasant dreams that haunted his mornings. Then he realized the time, and the day. "Sorry, sorry. I'll be right down." He rolled out of bed and staggered into the bathroom. Who had decided on this early start, anyway? Then he remembered it had been himself; something about time zones.

Even downstairs, he was still a bit foggy. He grabbed a box lunch from the kitchen. The bright colors on the package were advertising fifty million years old. When Korolev said she was providing twenty-first-century support, she meant it. The autofactories were running off the same programs as the original manufacturers. The effect was more weird than homey. He tucked the lunch into his shoulder bag along with his data set. Something in the back of his mind was saying he should take more; after all, he was going a third of the way around the world today. He shook his head. Sure, and he'd probably be back in five hours. Even the lunch was unnecessary. Wil gave final instructions to the house and stepped into the morning coolness.

It was the sort of morning that should change the ways of

night owls. Green loomed high around the house, the trees glistening damply in the sun. Everything felt clean and bright, just created. Except for the birds, it was quiet. He walked across the mossy street toward Lu's enclosed flier. Two protection devices—one from Yelén and one from Della—left their posts above his house and drifted along with him.

"Hey, Wil! Wait a minute." Dilip Dasgupta waved from his house, fifty meters down the road. "Where are you going?"

"Calafia," Brierson called back.

"Wow." Rohan and Dilip were both up and dressed. They jogged down the road to him.

"This part of the murder investigation?" said Dilip.

"You look awful, Wil," said Rohan.

Brierson ignored Rohan. "Yeah. We're flying out to see Monica Raines."

"Ah! A suspect."

"No. We're still fact-finding, Dilip. I want to talk to all the high-techs."

"Oh." He sounded like a football fan disappointed by his team's hard luck. A few days earlier, the disappointment would have been tinged with fear. Everyone had been edgy then, guessing that Marta's murder might be the prelude to a massive assault on the settlement.

"Wil, I mean it." Rohan was not to be sidetracked. "You really looked dragged out. And it's not just this morning, so early and all. Don't let this case shut you off from your friends. You gotta mingle, Wil. . . . Like, this morning we're going on a fishing expedition off North Shore. It's something the Peacers organized. That Genet fellow is coming along in case we run into anything too big to handle. You know, I don't see why governments got such a bad name. Both the Peacers and the New Mexicans aren't much different from social clubs or college fraternities. They've been real nice to everybody."

"Yes, and face it, Wil, we're starting new lives here. Most of the human race is tied up in those two groups now. There are lots of women there, lots of people you'd like to know."

Brierson grinned, embarrassed and a bit touched. "You're right. I should keep up with things."

Rohan reached up to slap him on the shoulder. "Hey, if you

get back in the afternoon, you might have the Lu person drop you off at North Shore. I bet there'll still be something going."

"Okay!" Wil turned and walked toward Lu's aircraft. The Dasguptas were right about some things. How wrong they were about others: A smile came back to his lips as he imagined Steve Fraley's reaction to hearing the Republic of New Mexico likened to a social club.

"Good morning, Wil." Lu's face was impassive. She seemed not at all impatient at the delay. "Is 1.5 g's okay?"

"Sure, sure." Brierson settled into a chair, not quite sure what she was talking about. At least he didn't have to worry about *her* questioning his mood. Short of laughter or smiles or tears, she still seemed incapable of reading facial expressions.

He sank slowly into the seat cushions as the flier's acceleration added a physical lassitude to his mental one. He'd been using the GreenInc database for more than the investigation of Marta's murder. Last night he'd tracked his family to the end of the twenty-second century. He was proud of what his children had become: Anne the astronaut, Billy the cop and later the story-maker. As far as he could tell, Virginia had never remarried. The three of them had disappeared into the twenty-third century, along with his parents, his sister, and all the rest of humanity.

In 2140 and 2180 they had bobbled gifts to accompany him. GreenInc said it was the best survival equipment their money could buy. It had all been lost to the graverobbers, the scavenging travelers that existed in the first megayears after Man. Perhaps that was just as well. There would have been family video in those care packages. That would have been very hard to view.

. . . But all along he'd had the secret dream that Virginia might come after him herself, at least when the kids had their own families. It was strange: He would have pleaded with her not to come, yet now he felt . . . betrayed.

The faint whistling from beyond the windows had long faded, but the gut-tugging acceleration continued. Wil's attention returned to the flier. He looked straight out. Cloud-speckled ocean stood like a blue wall beside them. He looked up through the transparent dome—and saw the curve of the Earth, pale blue meeting the black of space. They were hundreds of klicks up, driving forward at a steady acceleration that was nothing like the ballistic trajectories he was used to.

"How long?" he managed to say.

"It is slow, isn't it?" Della said. "Now that the settlement is founded, Yelén doesn't want us to use nukes in near space. At this acceleration, it'll be another half hour to North America."

An island chain trundled rapidly across his field of view. Much nearer, he saw the autons that protected him at home; the two flew formation with Della's craft.

"I still don't understand why you want to go out of your way to interview Ms. Raines. How is she special?"

Wil shrugged. "I like to do the reluctant ones first. She's not interested in coming back in person, and I want these interviews to be face to face."

Della said, "That's wise. Most of us could do almost anything on a holo channel. . . . But she's one of the least powerful of the high-techs. I can't imagine her as the killer."

A few minutes later, Della turned the flier over. It was a skew turn that for a moment had them accelerating straight down into the Pacific. Wil was glad there had not been time for breakfast. When they entered the atmosphere off the west coast of Calafia, they were moving barely fast enough to put a glow in the flier's hull.

Calafia. It was one of the Korolevs' more appropriate namings. In Wil's time, one of the clichés of regional insult was the prediction that California would one day fall into the sea. It never happened. Instead, California had *put* to sea, sliding along the San Andreas Fault, earthquake by earthquake, millennium after millennium—till the southwest coast of North America became a fifteen-hundred-kilometer island. It was indeed Calafia, the vast, narrow island that Spanish mariners had (prematurely) identified fifty million years earlier.

Della covered the last few hundred kilometers in a low approach. The beach passed quickly beneath. North and south, for as far as he could see, breakers marched on perfect sand. Nowhere was there town or road. The world was in an interglacial period now, much as in the Age of Man. That coastline really *did* look like California's. It didn't raise the same nostalgia as Michigan might, but he felt his throat tighten nevertheless. He and Virginia had often visited southern California in the 2090s, after the disgovernance of Aztlán.

They scudded over hills mantled with evergreens. Afternoon sunlight cast everything in jagged relief. Beyond the hills, the vegetation was sere and grayish green. Beyond that was prairie and the Calafia straits.

"Okay. So what dumb questions do you want to ask?" Monica Raines did not look back as she led them down to her —blind, she called it. Wil and Della hurried after her. He was not put off by the artist's brusqueness. In the past, she'd made no secret of her dislike for the Korolevs and their plans.

The wood stairs descended through tree-shrouded dimness. The smell of mesquite hung in the air. At the bottom, invisible among vines and branches, was a small cabin. Its floor was deeply carpeted, with pillows scattered about. One side of the room had no wall, but overlooked the beginning of the plainsland. A battery of equipment—optics?—was mounted at the edge of this open side.

"I'd appreciate it if you'd keep your voices down," said Monica. "We're less than one hundred meters from the starter nest." She fiddled with the equipment; she was not wearing a headband. A display flat lit with the picture of two . . . vultures? They strutted around a small pile of stones and brush. The picture was wavery with heat shimmers. Wil sighted over the optics: Sure enough, he could just make out two birds in the valley below the blind.

"Why use a telescope?" Lu asked softly. "With tracer cameras, you could—"

"Yeah, I use them, too. Gimme remotes," she said to the thin air. Several other displays came to life. The pictures were dim even in the darkened room. "I don't like to scatter tracers all around; they mess up the environment. Besides, I don't have any good ones left." She jerked a thumb at the main display. "If you're lucky, these dragon birds are gonna give you a real show."

Dragon birds? Wil looked again at the misshapen bodies, the featherless heads and necks. They still looked like vultures to him. The dun-colored creatures strutted round and round the pile, occasionally puffing out their chests. Off to one side, he saw a smaller one, sitting and watching. The strangest thing about them was the bladelike ridge that ran across the top of their beaks.

Monica sat cross-legged on the floor. Wil sat down more awkwardly and punched up some notes on his data set. Della Lu remained standing, drifting around the room, looking at the pictures on the wall. They were famous pictures: *Death on a Bicycle, Death Visits the Amusement Park*. . . . They'd been a fad in the 2050s, at the time of the longevity breakthrough, when people realized that but for accidents or violence, they could live forever. Death was suddenly a pleasant old man, freed from his longtime burden. He rolled awkwardly along on his first bicycle ride, his scythe sticking up like a flag. Children ran beside him, smiling and laughing. Wil remembered the pictures well; he'd been a kid himself then. But here, fifty million years after the extinction of the human race, they seemed more macabre than cute.

Wil pulled his attention back to Monica Raines. "You know that Yelén Korolev has commissioned Ms. Lu and me to investigate the murder. Basically, I'm to provide the old-fashioned nosing around—like in the detective stories—and Della Lu is doing the high-tech analysis. It may seem frivolous, but this is the way I've always operated: I want to talk to you face to face, get your thoughts about the crime." *And try to find out what you had to do with it,* he didn't say; Wil's approach was as nonthreatening and casual as possible. "This is all voluntary. We aren't claiming any contractual authority."

The corner of Raines' mouth turned down. "My 'thoughts about the crime,' Mr. Brierson, are that I had nothing to do with it. To put it in your detective jargon: I have no motive, as I have no interest in the Korolevs' pitiful attempt to resurrect mankind. I had no opportunity, as my protection equipment is much more limited than theirs."

"You are a high-tech, though."

"Only by the era of my origin. When I left civilization, I took the bare necessities for survival. I didn't bring software to build autofactories. I have air/space capability and some explosives, but they're the minimum needed to exit stasis safely." She gestured at Lu. "Your high-tech partner can verify all this."

Della dropped bonelessly to a cross-legged position and propped her chin on her hands. For an instant she looked like a young girl. "You'll give me access to your databases?"

"Yes."

The spacer nodded, and then her attention drifted away again. She was watching the picture off the telescope. The dragon birds had stopped their strutting. Now they were taking turns *throwing* small rocks into the nestlike structure between them. Wil had never seen anything like it. The birds would hunt about at the edge of the pile of stones and brush. They seemed very selective. What they grasped in their beaks glittered. Then, with a quick flip of the head, the pebble was cast into the pile. At the same time, the thrower flapped briefly into the air.

Raines followed Della's glance. The artist's face split with a smile less cynical than usual. "Notice how they face downwind when they do that."

"They're fire makers?" asked Lu.

Raines' head snapped up. "You're the spacer. You've seen things like this before?"

"Once. In the LMC. But they weren't . . . birds, exactly."

Raines was silent for a moment. Curiosity and wonder seemed to battle against her natural desire to remain one up on her visitors. The latter won, but she sounded friendlier as she continued. "Things have to be just right before they'll try. It's been a dry summer, and they've built their starter-pyre at the edge of an area that hasn't burned in decades. Notice that there's a good breeze blowing along the hillsides."

Lu was smiling now, too. "Yes. So that flapping reflex when they throw—that's to give the sparks a little help?"

"Right. It can be—oh, look, look!" There wasn't much to see. Wil had noticed a faint spark when the last pebble struck the rocks in the nest—the starter-pyre, Monica called it. Now a wisp of smoke rose from the straw that covered the leeward side of the pile. The vulture stayed close to the smoke, moved its wings in long sweeps. Its rattling call echoed up the ravine. "Nope. It didn't quite catch. . . . Sometimes the dragon's *too* successful, by the way. They burn like torches if their feathers catch fire. I think that's why the males work in pairs: one's a spare."

"But when the game works . . ." said Lu.

"When the game works, you get a nice brush fire sweeping away from the dragon birds."

"How do they benefit by starting fires?" asked Wil; he already had a bad feeling he knew the answer.

"It makes for good eating, Mr. Brierson. These scavengers don't wait for lunch to drop dead on its own. A fire like this can spread faster than some animals can run. After it's over, there's plenty of cooked meat. Those beak ridges are for scraping the char off their prey. The dragons get so fat afterwards, they can barely waddle. A good burn marks the start of a really successful breeding season."

Wil felt a little sick. He'd watched nature films all the way back to the flat-screen Disneys, but he never could accept the talk about the beauty and balance of nature—when illustrated by grotesque forms of sudden death.

Things got worse. Della asked, "So they get mainly small animals?"

Raines nodded. "But there are a few interesting exceptions." She brought another display to life. "These pictures are from a camera about four thousand meters east of here." The picture jogged and bounced. Wil glimpsed shaggy creatures rooting through dense brush. They were built low to the ground, yet seemed vaguely apelike.

"Marvelous what the primates can become, isn't it? The design is so multipurpose, so *centered*. Except for one disastrous dead end, they are by far the most interesting of the mammals. At one time or another, I've seen them adapt to almost every slot available for large land animals, and more: the fishermonkeys are almost in the penguin slot. I'm watching them very closely; someday they may become exclusively water animals." Enthusiasm was bright on her normally saturnine features.

"You think mankind *devolved* into the fishermonkeys and these . . . things?" Wil pointed at the display. He couldn't keep the revulsion from his voice.

Raines sniffed. "That's absurd. And presumptuous, really. Homo sapiens was about the most self-deadly variation in the theme of life. The species insulated itself from physical stress for so long that what few individuals survived the destruction of technology would have been totally unable to live on their own. No, the present-day primates are descended from those in wilderness estates at the time mankind did itself in."

She laughed softly at the look on Wil's face. "You have no business making value judgments on the dragons, Mr. Brierson. Theirs is a beautiful variation. It's survived half a million years —almost as long as Man's experiment with fire. The starter-pyres began as small piles of glitter, a kind of sexual display for the males. The first fires were accidental, but the adaptation has been refined over hundreds of thousands of years. It doesn't provide them with all their food, or even most of it. But it's an extra advantage. As a mating ritual, it even survives climatic wet spells. When summers are dry again, it is still ready to use.

"This is how fire was meant to be used, Mr. Brierson. The dragons have little impact on the average tonnage burned; they just redistribute the fires to their advantage. Their way is self-limiting, fitting the balance of nature. Man perverted fire, used it for unlimited destruction."

Every one crazier than the last, thought Wil. Monica Raines sat surrounded and served by the fruits of that "perversion," and all she could do was bitch. She sounded like something out of the twentieth century. "So you don't believe Juan Chanson's theory that man was exterminated by aliens?"

"There's no need for such an invention. Can't you see, Mr. Brierson? The trends were all there, undeniable. Mankind's systems grew more and more complicated, their demands more and more rapacious. Have you seen the mines the Korolevs built west of the Inland Sea? They stretch for dozens of kilometers—open pits, autons everywhere. By the late twenty-second century, *that's* the scale of resources demanded by a single individual. Science gave each human animal the presumption to act like a little god. The Earth just couldn't take it. Hell, I'll bet there wasn't even a war. I'll bet the whole structure collapsed under its own weight, leaving the rapists at the mercy of their victim—nature."

"There's the asteroid belt. Industry could be moved off-planet." In fact, Wil had seen the beginnings of that in his time.

"No. This was an exponential process. Moving into space just postponed the debacle a few decades." She rose to her knees and looked at the telescope display. The vultures had resumed their slow strutting about the rock pile. "Too bad. I don't think we'll get a fire today. They try hardest in the early afternoon."

"If you feel this way about humans, why are you out of stasis just now?" said Lu.

Wil added, "Did you think you could persuade the new settlement to behave more . . . respectfully toward nature?"

Raines made one of her turned-down smiles. "Certainly not. You haven't seen any propaganda from me, have you? I couldn't care less. This settlement is the biggest I've seen, but it will fail like all the others, and there will be peace on Earth once more. I, um . . . it's just a coincidence we're all out of stasis at the same time." She hesitated. "I—I am an artist, Ms. Lu. I use the scientist's tools, but with the heart of an artist. Back in civilization, I could see the Extinction coming: there would be no one left to rape nature, but neither would there be anyone to praise her handiwork.

"So I proceed down through time, averaging a year alive in each megayear, making my pictures, taking my notes. Sometimes I stay out for just a day, sometimes for a week or a month. The last few megayears, I've been very active. The social spiders are fascinating, and now—just in the last half million years —the dragon birds have appeared. It's not surprising that we all should be living at the same time."

71

There was something fishy about the explanation. A year of observing time spread through a million years left an awful lot of empty space. The settlement had only been active for a few months. The odds against meeting her seemed very high. Raines sat uneasily, almost fidgeting under his gaze. She was lying, but why? The obvious explanation was certainly an innocent one. For all her hostility, Monica Raines was still a human being. Even if she could not admit it to herself, she still needed others to share the things she did.

"But my staying is no coincidence, Mr. Brierson. I've got my pictures; I'm ready to go. Besides, I expect the next few centuries—the time it takes you people to die off—will be ugly ones. I'd be long gone except for Yelén. She demands I stay in this era. She says she'll drop me into the sun if I bobble up. The bitch." Apparently Raines didn't have as much firepower as the Robinsons. Wil wondered if any of the other high-techs were staying under duress. "So you can see why I'm willing to cooperate. Get her off my back."

Despite the sour words, she was eager to talk. She showed them her video of the early dragon birds, back when starting fires was almost an accident. In her fifty-year voyage she had created archives that would have shamed the national libraries of the twentieth century. And Don Robinson was not the only one who made home movies. Monica's automation could rearrange her data into terrifying homotopies, where creatures caught in the blowtorch of time flowed and melted from one form to another. She seemed determined to show them everything, and Della Lu, at least, seemed willing to watch.

When they left the blind, deep twilight lay across the grassland. Raines accompanied them to the top of her little canyon. A dry, warm wind rattled through the chaparral; the dragon birds should have no trouble starting their fire if the weather stayed like this. They stood for a moment at the top of the ridgeline. They could see for kilometers in all directions. Bands of orange and red crossed the western horizon. A hint of green lay above that, then violet and starry blackness. Nowhere was there a single artificial light. A smell like honey floated in the breeze.

"It's beautiful, isn't it?" Raines said softly.

Untouched forever and ever. Could she really want that? "Yes, but someday intelligence will evolve again. Even if you're right about humanity, the world won't stay peaceful forever."

She didn't answer immediately. "It could happen. There are a couple of species that seem to be at the brink of sentience —the spiders for one." She looked back at him, her face lit by the twilight band. Was she blushing? Somehow, his question had hit home. "If it happens . . . well, I'll be here, right from the beginning of their awareness. I'm not against intelligence by itself, just the abuse of it. Perhaps I can nudge them away from the arrogance of my race." Like an elder god, leading the new creatures in the way of the right. Monica Raines would find people who could properly appreciate her—even if she had to help in their creation.

Lu's flier drove steadily back over the Pacific. The sun rose swiftly from around the shoulder of the Earth. According to his data set it was barely noon in the Asian time zone. The bright sunlight and blue sky (which was really the Pacific below) made such an emotional difference. Just minutes ago all had been darkness and poor Monica's murky thoughts.

"Crazies," said Wil.

"What?"

"All these advanced travelers. I could go a year in police work and not meet anyone as strange: Yelén Korolev, who seems to be jealous of me just for liking her girlfriend, and who moped alone for a century after we jumped forward; cute little Tammy Robinson—who is old enough to be my mother—and whose object in life is to celebrate New Year's at the end of time; Monica Raines, who would make a twentieth-century ecofanatic look like a strip miner." *And then there's Della Lu, who has lived so long she has to study to seem human at all.*

He stopped short and looked guiltily at Della. She grinned knowingly at him, and the smile seemed to reach all the way to her eyes. Damn. There were times now she seemed totally aware. "What do you expect, Wil? We were all a little strange to begin with; we left civilization voluntarily. Since then, we have spent hundreds—sometimes thousands—of years getting here. That takes a power of will you would call monomania."

"Not all the high-techs started out crazy. I mean . . . your original motive was short-range exploration, right?"

"By your standards it wasn't short range. I had just lost someone I cared about very much; I wanted to be alone. The Gatewood's Star mission was a twelve-hundred-year round trip. By the time I got back, I had overshot the Singularity—what Monica and Juan call the Extinction. That's when I left on my really long missions. You've missed all the reasonable high-techs, Wil. They settled down in the first few megayears after Man and made the best of it. You're left with *la crud de la crud*, so to speak."

She had a point. The low-techs were a lot easier to talk to. Wil had thought that a matter of culture similarity, but now he saw that it went deeper. The low-techs were people who had been shanghaied, or had short-term goals (like the Dasguptas and their foolish investment schemes). Even the New Mexicans, who had an abundance of unpleasant notions, had not spent more than a few years in realtime since leaving civilization.

Okay, so all the suspects were nuts. The problem was to find the nut that was also rotten.

"What about Raines? For all her talk of indifference, she's clearly hostile to the Korolevs. Perhaps she killed Marta just to speed up the 'natural process' of the settlement's collapse."

"I don't think so, Wil. I snooped around while we were talking with her. She has good bobbling equipment, and enough automation to run her observation program, but she's virtually defenseless. She doesn't have the depth to fool the Korolev scheduling programs. . . . In fact, she's terribly underequipped. If she keeps living a year per megayear, she won't last more than a couple of hundred megayears before her autons begin to fail. Then she's going to find out about nature firsthand. . . . You should compliment me, Wil; I'm following your advice about the interviews. I didn't laugh when she started on peace and the balance of nature."

Brierson smiled. "Yes. You were a good cointerrogator.

. . . But I don't think she plans on traveling forever. Her real goal is to play god to the next intelligent race that evolves on Earth."

"The *next* intelligent race? Then she doesn't realize how rare intelligence is. You may think those fire-making birds are freaks, but let me tell you something: Such developments are a thousand times more common than the evolution of intelligence. Chances are the sun will go red giant long before intelligence reappears on Earth."

"Hmm." He was scarcely in a position to argue. Della Lu was the only living human, perhaps the only person in history, who really knew about such things. "Okay, so she's unrealistic . . . or maybe she's hiding her true resources, at the Lagrange zones or in the wilderness. Can you be sure she's not playing dumb?"

"Not yet. But when she gives me access to her records, I'll run consistency checks. I have faith in my automation. Raines left civilization seven years before me. Whatever automation she took, mine is better. If she's hiding anything, I will know."

One less suspect, probably. That was a sort of progress.

They flew silently for several minutes, the blue of the Earth on one side, the sun sliding down the other. He could see one of the protection autons, a bright fleck floating against the clouds.

Perhaps he should take the afternoon off, go to the Peacer meeting at North Shore. Still, there was something about Monica Raines. "Della, how do you think Raines would feel if the settlement were a success? Would she be so indifferent to us if she thought we might do permanent damage?"

"I think she would be surprised, and very angry . . . and impotent."

"I wonder. Let's suppose she doesn't have the usual high-tech battle equipment. If she simply wanted to destroy the settlement, she might not need anything spectacular: perhaps a disease, something with a long incubation period."

Lu's eyes widened almost comically. He had noticed the same mannerism in Yelén Korolev. It had something to do with their direct data interface: When confronted with a surprising question demanding heavy analysis, they seemed first startled and then dazed. Several seconds passed. "That's just barely possible. She has a bioscience background, and a small autolab would be hard to spot. The Korolevs' medical automation is good, but it's not designed for warfare. . . ."

She smiled. "That's an interesting idea, Wil. A properly designed virus could evade the panphages and infect everyone before any symptoms appeared. Bobbling out of the area would be no defense."

"Interesting" was not the word Brierson would have used. The diseases spread after the 1997 war had killed most of the human race. Even in Wil's time, less than forty million people lived in North America. By then the terror was gone, and the world was a friendly place, but still—better bombs and bullets than bugs. He licked his lips. "I suppose we don't have to worry about it immediately. She must know how deadly the high-tech response would be. But if our settlement is *too* successful . . ."

"Yes. I've put this on my list. Now that we're aware of the possibility, it shouldn't be hard to guard against. I have exploration-duty medical equipment. It's smart and very paranoid."

"Yeah." *Nothing to worry about, Wil.* They had lost a murder suspect—and possibly gained a genocidal maniac.

EIGHT

Wil didn't make it to the party at North Shore.

At first, the Raines thing had him wound up, and then—well, someone had killed Marta. Most likely that someone wanted the settlement to fail. And he was no nearer cracking the case today than a week ago. Parties would have to wait.

He meshed his data set with the house archives. He could have used the house displays direct, but he felt more at ease with his portable. . . . Besides, it was one of the few things that had come with him through time. Its memory was an attic filled with a thousand private souvenirs; the date it displayed, 16 February 2100, was when he would be if his old life had continued.

Wil heated his lunch pack and munched absentmindedly at hot vegetables as he scanned his progress. He was behind in his reading; just another good reason to stay home this afternoon. People outside police work didn't realize how much of criminal investigation involved drawing conclusions from databases—usually public databases, at that. Wil's "reading" was the most likely source of real evidence. There was no shortage of things to look at. His house archive was far bigger than any other low-tech's. In addition to the 2201 edition of GreenInc, he had copies of parts of Korolev's and Lu's personal databases.

Wil had insisted on having his own copies. He didn't want networked stuff. He didn't want it changing mysteriously depending on the whim of the original owners. The price of such independence was a certain incoherence. His own processors had to accommodate idiosyncrasies in the structure of the imported data. With Yelén's databases, it wasn't too bad. They were designed both for headband use and for old-fashioned query languages. Her engineering jargon was sometimes incomprehensible, but he could get by.

Della's db's were a different story. Her copy of GreenInc was a year more recent than Yelén's, but a note announced that the later parts had been severely damaged during her travels. That was an understatement. Whole sections from the late twenty-second were jumbled or just plain missing. Her personal database appeared to be intact, but it used a customized headband design. His processors found it almost impossible to talk to the retrieval programs. Usually the output seemed to be allegorical hallucinations; occasionally he was blocked by the fragments of a personality simulator. Not for the first time in his life, Wil wished he could use interface headbands. They had existed in his time. If you had great native intelligence and a certain turn of imagination, they made computers a direct extension of your mind; otherwise, the bands were little more than electronic drug-tripping. Wil sighed. Yelén said the headbands from her era were easier to use; if only she had given him the time to learn how.

Della had nine thousand years of exploration packed away in her database. He'd had tantalizing glimpses—a world where plants floated in the sky, pictures of stars crowding close about something dark and *visibly* moving, a low-orbit shot of a planet green and cratered. On one planet, bathed in the glow of a giant red sun, he saw something that looked like ruins. Nowhere else had he seen any sign of intelligence. Was it so rare that all Della ever saw were ruins or fossils of ruins—of civilizations lasting a few millennia, and missed by millions of years? He hadn't yet asked her about what she'd seen. The murder was their immediate business, and until recently she'd been difficult to talk to. But now that he thought about it, she was awfully closemouthed about her travels.

His other researches were going better. He'd studied most of the high-techs. None of them—except Yelén and Marta—had any special relationship back in civilization. The conclusion couldn't be absolute, of course. The biography companies only had so many spies. If someone was hiding something, and was also out of the public eye, then that something could stay hidden.

Philippe Genet was one of the least documented. Wil couldn't find any reference to him before 2160, when he began advertising his services as a construction contractor. At that time, he was at least forty years old. You'd have to live like a hermit or have lots of money to go forty years and not get on a junk-mail list or have a published credit rating. There was another possibility: Perhaps Genet had been in stasis before 2160. Wil had not pursued that very far; it would open a whole new tree of investigation. Between 2160 and when Genet left civilization in 2201, the trail was sparse but visible. He had not been convicted of any crimes that involved public punishment. He hadn't been seen at public events, or written anything for public scrutiny. From his advertising—and the advertising that was focused back on him—it was clear that his construction business was successful, but not so successful as to attract the attention of the trade journals. Consumer ratings of his work were solid but not spectacular; he came out low in "customer relations." In the 2190s, he followed the herd and began specializing in space construction. Nowhere could Wil find anything that might be a motive. However, with his construction background, Genet was probably one of the best armed of the travelers.

Genet's conservative, quiet background hardly seemed to fit jumping into the future. He was a must for an early interview; at the least, it would be nice to meet a high-tech who was not a crazy.

In terms of documentation, Della Lu was at the other extreme. Brierson should have recognized her name the first time he heard it, even attached to its present owner. That name was important in the history books of Wil's childhood. If not for her, the 2048 revolt against the Peace Authority would have been a catastrophic failure. Della had been a double agent.

Wil had just reread the history of that war. To the Peacers, Lu was a secret-police cop who had infiltrated the rebels. In fact, it was the other way around: During the rebel assault on Livermore, Della Lu was stationed at the heart of the Peacer command. Right under her bosses' noses, she bobbled the Peace's command center and herself. End of battle; end of Peace Authority. The rest of their forces surrendered, or bobbled themselves. The Peacers now living on North Shore had been a secret Asian garrison designed to take the war into the future; unfortunately for them, they took it a little too *far* into the future.

What Della did took guts. She had been surrounded by the people she betrayed; when the bobble burst she could expect little better than a quick death.

All that had happened in 2048, two years before Wil was born. He could remember, as a kid, reading the histories and hoping that some way would be found to save the brave Della Lu when the Livermore bobble finally burst. Brierson hadn't lived to see that rescue. He was shanghaied in 2100, just before Della came out of stasis. His entire life in civilization had passed in what was no time at all to Della Lu.

Now he could view the rescue, and follow Lu through the twenty-second century. From the beginning, she was a celebrity. The biographers paid their *paparazzi,* and no part of her life was free of scrutiny. How much she had changed. Oh, the face was the same, and the twenty-second-century Della Lu often wore her hair short. But there was a precision and a force to her movements then. She reminded Wil of a cop, even a soldier. There were also humor and happiness in the recordings, things the present Lu seemed to be relearning. She'd married a Tinker, Miguel Rosas—and here Wil recognized the model for the personality simulator he'd found in Della's database. In the 2150s, they'd been famous all over again, this time for exploring the outer Solar System. Rosas died on their expedition to the Dark Companion. Della had left civilization for Gatewood's Star in 2202.

Wil finished lunch, letting the display roll through the bio summaries he'd constructed so far. It was an ironic thing, impossible before the invention of the bobble: Della Lu was an historical figure in his past, yet *he* was an historical figure in hers. She'd mentioned reading of him after her rescue, admiring someone who had "single-handedly stopped the New Mexican incursion." Brierson smiled sourly. He'd just been at the right place at the right time. If he hadn't been there, the invasion would have ended a little later, a little more bloodily; it was people like Kiki van Steen and Armadillo Schwartz who really stopped the invasion of Kansas. All through his police career, his company had hyped Wil. It was good for business, and usually bad for Wil. The customers seemed to expect miracles when W. W. Brierson was assigned to their case. His reputation almost got him killed during the Kansas thing. *Hell. Fifty million years later, that propaganda is still haunting me.* If he'd been just another policeman, Yelén Korolev might never have thought to give him this case. What she needed was a real investigator, not an enforcement type who had been promoted beyond all competence.

So what if he "knew" people? It scarcely seemed to help here. He had plenty of suspects, plenty of motives, and no hard facts. GreenInc was big and detailed; there were hundreds of possibilities he should look into. But what would get him closer to finding Marta's killer?

Wil put his head in his hands. Virginia had always said it was healthy for a person to wallow in self-pity every once in a while.

"You have a call from Yelén Korolev."

"Ugh." He sat back. "Okay, house. Put her on."

The conference holo showed Yelén sitting in her library. She looked tired, but then she always looked tired these days. Wil restrained the impulse to brush at his hair; no doubt he looked equally dragged out.

"Hello, Brierson. I just talked to Della about Monica Raines. You've eliminated her as a suspect."

"Uh, yes. But did Della tell you that Raines might be—"

"Yeah, the biowar thing. That's . . . good thinking. You know, I told Raines I'd kill her if she tried to bobble out of this era. Now I wonder. If she's not a suspect in the murder and yet is a threat to the settlement, perhaps I should 'persuade' her to take a jump—at least a megayear. What do you think?"

"Hmm. I'd wait till we've studied her personal database. Lu says she can protect us against biological attack. In any case, I don't think Raines would try something unless mankind looks like a successful rerun. It's even possible she'd be more of a threat to humanity a million years from now."

"Yeah. I can't be absolutely sure of our own dispersion in time. I hope we're successfully rooted here, but—" She nodded abruptly. "Okay. That scheme is on hold. How's the investigation going otherwise?"

Brierson suggested Lu survey the weapon systems of the advanced travelers, and then outlined his own efforts with GreenInc. Korolev listened quietly. Gone was the blazing anger of their original confrontation. In its place was a kind of dogged determination.

When he finished, she didn't look pleased, but her words were mild. "You've spent a lot of time searching the civilized eras for clues. That's okay; after all, we come from there. But you should realize that the advanced travelers—excepting Jason Mudge—have lived most of their lives *since* the Singularity.

"At one time or another, there were about fifty of us. Physically we were independent, living at our own rates. But there was communication; there were meetings. Once it became clear that the rest of humanity was gone, all of us had our plans. Marta said it was a loose society, maybe a society of ghosts. And it got smaller and smaller. The high-techs you see now are the hard cases, Inspector. The overt criminals, the graverobbers, were killed thirty million years ago. The easygoing travelers, like Bil Sánchez, dropped off early. People would stop for a few hundred years, and try to start a family or a town; you could have a whole world for the stopping. Most we never saw again, but then sometimes a group—or parts of it—would appear megayears down time. Our lives are threaded loosely around one another. You should be studying my personal databases about that, Brierson."

"Hmm. These early settlements—they all failed. Was there evidence of sabotage?" If Marta's murder was part of a pattern. . .

"That's what I want *you* to look for, Inspector." A little of the old scorn appeared. "Till now I never thought so. From the standpoint of the dropouts, they weren't all failures. Several couples simply wanted to live their lives stopped in one era. Modern health care can keep the body alive a very long time; we discovered other limits. Time passes, personalities change. Very few of us have lived more than a thousand years. Neither our minds nor our machines last forever. To reestablish civilization, you need the interactions of many people, you need a good-sized gene pool and stability over several generations of population growth. That's almost impossible with small groups —especially when everyone has bobblers and every quarrel has the potential for breaking up the settlement."

Yelén leaned forward abruptly. "Brierson, even if Marta's murder is not part of a conspiracy against the settlement— even then, I–I'm not sure if I can hold things together."

Yelén really had changed. He had never expected her to come crying on *his* shoulder. "The low-techs won't stay in this era?"

She shook her head. "They have no choice. You're familiar with the Wáchendon suppressor field?"

"Sure. No new bobbles can be generated in a suppressor field." The invention had cost as many lives as it had saved, since the field made it impossible to escape the weapons that burn and maim.

Yelén nodded. "That's close enough. I've got most of Australasia under a Wáchendon field. The New Mexicans and the Peacers and the rest of the low-techs are stuck in this era until they discover how to counter the field. That should take at least ten years. We hoped they'd put down roots and be willing to stay by then." Yelén stared at the pink marble of her library table. "And the plan would work, Inspector," she said softly, taking her turn at self-pity. "Marta's plan would work if it weren't for those goddamned statist bastards."

"Steve Fraley?"

"Not just him. The top Peacers—Kim Tioulang and his gang—are as bad. They just won't cooperate with me. There are one hundred and one NMs and one hundred and fifteen Peacers. That's better than two-thirds of the settlement. Fraley and Tioulang think they *own* their groups. The hell of it is, the rank and file seem to agree! It's twentieth-century insanity, but it makes them powerful beyond all reason. They both want to run the whole show. Have you noticed their recruiting? They want the rest of the low-techs to become their 'citizens.' They won't be satisfied till one is supreme. They may reinvent high-tech just for the privilege of breaking up the settlement."

"Have you talked about this with the other high-techs?"

She rubbed nervously at her chin. *If only Marta were here;* the words all but spoke themselves. "A little, but most of 'em are more confused than I. Della was some help; she actually *was* a statist once. But she's hard to talk to. Have you noticed? She shifts personalities like clothes, as though she's trying to find something that fits.

"Inspector, you don't go back quite as far as Della, but there were still governments in your time. Hell, you caused the collapse of one of them. How can this sort of primitivism be successful now?"

Brierson winced. So now he had caused the disgovernance of New Mexico, had he? Wil sat back and—just like in the old days—tried to come up with something that would satisfy the inflated expectations of his customer. "Yelén, I agree that governments are a form of deception—though not necessarily for the rulers, who usually benefit from them. Most of the citizens, most of the time, must be convinced that the national interest is more important than their own. To you this must seem like an incredible piece of mass hypnotism, backed up by the public disciplining of dissenters."

Yelén nodded. "And the 'mass hypnotism' is the important thing. Any time they want, the NM rank and file could just give Fraley the finger and walk away; he couldn't kill 'em all. Instead they stay, his tools."

"Yes, but in a way this gives *them* power, too. If they walk, where's to go? There are no other groups. There is no ungoverned society like in my time."

"Sure there is. The Earth is empty, and almost a third of the low-techs are ungovs. There's nothing to keep people from settling down to their own interests."

Wil shook his head, surprised at his own insight, surprised at his voicing it to Yelén. Before, he wouldn't have thought to argue with her. But she seemed sincerely interested in his opinion. "Don't you see, Yelén? There are no ungoverned now. There are the Peacers, the NMs—but over all the low-techs there is the government of Yelén Korolev."

"What? I am *not* a government!" Red rose in her face. "I don't tax. I don't conscript. I only want to do what's right for people." Even if she was changed, at that moment Wil was glad for Lu's auton hovering above his house.

Wil chose his next words carefully. "That's all true. But you have two of the three essential attributes of government: First, the low-techs believe—correctly, I think—that you have the power of life and death over them. Second, you use that belief —however gently—to make them put your goals ahead of theirs."

It was pop social science from Wil's era, but it seemed to have a real effect on Korolev. She rubbed her chin. "So you figure that, at least subconsciously, the low-techs feel they have to choose sides?"

"Yes. And as the most powerful governing force, you could easily come out the most distrusted."

"What is your advice, then?"

"I, uh . . ." Wil had painted himself into a corner. *Yes. Suppose I'm right. What then?* The little settlement at fifty megayears was totally different from the society of Wil's time. It was entirely possible that without Korolev force, the handful of seeds collected here would be blown away on the winds of time. And separately, those seeds would never bloom.

Back in civilization, Wil had never thought much on "great

85

issues." Even in school, he hadn't liked nitpicking arguments about religion or natural rights. The world made sense and seemed to respond appropriately to his actions. Since he had lost Virginia, everything was so terribly on its head. Could there really be a situation so weird that he would advocate government? He felt like a Victorian pushing sodomy.

Yelén gave him a lopsided grin. "You know, Marta said some of the same things. You don't have her training, but you seem to have her sense. My gentle Machiavelli didn't shrink from the consequences, though. I've got to be popular, yet I've still got to have my way. . . ."

She looked at him, seemed to reach a decision. "Look, Inspector, I want you to mix more. Both the NMs and the Peacers have regular recruiting parties. Go to the next Peacer one. Listen to what they're saying. Maybe you can explain them to me. And maybe you can explain *me* to *them*. You were a popular person in your time. Tell people what you think— even what you don't like about me. If they have to choose sides, I think I'm their best bet."

Wil nodded. First the Dasguptas and now Korolev: Was there a conspiracy to get W. W. Brierson back in circulation? "What about the investigation?"

Yelén was silent for a moment. "I need you for both, Brierson. I mourned Marta for a hundred years. I traced her around the Inland Sea a meter at a time. I've got records or bobble samples of everything she did and everything she wrote. I—I think I'm over the rage. The most important thing in my life now is to see that Marta didn't die in vain. I will do *anything* to make the settlement succeed. That means finding the killer, but it also means selling my case to the low-techs."

NINE

That night he took another look at Marta's diary. It was a very low-priority item now, but he couldn't concentrate on anything more technical. Yelén had read the diary several times. In their literal-minded way, her autons had gone over the text in even more detail, and Lu's had cross-checked the analysis. Marta knew she had been murdered, but said again and again that she had no clues beyond her description of the evening of the party. According to the overdoc, she rarely repeated the details in later years, and when she did it was clear that her earlier memories were the more precise.

Now Will browsed the earliest sections. Marta had stayed near Town Korolev for more than a year. Though she said otherwise, it was clear she hoped for rescue in some small multiple of ninety days. Even if that rescue didn't come, she had lots of preparing to do: She planned to walk to Canada, halfway around the world.

≪ . . . but klick for klick it barely qualifies as an intermediate survival course, ≫ she wrote. ≪ It will take years, and I may miss a lookabout back here at Town Korolev, but that's okay. Along the way, I'll put billboards at the West End mines and the Peacer bobble. Once I get your attention, give me a sign, Lelya: Nuke the sky for a week of nights. I'll find open ground, and wait for the autons. >>

Marta knew the territory near Korolev. Her shelter in the realtime wing of the castle was secure, close to water and adequate hunting. It was a good place to collect her energy for the trek ahead. She experimented with the weapons and tools she'd known from survival sport. In the end she settled on a diamond-bladed pike and knife and a short bow. She kept the other diamond blades in reserve; she wasn't going to waste them on arrowheads. She built a travois from a section of Fred's hull. It was enough to do some testing. She made several cautious trips covering a few kilometers.

<< Dearest Lelya— If I am ever to leave, I suppose it should be now. The plan is still to sail to our mines at West End and then head north to the Peacer bobble, and Canada far beyond that. Tomorrow I depart for the coast; tonight I finish packing. Would you believe, I have made so much equipment, I actually have *lists;* the age of data processing has arrived!

<< Hope I see you before I write more. —Love, Marta. >>

That was the last of the bark tablets she left at the castle. Two hundred kilometers along the southern coast of the sea, Yelén found the second of Marta's cairns, a three-meter-high pile of rock at the edge of the jacaranda forests. This was one of the best preserved of Marta's sites. She'd built a cabin there; it was still standing when Yelén studied it a century later.

Six months had passed since Marta left the castle in the mountains. She was still optimistic, though she had hoped to reach the mines before stopping. There had been problems, one of them painful and deadly. During her time at the cabin, Marta described her adventures since leaving the castle.

<< I followed our monorail to the coast. You know I said it was a waste to build that thing when we were going to leave it behind anyway. Well, now I'm glad you listened to Genet and not me. That right-of-way cuts straight through the forest. I avoided some tricky rock climbing just by sliding the travois along the rail's underframe. It was like a practice hike—which I needed more than I realized.

<< I've forgotten a lot, Lelya. I have just one poor brainful

of memories now. If I'd known I was to be marooned, I would have loaded quite a different set. (But if I'd foreseen that, I probably could have avoided the whole adventure! Sigh. I should be glad I never offloaded our survival courses.) Anyway, my mind is full of our plans for the settlement, the stuff I was thinking about the night of the party. I have only a casual recollection of maps. I know we did lots of wildlife studies, and were hooked into Monica's work, too. But that's all gone. Where the plants are like the ones back in civilization, I recognize them.

≪ For the rest, I have fragments of memory that are sometimes worse than useless: take the spiders and their jacaranda forests. These are *nothing* like the scattered trees and isolated webs up at Town Korolev. Here the trees are huge, and the forests go on forever. That much was obvious from the ground, walking along the monorail. We had slashed through that forest, but it towered on either side. The brush that had grown along the path was already covered by matted spider webbing. Ah, if I had remembered then what I've learned since, I'd probably be at the mines by now!

≪ Instead, I wandered along beneath the rail (where for some reason the webs didn't come) and admired the gray silk that spread down from the jacarandas. I didn't dare cut through the webs to look into the forest; at that time, I was still scared of the spiders. They're little things, like the ones in the mountains, but if you look close you can see thousands of them moving in the webs. I was afraid they might be like army ants, ready to swarm down on whoever jiggled their silk. Eventually, I found a break in the shroud where I could step through without touching the threads. . . . Lelya, it's a different world in there, quieter and more peaceful than the deepest redwood grove. Dim green light is everywhere—the really thick webs are at the fringes of the forests. (And of course I didn't find the explanation for that till later.) There's no underbrush, no animals—only a musty smell and a greenish haze in the air. (I'll bet you're laughing at me now, because *you* already know what made that smell.) Anyway, I was impressed. It's like a cathedral . . . or a tomb.

≪ I only spent an hour in there the first time; I was still nervous about the spiders. Besides, the point of this trip was to reach the sea. I still planned to make a raft and sail direct to the West End. Failing that, short hops along the coast ought to bring me to the mines faster than any overland walk. So I thought.

≪ It was storming the day I came in sight of the shore. I knew we had wrecked the coast with our tsunami, but I wasn't prepared for what I saw. The jungle was blasted flat for kilometers back from the sea. The tree trunks were piled three and four deep, all pointing away from the water. I remember thinking that at least I would have plenty of lumber for my raft.

≪ I sheltered the travois and went a ways onto the coastal plain. The going was treacherous. Rotted vines swathed the trunks. Tree bark sloughed away under my weight. The topmost trunks were relatively clear, but slime slick. I crawled/walked from trunk to trunk. All the while, the storm was getting worse. The last time I'd been to the beach was to round up Wil Brierson . . . ≫

A reader smiled. *She did remember my name!* Somewhere in the adventures of her next forty years she forgot, but for a while she had remembered.

≪ . . . just before we raised the Peacers. It had been a warm, misty place. Today was different: lightning, thunder, wind-driven rain. No way was I going to get to water's edge this afternoon. I crawled along a tree trunk to its uptorn fan of roots, and peeked over. Fantasyland. There were three waterspouts out there. They slid back and forth, the further ones pale and translucent. The third had drifted inland, though it was still a couple of klicks away. Dirt and timber splashed up from its tip. I crawled out of the wind and listened to the roar. As long as it didn't get louder, I should be safe from heaven's dirty finger.

≪ All this raised serious questions about my plan to take a shortcut across the sea. No doubt this was an exceptional storm, but what about ordinary squalls? How common were they? The Inland Sea is a lot like the old Mediterranean. I thought of a guy named Odysseus who spent half his life being blown from one side of that pond to the other. I wished we had taken maritime sports more seriously. Sailing to Catalina barely qualified us as novices; we didn't even make our own boat. The notion of hugging the coast didn't look good either. I remembered the pictures: our tsunami had smashed the whole southern coast. There were no beaches or harbors left on this side of the sea, just millions of tonnes of broken wood and mud. I would have to carry all my food even if I stayed close to the shore.

≪ So there I was, kind of discouraged and awfully wet. My schedule was in shambles. And that was a laugh. I have all the time in the world; that's the problem.

≪ There was a super-close lightning bolt. From the corner of my eye I saw *something* rushing me. As I turned, it dropped on my shoulder, grabbing for my neck. An instant later something else landed on my middle, and on my leg. I bet I screamed as loud as ever in my life; it was lost in the thunder.

≪ . . . They were *fishermonkeys*, Lelya. Three of them. They clung tight as leeches; one had its face buried in my middle. But they weren't biting. I sat rigid for a moment, ready to start smashing in all directions. The one on my leg had its eyes screwed shut. All three were shivering, and holding me so tight it hurt. I gradually relaxed, and set my hand on the fellow who had grabbed my middle. Through the seallike fur, I could feel its shivering ease a little.

≪ They were like little children, running to Momma when the lightning got too bad. We sat in the lee of that root fan through the worst of the storm. They scarcely moved the whole time, their warm bodies stuck to my leg, belly, and shoulder.

≪ The storm gentled to an even rain, and the temperature climbed back into the thirties. The three didn't rush off. They sat, looking at me solemnly. Now, even *I* don't believe that nature is full of cuddly creatures just waiting to love a human. I began to have some unhappy suspicions. I got up, climbed over the side of the trunk. The three followed, then ran a little way to one side, stopped, and chittered at me. I walked to them, and they ran off again, and stopped again. Already I was thinking of them as Hewey, Dewey, and Lewey. (How did

Disney spell those names?) Of course, fishermonkeys look nothing like ducks, either real or caricatured. But there was a cooperative madness about them that made the names inescapable.

<< Our lurching game of tag went on for fifty meters. Then we came to a pile that had recently slipped: I could see where the trunks had turned, exposing unweathered wood. The three didn't try to climb these. They led me around them . . . to where a larger monkey was pinned between two trunks. It wasn't hard to guess what had happened. A good-sized stream flowed beneath the pile. Probably the four had been fishing there. When the storm came up, they hid in the wooden cave formed by the tree trunks. No doubt the wind and the added water in the stream had upset the woodpile.

<< The three patted and pulled at their friend, but halfheartedly; the body wasn't warm. I could see that its chest was crushed. Perhaps this had been their mother. Or maybe it was the dominant male—Unca Donald even.

<< It made me sadder than it should, Lelya. I knew our rescuing the Peacers was going to blow a hole in the ecosystem; I'd already done my rationalizing, cried my tears. But . . . I wondered how many fishermonkeys were left on the south shore. I bet they were scattered in small groups all through the dead jungle. And now this. The four of us sat for a time, consoling each other, I hope. >>

<< If sea travel was out, my options were a bit constrained. The jungle parallels the coast and extends inland to the two-thousand-meter level. It would take me a hundred years to get around the sea by hacking my way through that, with every stream at right angles to my line of travel. That left the jacaranda forests—back up where the air is cool, and the spiders spin their webs.

<< Oh. I took the fishermonkeys with me. In fact, they refused to be left behind. I was now mother, or dominant male, or whatever. These three had all the mobility of penguins. During the days, they spent most of the time on the travois. When I stopped to rest, they'd be off—racing each other

around, trying to tease me into the chase. Then Dewey would come to sit by me. He was the odd man out. Literally. Hewey was a girl and Lewey the other male. (It took a while to figure this out. The fishers' sexual equipment is better hidden than in the monkeys of our time.) It was all very platonic, but sometimes Dewey needed another friend.

<< I can just see you, Lelya, shaking your head and muttering about sentimental weakness. But remember what I've said so many times: If we can survive and still be sentimental, life is a lot more fun. Besides, there were coldly calculated reasons for lugging my little friends back to the jac forest. The fishers are not entirely sea creatures. The fact that they can fish from streams shows that. These three ate berries and roots. Plants haven't changed as much as animals over these fifty megayears, but some of the changes can be inconvenient. For instance, Dewey *et al.* wouldn't touch the water I got from a traveler's palm; on the way down, that stuff had made me sick. >>

Here the diary had many pages of drawings, enhanced by Yelén's autons to show the dyes' original colors. These were not as skillfully drawn as those Wil had seen later in the diary—when Marta had had years of practice—but they were better than anything he could do. She had brief notes by each picture: << Dewey wouldn't touch this when green, otherwise okay . . . >> or << Looks like trillium; raises blisters like poison ivy. >>

Wil looked carefully at the first few pages, then skipped ahead to where Marta entered the jacaranda forest.

<< I was a bit frightened at first. The fishers picked up on it, edging moodily around on the travois and whimpering. Walking through the jac forest just seemed too *easy*. The air is wet and moist, yet not nearly so uncomfortable as in a rain forest. The mist I'd seen earlier is always present. The musky, choking smell is there, too, though you don't notice it after the first few minutes. The light coming through the canopy is shadowless and green. Floating down from the heights are occasional leaves and twigs. There are no animals; except at the edges of the forest, the spiders stick to the canopy. There are no trees but the jacs, and no vines. The ground cover is a moist

carpet. In the top few centimeters you can see leaf fragments, perhaps little bits of spiders. Walking through it kicks up a murkier version of what hangs all through the air. A thousand meters into the forest, the only sounds you hear are those you make yourself. The place is beautiful, and heaven to hike through.

≪ But you see why I was nervous, Lelya? Just a few hundred meters downslope was a *jungle*, a thickly grown, life-gone-to-crazy-excess jungle. There had to be something pretty fearsome keeping all competing plants and all animal pests out of the jac forest. I still had visions of spider armies sweeping down the trees and sucking the juice out of intruders.

≪ I was very cautious the first few days. I walked close to the northern edge of the forest, close enough so I could hear the sounds of the jungle.

≪ It didn't take long to see that the jungle/jac border is a war zone. As you walk toward the border, the forest floor is broken by the corpses of ordinary trees. The deadwood furthest in is scarcely recognizable lumps; closer to the border you can see whole trees, some still standing. What had been the leafy parts are drowned in ancient webs. Rank on rank of mushrooms cover the wood. Their colors are beautiful pastels . . . and the fishers wouldn't touch them.

≪ Walk a bit further and you're out from under the jacs. Here the jungle is alive and fighting to stay that way. Here the spiderwebs are thickest, a tight dark layer across the treetops. Those webs are silver kudzu, Lelya. The critical battle in this war is the jungle top trying to grow past the shroud, and the spiders trying to lay still more silk on top. You know how fast things grow in a rain forest; the plants themselves play the shade-out game, growing a dozen centimeters in twenty-four hours. The spiders have to hustle to keep ahead. Since those first days, I've climbed into the jungle canopy just outside the jac forest and watched. On a busy day, the top of the kudzu web almost seems to froth, the little buggers are pumping out so much new silk.

≪ Where the jungle trees are still living, you do see animals. Webs fan from tree to tree, black with trapped insects.

For larger animals, the silk is no barrier. Snakes, lizards, catlike predators—I've seen them all in the thirty-meter-wide band that the spiders' kudzu shades. But they don't have dens there. They are fleeing, or chasing, or very sick. There are no monsters to scare them back; they just don't like to stay. By now I had some theories, but it was almost a week before I knew for sure.

≪ Once or twice a day, we walked to the jungle's edge. There I did some easy hunting and we ate the berries the fishers liked. At night, we slept several hundred meters into the jacs, farther than any other animals dared come. And as long as I stayed far enough inside the forest, we made very good time. Even old jac trunks molder quickly away and the ubiquitous mulch smooths out most ground irregularities. The only obstacles were the many streams that crossed our path. Down in the jungle, the brush along these streams would have been virtually impassable. Here, the mulch extended right to the water's edge. The water itself was clear, though where a stream broadened and the water slowed, there was greenish scum on the surface. There were fish.

≪ Ordinarily, I don't mind drinking from a stream, even in the tropics. Any blood or gut parasites are just a tasty meal for my panphages. Here I was more careful. The first one we came to, I hung back and watched my committee of experts. They sniffed around, took a drink or two, and jumped in. A few seconds later they had their dinner. From then on, I didn't hesitate to ford the streams, floating the travois ahead of me.

≪ But by the fifth day, Hewey was beginning to drag. She didn't come off the travois to play. Dewey and Lewey patted and groomed her, but she would not be jollied. By the next afternoon, they were equally droopy. There were sniffles and tiny coughs. It was about what I had expected. Now for the important questions:

≪ I found a campsite on the jungle side of the border. It was hell compared to the comfort we'd enjoyed in the jacs, but it was defensible and at the edge of a lake. By then the three were so weak I had to fish and forage for them.

≪ I watched them for a week, trying to analyze the odds, trying to guess what once I could have remembered in an

instant. It was the greenish mist, I was sure. The stuff floated
down endlessly from the top of the jacarandas. Other stuff
came down too, but most of it was identifiable—leaves, bits of
spider, things that might have been caterpillar parts. I had a
fair estimate of the spider biomass; the jac tops were actually
bowed down in places. The green mist . . . it was spider shit.
That by itself was no big deal. The thing is, if you lived in the
forest, you breathed a lot of it. Almost anything that fine would
eventually cause health problems. It was clear now the spiders
had gone a step further. There was something downright poi-
sonous in that haze. Mycotoxins? The word pops to mind, but
damn it, I have nowhere to remember more. It had to be more
than an irritant. Apparently nothing had evolved a defense.
Yet it wasn't super fast-acting. The fishers had lasted several
days. The big question was, how fast would it affect a larger
animal (such as yours truly)? And was recovery a simple matter
of leaving the forest?

<< I got the answer to the second question in a couple of
days. All three came out of their funk. Eventually they were
fishing and rowdying as enthusiastically as ever. So I had the
old decision to make, this time with a bit more information:
Should I hike through the jac forest as far and fast as I was able?
Or should I hack my way crosswise through a thousand klicks
of jungle? My guinea pigs looked as good as new; I decided to
continue with the forest route, till I had symptoms.

<< It would mean leaving Dewey and Hewey and Lewey. I
hoped I was leaving them better off than when I found them.
That pond was alive with fish, as good as anything back in
civilization. The fishermonkeys were quick to rush into the
water at the first hint of land predators. The only threat from
the water was something large and croc-like that didn't look
very fast. It wasn't precisely like the jungle they had once
known by the seashore, but I would stay long enough to build
them a sanctuary.

<< I ignored the fact that my survival craft was from a
different era. For once, being sentimental was deadly.

<< The morning of the seventh day, it was obvious that
something big had died nearby. The moist air always carried

the scents of life and death, but a heavy overtone of putrefaction had been added. Hewey and Lewey ignored it, were busy chasing each other around the water's edge. Dewey was not in sight. Usually when the others squeezed him out he came to me; sometimes he just went off to sulk. I called to him. No answer. I'd seen him an hour earlier, so it couldn't be his demise the breeze announced.

<< I was just getting worried when Dewey raced out of the bushes, chittering gleefully. He held a huge black beetle between his hands. >>

A drawing covered the rest of the page. The creature looked like a stinkbug, but according to the overdoc it was more than ten centimeters long. Its enormous abdomen accounted for most of that size. The chitin was thick and black, laced by a network of deep grooves.

<< Dewey ran right up to Hewey, brushing Lewey aside. For once he had an offering that might give him precedence. And Hewey was impressed. She poked at the armored ball, jumped back in surprise when the bug gave a whistling *tweet*. In seconds they were rolling it back and forth between them, entranced by the teakettle noises and acrid bursts of steam that came from the thing.

<< I was as curious too. As I started toward them, Dewey grabbed the beetle to hold it up to me. Suddenly he screamed and tossed the bug toward me. It struck the top of my right foot—and exploded.

<< I didn't know such pain could exist, Lelya. Even worse, I couldn't turn it *off*. I don't think I lost consciousness, but for a while the world beyond that pain scarcely existed. Finally I came back far enough to feel the wetness that flowed from the wound. The small bones in my foot were shattered. Chitin fragments had cut deep into my foot and lower leg. Dewey was bleeding too—but his wound was a nick compared to mine.

<< I've named them grenade beetles. I know now they're a carrion eater—with a defense worthy of a twenty-first-century armadillo. When hassled, their metabolism becomes an acidulous pressure cooker. They don't want to die; they give plenty of warning. No creature from this region would deliberately

give them any trouble. But if goaded to the bursting point, their death is an explosion that will kill any small attacker outright, and bring lingering death to most larger ones.

<< I don't remember much of the next few days, Lelya. I had to cause myself even greater pain trying to set the bones of my foot. It hurt almost as much to pick out the fragments of chitin. They smelled of rot, of the corpse that beetle had been into. God only knows what infections my panphages saved me from.

<< The fishermonkeys tried to help. They brought berries and fish. I improved. I could crawl, even walk with a makeshift crutch—though it hurt like hell.

<< Other creatures knew I was hurt. Various things nosed about my shelter, but were chased off by the fishers. I woke one morning to loud fishermonkey screeching. Something big shuffled by, and the monkey's cry ended in a horrible squeak.

<< That afternoon, Hewey and Lewey were back, but I never saw Dewey again.

<< A jungle does not tolerate convalescents. Unless I could get back to the jac forest, I would be dead very soon. And if the remaining fishers were half as loyal as Dewey, they would be dead, too. That evening, I put the berries and freshest fish onto my travois. Meter by meter, I dragged it back to the jac forest. Hewey and Lewey followed me partway in. Even their foolish penguin walk was enough to keep up. But they feared the forest now, or maybe they weren't as crazy as Dewey, for eventually they fell behind. I still remember their calling after me. >>

This was Marta's closest brush with death for many years. If there had not been good fishing in the first stream she found or if the jac forest had been any less gentle than she imagined, she would not have survived.

The weeks passed, and then a month. Her shattered foot slowly healed. She spent nearly a year by that stream just inside the forest, returning to the jungle only occasionally—for fresh fruit, and to check on the fishers, and to hear some sounds beyond herself. It became her second major camp, the one with the cabin and the cairn. She had plenty of time to bring her diary up to date, and to scout the forest. It was not everywhere the same. There were patches of older, dying jacarandas. The spiders hung their display webs across those trees, turning the light blue and red. Most of her descriptions of the forest gave Wil the impression of unending catacombs, but this was a cathedral, the webs stained glass. Marta couldn't remember the purpose of the display webs. She stayed for days under one of them, trying to fathom the mystery. Something sexual, she guessed: but for the spiders . . . or the trees? For a weird instant, Wil felt impelled to look up the answer for her; she of all people deserved to know. Then he shook his head and deliberately paged his data set.

Marta figured out most of the spiders' life cycle. She'd seen the enormous quantities of insect life trapped on the perimeter barriers, and she guessed at the tonnage that must be captured on the canopy. She also noticed how often the fallen leaves were fragmented, and correctly guessed that the spiders maintained caterpillar farms much as ants keep aphids. She did as much as any naturalist without tools could.

<< But the forest never made me sick, Lelya. A mystery. In fifty million years, has Evolution's arms race drifted so far that I'm outside the range of the spider-shit toxin? I can't believe that, since the poison seems to work on everything that moves. More likely, there's something in my medical systems, the panphages or whatever, that's protecting me. >>

Wil looked up from the transcript. There was more, of course, almost two million words more.

He stood, walked to the window, and turned off the lights. Down the street, the Dasguptas' place was still dark. It was a clear night; the stars were a pale dust across the sky, outlining the treetops. This day seemed awfully long. Maybe it was the trip to Calafia and going through two sunsets in one day. More likely it was the diary. He knew he was going to keep reading it. He knew he was going to give it more time than the investigation justified. Damn.

TEN

For Wil Brierson, dreams had always waited at the end of sleep. In earlier times, they had waited to entertain and enlighten. Now, they lay in ambush.

Goodbye, goodbye, goodbye. Wil cried and cried, but no sounds came and scarcely any tears. He was holding hands with someone, someone who didn't speak. Everything was shades of pale blue. Her face was Virginia's, and also Marta's. She smiled sadly, a smile that could not deny the truth they both knew. . . . *Goodbye, goodbye, goodbye.* His lungs were empty, yet still he cried, forcing out the last of his breath. He could see through her now, to blue beyond. She was gone, and what he might have saved was lost forever.

Wil woke with an abrupt gasp for breath. He had exhaled so far it hurt. He looked up at the gray ceiling and remembered an advertisement from his childhood. They'd been pushing medical monitors; something about 6:00 AM being a good time to die, that lots of people suffered sleep apnea and heart attacks just before waking—and wouldn't everyone be safer if everyone bought automatic monitors.

It couldn't happen with modern medical treatment. Besides, the autons Yelén and Della had floating above the house were monitoring him. And a second besides—Wil smiled sourly to himself—the clock said 10:00 AM. He had slept nearly nine hours. He swung his bulk out of bed, feeling as if he had slept less than half that.

He lumbered into the bathroom, washed away the strange wetness he found around his eyes. All through his career, he'd done his best to project an appearance of calm strength. It hadn't been hard: He was built like a tank, and he was naturally a low-blood-pressure type. There were a few cases that had made him nervous, but that had been reasonable, since bullets were flying. In police work, he'd seen a fair number of people crack up. For all the publicity given cases like the Kansas Incursion, most of the violence in his era was simple domestic stuff, folks driven around the bend by job or family pressures.

He smiled wryly at the face in the mirror. He had never imagined it could happen to him. The end of sleep was a walk down night paths now. He had a feeling things were going to get worse. Yet there was a part of him that was as analytical as always, that was following his morning dreams and daytime tension with surprised interest, taking notes at his own dismemberment.

Downstairs, Wil threw open the windows, let the morning sounds and smells drift in. He was damned if he'd let this funk paralyze him. Later in the day, Lu was coming over. They would talk about the weapons survey, and decide who to interview next. In the meantime, there was lots of work to do. Yelén was right about studying the high-techs' lives since the Extinction. In particular, he wanted to learn about Sánchez's aborted settlement.

He was barely started on this project when Juan Chanson dropped by. In person. "Wil, my boy! I was hoping we might have a chat."

Brierson let him in, wondering why the high-tech hadn't called ahead. Chanson strode quickly around the living room. As usual, he was energetic to the point of twitchiness. " 'Blas Spañol, Wil?" he said.

"Sí," Brierson replied without thinking; he could get by, anyway.

"Buen," the archeologist continued in Spañolnegro. "I really get tired of English, you know. Never can get just the right word. I'll wager some people think me a fool because of it."

Wil nodded at the rush of words. In Spañolnegro, Chanson talked even faster than in English. It was an impressive—and nearly unintelligible—achievement.

Chanson stopped his nervous tour of the living room. He jerked a thumb at the ceiling. "I suppose our high-tech friends are taking in every word?"

"Uh, no. They're monitoring body function, but I would have to call for help before our words would be interpreted." *And I asked Lu to make sure Yelén did no eavesdropping.*

Chanson smiled knowingly. "So they tell you, no doubt." He placed a gray oblong on the table; a red light blinked at one end. "Now the promises are true. Whatever we say goes unrecorded." He waved for Brierson to be seated.

"We've talked about the Extinction, have we not?"

"Sí." Several times.

Chanson waved his hand. "Of course. I talk to everybody about it. Yet how many believe? Fifty million years ago, the human race was *murdered*, Wil. Isn't that important to you?"

Brierson sat back. This would shoot the morning. "Juan, the Extinction is very important to me." Was it really? Wil had been shanghaied more than a century before it. To his heart, that was when Virginia and Anne and W. W. Jr. had died—even if the biographies said they lived into the twenty-third century. He had been shanghaied across a hundred thousand years; that was many times longer than all recorded history. Now he lived at fifty megayears. Even without the capital-e Extinction, this was so deep in the future that no one could expect the human race to still exist. "But most high-techs don't think there was an alien invasion. Alice Robinson said the race died out over the whole twenty-third century, and that there weren't signs of violence until very late. Besides, if there were an invasion, you'd think we'd have all sorts of refugees from the twenty-third. Instead we have *nobody*—except the last of you high-techs from 2201 and 2202."

Chanson sniffed. "The Robinsons are fools. They fit the

facts to their rosy preconceptions. I've spent thousands of years of my life piecing this together, Wil. I've mapped every square centimeter of Earth and Luna with every diagnostic known to man. Bil Sánchez did the same for the rest of the Solar System. I've interviewed the rescued low-techs. Most of the high-techs think I'm a crank, I've so thoroughly abused their hospitality. There's a lot I don't understand about the aliens—but there's a lot that I do. There are no refugees from the twenty-third because the invaders could jam bobble generators; they had some superpowerful version of the Wáchendon suppressor. The extermination was not like twentieth-century nuclear war, over in a matter of weeks. I've dated the Norcross graffiti at 2230. Apparently, the aliens were using specifically antihuman weapons early in the war. On the other hand, the vanadium tape Billy Sánchez found on Charon appears to be from late in the century. It ties in with the new craters there and in the asteroids. At the end, the aliens dug out the deep resistance with nukes."

"I don't know, Juan. It's so far in the past now—how can we prove or disprove anyone's theories? What's important is to make sure our settlement succeeds and humanity has another chance."

Chanson leaned across the table, even more intense than before. "Exactly. But don't you see? The aliens had bobblers, too. What destroyed civilization threatens to destroy us now."

"After fifty million years? What could be the motive?"

"I don't know. There are limits to physical investigation, no matter how patient. But I think it was a close thing back in the twenty-third. The aliens pulled out all the stops at the end, and it was barely enough. After the war, they were very weak—perhaps on the edge of extinction themselves. They were gone from the Solar System for millions of years. But make no mistake, Wil. They have not forgotten us."

"You expect another invasion."

"That's what I've always feared, but I'm beginning to feel otherwise. There are too few of them; their game is stealth now. They aim to divide and destroy. Marta's murder was only the beginning."

"*What?*"

Chanson flashed a quick, angry smile. "The game is not so academic now, is it, my boy? Think on it: With that murder, they crippled us. Marta was the brains behind the Korolev plan."

"You claim they're here *among* us? I should think you high-techs can monitor things coming into the system."

"Certainly, though the others don't bother. One of the safest places for long-term storage is on cometary orbits. Such bobbles return every hundred thousand years or so. Only *I* seem to realize that a few more return than go out. At least half my time has been spent building a surveillance net. Over the megayears I intercepted three coming in with substantial hyperbolic excess. Two came out of stasis in the inner Solar System, surrounded by my forces. *They came out shooting,* Wil."

"Did they use the super Wáchendon suppressor?"

"No. I think their surviving equipment is scarcely better than ours. With my superior position, I managed to destroy both of them."

Wil looked at the little man with new respect. Like all the high-techs, he was a monomaniac; anyone who pursued one objective for centuries would be. His conclusions had been ridiculed by most of the others, yet he stuck by them and had done his best to protect the others from a threat only he could see. If Chanson was right . . . Wil's mouth was suddenly dry. He could see where this was leading. "What about the third one, Juan?" he said quietly.

Again that angry smile. "That one was much more recent, *much* more clever. It did a lookabout before I was in position. I was outmaneuvered. By the time I got back to Earth, it was already here, claiming to be human—claiming to be Della Lu, long-lost spacer. Your partner is a monster, my boy."

Wil tried not to think about the firepower that floated over their heads. "Is there any solid evidence? Della Lu was a real person."

Chanson laughed. "They're weak now. Subterfuge may be all that's left them—and surely they have copies of GreenInc. Did you see this 'Della Lu' right after she arrived? It would be a joke to call that thing human. The claim she's so old that normal human attributes have faded is nonsense. *I'm* more than two thousand years old, and *my* behavior is perfectly normal."

"But she was alone all that time." Wil's words defended her, but he was remembering the encounter on the beach, Lu's insectile manner, her cold stare. "Surely a medical exam would settle this."

"Maybe. Maybe not. I have reason to think the exterminators are of nearly human structure. If their life sciences are as good as ours, they could rearrange their innards to human standards. As for subtle chemical tests—our ignorance of them and their technology is simply too great to risk accepting negative evidence as proof."

"Who else have you told?"

"Yelén. Philippe. You can be sure I'm making no public accusations. The Lu creature knows *someone* attacked her coming in, but I don't think she knows who. She may even think it was an automatic action. Even if she's alone, she is terribly dangerous, Wil. We can't afford to move against her until all the high-techs are willing to act together. I pray this will happen before she destroys the settlement.

"I don't know if Philippe believes me, but I think he'd act if the rest could be won over. As for Yelén, well . . . I already said she was the lesser of the Korolevs. She's done some passive testing and can't believe the enemy could make such a good counterfeit. She's totally unimpressed by Lu's erratic behavior. Basically, Yelén has no imagination.

"You may be the key, Wil. You see Lu every day. Sooner or later she is going to slip, and you will *know* that what I say is true. It is vitally important you prepare yourself for that moment. With luck, it will be something small, something you can pretend to ignore. If you can cover your knowledge, she may let you live.

"And if she lets you live, then maybe we can convince Yelén."

And if she doesn't let me live, no doubt that will be evidence too. One way or another, Chanson had a use for him.

ELEVEN

Della Lu arrived in early afternoon. Wil stepped outside to watch her land. The autons supplied by Yelén and Della were faithfully keeping station several hundred meters above the house. He wondered what a battle between those two machines would be like, and whether he could survive it. Before, he'd been grateful for Lu's protection against Yelén. Now it worked both ways. Brierson kept his face placid as the spacer walked toward him.

"Hi, Wil." Even with his recollection of the early Della, it was hard now to believe that Chanson could be right. Lu wore a pink blouse and belled pants. Her hair was cut in bangs that swayed girlishly as she walked. Her smile seemed natural and spontaneous.

"Hi, Della." He grinned back with a smile he hoped seemed just as natural and spontaneous. She entered the house ahead of him.

"Yelén and I have a disagreement we'd like you to . . ." She stopped talking and her body tensed. She sidled around the living-room table, her eyes flicking across its surface. Abruptly something round and silver gleamed there. She picked it up. "Did you know you were bugged?"

"No!" Wil walked to the table. A spherical notch about a

centimeter across had been cut from it. The notch was where Chanson had set his bug stomper.

She held up the silver sphere—an exact match for the notch —and said, "Sorry to nick your table. I wanted to bobble it first thing. Some bugs bite when they are discovered."

Wil looked at his face reflected perfect and tiny in the ball. It could contain anything. "How did you spot it?"

She shrugged. "It was too small for my auton to see. I've got some built-in enhancements." She tapped her head. "I'm a little more capable than an ordinary human. I can see into the UV and IR, for instance. . . . Most of the high-techs don't bother with such improvements, but they can be useful sometimes."

Hmm. Wil had lived several years with medical electronics jammed inside his skull; he hadn't liked it one bit.

Della walked across the room and sat on the arm of one of his easy chairs. She swung her feet onto the seat and braced her chin on her hands. The childlike mannerisms were a strange contrast to her words. "My auton says Juan Chanson was your last visitor. Did he get near the table?"

"Yes. That's where we were sitting."

"Hmm. It was a dumb trick, ran a high risk of detection. What did he want, anyway?"

Wil was ready for the question. His response was prompt but casual. "He rambled, as usual. He's discovered I speak Spañol-negro. I'm afraid I'll be his favorite audience from now on."

"I think there's more to it than that. I haven't been able to get an appointment for us to interview him. He won't say no, but he has endless excuses. Philippe Genet is the only other person who seems to be avoiding us. We should put these people at the top of our interview list."

She was doing a better job of proving Juan's case than Juan himself. "Let me think about it. . . . What was it you and Yelén wanted to know?"

"Oh, that. Yelén wants to keep Tammy bobbled for a century or so, till the low-techs are 'firmly rooted.' "

"And you don't."

"No. I have several reasons. I promised the Robinsons

Tammy would be safe. That's why I refuse to turn her over to Yelén. But I also promised them that Tammy would be given a chance to clear the family name. She claims that means she should be free to operate in the present."

"I'll bet Don Robinson couldn't care less about his good name. Things are too hot for the family, but he still wants recruits. If Tammy is bobbled she won't be doing any recruiting."

"Yes. Those are almost Yelén's words." Della moved off the chair arm and sat like an adult. She steepled her hands and stared at them a moment. "When I was very young—even younger than you—I was a Peacer cop. I don't know if you understand what that means. The Peace Authority was a government, no matter what its claims. As a government cop, my morality was very different from yours. The long-range goals of the Authority were the basis of that morality. My own interests and the interests of others were secondary—though I truly believed that survival depended on achieving the Authority's goals. The history books talk mostly about how I stopped Project Renaissance and brought down the Peacers, but I also did some . . . pretty rough things for the Authority; look up my management of the Mongolian Campaign.

"That youngest version of Della Lu would have no problem here: leaving Tammy free is a risk—a very small risk—to the goal of a successful colony. That Della Lu would not hesitate to bobble her, perhaps even execute her, to avoid that risk.

"But I grew out of that." Her steepled hands collapsed, and her expression softened. "For a hundred years I lived in a civilization where individuals set their own goals and guarded their own welfare. That Della Lu sees what Tammy is going through. That Della Lu believes in keeping promises made."

Wil forced himself to think on the question. "I believe in abiding by contracts, too, though I'm not quite sure what was agreed to here. I'm inclined to release Tammy. Let her proselytize, but without her headband. I doubt she remembers enough technology to make any difference."

"It's possible the Robinsons left an equipment cache someplace where Tammy and her recruits could get it."

"If they did, that would be pretty good evidence they knew about the murder beforehand. Why don't we release her, but bug her mercilessly. If she does more than talk, we'll bobble her. Tammy and her family are the best suspects. If we keep her locked up, it's possible we'll never solve the murder. . . . Do you think Yelén would go for that?"

"Yes. That's more or less the argument I made. She said okay if you agreed."

Wil's eyebrows rose. He was both surprised and flattered. "That's settled, then." He looked through the window, trying to think how the conversation might be turned to the topic that was really bothering him. "You know, Della, I had a family. From what I read in GreenInc, they lived right through to the Extinction. I hate to think that Monica is right—that humankind just committed suicide. And Juan's theories are just as obnoxious. How do you think it ended?" He hoped the camouflage hid his real interest. And it wasn't entirely camouflage: He'd be grateful to get a nonviolent explanation for the end of civilization.

Della smiled at the question. She seemed without suspicion. "It's always easier to seem wise if you're selling pessimism. That makes Juan and Monica seem smarter than they really are. The truth is . . . there was no Extinction."

"What?"

"*Something* happened, but we have only circumstantial evidence what it was."

"Yes, but that 'something' killed every human outside of stasis." He could not disguise his sarcasm.

She shrugged. "I don't think so. Let me give you my interpretation of the circumstantial evidence:

"During the last two thousand years of civilization, almost every measure of progress showed exponential growth. From the nineteenth century on, this was obvious. People began extrapolating the trends. The results were absurd: vehicles traveling faster than sound by the mid-twentieth century, men on the moon a bit later. All this was achieved, yet progress continued. Simple-minded extrapolations of energy production and computer power and vehicle speeds gave meaninglessly large answers for the late twenty-first century. The more so-phisticated forecasters pointed out that real growth eventually saturates; the numbers coming out of the extrapolations were just too big to be believed."

"Hmph. Seems to me they were right. I really don't think 2100 was more different from 2000 than 2000 was from 1900. We had prolongevity and economical space travel, but those were in the range of conservative twentieth-century predic-tion."

"Yes, but don't forget the 1997 war. It just about eliminated the human race. It took more than fifty years to dig out of that. After 2100 we were back on the exponential track. By 2200, all but the blind could see that something fantastic lay in our immediate future. We had practical immortality. We had the beginnings of interstellar travel. We had networks that effec-tively increased human intelligence—with bigger increases coming."

She stopped, seemed to change the subject. "Wil, have you ever wondered what became of your namesake?"

"The original W.W.? . . . Say," he said, with sudden realiza-tion, "you actually *knew* him, didn't you?"

She smiled briefly. "I *met* Wili Wáchendon a couple of times. He was a sickly teenager, and we were on the opposite sides of a war. But what became of him after the fall of the Peacers?"

"Well, he invented too many things for me to remember. He spent most of his time in space. By the 2090s, you didn't hear much about him."

"Right. And if you follow him in GreenInc, you'll see the trend continued. Wili was a first-rate genius. Even then he could use an interface band better than I can now. I figure that, as time passed, he had less and less in common with people like us. His mind was somewhere else."

"And you think that's what happened to all mankind even-tually?"

She nodded. "By 2200, we could increase human intelli-gence itself. And intelligence is the basis of all progress. My guess is that by midcentury, any goal—any goal you can state objectively, without internal contradictions—could be achieved. And what would things be like fifty years after *that?* There would still be goals and there would still be striving, but not what we could understand.

"To call that time 'the Extinction' is absurd. It was a Singularity, a place where extrapolation breaks down and new models must be applied. And those new models are beyond our intelligence."

Della's face was aglow. It was hard for Wil to believe that this was the fabrication of an "exterminator." In the beginning at least, these had been human ideas and human dreams.

"It's a funny thing, Wil. I left civilization in 2202. Miguel had died just a few years earlier. That meant more to me than any Big Picture. I wanted to be alone for a while, and the Gatewood's Star mission seemed ideal. I spent forty years there, and was bobbled out for almost twelve hundred. I fully expected that when I got back, civilization would be unintelligible." Her smile twisted. "I was very surprised to find Earth empty. But then, what could be less intelligible than a total absence of intelligence? From the nineteenth century on, futurists wondered about the destiny of science. And now, from the other side of the Singularity, the mystery is just as deep.

"There was no Extinction, Wil. Mankind simply graduated, and you and I and the rest missed graduation night."

"So three billion people just stepped into another plane. This begins to sound like religion, Della."

She shrugged. "Just talking about superhuman intelligence gets us into something like religion." She grinned. "If you really want the religious version . . . have you met Jason Mudge? He claims that the Second Coming of Christ was sometime in the twenty-third century. The Faithful were saved, the unfaithful destroyed—and the rest of us are truant."

Wil smiled back; he had heard of Mudge. His notion of the Second Coming could explain things too—in one respect better than Lu's theory. "I like your ideas better. But what's your explanation for the physical destruction? Chanson isn't the only person who thinks that nukes and bioweapons were used towards the end of the twenty-third."

Della hesitated. "That's the one thing that doesn't fit. When I returned to Earth in 3400, there was plenty of evidence of war. The craters were already overgrown, but from orbit I could see that metropolitan areas had been hit. Chanson and the Korolevs have better records; they were active all through the fourth millennium, trying to figure out what had happened, and trying to rescue short-term low-techs. It looks like a classic nuclear war, fought without bobbles. The evidence of biowarfare is much more tenuous.

"I don't know, Wil. There must be an explanation. The trends in the twenty-second century were *so* strong that I can't believe the race committed suicide. Maybe it was a fireworks celebration. Or maybe . . . do you know about survival sport?"

"That was after my time. I read about it in GreenInc."

"Physical fitness has always been a big thing in civilization. By the late twenty-second, medical care automatically maintained body fitness, so people worked on other things. Most middle-class folk had Earthside estates of several thousand hectares. There were shared estates bigger than some twentieth-century nations. Fitness came to mean the ability to survive without technology. The players were dropped naked into a wilderness—arctic, rain forest, you name it—that had been secretly picked by the judges. No technology was allowed, though medical autons kept close track of the contestants; it could get to be pretty rough. Even people who didn't compete would often spend several weeks a year living under conditions that would be deadly to twentieth-century city-dwellers. By 2200, individuals were probably tougher than ever before. All they lacked was the bloody-mindedness of earlier times."

Wil nodded. Marta had certainly demonstrated what Lu was saying. "How does this explain the nuke war?"

"It's a little farfetched, but . . . imagine things just before the race fell into the Singularity. Individuals might be only 'slightly' superhuman, and might still be interested in the primitive. For them, nuclear war might be a game of strength and fitness."

"You're right; that does sound farfetched."

She shrugged.

"Would you say Juan is in the minority, thinking mankind was exterminated?"

"I think so; I know Yelén agrees with me. But remember that—until very recently—I didn't have much chance to talk to anyone. I was back in the Solar System for a few years around 3400. During that time, no one was out of stasis. They'd left plenty of messages, though: The Korolevs were already talking about a rendezvous at fifty megayears. Juan Chanson had an auton at L4 blatting his theories to all who would listen. It was clear to me that with the evidence at hand, they could argue forever without proving things one way or the other.

"I wanted certainty. And I thought I could have it." She made that twisted smile again.

"So *that's* why you went back into space."

"Yes. What had happened to us must have happened—must *be happening*—over and over again throughout the universe. From the twentieth century on, astronomers watched for evidence of intelligence beyond the Solar System. They never saw any. We wonder about the great silence on Earth after 2300. They wondered about the silence among the stars. Their mystery is just the spacelike version of ours.

"There is a difference. In space, I can travel any direction I wish. I was sure that eventually I would find a race at the edge of the Singularity."

Listening to her, Wil felt a strange mix of fear and frustration. One way or another, this person must *know* where others could only speculate. Yet what she told him and the truth could be entirely different things. And the questions that might distinguish lie from truth might provoke a deadly response. "I've tried to use your databases, Della. They're very hard to understand."

"That's not surprising. Over the years, there was some non-repairable damage; parts of my GreenInc are so messed up I don't even use them. And my personal db's . . . well, I've customized them quite a bit."

"Surely you want people to know what you've seen?" Yet Della had always been strangely closemouthed about her time Out There.

She hesitated. "Once I did. Now I'm not sure. There are people who don't want to know the truth. . . . Wil, someone fired on me when I entered the Solar System."

"What?" Brierson hoped his surprise sounded real. "Who was it?"

"I don't know. I was a thousand AUs out, and the guns were automatic. My guess is Juan Chanson. He seems to be the most paranoid about outsiders, and I was clearly hyperbolic."

Wil suddenly wondered about the "aliens" Juan said he had destroyed. How many of them had been returning spacers? Some of Juan's theories could be self-proving. "You were lucky," he said, probing gently, "to get past an ambush."

"Not lucky. I've been shot at before. Any time I'm less than a quarter light-year from a star, I'm ready to fight—usually ready to run, too."

"So there *are* other civilizations!"

For a long moment, Della didn't answer. Her personality shifted yet again. Expression drained from her face, and she seemed almost as cold as in their first meetings.

"Intelligent life is a rare development.

"I spent nine thousand years on this, spread across fifty million years of realtime. I averaged less than a twentieth light speed. But that was fast enough. I had time to visit the Large Magellanic Cloud and the Fornax System, besides our own galaxy. I had time to stop at tens of thousands of places, at astrophysical freaks and normal stars. I saw some strange things, mostly near deep gravity wells. Maybe it was engineering, but I couldn't prove it, even to myself.

"I found that most slow-spinning stars have planets. About ten percent of these have an Earth-type planet. And almost all such planets have life.

"If Monica Raines loves the purity of life without intelligence, she loves one of the most common things in the universe. . . . In all my nine thousand years, I found two intelligent races." Her eyes stared into Wil's. "Both times I was too late. The first was in Fornax. I missed them by several billion years; even their asteroid settlements were ground to dust. There were no bobbles, and it was impossible to tell if their ending had been abrupt.

"The other was a nearer thing, both in space and time: a G2 star about a third of the way around the Galaxy from here. The world was beautiful, larger than Earth, its atmosphere so dense that many plants were airborne. The race was centaurlike; I learned that much. I missed them by a couple of hundred megayears. Their databases had evaporated, but their space settlements were almost undamaged.

"They had vanished just as abruptly as humankind did from Earth. One century they were there, the next—nothing. But there were differences. For one thing, there was no sign of nuclear war. For another, the centaur-folk had started a couple of interstellar colonies. I visited them. I found evidence of growing population, of independent technological progress, and then . . . their own Singularities. I lived two thousand years in those systems, spread out over a half megayear. I studied them as carefully as Chanson and Sánchez did our solar system.

"There were bobbles in the centaur systems. Not as many as near Earth, but this was a lot longer after their Singularity. I knew if I hung around, I'd run into somebody."

"Did you?"

Della nodded. "But what sort of person would you expect two hundred megayears after civilization? . . . The centaur came out shooting. I nuked out; I ran fifty light-years, past where the centaur had any interest. Then, over the next million years, I sneaked back. Sure enough, he was back in stasis, depending on occasional lookabouts and his autons for protection. I left plenty of robot transmitters, some with autons. If he gave them half a chance, they would teach him my language and convince him I was peaceful. . . .

"His realtime forces attacked the minute they heard my transmissions. I lost half my auton defense holding them off. I almost lost my life; that's where my db's were damaged. A thousand years later, the centaur himself came out of stasis. Then *all* his forces attacked. Our machines fought another thousand years. The centaur stayed out of stasis the whole time. I learned a lot. He was willing to talk even if he had forgotten how to listen.

"He was alone, had been the last twenty thousand years of his life. Once upon a time, he'd been no nuttier than most of us, but those twenty thousand years had burned the soul from him." She was silent for a moment—thinking on what nine thousand years could do? "He was caught on behavior tracks he could never—could never want to—break. He thought of his solar system as a mausoleum, to be protected from desecration. One by one, he had destroyed the last centaurs as they came out of stasis. He had fought at least four travelers from outside his system. God knows who they were—centaur spacers, or 'Della Lus' of other races.

"But, like us, he couldn't replace his autons. He had lost most of them when I found him; I wouldn't have stood a chance a hundred megayears earlier. I suppose, if I had stayed long enough, I could have beaten him. The price would have been my living more thousands of years; the price would have been *my* soul. In the end, I decided to let him be." She was silent for a long while, the coldness slowly departing from her face, to be replaced by . . . tears? Were they for the last centaur—or for the millennia she had spent, never finding more than the mystery she began with?

"Nine thousand years . . . was not enough. Artifacts from beyond the Singularity are so vast that doubters can easily deny them. And the pattern of progress followed by vanishment can be twisted to any explanation—especially on Earth, where there are signs of war."

There was a difference between Della's propaganda and the others', Wil realized. She was the only one who seemed plagued by uncertainty, by any continuing need for proof. It was hard to believe that such an ambiguous, doubt-ridden story could be an alien cover. Hell, she seemed more human than Chanson.

Della smiled but did not brush the wetness from her lashes. "In the end, there is only one way to know for a fact what the Singularity is. You have to be there when it happens. . . . The Korolevs have brought together everybody that's left. I think we have enough people. It may take a couple of centuries, but if we can restart civilization *we will make our own Singularity*.

"And *this* time, I won't miss graduation night."

116

TWELVE

Wil was at the North Shore party later that week.
Virtually everyone was there, even some high-techs. Della and Yelén were absent—and Tammy was more or less forbidden from attending these outings—but he saw Blumenthal and Genet. Today they looked almost like anyone else. Their autons hovered high, all but lost in the afternoon light. For the first time since taking the Korolev case, Wil didn't feel like an outsider. His own autons were indistinguishable from the others, and even when visible, the fliers seemed no more intimidating than party balloons.

There were two of these affairs each week, one at Town Korolev sponsored by New Mexico, the other run by the Peacers here at North Shore. Just as Rohan said, both groups were doing their best to glad-hand the uncommitted. Wil wondered if ever in history governments had been forced to tread so softly.

Clusters of people sat on blankets all across the lawn. Other folks were lining up at the barbecue pits. Most were dressed in shorts and tops. There was no sure way of telling Peacers from NMs from ungovs, though most of the blue blankets belonged to the Republic. Steve Fraley himself was attending. His staff seemed a little stiff, sitting on lawn chairs, but they

117

were not in uniform. The top Peacer, Kim Tioulang, walked over and shook Steve's hand. From this distance, their conversation looked entirely cordial. . . .

So Yelén figured he should mingle, observe, find out just how unpopular her plans were. Okay. Wil smiled faintly and leaned back on his elbows. It had been a matter of duty to come to this picnic, to do just what the Dasgupta brothers—and simple common sense—had already suggested. Now he was very glad he was here, and the feeling had nothing to do with duty.

In some ways, the North Shore scenery was the most spectacular he'd seen. It was strikingly different from the south side of the Inland Sea. Here, forty-meter cliffs fell straight to narrow beaches. The lawns that spread inland from the cliffs were as friendly as any park in civilization. A few hundred meters further north, the clifftop bench ended in steep hills shrouded by trees and flowers—climbing and climbing, till they stood faintly bluish against the sky. Three waterfalls streamed down from those heights. It was like something out of a fairy tale.

But the view was only the smallest part of Wil's pleasure. He'd seen so much beautiful country the last few weeks—all untouched and pristine as any city-hater could wish. Something in the back of his mind thought it the beauty of a tomb —and he a ghost come to cry for the dead. He brought his gaze back from the heights and looked across the crowds of picnickers. *Crowds*, by God! His smile returned, unthinking. Two hundred, three hundred people, all in one spot. Here he could see that they really did have a chance, that there could be children and a human future, and a use for beauty.

"Hey, lazybones, if you're not going to help with the food, at least give us room to sit down!" It was Rohan, a big grin on his face. He and Dilip were back from the food lines. Two women accompanied them. The four sat down, laughing briefly at Wil's embarrassment. Rohan's friend was a pretty Asian; she nodded pleasantly to him. The other woman was a stunning, dark-haired Anglo; Dilip really knew how to pick 'em. "Wil, this is Gail Parker. Gail's an EMC—"

"ECM," the girl corrected.

"Right, an ECM officer on Fraley's staff."

She wore thigh-length shorts, with a cotton top; he'd never have guessed she was an NM staffer. She stuck out her hand. "I've always wondered what you were like, Inspector. Ever since I was a little girl, they've been telling me about that big, black, badass northerner name of W. W. Brierson. . . ." She looked him up and down. "You don't look so dangerous." Wil took her hand uncertainly, then noticed the mischievous gleam in her eyes. He'd met a number of New Mexicans since the failed NM invasion of the ungoverned lands. A few didn't even recognize his name. Many were frankly grateful, thinking he had speeded the disgovernance of New Mexico. Others—the die-hard statists of Fraley's stripe—hated Wil out of all proportion to his significance.

Gail Parker's reaction was totally unexpected . . . and fun. He smiled, and tried to match her tone. "Well, ma'am, I'm big and black, but I'm really not such a badass."

Gail's reply was interrupted by an immensely loud voice echoing across the picnic grounds. "FRIENDS—" There was a pause. Then the amplified voice continued more quietly. "Oops, that was a bit much. . . . Friends, may I take a few moments of your time."

Rohan's friend said quietly, "So wonderful; a speech." Her English was heavily accented, but Wil thought he heard sarcasm. He had hoped that with Don Robinson's departure he would be spared any more "friends" speeches. He looked down the lawn at the speaker. It was the Peacer boss who had been talking to Fraley a few moments earlier. Dilip handed a carton of beer over Wil's shoulder. "I advise you to drink up, 'friend,' " he said. "It may be the only thing that saves you." Wil nodded solemnly and broke the seal on the carton.

The spindly Peacer continued. "This is the third week we of the Peace have hosted a party. If you have been to the others, you know we have a message to get across, but we haven't bothered you with speeches. Well, by now we hope we've 'sucked you in' enough so you'll give me a hearing." He laughed nervously, and there were responding chuckles from the audience, almost out of sympathy. Wil chugged some beer and watched the speaker narrowly. He'd bet anything the guy really was nervous and shy—not used to haranguing the masses. But Wil had read up on Tioulang. From 2010 till the fall of the Peace Authority in 2048, Kim Tioulang had been the Director for Asia. He had ruled a third of the planet. So maybe his diffidence reflected nothing more than the fact that if you're a big-enough dictator, you don't have to impress anyone with your manner.

"Incidentally, I warned President Fraley of my intention to propagandize this afternoon, and offered him the 'floor' in rebuttal. He graciously declined the offer."

Fraley stood up and made a megaphone of his hands. "I'll get you all at *our* party." There was laughter, and Wil felt the corners of his mouth turn down. He *knew* Fraley was a martinet; it was annoying to see the man behave with any grace.

Tioulang turned back to the mass of picnickers. "Okay. What am I trying to convince you of? To join the Peace. Failing that, to show solidarity with the interests of the low-techs—as represented by the Peace and the Republic of New Mexico. . . . Why do I ask this? The Peace Authority came and went before many of you were born—and the stories you've heard about it are the usual ones that history's winners lay on the losers. But I can tell you one thing: The Peace Authority has always stood for the survival of humanity, and the welfare of human beings everywhere."

The Peacer's voice went soft. "Ladies and gentlemen, one thing is beyond argument: What we do during the next few years will determine if the human race lives or dies. It depends on *us*. For the sake of humanity, we can't afford to follow blindly after Korolev or any high-tech—Don't mistake me: I admire Korolev and the others. I am deeply grateful to them. They gave the race a second chance. And the Korolev scheme seems very simple, very generous. By running her factories way over redline, Yelén has promised to keep us at a moderate standard of living for a few decades." Tioulang gestured at the beer freezers and the barbecue pits, acknowledging their provenance. "She tells us that this will wreck her equipment centuries before it would otherwise break down. As the years pass, first one and then another of her systems will fail. And we will be left dependent on whatever resources we have developed.

"So we have a few decades to make it . . . or fade into savagery. Korolev and the others have provided us with tools and the databases to create our own means of production. I think we all understand the challenge. I shook some hands this afternoon. I noticed calluses that weren't there earlier. I talked to people that have been working twelve-, fifteen-hour days. Before long, these little meetings will be our only break from the struggle."

Tioulang paused a moment, and the Asian girl laughed softly. "Here it comes, everybody."

"To this point, no sane person can have disagreement. But what the Peace Authority—and our friends of the Republic— do resist is Yelén Korolev's method. Hers is the age-old story of the absentee landlord, the queen in the castle and the serfs in the fields. By some scheme that is never revealed, she parcels out data and equipment to individuals—never to organizations. The only way individuals can make sense of such a hopeless jumble is by following Korolev directions . . . by developing the habit of serfdom."

Wil set the beer down. The Peacer had one hundred percent of his attention now. Certainly Yelén was listening to the spiel, but would she understand Tioulang's point? Probably not; it was something new to Wil, and he'd thought he appreciated all the reasons for resenting Korolev. Tioulang's interpretation was a subtle—perhaps even an unconscious—distortion of Marta's plan. Yelén gave tools and production equipment to individuals, according to what hobbies or occupations they had had back in civilization. If those individuals chose to turn the gear over to the Peace or the Republic, that was their business; certainly Yelén had not forbidden such transfers.

In fact, she hadn't given any orders about how to use the gifts. She had simply made her production databases and planning programs public. Anyone could use those data and programs to make deals and coordinate development. The ones who coordinated best would certainly come out ahead, but it was scarcely a "jumble" . . . except perhaps to statists. Wil looked across the picnickers. He couldn't imagine the ungoverned being taken in by Tioulang's argument. Marta's plan was about as close to "business as usual" as you could come under the present circumstances, but it was alien weirdness to the Peacers and most of the NMs. That difference in perception might be enough to bring everything down.

Kim Tioulang was also watching the audience, waiting to see if his point had sunk in. "I don't think any of us want to be serfs, but how can we prevent it, given Korolev's overwhelming technical superiority? . . . I have a secret for you. The high-techs need us more than we need them. Without any high-techs at all, the human race would still have a chance. We have—we *are*—the one thing that is really needed: people. Between the Peace, the Republic, and the, uh, unaffiliated, we low-techs are almost three hundred human beings. That's more than in any settlement since the Extinction. Our biologists tell us it is enough—just barely enough—genetic diversity to restart the human race. Without our numbers, the high-techs are doomed. And they know it.

"So the most important thing is that we hang together. We are in a position to reinvent democracy and the rule of the majority."

Behind Wil, Gail Parker said, "God, what a hypocrite. The Peace never had any interest in elections when *they* were in the saddle."

"If I've convinced you of the need for unity—and frankly, the need is so obvious that I don't need much persuasiveness there—there is still the question of why the Peace is a better bet for you than the Republic.

"Think about it. The human race has been at the brink before. In the early part of the twenty-first century, plagues destroyed billions. Then, as now, technology remained widely available. Then, as now, the problem was the depopulation of the Earth. In all humility, my friends, the Peace Authority has more experience in solving our present problem than any group in history. We brought the human race *back* from the brink. Whatever else may be said of the Peace, *we* are the acknowledged experts in these matters. . . ."

Tioulang shrugged diffidently. "That's really all I had to say.

These are important things to think about. Whatever your decisions, I hope you'll think about them carefully. My people and I are happy to take any questions, but let's do it one on one." He cut the amplifier.

There was a buzz of conversation. A fair-sized crowd followed Tioulang back to his pavilion by the beer locker. Wil shook his head. The guy had made some points. But people didn't believe everything he said. Just behind Wil, Gail Parker was giving the Dasguptas a quick rehash of history. The Peace Authority was the great devil of the early twenty-first century, and Wil had lived near enough to that era to know that their reputation could not be entirely a smear. Tioulang's diffident, friendly manner might soften the harsh outlines of history, but few were going to buy his view of the Peace.

What some *did* buy—Wil realized unhappily as he listened to nearby ungovs—was Tioulang's overall viewpoint. They accepted his claim that Korolev's policies were designed to keep them down. They seemed to agree that "solidarity" was their great weapon against the "queen on the hill." And the Peacer's call for a reestablishment of democracy was especially popular. Wil could understand the NMs buying that; majority rule was the heart of their system. But what if the majority decided that everyone with dark skin should work for free? Or that Kansas should be invaded? He couldn't believe the ungoverned would accept such a notion. But some appeared to. This was a matter of survival, and the will of the majority was working in their favor. How quickly cracks the veneer of civilization.

Brierson rolled to his feet. "I'm getting some food. Need anything more?"

Dilip looked up from the discussion with Parker. "Er, no. We're stocked."

"Okay. Be back in a little while." Wil wandered down the lawn, treading carefully around blankets and people. There seemed the same discouraging set of responses: the Peacers enthusiastic, NMs distrustful but recognizing the "basic wisdom" of Tioulang's speech, the ungovs of mixed opinions.

He reached the food, began filling a couple of plates. One

good thing about all this deep philosophical debate: He didn't have to wait in line.

The voice behind him was a sardonic bass. "That Tioulang is really a clown, isn't he?"

Wil turned. An ally!

The speaker was a brown-haired Anglo, dressed in a heavy —and none too clean—robe. At one meter seventy, he was short enough so Wil could see the shaved patch on the top of his skull. The fellow had a permanent grin pasted on his face.

"Hello, Jason." Brierson tried to keep the irritation out of his voice. Of all the people here, that the only one to echo his thoughts was Jason Mudge, the cheated chiliast and professional crank! It was too much. Wil continued down the food line, piling his plates precariously high. Jason followed, not taking anything to eat, but bombarding Wil with the Mudge analysis of Tioulang's lunacy: Tioulang totally misunderstood Man's crisis. Tioulang was taking humanity back from the Faith. The Peacers and the NMs and the Korolevs—in fact, everybody—had closed their eyes to the possibility of redemption and the perils of further dis-Belief.

Wil grunted occasionally at the other's words, but avoided any meaningful response. Reaching the end of the line, he realized there was no way to get all this food across the lawn without slopping; he'd have to scarf some of it right here. He set the plates down and attacked one of the hot dogs.

Mudge circled closer, thinking Brierson had stopped to listen. Once his spiel began, he was a nonstop talker. Right now, his voice was "powered down." Earlier, he'd stood on the high ground north of the lawn and harangued them for a quarter hour. His voice had boomed across the picnic grounds, as loud as Tioulang's had been with amplification. Even at that volume, he'd spoken as fast as now, every word standing in block capitals. His message was very simple, though repeated again and again with different words: Present-day humans were Truants from the Second Coming of the Lord. (That Second Coming was presumably the Extinction.) He, Jason Mudge, was the prophet of the Third and Final Coming. All must repent, take the robes of the Forgiven, and await the Salvation that was soon to come.

At first, the harangue had been amusing. Someone shouted that with all these Comings, Mudge must not only be a prophet, but the Lord's Sexual Athlete as well. Such taunts only increased Jason's zeal; he would talk till the Crack of Doom if there remained any unrepentant. Finally, the Dasgupta brothers walked up from the lawn and had a brief chat with the prophet. That had been the end of the speechifying. Afterwards, Will had asked them about it. Rohan had smiled shyly and replied, "We told him we'd throw him over the cliffs if he continued shouting at us." Knowing Dilip and Rohan, the threat was completely incredible. However, it worked on Mudge; he was a prophet who could not afford to become a martyr.

So now Jason toured the picnic grounds, looking for stragglers and other targets of opportunity. And W. W. Brierson was the current victim. Wil munched a curried egg roll and eyed the other man. Perhaps this wasn't entirely wasted time. Della and Yelén had lost all interest in Mudge, but this was the first time Wil had seen him up close.

Strictly speaking, Jason Mudge was a high-tech. He had left civilization in 2200. The GreenInc database showed him as a (very) obscure religious nut, who proclaimed that the Second Coming of Christ would occur at the end of the next century. Apparently ridicule is a constant of history: Mudge couldn't take the pressure, and bobbled through to 2299, thinking to come out during the final throes of the world of sin. Alas, 2299 was after the Singularity; Mudge arrived on an empty planet. As he would willingly—and at great length—explain, he had erred in his biblical computations. The Second Coming had in fact occurred in 2250. Furthermore, his errors were fated, as punishment for his arrogance in trying to "skip ahead to the good part." But the Lord in His infinite compassion had given Jason one more chance. As the prophet who had missed the Second Coming, Jason Mudge was the perfect shepherd for the lost flock that would be saved at the Third.

So much for religion. GreenInc had shown another side of

the man. Up until 2197, he had worked as a systems programmer. When Wil noticed that, Mudge's name had moved several notches up the suspect list. Here was a certified nut who could reasonably want to see the Korolev effort fail. And the nut's specialty involved the sort of skills needed to sabotage the bobble fail-safes and maroon Marta.

Yelén was not so suspicious of him. She had said that by the late twenty-second century, most occupations involved systems. And with prolongevity, many people had several specialties. Mudge's path had crossed the Korolevs' several times since the Age of Man. The encounters were always the same: Mudge needed help. Of all the high-techs who had left civilization voluntarily, he was the most poorly equipped: He had a flier but no space capability. He owned no autons. His databases consisted of a couple of religion cartridges.

Yet he was still on Wil's list. It was a bit implausible that anyone would go this far to disguise his abilities, but Mudge *might* have something cached away. He had asked Yelén to put Mudge under surveillance, to see if he was communicating with hidden autons.

Now Wil had a chance to apply the "legendary Brierson savvy" firsthand. Watching Mudge, Wil realized the little man required virtually no feedback. As long as Wil was standing here facing him, the harangue would continue. No doubt he rarely talked to anyone who gave more. Could he respond at all once he got rolling? *Let's see.* Wil raised his hand and injected a random comment. "But we don't *need* supernatural explanations, Jason. Why, Juan Chanson says invaders caused the Extinction."

The Mudge diatribe continued for almost a second before he noticed there had been some real interaction. His mouth hung open for an instant, and then—he laughed. "*That* backslider? I don't see why you people believe anything he says. He has fallen from the Way of Christ, into the toils of science." The last was a dirty word in Jason's mouth. He shook his head, and his smile came back broader than ever. "But your question shows something. Indeed we must consider that—" The last prophet moved closer and launched still another attempt to make him understand . . .

. . . and Wil really did. Jason Mudge needed people. But somewhere in his past, the little man had concluded that the only way to get others' attention was with the cosmically important. And the harder he tried to explain, the more hostile was his audience—until it was a triumph to have an audience at all. If there was anything to the Brierson intuition, Yelén was right: Jason Mudge should come off the suspect list.

It might seem a small thing, the twenty-five-hour day. But that extra hour and bit was one of the nicest things about the new world. Almost everyone felt it. For the first time in their lives, there seemed to be enough time in the day to get things done, enough time to reflect. Surely, everyone agreed, they would soon adjust, and the days would be just as crowded as always. Yet the weeks passed and the effect persisted.

The picnic stretched through the long afternoon, lost much of the intentness that followed Tioulang's speech. Attention shifted to the volleyball nets on the north side of the lawn. For many, it was a mindless, pleasurable time.

It should have been so for Wil Brierson; he had always enjoyed such things. Today, the longer he stayed, the more uncomfortable he became. The reason? If all the human race was here, then the person who had shanghaied him was, too. Somewhere within two hundred meters was the cause of all his pain. Beforehand, he'd thought he could ignore that fact; he'd been faintly amused at the Korolev fears he might launch a vendetta against the shanghaier.

How little he knew himself. Wil found himself watching the other players, trying to find a face from the past. He muffed easy shots; worse, he crashed into a smaller player. Considering Brierson's ninety kilos, that was a distinct breach of etiquette.

After that, he stood on the sidelines. Did he really know what he was looking for? The embezzlement case had been so simple; a blind man could have tagged the culprit. Three suspects there had been: the Kid, the Executive, and the Janitor

—that was how he'd thought of them. And given a few more days, he'd have had an arrest. Brierson's great mistake was to underestimate the crook's panic. Only trivial amounts had been stolen; what kind of crazyman would bobble the investigating officer, and guarantee a terrible punishment?

The Kid, the Exec, the Janitor. Wil wasn't even sure of their names just now, but he remembered their faces so clearly. No doubt, the Korolevs had disguised the fellow, but Wil was sure that given time he could see through such.

This is insane. He'd all but promised Yelén—and Marta before her—that he wouldn't go after the shanghaier. And what could he do if he found the bastard? If anything, life would be more unpleasant than before. . . . Still, his eyes wandered, thirty years of police skill in harness to his pain. Wil left the games and began a circuit of the grounds. More than half the picnickers were not involved with the volleyball. He moved with apparent aimlessness but kept track of everything in his field of vision, watching for any sign of evasion. Nothing.

After walking around the field, Brierson moved from group to group. His approach was relaxed, cheerful. In the old days, this appearance had almost always been genuine, even when he was on the job. Now it was a double deception. Somewhere above him, Yelén was watching his every move. . . . She should be pleased. He appeared to be doing exactly what she wanted of him: in the course of two hours, he interviewed about half the ungovs—all without giving the appearance of official scrutiny. He learned a lot. For instance, there were many people who saw through the governments' line. Good news for Yelén.

At the same time, Wil's private project continued. After ten or fifteen minutes of chatting, Wil could be sure that yet one more was not his quarry. He kept track of the faces and the names. Something inside him took pleasure in so thoroughly fooling Yelén.

The shanghaier was almost certainly a loner. How would such a type hide himself? Wil didn't know. He did discover that almost no one was really alone now. Faced with an empty Earth, people were hanging together, trying to help those who hurt the most. And he could see terrible grief in many, often hidden behind cheerfulness. The basket cases were the folks who had been out of stasis only a month or two; for them, the loss was so painfully fresh. Surely there had been some outright psychiatric breakdowns; what was Yelén doing about those? Hmm. It was entirely possible the shanghaier *wasn't* here. No matter. When he got home, he would match the people he'd met with the settlement lists. The holes would stand out. After the next party or the next, he'd have a good idea who he was after.

The sun slowly fell, a straight-down path that seemed faintly unreal to someone raised in midlatitudes. Shadows deepened. The green of lawn and hillsides was subtly changed by the reddening light; more than ever, the land looked like a fantasist's painting. The sky turned to gold and then to red. As twilight passed quickly into night, light panels came on by two of the volleyball courts. There were several bonfires—cheerful yellow light compared to the blue around the courts.

Wil had talked with most of the ungovs and perhaps twenty Peacers. Not an enormous group, but then he'd had to move slowly—to fool Yelén and to assure that *he* wasn't fooled by any disguise.

Darkness released him from the terrible compulsion; there was no point to an interview unless he was confident of the results. He wandered back towards the courts, relief verging on elation. Even his feeling of shame at deceiving Yelén was gone. In spite of himself, he had done good work for her this day. He'd seen issues and attitudes that she had never mentioned.

For instance:

There were people sitting away from the lights. Their talk was low and intense. He was almost back to the courts when he came on a large group—almost thirty people, all women. By the light of the nearest bonfire, he recognized Gail Parker and a few others. There were both ungovs and NMs here, maybe a few Peacers. Wil paused, and Parker looked up. Her gaze had none of its earlier friendliness. He drifted away, aware of several pairs of eyes following his retreat.

He knew the shape of their discussions. People like Kim

Tioulang could make grandiose talk about reestablishing the human race. But that reestablishment demanded tremendous birth rates, for at least a century. Without womb tanks and postnatal automation, the job would fall on the women. It meant creating a serf class, but not the one Tioulang was so eager to warn against. These serfs might be beloved and cherished—and might believe in the rightness of it all as much as anyone—but they would carry the heavy burden. It had happened before. The plagues of the early twenty-first century had killed most of the race, and left many of the survivors sterile. The women of that period had a very restricted role, very different from women before or after. Wil's parents had grown up in that time: The only serious fights he could remember between them involved his mother's efforts to start her own business.

A motherhood serfdom would be much harder to establish this time around. These people were not coming back from plagues and a terrible war. Except for the Peacers, they were from the late twenty-first and the twenty-second. The women were highly trained, most with more than one career. As often as not, they were the bosses. As often as not, they initiated romance. Many of those from the twenty-second were sixty or seventy years old, no matter how young and lush their bodies. They were not people you could push around.

. . . And yet, and yet Gail and the others could see final extinction waiting irrevocably in the very near future . . . unless they made some terrible sacrifices. He understood their intent discussion and Gail's unfriendly stare. Which sacrifices to make, which to decline. What to demand, what to accept. Wil was glad he wasn't welcome in their councils.

Something moon-bright rose into the air ahead of him, quickly fell back. Wil looked up and broke into a trot, forcing the problem from his mind. The light rose again, sweeping fast-moving shadows across the lawn. Someone had brought a glowball! A crowd had already gathered along three sides of the volleyball court, blocking his view. Brierson edged around till he could see the play.

Wil found himself grinning stupidly. Glowballs were something new, just a couple of months old . . . at the time he was shanghaied. It might be old hat to some, but it was a complete novelty to the Peacers and even to the NMs. The ball had the same size and feel as a regulation volleyball—but its surface was brightly aglow. The teams were playing by this light alone, and Wil knew the first few games would be comic relief. If you kept your eye on the ball, then little else was bright enough to see. The ball became the center of the universe, a sphere that seemed to swell and shrink while everything else swung around it. After a few moments, you couldn't find your teammates— or even the ground. The NM and Peacer players spent almost as much time on their butts as standing. Laughter swept the far side of the court as three *spectators* fell down. This ball was better than the others Wil had seen. Whenever it touched out-of-bounds, it chimed and the light changed to yellow. *That* was an impressive trick.

Not everyone had problems. No doubt Tunç Blumenthal had always played with glowballs. In any case, Wil knew that Tunç's biggest problem was playing down to everyone else's level. The high-tech massed as much as Wil, but stood over two meters tall. He had the speed and coordination of a professional. Yet, when he held back and let others dominate the play, he didn't seem condescending. Tunç was the only high-tech who really mixed with the lows.

After a time, all players learned the proper strategy: less and less did they watch the ball directly. They watched each other. Most important, they watched the *shadows*. With the glow-ball, those shadows were twisting, shifting fingers—showing where the ball was and where it was going.

The games went quickly, but there was only one ball and many wanted to play. Wil gave up any immediate plans to get on the court. He wandered around the edge of the crowd, watching the shadows flick back and forth, highlighting a face for an instant, then plunging it into darkness. It was fun to see adults as fascinated as kids.

One face stopped him short: Kim Tioulang stood at the outskirts of the crowd, less than five meters from Brierson. He was alone. He might be a boss, but apparently he didn't need

a herd of "aides" like Steve Fraley. The man was short, his face
in shadow except when a high shot washed him in a quick
down-and-up of light. His concentration was intense, but his
expressionless gaze contained no hint of pleasure.

The man was strikingly frail. He was something that did not
exist in Wil's time—except by suicidal choice or metabolic
accident. Kim Tioulang's body was *old*; it was in the final
stages of the degeneration which, before the mid-twenty-first,
had limited life spans to less than a century.

There were so many different ways to think of time now.
Kim had lived less than eighty years. He was young by comparison with the "teenagers" from the twenty-second. He had
nothing on Yelén's three hundred years of realtime experience
or the mind-destroying stretch of Della's nine thousand. Yet,
in some ways, Tioulang was a more extreme case than either
Korolev or Lu.

Brierson had read the GreenInc summary on the man. Kim
Tioulang was born in 1967. That was two years before Man
began the conquest of space, thirty years before the war and
the plagues, at least fifty years before Della Lu was born. In a
perverse sense, he *was* the oldest living human.

Tioulang had been born in Kampuchea, in the middle of one
of the regional wars that pocked the late twentieth. Though
limited in space and time, some of those wars were as horrible
as what followed the 1997 collapse. Tioulang's childhood
was drenched in death—and unlike the twenty-first-century
plagues, where the murderers were faceless ambiguities, death
in Kampuchea came person to person via bullets and hackings
and deliberate starvation. GreenInc said the rest of Tioulang's
family disappeared in the maelstrom . . . and little Kim ended
up in the USA. He was a bright kid; by 1997 he was finishing
a doctorate in physics. And working for the organization that
overthrew the governments and became the Peace Authority.

From there, GreenInc had little but Peacer news stories and
historical inference to document Tioulang's life. No one knew
if Tioulang had anything to do with starting the plagues. (For
that matter, there was no absolute proof the Peace had started
them.) By 2010, the man was Director for Asia. He'd kept his

third of the planet in line. He had a better reputation than the other Directors; he was no Christian Gerrault, "Butcher of Eurafrica." Except during the Mongolian insurrection, he managed to avoid large-scale bloodshed. He remained in power right up to the fall of the Peace in 2048—and that fall was for Tioulang less than four months past.

And so, even though Kim Tioulang predated the rest of living humanity by scant decades, his background put him in a class by himself. He was the only one who had grown up in a world where humans routinely killed other humans. He was the only one who had ruled, and killed to stay in power. Next to him, Steve Fraley was a high-school class president.

An arcing shot lifted the glowball above the crowd, putting Tioulang's face back in the light—and Wil saw that the Peacer was staring at him. The other smiled faintly, then stepped back from the crowd to stand beside Brierson. Up close, Wil saw that his face was mottled, pocked. Could old age alone do that?

"You're Brierson, the one who works for Korolev?" His voice was just loud enough to be heard over the laughs and shouting. Light danced back and forth around them.

Wil bridled, then decided he wasn't being accused of betraying the low-techs. "I'm investigating Marta Korolev's murder."

"Hmm." Tioulang folded his arms and looked away from Wil. "I've done some interesting reading the last few weeks, Mr. Brierson." He chuckled. "For me, it's like future history to see where the next hundred and fifty years took the world. . . . You know, those years turned out as well as ever I could hope. I always thought that without the Peace, humankind would exterminate itself. . . . And maybe it did eventually, but you went for more than a century without our help. I think the immortality thing must have something to do with it. Does it really work? You look around twenty years old—"

Brierson nodded. "But I'm fifty."

Tioulang scuffed at the lawn with his heel. His voice was almost wistful. "Yes. And apparently I can have it now, too. The long view—I can already see how it softens things, and how that's probably for the best.

"I've also read your histories of the Peace. You people make

133

us out as monsters. The hell of it is, you have some of it right."
He looked up at Wil, and his voice sharpened. "I meant what
I said this afternoon. The human race is in a bind here; we of
the Peace would make the best leaders. But I also meant it
when I said we're willing to go with democracy; I see now it
could really work.

"You are very important to us, Brierson. We know you have
Korolev's ear—don't interrupt, please! We can talk to her
whenever we wish, but we think she respects your opinions. If
you believe what I am telling you, there is some chance she may
too."

"Okay," said Wil. "But what *is* the message? You oppose
Yelén's policies, want to run things under some government
system with majority rule. What if your people don't win out?
The NMs have a lot more in common with the ungovs and the
high-techs than you. If we fall back to a government situation,
they are more likely to be the leaders than you. Would you
accept that?" *Or grab for power like you did at the end of the
twentieth?*

Tioulang looked around, almost as though checking for
eavesdroppers. "I expect we'll win, Brierson. The problems we
face here are problems the Peace is especially well equipped to
handle. Even if we don't win, we'll still be needed. I've talked
to Steven Fraley. He may seem rough and tough to you . . .
but not to me. He's a little bit of a fool, and likes to boss people
around, but left to ourselves, we could get along."

"Left to yourselves?"

"That's the other thing I want to talk to you about." He shot
a furtive glance past Wil. "There are forces at work Korolev
should know about. Not everyone wants a peaceful solution. If
a high-tech backs one faction, we—" The swinging light
splashed over them. Tioulang's expression suddenly froze into
something that might might have been hatred . . . or fear. "I
can't talk more now. I can't talk." He turned and walked stiffly
away.

Wil glanced in the opposite direction. There was no one
special in the crowd there. What had spooked the Peacer? Wil
drifted around the court, watching the game and the crowd.

Several minutes passed. The game ended. There were the usual cheerful arguments about who should be on the new teams. He heard Tunç Blumenthal say something about "trying something new" with the glowball. The random chatter lessened as Tunç talked to the players and they pulled down the volleyball net. When the new game started, Wil saw that Blumenthal had indeed tried something new.

Tunç stood at the serving line and punched the glowball across the court, over the heads of the other team. As it passed across the far court out-of-bounds, there was a flash of green light and the ball *bounced* as if from some unseen surface. It sailed up and back—and bounced downwards off an invisible ceiling. As it hit the ground, the glow turned to out-of-play yellow. Tunc served again, this time to the side. The ball bounced as from a side wall, then against the invisible far-court wall, then off the other side. The green flashes were accompanied by the sounds of solid rebounds. The crowd was silent except for scattered gasps of surprise. Were the teams trapped in there? The idea occurred to several of the players simultaneously. They ran to the invisible walls, reached out to touch them. One fellow lost his balance and fell off the court. "There's nothing there!"

Blumenthal gave some simple rules and they volleyed. At first it was chaos, but after a few minutes they were really playing the new game. It was fast, a strange cross between volleyball and closed-court handball. Wil couldn't imagine how this trick was managed, but it was spectacular. Before, the ball had moved in clean parabolas, broken only by the players' strokes. Now it careened off unseen surfaces, the shadows reversing field instantly.

"Ah, Brierson! What are you doing out here, man? You should be playing. I watched you earlier today. You're good."

Wil turned to the voice. It was Philippe Genet and two Peacer women friends. The women wore open jackets and bikini bottoms. Genet wore only shorts. The high-tech walked between the women, his hands inside their jackets, at their waists.

Wil laughed. "I'd need lots of practice to be good with

135

something that wild. I imagine you could do pretty well, though."

The other shrugged and drew the women closer. Genet was Brierson's height but perhaps fifteen kilos less massive, verging on gauntness. He was a black, though several shades paler than Wil. "Do you have any idea where that glowball came from, Brierson?"

"No. One of the high-techs."

"That's certain. I don't know if you realize what a clever gadget that is. Oh, I'll bet you twenty-first-century types had something like it: put a HI light and a navigation processor in a ball and you could play a simple game of night volley. But look at that thing, Brierson." He nodded at the glowball, caroming back and forth off invisible barriers. "It has its own agrav unit. Together with the navigation processor, it's simulating the existence of reflecting walls. I was in the game earlier. That ball's a Collegiate Mark 3, a whole athletic department. If one team is short a player, just tell the ball—and in addition to boundary walls, it'll simulate the extra player. You can even play solitaire with it, specify whatever skill level and strategy you want for the other players."

Interesting. Wil found his attention divided between the description and the high-tech himself. This was the first time he'd talked to Genet. From a distance, the man had seemed sullen and closemouthed, quite in keeping with the business profile GreenInc had on him. Now he was talkative, almost jovial . . . and even less likable. The man had the arrogance of someone who was both very foolish and very rich. As he talked, Genet's hands roamed across the women's torsos. In the shifting of light and shadow, it was like watching a stop-action striptease. The performance was both repellent and strange. In Brierson's time, many people were easygoing about sex, whether for pleasure or pay. This was different; Genet treated the two like . . . property. They were fine furniture, to be fondled while he talked to Brierson. And they made no objection. These two were a far cry from the group with Gail Parker.

Genet glanced sidelong at Wil and smiled slowly. "Yes, Brierson, the glowball is high-tech. Collegiate didn't market the M.3 till . . ." He paused, consulting some database. "Till 2195. So it's strange, don't you think, that the New Mexicans are the people who brought it to the party?"

"Obviously some high-tech gave it to them earlier." Wil spoke a bit sharply, distracted by the other's hands.

"Obviously. But consider the implications, Brierson. The NMs are one of the two largest groups here. They are absolutely necessary to the success of the Korolev plan. From history—my history, your personal experience—we know they're used to running things. The only thing that keeps them from bulldozing the rest of you low-techs is their technical incompetence. . . . Now, just suppose some high-tech wanted to take over from Korolev. The easiest way to destroy her plan might be to back the NMs and feed them some autons and agravs and advanced bobblers. Korolev and the rest of us high-techs could not afford to put the NMs down; we need them if we are to reestablish civilization. We might just have to capitulate to whoever was behind the scheme."

Tioulang was trying to tell me something similar. The evening cool was suddenly chill. Strange that a thing as innocent as the glowball should be the first evidence since Marta's murder that someone was trying to take over. What did this do to his suspect list? Tammy Robinson might use such a bribe to recruit. Or maybe Chanson was right, and the force that ended civilization in the twenty-third was still at work. Or maybe the enemy simply desired to *own,* and was willing to risk the destruction of them all to achieve that end. He looked at Genet. Earlier in the day, Brierson had been upset to think they might slide back to governments and majority rule. Now he remembered that more evil and primitive institutions were possible. Genet oozed confidence, megalomania. Wil was suddenly sure the other was capable of planting such a clue, pointing it out, and then enjoying Wil's consternation and suspicion.

Some of that suspicion must have shown on his face. Genet's smile broadened. His hand brushed aside one girl's jacket, flaunting his "property." Wil relaxed fractionally; over the years, he had dealt with some pretty unpleasant people. Maybe this high-tech was an enemy and maybe not, but he wasn't going to get under Wil's skin.

"You know I'm working for Yelén on Marta's murder, Mr. Genet. What you tell me, I'll pass on to her. What do you suggest we do?"

Genet chuckled. "You'll 'pass it on,' will you? My dear Brierson, I don't doubt that every word we say is going directly to her. . . . But you're right. It's easier to pretend. And you low-techs are a good deal more congenial. Less back talk, anyway.

"As for what we should do: nothing overt just yet. We can't tell whether the glowball was a slip, or a subtle announcement of victory. I suggest we put the NMs under intense surveillance. If this was a slip, then it will be easy to prevent a takeover. Personally, I don't think the NMs have received much help yet; we'd see other evidence if they had." He watched the game for a few moments, then turned back to Wil. "You especially should be pleased by this turn of events, Brierson."

"I suppose so." Wil resented admitting anything to Genet. "If this is connected to Marta's murder, it may break the case."

"That's not what I meant. You were shanghaied, right?"

Wil gave a brief nod.

"Ever wonder what became of the fellow who bushwhacked you?" He paused, but Brierson couldn't even nod to that. "I'm sure dear Yelén would like this kept from you, but I think you deserve to know. They caught him; I've got records of the trial. I don't know how the skunk ever thought he could evade conviction. The court handed down the usual sentence: He was bobbled, timed to come out about a month after you. Personally, I think he deserved whatever you might do to him. But Marta and Yelén didn't work that way. They rescued everyone they could. They figured every warm body increases the colony's chances.

"Marta and Yelén made him promise to stay out of your way. Then they gave him a shallow disguise and turned him over to the NMs. They figured he could fade into the crowd there." Genet laughed. "So you see why I say this is an enjoyable twist of fate for you, Brierson. Putting pressure on the NMs gives you a chance to step on the insect who put you here." He saw the blank expression on Wil's face. "You think I'm putting you on? You can check it out easily enough. The NM Director, President—whatever they call him—has taken a real shine to your friend. The twerp is on Fraley's staff now. I saw them a few minutes ago, on the other side of this game."

Genet's gaunt face parted in a final smile. He gathered his "property" close and walked into the darkness. "Check it out, Brierson. You'll get your jollies yet."

Wil stood quietly for several minutes after the other left. He was looking at the game, but his eyes did not track the glowball anymore. Finally, he turned and walked along the outskirts of the crowd. The way was lit whenever the ball rose above the fans. That light flickered white and green and yellow, depending on whether the ball was live, striking a "wall," or out of play. Wil didn't notice the colors anymore.

Steve Fraley and his friends were sitting on the far side of the court. Somehow they had persuaded the other spectators to stand clear of the sidelines, so they had a good view even sitting down. Wil stayed in the crowd. From here he could observe with little chance that Fraley would notice.

There were fifteen in the group. Most looked like staff people, though Wil recognized a few ungovs. Fraley sat near the middle, with a couple of his top aides. They spent more time talking to the ungovs than watching the game. For a government type, ol' Steve had plenty of experience with the soft sell. Twice back in the 2090s he'd been elected President of the Republic.

It was an impressive achievement—and an empty one: By the end of the twenty-first, the New Mexico government was like a beach house when the dunes shift. War and territorial expansion were not feasible—the failure of the Kansas Incursion had shown that. And the Republic couldn't compete economically with the ungoverned lands. The grass was truly greener on the other side of the fence, and with unrestricted emigration, the situation only got worse. As a matter of frank competition, the government repealed regulation after regulation. Unlike Aztlán, the Republic never formally disgoverned. But in 2097, the NM Congress amended the constitution—over Fraley's veto—to renounce all mandatory taxing authority. Steve Fraley objected that what was left was not a government. ¹He was obviously correct, but it didn't do him much good. What *was* left was a viable business. The Republic's police and court system didn't last; it simply wasn't competitive with existing companies. But the NM Congress did. Tourists from all over the world visited Albuquerque to pay "taxes," to vote, to see a real government in action. The ghost of the Republic lived for many years, a source of pride and profit to its citizens.

It was not enough for Steve Fraley. He used what was left of presidential authority to assemble the remnants of the NM military machine. With a hundred fellow right-thinkers he bobbled forward five hundred years—to a future where, it was hoped, sanity had returned.

Wil grimaced to himself. So, like all the cranks and crooks and victims who overshot the Singularity, Fraley and his friends ended up on the shore of a lake that had once been open ocean—fifty million years after Man.

Wil's eyes slid from Fraley to the aides beside him. Like many self-important types, these two kept their apparent age in the middle forties. Sleek and gray, they were the NM ideal of leadership. Wil remembered both from twenty-first-century news stories. Neither could be the . . . creature . . . he sought. He pushed through the crowd, closer to the open space around the NMs.

Several of those listening to Fraley's sales pitch were strangers. Wil stared at them, applying all the tests he had invented during the day.

Scarcely conscious of the movement, Wil edged out of the crowd. Now he could see all the NMs in Fraley's group. A few were paying attention to the discussions around Fraley; the rest were watching the game. Wil studied each one, matching what he saw with the Kid, the Exec, and the Janitor. There were several vague resemblances, but nothing certain. . . . He stopped, eyes caught on a middle-aged Asian. The fellow didn't resemble any of the three, yet there was something strange about him. He was as old as Fraley's top advisers, yet the game had all his attention. And this guy didn't have the others' air of assurance. He was balding, faintly pudgy. Wil stared at him, trying to imagine the man with a head of hair, and without eyefolds or facial flab.

Make those changes, and take thirty years off his apparent age . . . and you'd have . . . the Kid. The nephew of the guy who was robbed. This was the *thing* that had taken Virginia from him, that had taken Billy and Anne. This was the thing that had destroyed Brierson's whole world . . . and done it just to avoid a couple of years of reparation surcharge.

And what can I do if I find the bastard? Something cold and awful took over then, and thought ceased.

Wil found himself in the open area between the volleyball court and the NMs. He must have shouted; everyone was looking at him. Fraley stared openmouthed. For an instant, he looked afraid. Then he saw where Wil was headed, and he laughed.

There was no humor in the Kid's response. His head snapped up, instant recognition on his face. He sprang to his feet, his hands held awkwardly before him—whether an inept defense or a plea for mercy was not clear. It didn't matter. Wil's deliberate walk had become a lumbering run. Someone with his own voice was screaming. The NMs in his way scattered. Wil was barely conscious of body-blocking one who was insufficiently agile; the fellow simply bounced off him.

The Kid's face held sheer terror. He backpedaled frantically, tripped; this was one bind he would not escape.

THIRTEEN

Something flashed in the air above Wil, and his legs went numb. He went down, just short of where the Kid had been standing. Even as the breath smashed out of him, he was trying to get back to his knees. It was no good. He snorted blood, and rational thought resumed. Someone had stungunned him.

Around him there was shouting and people were still backing away, unsure if his berserker charge might continue. The game had broken off; the glowball's light was steady and unmoving. Wil touched his nose; bloodied but unbroken.

When he twisted back onto his elbows, the babble quieted. Steve Fraley walked toward him, a wide grin on his face. "My, my, Inspector. Getting a little carried away, aren't you? I thought you were cooler than that. You, of all people, should know that we can't support the old grudges." As he got closer, Wil had to strain to look up at his face. Wil gave up and lowered his head. Beyond the NM President, at the limit of the glowball's illumination, he saw the Kid puking on the grass.

Fraley stepped close to the fallen Brierson, his sport shoes filling most of the near view. Wil wondered what it would be like to get one of those shoes in the face—and somehow he was sure that Steve was wondering the same thing.

"President Fraley." Yelén's voice spoke from somewhere above. "I certainly agree with you about grudges."

"Um, yes." Fraley retreated a couple of steps. When he spoke, it sounded as if he were looking upwards. "Thanks for stunning him, Ms. Korolev. Perhaps it's for the best that this happened. I think it's time you realized who you can trust to behave responsibly—and who you cannot."

Yelén did not reply. Several seconds passed. There was quiet conversation around him. He heard footsteps approach, then Tunç Blumenthal's voice. "We just want to move him away from the crowd, Yelén, give him a chance to get his legs back. Okay?"

"Okay."

Blumenthal helped Wil roll onto his back, then picked him up under the shoulders. Looking around, Wil saw that Rohan Dasgupta had grabbed his legs. But all Wil could feel was Blumenthal's hands; his legs were still dead meat. The two lugged him away from the light and the crowd. It was a struggle for the slender Rohan. Every few steps, Wil's rear dragged on the ground, a noise without sensation.

Finally, it was dark all around. They set him down, his back against a large boulder. The courts and bonfires were pools of light clustered below them. Blumenthal sat on his heels beside Wil. "Soon as you feel a tingling in those legs, I suggest you try walking, Wil Brierson. You'll have less an ache that way."

Wil nodded. It was the usual advice to stungun victims, at least when the heart wasn't involved.

"My God, Wil, what happened?" Curiosity struggled with embarrassment in Rohan's voice.

Brierson took a deep breath; the embers of his rage still glowed. "You've never seen me blow my stack, is that it, Rohan?" The world was so empty. Everybody he'd cared about was gone . . . and in their place was an anger he had never known. Wil shook his head. He'd never realized what an uncomfortable thing continuing anger could be.

They sat in silence a minute more. Pins-and-needles prickling started up Wil's feet. He'd never known a stun to wear off so quickly; another high-tech improvement, no doubt. He rolled onto his knees. "Let's see if I can walk." He climbed to his feet, using Dasgupta and Blumenthal as crutches.

"There's a path over here," said Blumenthal. "Just keep walking and it'll get easier."

They tottered off. The path turned downwards, leaving the picnic grounds behind the crest of a hill. The shouts and laughter faded, and soon the loudest sounds were the insects. There was a sweetish smell—flowers?—that he'd never noticed around Town Korolev. The air was cool, downright cold on those parts of his legs that had regained sensation.

At first, Wil had to put all his weight on Blumenthal and Dasgupta. His legs seemed scarcely more than stumps, his knees now locking, now bending loose with no effective coordination. After fifty meters his feet could feel the pebbles in the path and he was doing at least part of the navigating.

The night was clear and moonless. Somehow the stars alone were enough to see by—or maybe it was the Milky Way? Wil looked into the sky ahead of them. The pale light was strangely bright. It climbed out of the east, a broad band that narrowed and faded halfway up the sky. *East?* Could the megayears change even that? Wil almost stumbled, felt the others' grasp tighten. He looked higher, saw the real Milky Way slicing down from another direction.

Blumenthal chuckled. "There wasn't much going on at the Lagrange zones in your time, was there?"

"There were habitats at L4 and L5. They were easy to see, like bright stars," nothing like this stardust haze.

"Put enough stuff in Luna's orbit and you'll see more than just a few new stars. In my time, millions lived there. All Earth's heavy industry was there. Things were getting crowded. There's only so much thermal and chemical pollution you can dump before your factories begin to poison themselves."

Now Wil remembered things Marta and Yelén had said. "But it's mainly bobbles there now."

"Yes. This light isn't caused by factories and civilization. Third-body perturbations have long since flushed the original

144

artifacts. Now it's a handy place for short-term storage, or to park observing equipment."

Wil stared at the pale glow. He wondered how many thousands of bobbles it took to make such a light. He knew Yelén still had much of her equipment off Earth. How many millions of tonnes were in "short-term storage" out there? For that matter, how many travelers were still in stasis, ignoring all the messages the Korolevs had laid down across the megayears? The light was ghostly in more ways than one.

They went another couple of hundred meters eastwards. Gradually Wil's coordination returned, till he was walking without help and only an occasional wobble. His eyes were fully dark-adapted now. Light-colored flowers floated in the bushes to the side of the path, and when they nodded close the sweetish smell came stronger. He wondered if the path was natural or a piece of Korolev landscaping. He risked his balance by looking straight up. Sure enough, there was something dark against the stars. Yelén's auton—and probably Della's, too— was still with them.

The path meandered southwards, to the naked rock that edged the cliffs. From below came a faint sighing, the occasional slap of water against rock. It could have been Lake Michigan on a quiet night. Now for some mosquitoes to make him feel truly at home.

Blumenthal broke the long silence. "You were one of my childhood heroes, Wil Brierson." There was a smile in his voice.

"What?"

"Yes. You and Sherlock Holmes. I read every novel your son wrote."

Billy wrote . . . about me? GreenInc had said Billy's second career was as a novelist, but Wil hadn't had time to look at his writing.

"The adventures were fiction, even though you were the hero. He wrote 'em under the assumption that Derek Lindemann hadn't bumped you off. There were almost thirty novels; you had adventures all through the twenty-second."

"Derek Lindemann?" Dasgupta said. "Who . . . Oh, I *see.*"

Wil nodded. "Yeah, Rohan." Wimpy Derek Lindemann . . . the Kid. "The guy I tried to kill just now." But for a moment his anger seemed irrelevant. Wil smiled sadly in the darkness. To think that Billy had created a synthetic life for the one that had been ended. By God, he was going to read those novels!

He glanced at the high-tech. "Glad you enjoyed my adventures, Tunç. I assume you grew out of it. From what I hear, you were in construction."

"True and true. But had I wished to be a policeman, it would've been hard. By the late twenty-second, most habitats had fewer than one cop per million population. It was even worse in rural areas. A deplorable scarcity of crime, it was." Wil smiled. Blumenthal's accent was strange—almost singsong, a cross between Scottish and Amerasian. None of the other high-techs talked like this. In Wil's time, English dialect differences had been damping out; communication and travel were so fast in the Earth-Luna volume. Blumenthal had grown up in space, several days' travel time from the heartland.

"Besides, I wanted more to build things than to protect folks. At the beginning of the twenty-third, the world was changing faster than you can imagine. I'll wager there was more technical change in the first decade of the twenty-third than in all the centuries to the twenty-second. Have you noticed the differences among the advanced travelers? Monica Raines left civilization in 2195; no matter what she claims now, she bought the best equipment available. Juan Chanson left in 2200—with a much smaller investment. Yet Juan's gear is superior in every way. His autons have spent several thousand years in realtime, and are good for at least as much more. Monica has survived sixty years and has only one surviving auton. The difference was five years' progress in sport and camping equipment. The Korolevs left a year after Chanson. They bought an immense amount of equipment, yet for about the same investment as Chanson; a single year had depreciated the 2200 models that far. Juan, Yelén, Genet—they're aware of this. But I don't think any of them understand what nine more years of progress could bring. . . . You know I'm the last one out?"

Wil had read that in Yelén's summaries. The difference hadn't seemed terribly important. "You bobbled out in 2210?"

"True. Della Lu was latest before me, in 2202. We've never found anyone who lived closer to the Singularity."

Rohan said softly, "You should be the most powerful of all."

"Should be, perhaps. But the fact is, I'm not one of the willing travelers. I was more than happy to live when I was. I never had the least inclination to hop into the future, to start a new religion or break the stock market. . . . I'm sorry, Rohan Dasgupta, I—"

"It's okay. My brother and I were a little too greedy. We thought, 'What can go wrong? Our investments seem safe; after a century or two, they should make us very rich. And if they don't, well, the standard of living will be so high, even being poor we'll live better than the rich do now.'" Rohan sighed. "We bet on the progress you speak of. We didn't count on coming back to jungles and ruins and a world without people." They walked several paces in silence. Finally Rohan's curiosity got the better of him. "You were shanghaied, then, like Wil?"

"I . . . don't think so; since no one lived after me, it's impossible to know for sure. I was in heavy construction, and accidents happen. . . . How's the legs, Wil Brierson?"

"What?" The sudden change of topic took Wil by surprise. "Fine now." There were still pins and needles, but he had no trouble with coordination.

"Then let's start back, okay?"

They walked away from the cliffs, past the sweet blossoms. The campfires were invisible behind several ridgelines; they had come almost a thousand meters. They walked most of the way back with scarcely a word. Even Rohan was silent.

Wil's rage had cooled, leaving only ashes, sadness. He wondered what would happen the next time he saw Derek Lindemann. He remembered the abject terror on Lindemann's face. The disguise had been a good one. If Phil Genet hadn't

pointed Wil right at the Kid, it might have been weeks before
he nailed him. Lindemann had been seventeen, a gawky Anglo;
now he looked fifty, a somewhat pudgy Asian. Clearly there
had been cosmetic surgery. As for his age ... well, when Yelén
and Marta decided to do something, they could be brutally
direct. Somewhere in the millions of years that Wil and the
others spent bobbled, Derek Lindemann had lived thirty years
of realtime without medical support. Perhaps the Korolevs had
been out of stasis then, perhaps not; the autons that attended
their bobble farm on the Canadian Shield would have been
competent to provide for him. Thirty years the Kid lived essen-
tially alone. Thirty years inward turning. The Lindemann that
Wil knew had been a wimp. No doubt his embezzling was
petty revenge against his relatives in the company. No doubt
he bobbled Brierson out of naive panic. And for thirty years the
Kid had lived with the fear that one day W. W. Brierson would
recognize him.

"Thanks for ... talking to me. I-I'm not usually like this."
That was true, and perhaps the most unnerving part of the
whole day. In thirty years of police work, he'd never blown up.
Perhaps that wasn't surprising; knocking customers around was
a quick way to get fired. But in Wil's case, being cool had come
easy. He was truly the low-pressure type he seemed. How often
he had been the calm one who talked others down from the
high ledges of panic and rage. He'd never been the kind who
went from anger to anger. In the last weeks, all that had
changed, yet ... "You've both lost as much as I, haven't you?"
He thought back to all the people he had talked to this afternoon, and shame replaced his embarrassment. Maybe ol' W.
W. Brierson had always been unflappable because he never had
any real problems. When the crunch came, he was the weakest
of all.

"It's okay," Blumenthal said. "There have been fights before. Some people are hurting more than others. And for each
of us, some days are worse than others."

"Besides, you're special, Wil," said Rohan.

"Huh?"

"The rest of us have our hands full rebuilding civilization.

Korolev is giving us enormous amounts of equipment. It needs lots of supervision; there's not enough automatic stuff to go around. We're working as hard as anyone in the twentieth century. I think most of the high-techs are, too. I know Tunç is.

"But you, Wil, what is your job? You work just as hard as any of us—but doing what? Trying to figure out who killed Marta. I'll bet that's fun. You have to spend all your time, off by yourself, thinking about things that have been lost. Even the laziest low-tech isn't in that bind. If someone wanted to drive you crazy, they couldn't have invented a better job for you."

Wil found himself smiling. He remembered the times Rohan had tried to get him to these picnics. "Your prescription?" he asked lightly.

"Well . . ." Rohan was suddenly diffident. "You could get off the case. But I hope you won't. We all want to know what happened to Marta. I liked her the most of all the high-techs. And her murder might be part of something that could kill the rest of us. . . . I think the important thing is that you realize what the problem is. You're not falling apart. You're just under more pressure than most of us.

"Also, there's no point in working on it all the time, is there? I'll bet you spend hours staring into blind alleys. Spend more time with the rest of humanity. Ha! You might even find some clues here!"

Wil thought back over the last two hours. On Rohan's last point there was no possible disagreement.

FOURTEEN

rom North Shore to Town Korolev was about a thousand kilometers, most of it over the Inland Sea. Yelén didn't stint with the shuttle service between the two points. The two halves of the settlement were physically separate, but she was determined to make them close in every other way. When Wil left the picnic, there were three fliers waiting for southbound passengers. He ended up in one that was empty except for the Dasgupta brothers.

The agrav rose with the familiar silent acceleration that never became intense—and never ceased. The trip would take about fifteen minutes. Below them, the picnic fires dwindled, seemed to tilt sideways. The loudest sound was a distant scream of wind. It grew, then dwindled to nothing. The interior lighting turned the night beyond the windows into undetailed darkness. Except for the constant acceleration, they might have been sitting in an ordinary office waiting room.

They were going home ahead of most people. Wil was surprised to see Dilip leaving early. He remembered what the guy had been up to that afternoon. "What became of Gail Parker, Dilip? I thought . . ." Wil's voice trailed off as he remembered the unhappy caucus he'd stumbled onto.

The older Dasgupta shrugged, his normally rakish air

deflated. "She . . . she didn't want to play. She was polite enough, but you know how things are. Every week the girls are a bit harder to get along with. I guess we've all got some hard decisions to make."

Wil changed the subject. "Either of you know who brought the glowball?"

Rohan grinned. No doubt he was pleased by what he thought an innocuous topic. "Wasn't that something? I've seen glowballs before, but nothing like that. Didn't Tunç Blumenthal bring it?"

Dilip shook his head. "I was there from the beginning. It was Fraley's people. I saw them get off the shuttle with it. Tunç didn't come along till they had played a couple of games."

Just as Phil Genet claimed.

Still under acceleration, the shuttle did a slow turn, the only evidence being a faint queasiness in the passengers' guts. Now they were flying tailfirst into the darkness. They were halfway home.

Wil settled back in his seat, let his mind wander back over the day. Detective work had been easier in civilization. There, most things were what they seemed. You had your employers, their clients, collateral services. In most cases, these were people you had worked with for years; you knew who you could trust. Here, it was paranoid heaven. Except for Lindemann, he knew no one from before. Virtually all the high-techs were twisted creatures. Chanson, Korolev, Raines, Lu—they had all lived longer than he, some for thousands of years. They were all screwier than the types he was used to dealing with. And Genet. Genet was not so strange; Wil had known a few like him. There were lots of mysteries about Genet's life in civilization, but one thing was clear as crystal after tonight: Phil Genet was a people-owner, barely under control. Whether or not he had killed anyone, murder was in his moral range.

On the other hand, Blumenthal seemed to be a genuinely nice guy. He was an involuntary traveler like Wil, but without the Lindemann burden.

Brierson suppressed a smile. In the standard mystery plot, such all-around niceness would be a sure sign of guilt. In the real world, things rarely worked that way. . . . *Damn.* In *this* real world, almost anything could be true. Okay, what grounds could there be for suspecting Blumenthal? Motive? Certainly none was visible. In fact, very little was known about Blumenthal. The 2201 GreenInc listed him as ten years old, a child employee in a family-owned mining company. There was scarcely more information about the company. It was small, operating mainly in the comet cloud. Wil had less hard information on Blumenthal than on any other high-tech, Genet excepted. As the last human to leave civilization, there had been no one to write Tunç's biography. It was only Tunç's word that he'd been bobbled in 2210. It could have been later, perhaps from the heart of the Singularity. He claimed an industrial accident had blown him into the sun. Come to think of it, what corroboration could there be for that either? And if it wasn't an accident, then most likely he was the loser in a battle of nukes and bobbles, where the victors wanted the vanquished permanently dead.

Wil suddenly wondered where Tunç stood on Chanson's list of potential aliens.

Scattered streetlamps shone friendly through the trees, and then the flier was on the ground. Wil and the Dasguptas piled out, feeling light-headed in the sudden return to one gravity.

They had landed on the street that ran past their homes. Wil said good night to Rohan and Dilip and walked slowly up the street toward his place. He couldn't remember when so many things, both physical and mental, had been jammed into one afternoon. The residual effects of the stun added overwhelming fatigue to it all. He glanced upwards but saw only leaves, backlit by a streetlamp. No doubt the autons were still up there, hidden behind the trees.

Such an innocuous thing, the glowball. And the explanation might be innocuous, too: Maybe Yelén had simply given it to the NMs, or maybe they'd swiped it themselves. Surely it was a trivial item in a high-tech's inventory. The fact that she hadn't demanded a late-night session was a good sign. After he got a good sleep, he might be able to laugh at Genet.

152

Wil walked along the edge of his lot. He reached the gate
. . . and stopped cold. Crude letters were spraygunned across
the gate and surrounding wall. They spelled the words LO
TECH DONT MEAN NO TECH. The message had scarcely
registered on his mind when white light drenched the scene.
Yelén's auton had dropped to man-height beside Wil. Its spot-
light fanned across the gateway.

Brierson stepped close to the wall. The paint was still wet.
It glittered in the light. He stared numbly at the lettering.

Polka-dot paint, green on purple. The bright green disks
were perfectly formed, even where the paint had dribbled
downwards. It was the sort of thing you see often enough on
data sets—and never in the real world.

Yelén's voice came from the auton. "Take a good look,
Brierson. Then come inside; we've got to talk."

FIFTEEN

The lights came on even before he reached the house. Wil walked into the living room and collapsed in his favorite chair. Two conference holos were lit: Yelén was on one, Della the other. Neither looked happy. Korolev spoke first. "I want Tammy Robinson out of our time, Inspector."

Wil started to shrug, *Why ask me?* He glanced at Della Lu, remembered that he was damn close to being arbiter in this dispute. "Why?"

"It should be obvious now. The deal was that we would let her stay in realtime as long as she didn't interfere. Well, it's sure as hell clear someone is backing the NMs—and she's the best suspect."

"But suspect only," said Lu. The spacer's face and costume were a strange contrast. She wore frilly pants and halter, the sort of outfit Wil would have expected at the picnic. Yet he hadn't seen her there. Had she simply *peeped,* too shy or aloof to show up? Whatever personality matched the outfit, it scarcely fit her expression now. It was cold, determined. "I gave her my word that—"

Yelén slapped the table in front of her. "Promises be damned! The survival of the settlement comes first, Lu. You of all people should know that. If you won't bobble Robinson, then stand aside and let—"

154

Della smiled, and suddenly she seemed a lot deadlier, a lot more determined than Korolev—with all her temper—ever had. "I will not stand aside, Yelén."

"Um." Yelén sat back, perhaps remembering that Della was one of the most heavily armed of the travelers, perhaps thinking of the centuries of combat experience Lu had had with her weapons. She glanced at Brierson. "Will you talk some sense to her? We've got a life-and-death situation here."

"Maybe. But Tammy is only one suspect—and the one who is most carefully watched. If she was up to something, surely you'd have direct evidence?"

"Not necessarily. I figure I'll need a medium recon capability for at least another century of realtime. I can't afford a 'no-sparrow-shall-fall' network; I'd run out of consumables in a few months. I have kept a close watch on Robinson, but if her family stashed autons before they left, it wouldn't take much for her to communicate with them. All she has to do is give away some trinkets, make these low-techs a bit more dissatisfied. I'll bet she has high-performance bobblers hidden near the Inland Sea. If she can lead her little friends there, we'll be looking at a lot of long-term bobbles—and an end to the plan."

If the Robinsons had prepared their departure that carefully, they were probably responsible for Marta's murder, too. "How 'bout a compromise? Take her out of circulation for a few months."

"I promised her, Wil."

"I know. But this would be voluntary. Explain the situation to her. If she's innocent, she'll be as upset by all this as we are. A three-month absence won't hurt her announced goals, and will very likely prove her innocent. If it does, then she could have a lot more freedom afterwards."

"What if she doesn't agree?"

"I really think she will, Della." *If not, then we'll see if my integrity can stand up to Yelén as well as yours does.*

Yelén said, "I would buy a three-month bobbling—though we may go through this same argument again at the end of it."

"Okay. I'll talk to Tammy." Della looked down at her frilly outfit, and a strange expression crossed her face. Embarrassment? "I'll get back to you." Her image vanished.

Wil looked at the remaining holo. Yelén was in her library. Sunlight streamed through its fake windows. Night and day must have little meaning to Yelén; that made Wil feel even more tired.

Korolev diddled with something on her desk, then looked back at Wil. "Thanks for the compromise. I was on the verge of doing something . . . rash."

"You're welcome." He closed his eyes a moment, almost succumbing to stun-induced sleepiness.

"Yes. Now we know our worst fears are true, Inspector. Agrav glowballs. Polka-dot paint. These are completely trivial things compared to what we have already given away. *But they are not on the gift inventory.* It's just like Phil says. Marta's murderer is not done with us. Someone or some*thing* is out there, taking over the low-techs."

"You don't sound so sure the Robinsons are behind it."

". . . No, that was partly wishful thinking. They have the clearest motive. Tammy would be the easiest to handle. . . . No. It could be almost any of the high-techs."

Brierson was too tired to keep his mouth shut. "Do we even know who those are?"

"What do you mean?"

"What if the murderer is masquerading as a low-tech? Maybe there's a surviving graverobber."

"That's absurd." But her eyes went wide, and for nearly fifteen seconds she was silent. "Yes, that's absurd," she repeated, with a trace less certainty. "I've got good records on all the rescues; we made most of them. We never saw any unusual equipment. Now, a masquerader might have his high-tech gear in separate storage, but we'd know if he moved much of it. . . . I don't know if you can understand, Brierson: We've had total control of their stasis from the beginning. An advanced traveler couldn't tolerate such domination."

"Okay." But he wondered if Lu's reaction would be the same.

"Good. Now I want to get your impression of what you saw today. I watched it all myself, but—"

Wil held up a hand. "How about waiting till tomorrow, Yelén? I'll have things sorted out better."

"No." The queen on the mountain wasn't angry, but she was going to have things her way. "There are things I need to know right now. For instance, what do you think spooked Kim Tioulang?"

"I have no idea. Could you see who he was looking at when he panicked?"

"Into the crowd. I didn't have enough cameras to be more definite. My guess is he had lookouts posted, and one of them signaled that Mr. Bad was in the area."

Mr. Bad. Phil Genet. The connection was instantaneous, needed no supporting logic. "Why make a mystery of it? Give Tioulang some protection and ask him what he has in mind."

"I did. Now he won't talk."

"Surely you have truth drugs. Why not just bring him in and—" Wil stopped, suddenly ashamed. He was talking like some government policeman: "The needs of the State come first." He could rationalize, of course. This was a world without police contracts and legal systems. Till they were established, simple survival might justify such tactics. The argument was slippery, and Wil wondered how far he would slide into savagery before he found solid footing.

Yelén smiled at his embarrassment—whether from sympathy or amusement he could not tell. "I decided not to. Not yet, anyway. The low-techs hate me enough already. And it's just possible Tioulang might suicide under questioning. Some of the twentieth-century governments put pretty good psychblocks in their people. If the Peacers inherited that filthy habit . . . Besides, he may not know any more than we do: Someone is backing the NM faction."

Wil remembered Tioulang's sudden panic; the man feared someone in particular. "You have him protected?"

"Yes. Almost as well as you, though he doesn't know it. For the time being I won't risk snatching him."

"You want to know my favorite candidate for villain? Phil Genet."

Yelén leaned forward. "Why?"

"He showed up just a few minutes after Tioulang took off. The man reeks of evil."

" 'Reeks of evil'? That's a professional opinion, is it?"

Wil rubbed his eyes. "Hey, you wanted to get my 'impressions,' remember?" But she was right; he wouldn't have put it that way if he'd been thinking straight.

"Phil's a sadist. I've known that for years. And I think he's worse now that we've got all the low-techs out of stasis—you little guys are such easy victims. I saw how he worked you over about Lindemann. I'm sorry about stunning you, Wil, but I can't tolerate any of the old grudges."

Wil nodded, faintly surprised. There was something near sympathy in her voice. In fact, he was grateful she had stunned him down. "Genet is capable of murder, Yelén."

"Lots of people are. What would you have done to Lindemann if . . . ? Look, neither of us likes Phil. That by itself is no big deal: I don't especially like you, and yet we get along. It's a matter of common interest. He helped Marta and me a lot. I doubt if we could have rescued the Peacers without his construction equipment. He's more than proved he wants the settlement to succeed."

"Maybe. But now that everyone has been brought together, perhaps your 'common interest' is dead. Maybe he wants to run the whole show."

"Hmm. He knows none of us have a chance if we start shooting. You think he's really crazy?"

"I don't know, Yelén. Look at the recording again. I had the feeling he wasn't taunting just me. He knew you'd be listening. I think he was laughing at you, too. Like he was on the verge of some triumph, something the sadist in him couldn't resist hinting at."

"So you think he set up the glowball—and was laughing at us all the time he was 'clueing you in.'" She pursed her lips. "It doesn't make sense . . . but I guess I'm paying for your intuition as much as anything else. I'll break a few more autons out of stasis, try to keep better tabs on Phil."

She sat back, and for a moment Wil thought she might be done with him. "Okay. I want to go over your other conversations." She noticed his expression. "Look, Inspector. I didn't ask you to socialize for your health. You're my low-tech point of view. We've got a murder here, incipient civil war, and everybody's general dislike for me. Just about everything we saw today has a connection with these things. I want your reactions while they're fresh."

So they reviewed the picnic. Literally. Yelén insisted on playing much of the video. She really did need help. Whether it was the centuries of living apart or her high-tech viewpoint Wil didn't know, but there were many things about the picnic she didn't understand. She had no sympathy for the women's dilemma. The first time they viewed the women's meeting, she made an obscure comment about "people having to pay for other people's mistakes." Was she referring to the Korolev failure to bring womb tanks?

Wil had her play the scene again, and he tried to explain. Finally she became a little angry. "Sure they've got to make sacrifices. But don't they realize it's the survival of the human race that's at stake?" She waved her hand. "I can't believe their nature is that different from earlier centuries. When the crunch comes, they'll do what they must." Would the queen on the mountain also do her female duty? Would she have six kids—or twelve? Brierson didn't voice the question. He could do without a Korolev explosion.

The sunlight streaming through Yelén's windows slowly shifted from morning to afternoon. The clock on Wil's data set showed it was way past the Witching Hour. If they kept going, he'd be seeing *real* sunlight, through his own windows. Finally the analysis wound back to Wil's conversation with Jason Mudge. Korolev stopped him. "You can take Mudge off your list of suspects, Inspector."

Wil had been about to say the same. He simulated curiosity. "Why?"

"The jerk fell off the cliffs last night, right on his pointy head."

Brierson lurched to wakefulness. "You mean, he's *dead?*"

"Dead beyond all possible resuscitation, Inspector. For all his God-mongering, he was no teetotaler. The autopsy showed blood alcohol at 0.22 percent. He left the party a little before you ran into Lindemann. Apparently he couldn't find anyone who'd even pretend to listen. The last I saw he was weaving along the westward bluffs. He got about fifteen hundred meters down the path, must have slipped where it comes near the cliff edge. One of my routine patrols found the body just after you got back here. He'd been in the water a couple of hours."

He rested his chin in his palms and slowly shook his head. *Yelén. Yelén. We've talked all through the night, and all that time your autons have been investigating and dissecting . . . and never a word that a man has died.* "I asked you to keep an eye on him."

"Well, *I* decided not to. He just wasn't that important." Korolev was silent a moment. Something of his attitude must have penetrated. "Look, Brierson, I'm not happy he died. Eventually he might have dropped that 'Third Coming' garbage and been of some use. But face it: The man was a parasite, and having him out of the way is one less suspect—however farfetched."

"Okay, Yelén. It's okay."

He should have guessed the effect of his assurance. Yelén leaned forward. "Are you really that paranoid, Brierson? Do you think Mudge was murdered, too?"

Maybe. What might Mudge know that could make it worth silencing him? He owned little high-tech equipment, yet he did know systems. Maybe he'd been the murderer's pet vandal, now deemed a liability. Wil tried to remember what they had talked about, but all that came was the little guy's intent expression. Of course, Yelén would be willing to play the conversation back. Again and again. It was the last thing he wanted now. "Let our paranoias go their separate ways, Yelén. If I think of anything, I'll let you know."

For whatever reason, Korolev didn't push him. Fifteen minutes later she was off the comm.

Wil straggled up to his bedroom, relieved and disappointed to be alone at last.

SIXTEEN

As usual there was a morning dream, but not the dream in blue this time, not the dream of parting, of gasping sobs that emptied his lungs. This was the dream of the many houses. He woke again and again, always to a house that should have been familiar, yet wasn't. There were yards and neighbors, never quite understood. Sometimes he was married. Mostly he was alone; Virginia had just left or was at some other house. Sometimes he saw them—Virginia, Anne, Billy—and that was worse. Their conversations were short, about packing, a trip to be made. And then they were gone, leaving Wil to try to understand the purpose of the hidden rooms, the doors that wouldn't open.

When Wil really woke, it was with a desperate start, not the sobbing breathlessness of the blue dream. He felt a resentful relief, seeing the sun streaming past the almost-jacarandas into his bedroom. This was a house that didn't change from day to day, a house he had almost accepted—even if it was the source for some of the dreams. He lay back for a second; sometimes he almost recognized the others, too; one was a mixture of this place and the winter home they bought in California just before . . . the Lindemann case. Wil smiled weakly at himself. These morning entertainments had greater intensity than any

novel he'd ever played. Too bad he wasn't a fan of the tearjerk-
ers.

He glanced at his mail. There was a short note from Lu:
Tammy had agreed to a three-month bobblement, subject to
a ten-hour flicker. Good. The other items were from Yelén:
megabytes of analysis on the party. Ugh. She'd expect him to
know all this the next time they talked. He sat down, browsed
through the top nodes. There were a couple of things he was
especially curious about. Mudge, for instance.

Wil formatted the autopsy report in Michigan State Police
style. He scanned the lab results; the familiar forms brought
back memories, strangely pleasant for all that they involved the
uglier side of his job. Jason Mudge had been as drunk as Yelén
said. There was no trace of any other drug. She had not been
exaggerating about his fall, either. The little guy had struck the
rocks headfirst. Wil ran some simulations: A headfirst landing
was consistent with the cliff's height and Mudge's stature—
assuming he tripped and fell with no effort at recovery. Every
lesion, every trauma on poor Mudge's body was accounted for;
even the scratches on his arms were matched to microgram
specks of flesh left on bushes that grew close to the path.

It was all very reasonable: The man had been seen drinking,
had been seen leaving the picnic in a drunken state. From his
desperate eagerness of the afternoon, Wil could imagine his
state of mind by evening. He had wandered down the path,
self-pity and booze exaggerating every movement. . . . If it had
been anyone else, he might have been stopped. But to approach Jason Mudge was to risk sermons unending.

And so he was dead, like any number of drug-related semisui-
cides Wil had seen. Still, it was interesting that the actual cause
of death was so perfectly, instantly fatal. Even if Yelén's autons
had discovered Mudge immediately after his fall, they could
not have saved him. Except for multiple gunshot wounds and
explosions, Wil had never seen such thorough destruction of
a brain.

It might be worth going over the fellow's past once more,
in particular Wil's last conversation with Mudge. He remem-

bered now. There had been some strange comment about Juan Chanson. Wil replayed the video from Yelén's auton. Yes, he implied Juan had once been a chiliast, too.

Now, that was easy to check. Brierson asked Yelén's Green-Inc about the archeologist. . . . Chanson was well covered, despite his obscure specialty. As a kid, he had been involved with religion; both his parents had been Faithful of the Nde-lante Ali. But by the time he reached college, whatever belief remained was mild and ecumenical. He was awarded a doctor-ate in Mayan archeology from the Universidad Politécnica de Ceres. Wil smiled to himself. In his time, Port Ceres had been a mining camp—to think that a few decades later it could support a university granting degrees like Chanson's!

Nowhere was there evidence of religious fanaticism or of any connection with Jason Mudge. In fact, there was no hint of his later preoccupation with alien invasions. Chanson bobbled out in 2200, and his motive was no nuttier than most: He thought a century or two of progress might give him the tools for a definitive study of the Mayan culture.

. . . *Instead he wound up with the greatest archeological mystery of all time.*

Wil sighed. So in addition to the late Mr. Mudge's other flaws, he had been spreading lies about his rivals.

SEVENTEEN

The next few days fell into a pattern, mostly a pleasant one: The afternoons he spent with one or another group of low-techs.

He saw several mines. They were still heavily automated. Many were open-pit affairs; fifty million years had created whole new ore beds. (The only richer pickings were in the asteroid belt, and one of Yelén's retrenchments was to give up most space activities.) The settlement's factories were like nothing that had existed in history, a weird combination of high-tech custom construction and the primitive production lines which would eventually dominate. Thanks to Gail Parker he even saw an NM tractor factory; he was surprised by a generally friendly reception.

In some ways the North Shore picnic had been misleading. Wil discovered that, although most people agreed with Ti-oulang's complaints against Korolev, few ungovs seriously considered giving their sovereignty to either the Peace or New Mexico. In fact, there had already been some quiet defections from the statist camps.

People were as busy as Rohan claimed. Ten-, twelve-hour days were the rule. And much of the remaining time was filled with scheming to maximize long-term gain. Most of the high-

164

tech giveaways had already been traded several times. When he visited the Dasguptas' farm he saw they were also making farm machinery. He told them about the NM factory. Rohan just smiled innocently. Dilip leaned back against one of his home-brew tractors and crossed his arms. "Yes, I've talked to Gail about that. Fraley wants to buy us out. If the price is right, maybe we'll let him. Heh, heh. Both NMs and Peacers are heavy in tool production. I can see what's going on in their tiny brains. Ten years down the road, they figure on a classic peas-ant/factory confrontation—with them on top. Poor Fraley; sometimes I feel sorry for him. Even if the NMs and the Peace merged, they still wouldn't have all the factories, or even half the mines. Yelén says her databases and planning software will be available for centuries. There are ungov technical types better than anyone Fraley has. Rohan and I know commodity trading. Hell, a lot of us do, and market planning, too." He smirked happily. "In the end, he'll lose his shirt."

Wil grinned back. Dilip Dasgupta had never lacked for self-confidence. In this case he might be right . . . as long as the NMs and the Peace couldn't use force.

Wil's evening debriefings with Yelén were not quite so much fun, though they were more congenial than the one after the North Shore picnic. Her auton followed him everywhere, so she usually heard and saw everything he did. Sometimes it seemed that she wanted to rehash every detail; finding Marta's murderer was a goal never far from her mind, especially now that it seemed part of a general sabotage scheme. But just as often she wanted his estimate of the low-techs' attitudes and intentions. Their conversations were a weird mix of social sci-ence, paranoia, and murder investigation.

Tammy had been bobbled within hours of the picnic. Since then, there had been no signs of high-tech interference. Either she was responsible for it (and had been terribly clumsy), or the glowball and paint were part of something still inscrutable.

Apparently the low-techs were oblivious to this latest twist. Over the last few weeks they had seen and used an enormous amount of equipment; most had no way of knowing the source or "sanctity" of what was provided. And Yelén had erased the polka-dot graffiti from Wil's gate. On the other hand, it was certain that some NMs knew of the bootlegging, enough that Tioulang's spies had gotten the news. Knowing the NM organization, Wil couldn't imagine any conspiracy independent of Steve Fraley.

Yelén dithered with the notion of seizing Fraley and his staff for interrogation, in the end decided against it. There was the same problem as with grabbing Tioulang. Besides, Marta's plan seemed to be *working*. The first phases—the giveaway, the establishment of agreements among the low-techs—were delicate steps that depended on everyone's confidence and goodwill. Even in the best of circumstances—and the last few days did seem about as good as things could get—the low-techs had all sorts of reasons for disliking the queen on the mountain.

And that was one of Korolev's main interests in pumping Brierson. She took every complaint that appeared on the recordings and asked for Wil's analysis. More, she wanted to know the problems he sensed but that went unsaid. It was one of the happier parts of Wil's new job, one he suspected that most of the low-techs understood, too. . . . Would his reception at the NM tractor plant have been quite so cordial otherwise?

Yelén was amused by Dilip Dasgupta's dealings with New Mexico: "Good for him; no one should be taking any crap from those atavists.

"You know what Tioulang and Fraley did when I started Marta's giveaway?" she continued. "They told me how they had their disagreements, but that the future of the race was of supreme importance; their experts had gotten together, come up with a 'Unity Plan.' It specified production goals, resource allocation, just what every damn person was going to do for the next ten years. They expected me to jam this piece of wisdom down everyone's throat. . . . Idiots. I have software that's spent decades crunching on these problems, and *I* can't plan at the level of detail these jerks pretend to. Marta would be proud of me, though; I didn't laugh out loud. I just smiled sweetly and said anyone who wanted to follow their plan was certainly welcome to, but that I couldn't dream of enforcing it. They were insulted even so; I guess they thought I was being sarcastic. It was after that that Tioulang started peddling his line about majority rule and unity against the queen on the mountain."

Other items were more serious, and did not amuse her at all. There were 140 low-tech females. Since the founding of the settlement, her medical service had diagnosed only four pregnancies. "Two of the women requested abortions! I will *not* do abortions, Brierson! And I want every woman off contraceptive status."

They had talked around this problem before; Wil didn't know quite what to say. "This could just drive them into the arms of the NMs and Peacers." Come to think of it, this was one issue where Korolev and the governments probably saw eye to eye. Fraley and Tioulang might make a show of supporting reproductive freedom, but he couldn't imagine it as more than a short-term ploy.

The anger left Yelén's voice. She was almost pleading. "Don't they see, Wil? There have been settlements before. Most were just a family or two, but some—like Sánchez's— were around half our size. They all failed. I think ours may be big enough. Just barely. If the women can average ten children each over the next thirty years, and if their daughters can perform similarly, then we'll have enough people to fill the gaps left as automation fails. But if they can't, then the technology will fail, and we'll actually lose population. All my simulations show that what's left won't be a viable species. In the end, there'll be a few high-techs living a few more subjective centuries with what's left of their equipment."

Marta's vision of a flamed-out ramjet diving Earthwards passed through Wil's mind. "I think the low-tech women want humanity back as much as you, Yelén. But it takes a while to get hardened to this situation. Things were so different back in civilization. A man or a woman could decide where and when and whether—"

"Inspector, don't you think that I know that? I lived forty years in civilization, and I know that what we have here stinks. . . . But it's all we've got."

There was a moment's awkward silence, then: "One thing I don't understand, Yelén. Of all the travelers, you and Marta had the best intuition about the future. Why didn't . . ." The words slipped out before he could stop them; he really wasn't trying to provoke a fight. "Why didn't you think to bring along automatic wombs and a zygote bank?"

Korolev's face reddened, but she didn't blow up. After a second she said, "We did. As usual, it was Marta's idea. I made the purchase. But . . . I screwed up." She looked away from Brierson. It was the first time he'd seen shame in her manner. "I, I didn't test the shipment enough. The company was rated AAAA; it should have been safe as houses. And we were so busy those last few weeks . . . but I should have been more careful." She shook her head. "We had plenty of time later, on the future side of the Singularity. The equipment was junk, Brierson. The wombs and postnatal automation were shells, with just enough processing power to fake the diagnostics."

"And the zygotes?"

Yelén gave a bitter laugh. "Yes. With bobbles it should be impossible to mess that up, right? Wrong. The zygotes were malformed, the sort of nonviable stuff even Christians won't touch.

"I've studied that company through GreenInc; there's nothing that could have tipped us off. But after their last rating, the owners must have gutted their company. The behavior was criminal; when they were caught, it would take them decades to make reparations. Or maybe we were a one-shot fraud; maybe they knew I was making a long jump." She paused. The zip returned to her voice. "I wish they were here now. I wouldn't have to sue them; I'd just drop 'em into the sun.

"Sometimes innocent people have to pay for the mistakes of others, Inspector. That's how it is here. These women must start producing. Now."

Wil spread his hands. "Give them, give us some time."

"It may be hard for you to believe, but time is something we don't have a whole lot of. We waited fifty million years to get everyone together. But once this exercise is begun, there are certain deadlines. You've noticed that I haven't given away any medical equipment."

Wil nodded. Peacer and NM propaganda noticed it loudly. Everyone was welcome to *use* the high-techs' medical services, but, like their bobblers and fighting gear, their medical equipment had not been part of the giveaway.

"We have almost three hundred people here now. The high-end medical equipment is delicate stuff. It consumes irreplaceable materials; it wears out. This is already happening, Brierson, faster than a linear scale-up would predict. The synthesizers must constantly recalibrate to handle each individual."

There was a tightness in Wil's throat. He wondered if this was how a twentieth-century type might feel on being told of inoperable cancer. "How long do we have?"

She shrugged. "If we gave full support, and if the population did *not* increase, maybe fifty years. But the population must increase, or we won't be able to maintain the rest of our technology. The children will need plenty of health care. . . . Now, I don't know how long it will be before the new civilization can make its own medical equipment. It could take anywhere from fifty to two hundred years, depending on whether we have to mark time waiting for a really large population or can get exponential tech growth with only a few thousand people.

"No one need die of old age; I'm willing to bobble the deathbed cases. But there *will* be old age. I'm not supplying age maintenance—and, with certain exceptions, I will not for at least a quarter century."

Wil was a biological twenty. Once, he'd let it slide to thirty —and discovered that he was not a type that aged gracefully. He remembered the flab, the belly that swelled over his pants.

Yelén smiled at him coldly. "Aren't you going to ask me about the exceptions?"

Damn you, thought Wil.

When he didn't reply, she continued. "The trivial exception: those so foolish or unfortunate as to be over bio-forty right now. I'll set their clocks back once.

"The important exception: any woman, for as long as she stays pregnant." Yelén sat back, a look of grim satisfaction on her face. *"That* should supply any backbone that is missing."

Wil stared at her wonderingly. Just a few minutes before, Yelén had been acting as a civilized person might, all amused by the Peacer/NM plans for central control. Now she was talking about running the low-techs' personal lives.

There was a long silence. Yelén understood the point. He could tell by the way she tried to stare him down. Finally her gaze broke. "Damn it, Brierson, it has to be done. And it's moral, too. We high-techs each *own* our medical equipment. We've agreed on this action. Just how we invest our charity is surely our business."

They had argued the theory before. Yelén's logic was a thin thing, going a bit beyond what shipwreck law Wil knew. After all, the advanced travelers had brought the low-techs here, and would not allow them to bobble out of the era. More clearly than ever, he understood Yelén's reaction to Tammy. It would take so little to destroy the settlement. And over the next few years, disaffection was bound to grow.

Like it or not, Wil was working for a government. *Sieg Heil.*

EIGHTEEN

The mornings Wil devoted to research. He still had a lot of background to soak up. He wanted a basic understanding of the settlers, both low-tech and high. They all had pasts and skills; the more he knew, the less he might be surprised. At the same time, there were specific questions (suspicions) raised by his field trips and discussions with Yelén.

For instance: What corroboration was there for Tunç Blumenthal's story? Was he the victim of an accident—or a battle? Had it happened in 2210—or later, perhaps from within the Singularity itself?

It turned out there was physical evidence: Blumenthal's spacecraft. It was a small vehicle (Tunç called it a repair boat), massing just over three tonnes. The bow end was missing—not cut by the smooth curve of a bobble, but flash-evaporated. That hull had a million times the opacity of lead; some monstrous burst of gamma had vaporized a good hunk of it just as the boat bobbled out.

The boat's drive was "ordinary" antigravity—but in this case, it was a built-in characteristic of the hull material. The comm and life-support systems bore familiar trademarks; their mechanism was virtually unintelligible. The recycler was thirty

171

centimeters across; there were no moving parts. It appeared to be as efficient as a planetary ecology.

Tunç could explain most of this in general terms. But the detailed explanations—the theory and the specs—had been in the boat's database. And that had been in Tunç's jacket, in the forward compartment. The volatilized forward compartment. The processors that remained were compatible with the Korolevs', and Yelén had played with them quite a bit.

At one extreme was the lattice of monoprocessors and bobblers embedded in the hull. The monos were no smarter than a twentieth-century home computer, but each was less than one angstrom unit across. Each ran a simple program loop, 1E17 times a second. That program watched its processor's brothers for signs of catastrophe—and triggered an attached bobbler accordingly. Yelén's fighter fleet had nothing like it.

At the other extreme was the computer in Tunç's headband. It was massively parallel, and as powerful as a corporate mainframe of Yelén's time. Marta thought that, even without its database, Tunç's headband made him as important to the plan as any of the other high-techs. They had given him a good part of their advanced equipment in exchange for its use.

Brierson smiled as he read the report. There were occasional comments by Marta, but Yelén was the engineer and this was mainly her work. Where he could follow it at all, the tone was a mix of awe and frustration. It read as he imagined Benjamin Franklin's analysis of a jet aircraft might read. Yelén could study the equipment, but without Tunç's explanations its purpose would have been a mystery. And even knowing the purpose and the underlying principles of operation, she couldn't see how such devices could be built or why they worked so perfectly.

Wil's grin faded. Almost two centuries separated Ben Franklin from jet planes. Less than a decade stood between Yelén's expertise and this "repair boat." Wil knew about the acceleration of progress. It had been a fact of his life. But even in his time, there had been limits on how fast the marketplace could absorb new developments. Even if all these inventions could be made in just nine years—what about the installed base of older

equipment? What about compatibility with devices not yet
upgraded? How could the world of real products be turned
inside out in such a short time?

Wil looked away from the display. So there was physical
evidence, but it didn't prove much except that Tunç had been
as far beyond the high-techs as they were beyond Wil. It really
was surprising that Chanson had not accused Tunç—rescued
from the sun with inexplicable equipment and a story no one
could check—of being another alien. Perhaps Juan's paranoia
was not as all-encompassing as it seemed.

He really should have another chat with Blumenthal.

Wil used a comm channel that Yelén said was private. Blumenthal was as calm and reasonable as before. "Sure, I can talk.
The work I do for Yelén is mainly programming; very flexible
hours."

"Thanks. I wanted to talk more about how you got bobbled.
You said it was possible you were shanghaied. . . ."

Blumenthal shrugged. "It is possible. Yet most likely an
accident it was. You've read about my company's project?"

"Just Yelén's summaries."

Tunç hesitated, swapped out. "Ah, yes. What she says is fair.
We *were* running a matter/antimatter distillery. But look at
the numbers. Yelén's stations can distill perhaps a kilo per day
—enough to power a small business. We were in a different
class entirely. My partners and I specialized in close solar work,
less than five radii out. We had easements on most of the sun's
southern hemisphere. When I . . . left, we were distilling one
hundred thousand *tonnes* of matter and antimatter every *second.* That's enough to dim the sun, though we arranged things
so the effect wasn't perceptible from the ecliptic. Even so,
there were complaints. An absolute condition of our insurance
was that we move it out promptly and without leakage. A few
days' production would be enough to damage an unprotected
solar system."

"Yelén's summary said you were shipping to the Dark Companion?" Like a lot of Yelén's commentary, the rest of that
report had been technical, unintelligible without a headband.

"True!" Tunç's face came alight. "Such a fine idea it was. Our parent company liked big construction projects. Originally, they wanted to stellate Jupiter, but they couldn't buy the necessary options. Then we came along with a much bigger project. We were going to *implode* the Dark Companion, fashion of it a small Tipler cylinder." He noticed Wil's blank expression. "A naked black hole, Wil! A space warp! A gate for faster-than-light travel! Of course the Dark Companion is so small that the aperture would be only a few meters wide, and have tidal strains above 1E13 g's per meter—but with bobbles it might be usable. If not, there were plans to probe through it to the galactic core, and siphon back the power to widen it."

Tunç paused, some of his enthusiasm gone. "That was the plan, anyway. In fact, the distillery was almost too much for us. We were on site for days at a time. It gets on your nerves after a while, knowing that beyond all the shielding, the sun is stretched from horizon to horizon. But we had to stay; we couldn't tolerate transmission delays. It took all of us linked to our mainframe to keep the brew stable.

"We had stability, but we weren't shipping quite everything out. Something near a tonne per second began accumulating over the south pole. We needed a quick fix or we'd lose performance bonuses. I took the repair boat across to work on it. The problem was just ten thousand kilometers from our station —a thirty-millisecond time lag. Intellect nets run fine with that much lag, but this was process control; we were taking a chance. We'd accumulated a two-hundred-thousand-tonne backlog by then. It was all in flicker storage—a slowly exploding bomb. I had to repackage it and boost it out."

Tunç shrugged. "That's the last I remember. Somehow, we lost control; part of that backlog recombined. My boat bobbled up. Now, I was on the sun side of the brew. The blast rammed me straight into Sol. There was no way my partners could save me."

Bobbled into the sun. It was almost high-tech slang for certain death. "How could you ever escape?"

Blumenthal smiled. "You haven't read about that? There is no way in heaven *I* could have. On the sun, the only way you can survive is to stay in stasis. My initial bobbling was only for a few seconds. When it lapsed, the fail-safe did a quick look-about, saw where we were heading, and rebobbled—sixty-four thousand years. That was 'effective infinity' to its pinhead program.

"I've done some simulations since. I hit the surface fast enough to penetrate thousands of kilometers. The bobble spent a few years following convection currents around inside. It wasn't as dense as the inner sunstuff. Eventually I percolated back to near the surface. Then, every time the bobble floated over a blow-off, it was boosted tens of thousands of kilometers up. . . . For thirty thousand years a damn volleyball I was, flying up to the corona, falling back through the photosphere, float-ing around awhile, then getting thrown up again.

"That's where I was through the Singularity and during the time the short-term travelers were being rescued. That's where I would have died if it hadn't been for Bil Sánchez." He paused. "You never knew Bil. He dropped out, died about twenty million years ago. He was a nut about Juan Chanson's extermination theory. Most of Chanson's proof is on Earth; W. W. Sánchez traveled all over the Solar System looking for evidence. He dug up things Chanson never guessed at.

"One thing Bil did was scan for bobbles. He was convinced that sooner or later he'd find one containing somebody or somemachine that had escaped the 'Extinction.' When he spotted my bobble in the sun, he thought he'd hit the jackpot. Their latest records—from 2201—didn't show any such bob-bling. It was just the weird place you might expect to find a survivor; even the exterminators couldn't have reached some-one down there.

"But Bil Sánchez was patient. He noticed that every few thousand years, a really big solar flare would blast me way up. He and the Korolevs diverted a comet, stored it off Mercury. The next time I was boosted off the surface, they were ready: They dropped the comet into a sun-grazing orbit. It picked me off at the top of my bounce. Fortunately, the snowball didn't break up and my bobble stuck on its surface; we swung around the sun, up into the cool. From there, the situation was much like their other rescues. Thirty thousand years later, I was back in realtime."

"Tunç, you lived closer to the Extinction than anyone else. What do *you* think caused it?"

The spacer sat back, crossed his arms. "That's what they all ask. . . . Ah, Wil Brierson, if I only knew! I tell them I don't know. And they go away, seeing each his own theory reflected in my story." He seemed to realize the answer was not going to satisfy. "Very well, my theories. Theory Alpha: Possible it is that mankind was exterminated. What Bil found in the Charon catacombs is hard to explain any other way. But it can't be like Juan Chanson says. Bil had it better: Anything that could bump off the intellect nets in Earth/Luna would needs be superhuman. If it's still around, no brave talk will save us. That's why Bil Sánchez and his little colony dropped out. Poor man, he was frightened of what might happen to anything bigger.

"And Theory Beta: This is what Yelén believes, and probably Della too—though she is still so shy, I can't tell for sure. Humankind and its machines became something better, something . . . unknowable. And I saw things that fit with that, too.

"Ever since the Peace War there have been more or less autonomous devices. For centuries, folks had been saying that machines as smart as people were just around the corner. Most didn't realize how unimportant such a thing would be. What was needed was *greater* than human intelligence. Between our processors and ourselves, my era was achieving that.

"My own company was small; there were only eight of us. We were backward, rural; the rest of humanity was hundreds of light-seconds away. The larger spacing firms were better off. Their computers were correspondingly bigger, and they had thousands of people linked. I had friends at Charon Corp and Stellation Inc. They thought we were crazy to stay so isolated. And when we visited their habitats, when the comm lag got to less than a second, I could see what they meant. There was power and knowledge and joy in those companies. . . . And they could plan circles around us. Our only advantage was mobility.

"Yet even these corporations were fragments, a few thousand people here and there. By the beginning of the twenty-third, there were three *billion* people in the Earth/Luna volume. Three billion people and corresponding processing power —all less than three light-seconds apart.

"I . . . it was strange, talking to them. We attended a marketing conference at Luna in 2209. Even linked, we never did understand what was going on." He was quiet for a long moment. "So you see, either theory fits."

Wil was not going to let him off that easily. "But your project—you say it would have meant faster-than-light travel. Is there any evidence what became of that?"

Tunç nodded. "Bil Sánchez visited the Dark Companion a couple times. It's the same dead thing it always was. There's no sign it was ever modified. I think that scared him even more than what he found at Charon. I know it scares me. I doubt my accident was enough to scuttle the plan: our project would have given humanity a gate to the entire Galaxy . . . but it was also mankind's first piece of cosmic engineering. If it worked, we wanted to do the same to a number of stars. In the end, we might have built a small Arp object in this arm of the Galaxy. Bil thought we'd been 'uppity cockroaches'—and the real owners finally stepped on us. . . .

"But don't you be buying Theory Alpha just yet. I said the Singularity was a mirrored thing. Theory Beta explains it just as well. In 2207, we were the hottest project at Stellation Inc. They put everything they had into renting those easements around the sun. But after 2209, the edge was gone from their excitement. At the marketing conference at Luna, it almost seemed Stellation's backers were trying to sell our project as a *frivolity.*"

Tunç stopped, smiled. "So you have my thumbnail sketch of Great Events. You can get it all, clearer said with more detail, from Yelén's databases." He cocked his head to one side. "Do you like listening to others so much, Wil Brierson, that you visit me first?"

Wil grinned back. "I wanted to hear you firsthand." *And I still don't understand you.* "I'm one of the earlier low-techs, Tunç. I've never experienced direct connect—much less the mind links you talk about. But I know how much it hurts a high-tech to go without a headband." All through Marta's diary, that loss was a source of pain. "If I understand what you say about your time, you've lost much more. How can you be so *cool?*"

The faintest shadow crossed Tunç's face. "It's not a mystery, really. I was nineteen when I left civilization. I've lived fifty years since. I don't remember much of the time right after my rescue. Yelén says I was in a coma for months. They couldn't find anything wrong with my body; just no one was home.

"I told you my little company was backward, rural. That's only by comparison with our betters. There were eight of us, four women, four men. Maybe I should call it a group marriage, because it was that, too. But it was more. We spent every spare gAu on our processor system and the interfaces. When we were linked up, we were something . . . wonderful. But now all that's memories of memories—no more meaningful to me than to you." His voice was soft. "You know, we had a mascot: a poor, sweet girl, close to anencephalic. Even with prosthesis she was scarcely brighter than you or I. Most of the time she was happy." The expression on his face was wistful, puzzled. "And most of the time, I am happy, too."

NINETEEN

Then there was Marta's diary. He had started reading it as a casual cross-check on Yelén and Della. It had become a dark addiction, the place he spent the hours after his late-night arguments with Yelén, the hours after returning from his field trips.

What might have happened if Wil had been less a gentleman the night of the Robinson party? Marta was dead before he really knew her; but she looked a little like Virginia . . . and talked like her . . . and laughed like her. The diary was the only place where he could ever know her now. And so every night ended with new gloom, matched only by the dreams of morning.

Of course Marta found the West End mines bobbled. She stayed a few months, and left some billboards. It was not safe country. Packs of doglike creatures roamed. At one point she was trapped, had to start a grass fire and play mirror tag with the dogs among the bobbles. Wil read that part several times; it made him want to laugh and cry in the same breath. For Marta, it was just part of staying alive. She moved northwards, into the foothills of the Kampuchean Alps. That was where Yelén found her third cairn.

Marta reached the Peacer bobble two years after she was

marooned. She had walked and sailed around the Inland Sea to do it. The last six hundred kilometers had been a climb over the Kampuchean Alps. She was still an optimist, yet her words were sometimes tinged with self-mockery. She had started out to walk halfway around the world, and ended up less than two thousand kilometers north of where she started. Despite her year's layover, the shattered bones in her foot had not healed perfectly. Till she was rescued (her usual phrasing) she would walk with a limp. At the end of a long day's walk she was in some pain.

But she had plans. The Peacer bobble was at the center of a vitrified plain 150 kilometers across. Even now, not much life had returned. Her first walk in, she carried all her food on the travois.

≪ The bobble isn't super large, maybe three hundred meters across. But its setting is spectacular, Lelya; I had not remembered the details. It's in a small lake bordered by uniform cliffs. Concentrically around those cliffs are rings of ridges. I climbed to the edge of the cliffs and looked across at the bobble. My reflection looked back and we waved at each other. With its moat and the ringwall, it looks like a jewel in a setting. Equally spaced along the wall are five smaller gems —the bobbles around our lookout equipment. Whoever— whatever—marooned me has locked them up, too. But for how long? Those five were supposed to have a very high flicker rate. I still can't believe anyone could subvert our control systems for a jump of longer than a few decades.

≪ Wouldn't it be a joke if I were rescued by the *Peacers!* They thought they were making a fifty-year jump to renewed dominion. What a shock it would be to come out on an empty world, and find exactly one taxpayer left. Amusing, but I'd rather be rescued by you, Lelya. . . .

≪ The jewel's setting is cracked in places. There's a waterfall coming into the lake on the south side. The water exits through a break in the north wall. It's very clear; I can see fish in the lake. There are places where the cliff has collapsed. It looks like it could make decent soil. This is probably the most habitable spot in the whole destruction zone. If I have to stop,

Lelya, I think this is really the best place it could happen. It's the most likely to be monitored; it's at the center of a glazed flatland that should be easy to mark up. (Do you think our L5 autons would respond to KILROY IS HERE written in letters a kilometer long?)

<< So. This will be my base, forever till I'm rescued. I think I can make it a nice place to live, Lelya. >>

And Marta did. Through the first ten years she made steady improvements. Five times she trekked out of the glazed zone, sometimes for necessities like seed and wood, later to import some friends: she hiked three hundred kilometers north, to a large lake. There were fishermonkeys on that lake. She understood their matriarchal scheme now. It wasn't hard to find displaced trios wandering the shores, looking for something bigger than they that walked on two legs. The fishers loved the ringlake. By year twelve, there were so many that some left every year down the river.

From her cabin high on the ringwall she watched them by the hour:

<< Back and forth in water and bobble there are reflections of the ringwall and my cabin and our bobbled monitors. The fishers love to play with their reflections. Often they swim against its surface. I'll bet they feel the reflected body heat, even through their pelts. I wonder what mythology they have about the kingdom beyond the mirror. . . . Yes, Lelya. Sentiment is one thing, fantasy another. But, you know, my fishers are smarter than chimpanzees. If I'd seen them before we left civilization, I'd have bet they would evolve human intelligence. Sigh. After all our travels, I know better. In the short term, the marine adaptation is more profitable. Another five megayears, they'll be as agile as penguins—and not much brighter. >>

Marta gave names to the friendliest, and the weirdest. There was always a Hewey and a Dewey and a Lewey. Others she named after humans. Wil found himself chuckling. Over the years, there were several Juan Chansons and Jason Mudges— usually the most compulsive chitterers. There was also a succession of Della Lus—all small, pale, shy. And there was even one W. W. Brierson. Wil read that page twice, a trembling smile on his lips. Wil the fishermonkey was black-furred and large, even bigger than a dominant female. He could have run the whole show, but kept mostly to himself and watched everyone else. Every so often his reserve broke and he gave a great screeching display, rushing along the edge of the ringwall and slapping his sides. Like the first Dewey, he was odd man out, and especially friendly to Marta. He spent more time with her than any of them. They all played at imitating her, but he was the most successful. She actually got some useful work out of him, pulling small bundles. His most impressive game was the building of miniature versions of the pyramidal cairn Marta used to store the completed portion of her diary. Marta never said he was her favorite, yet she did seem fond of him. He disappeared on her last big expedition, around year fifteen.

≪ I'll never name one of my little friends after you, Lelya. The fishers live only ten or fifteen years. It's always sad when they go. I don't want to go through that with a fisher named Yelén. ≫

As the years passed, Marta concentrated on the diary. This was where the words piled into the millions. She had lots of advice for Yelén. There were some interesting revelations: It had been Phil Genet who persuaded Yelén to raise the Peacer bobble while the NMs were in realtime. It had been Phil Genet who was behind the ash-shoveling incident. Genet consistently argued that the key to success lay in the explicit intimidation of the low-techs. Marta begged Yelén not to take his advice again. ≪ We will be hated enough, feared enough, even if we act like saints. ≫

In the middle decades, her writing was scarcely a diary at all, but a collection of essays and stories, poems and whimsy. She spent at least as much time with her sketches and paintings. There were dozens of paintings of the ringlake and bobble, under every kind of lighting. There were landscapes done from sketches she had made on her trips. There were portraits of many of the fishers, as well as pictures of Marta herself. In one, the artist knelt at the edge of the ringlake, smiling at her own reflection as she painted it.

It came to Wil that though there were periods of depression, and physical pain, and occasional moments of stark terror, most of the time *Marta was having a good time.* She even said so:

≪ If I'm rescued, all this becomes a diversion, a few decades on top of the two centuries I have already lived. If I'm not . . . well, I know you'll be back sometime. I want you to know that I missed you, but that there were pleasures. Take all the pictures and poems as my evidence and as my gift. ≫

It was not a gift for W. W. Brierson. He tried to read it straight through, but the afternoon came when he couldn't go on. Someday he would read of those happy, middle times. Perhaps someday he could smile and laugh with her. Just now, all he felt was a horrid need to follow Marta Qen Korolev through her last years. Even as he skipped the data set forward, he wondered at himself. Unlike Marta, he *knew* how it all ended, yet he was forcing himself to see it all again through Marta's eyes. Was there some crazy part of him that thought that by reading her words he could take some of the pain from her onto himself?

More likely, this was like his daughter Anne's reaction to *The Worms Within.* The movie had been in a festival of twentieth-century film that came with the kid's new data set. It turned out that part of the festival was horror movies from the 1990s. The old USA had been at the height of its power and wealth then; for some perverse reason, slash-and-splash had its greatest flowering the same decade. Wil wondered if they would have spent so much time inventing blood and gore if they had known what was waiting for them just around the corner in the twenty-first; or maybe they feared such a future, and the gore was their way of knocking wood. In any case, Anne rushed out of her room after the first fifteen minutes, almost hysterical. They trashed the video, but she couldn't get the story out of her mind. Unknown to Wil and Virginia, she bought a replacement and every night watched a little more— just enough to make her sick again. Afterwards she said she kept watching it—even though it got more and more horrible —because there had to be *something* that would happen that would make up for the wounds she'd already suffered. Of course, there was no such redemption. The ending was even more imaginatively grotesque than she feared. Anne had been depressed and a little irrational for months afterwards.

Wil grimaced. Like daughter like father. And he didn't even have Anne's excuse; he knew how this one ended.

In those last years, Marta's life slowly darkened. She had completed her great construction, the sign that should alert any orbital monitors. It was a clever scheme: She had journeyed out of the glazed zone, to where a few isolated jacarandas grew. She gathered the spiders she found on the display webs and took them into the desolation. By this time she had discovered the relation of those webs to tree and spider reproduction. She set spiders and seeds at ten carefully selected sites along a line from the center of the glazed zone. Each was on a tiny stream; at each she had broken through the glaze and developed a real soil. Over the next thirty years, the spiders and their sprouts did most of the construction. The seedlings spread a small way down the streams, but not as much as ordinary plants. The spiders saw the faraway display webs of their brethren and thousands of seeds were deposited on the path between, each with a complement of arachnid paratroopers.

In the end, she had the vast green-and-silver arrow that did eventually alert an orbiter. But a problem came with that line of trees. They broke the glaze, made a bridge of soil from her base to the outside. The jacs and spiders were awesome defenders of their territory, but not perfect ones—especially when strung thin. Other plants infested the sides of their run. With those plants came herbivores.

<< The little buggers have added a couple of hours' work to each day, Lelya. And some of my favorite fruits I can't grow at all now. >>

Ten or even twenty years into the abandonment, this would have been an inconvenience. At thirty-five years, Marta's health was beginning to fail. Competing with the rabbity thieves was a slowly losing proposition for her.

<< Somewhere in a cairn on the far side of the sea, I said some very foolish things. Didn't I figure an unaided human lived about a century? And then I said something about being conservative and expecting I could last only seventy-five years. What a laugh.

≪ My foot has never gotten better, Lelya. I walk with a crutch now, and not very fast. Most of the time, my joints hurt. It's funny what not feeling good does to your attitude and your notion of time. I can scarcely believe there was a day when I expected to walk to Canada. Or that just fifteen years ago I still hiked out of the glazed zone regularly. Lelya, it's a major effort to climb down to the lake now. I haven't done it for weeks. I may not do it again. But I have a rain cistern . . . and the fishers are always happy to visit me up here. Besides, I don't like to see my reflection in the lake anymore. I'm not doing any more self-portraits, Lelya.

≪ Is this what it was like for people before decent medical care? The failed dreams, the horizons that shrink always inwards? It must have taken guts to do all they did. ≫

Two years later:

≪ Today the neighborhood went to hell. I have a pack of near-dogs camped just over the ringwall. They look a lot like the ones at the mines, though these are smaller. In fact, they're kind of cute, like big puppies with pointy ears. I'd like to kill the lot of them. An un-Marta-like thought, granted, but they've driven the fishers away from my cabin. They killed Lewey. I got a couple of the little murderers with my pike. Since then, they've been extremely wary of me. Now I carry a pike and knife when I'm out of doors. ≫

Marta spent most of her last year in the cabin. Outside, her garden went to weeds. There were edible roots and vegetables still, but they were scattered around. Getting out to gather them was an expedition as challenging as a hundred-kilometer walk had been before. The near-dogs grew bolder; they circled just outside the diamond tip of her pike, darted occasionally inwards. Marta had several pelts to prove that she was still the faster. But it could not last. She was eating poorly. That made it harder for her to gather food. . . . A downward spiral.

Wil paged the display and found himself looking at ordinary typescript. He felt his stomach drop. Was this the end? An ordinary entry and then . . . nothing? He forced his eyes through the words. It was a commentary from Yelén: Marta had not intended the next page to be seen. Her words had been rubbed out, then overwritten by a later diary entry. "You said you'd walk if you didn't see everything, Brierson. Well, here it is. Damn you." He could almost hear the bitterness in Yelén's words. He looked down the page.

<< *Oh God Yelen help me. If you ever lovd me save me now. I am dying dying. I dont want to die. Oh please please pleas* >>

He paged again, and was looking at Marta's familiar script. If anything, the letters were more finely drawn than usual. He imagined her in the dark cabin, patiently rubbing away the words of her despair, then overwriting them, cool and analytical. Wil wiped his face and tried not to breathe. A deep breath would start him sobbing. He read Marta's final entry.

<< Dearest Lelya,

<< I suppose there must be an end to optimism, at least locally. I've been holed up in my cabin for ten days now. There is water in the cistern, but I'm out of food. Damn dogthings; without them, I could have lasted another twenty years. They cut me up pretty bad the last time I was out. For a while, I thought to make a grand stand, give them a last taste of my diamonds. I've changed my mind about that; last week I saw them take on a grazer. Yes, one of those: bigger than I am, with a horn almost as effective as my pike. I couldn't see all of it, just when they were in view from my windows, but. . . . At first it looked like they were playing. They nipped at it, sending it scurrying round and round. But I could see the blood. Finally, it weakened, tripped.

<< I never noticed this when they got smaller animals, but the dogs don't deliberately kill their prey. They just eat them alive, usually from the guts out. That grazer was big; it took a while to die.

<< So. I'm staying inside. "Forever until you rescue me" was how I used to say it. I guess I don't expect a rescue anymore. With lookabouts scheduled every few decades (at best), the odds are against one happening in the next few days.

<< I figure it's been about forty years since I was marooned. It seems so much longer, longer than all the rest of my life. Nature's kindly way of stretching mortals' meager rations? I remember my fisher friends better than most of my human

ones. I can see the lake through one window. If they looked, they could see me up here. They rarely look. I don't think most of them remember me. It's been three years since they were driven away from the cabin. That's almost a fisher generation. The only one I think remembers is my last Juan Chanson. This one's not as loud as my earlier Juans. Mainly, he sits around, taking in the sun. . . . I just looked out the window. He's there now; I do think he remembers. >>

The handwriting changed. Wil wondered how many hours —or days—had passed from one paragraph to the next. The new lines were crossed out, but Yelén's magic made them clear:

<< I just remembered a strange word: taphonomy. Once upon a time, I could be an expert in a field just by remembering its name. Now . . . all I know . . . it's the study of death sites, no? A crumple of bones is all these mortal creatures leave . . . and I know that bones get swept away so fast. Not mine, though. Mine stay indoors. I'll be here a long time, my writing longer. . . . Sorry. >>

She didn't have the energy to erase the words. There was a gap, and her writing became regular, each letter carefully printed.

<< I have the feeling I'm saying things I've written you before, contingencies that now are certainties. I hope you get all my earlier writing. I tried to put all the details there, Lelya. I want you to have something to work for, dear. Our plan can still succeed. When it does, our dreams live.

<< You are for all time my dearest friend, Lelya. >>

Marta did not finish the entry with her usual sign-off. Perhaps she thought to write more later. Further down, there was a pattern of disconnected lines. Through an exercise of imagination, one might see them as the block letters L O V.

That was all.

It didn't matter; Wil wasn't reading anymore. He lay with his face in his arms, sobbing on empty lungs. This was the daytime version of the dream in blue; he could never wake from this.

Seconds passed. The blue changed to rage, and Wil was on his feet. *Someone had done this to Marta.* W. W. Brierson had been shanghaied, separated from his family and his world, thrown into a new one. But Derek Lindemann's crime was a peccadillo, laughable, hardly worth Wil's attention. *Compared to what was done to Marta.* Someone had taken her from her friends, her love, and then squeezed the life from her, year by year, drop by drop.

Someone must die for this. Wil stumbled across the room, searching. In the back of his mind, a rational fragment watched in wonder that his feelings could run so deep, that he could truly run amok. Then even the fragment was swallowed up.

Something hit him. A wall. Wil struck back, felt satisfying pain shooting through his fist. As he pulled his arm from the wall, he noticed motion in the next room. He ran towards the figure, and it towards him. He struck and struck. Glass flew in all directions.

Then he was in sunlight, and on his knees. Wil felt a penetrating coldness in the back of his neck. He sighed and sat down. He was on the street, surrounded by broken glass and what looked like parts of his living-room walls. He looked up. Yelén and Della were standing just beyond the pile of debris. He hadn't seen them in person and together for weeks. It must be something important. "What happened?" Funny. His throat hurt, as though he'd been shouting.

Yelén stepped over a fallen timber and bent to look at him. Behind her, Wil saw two large fliers. At least six autons hung in the air above the women. "That's what we would like to know, Inspector. Were you attacked? Our guards heard screaming and the sounds of a fight."

. . . and every so often he gave a great screeching display, rushing about and slapping his sides. Marta had named her fishers well. Wil looked at his bloody hands. The tranq Yelén had used on him was fast-acting stuff. He could think and remember, but emotions were distant, muted things. "I, I was reading the end of Marta's diary. Got carried away."

"Oh." Korolev's pale lips tightened. How could she be so cool? Surely she had gone through this, too. Then Wil remembered the century Yelén had spent alone with the diary and the cairns. Her harshness would be easier to understand in the future.

Della walked closer, her boots crunching on broken glass. Lu's outfit was dead black, like something from a twentieth-century police state. Her arms were folded across her chest. Her dark eyes were calm and distant. No doubt her current personality matched her clothes. "Yes. The diary. It's a depressing document. Perhaps you should choose other leisure-time reading."

The remark should have done something to his blood pressure, but Wil felt nothing.

Yelén was more explicit. "I don't know why you insist on mucking around in Marta's personal life, Brierson. She said everything she knew about the case right at the beginning. The rest is none of your damned business." She glanced at his hands, and a small robot swooped down. Wil felt something cold and soft work between his fingers. Yelén sighed. "Okay. I guess I understand; we are that much alike. And I still need you. . . . Take a couple of days off. Get yourself together." She started back to her flier.

"Uh, Yelén," said Della. "Are we going to leave him here alone?"

"Of course not. I'm wasting three extra autons on him."

"I mean, when the GriefStop wears off, Brierson may be very distressed." Something flickered in her eyes. She looked momentarily puzzled, searching through nine thousand years of memories—perhaps more important, nine thousand years of viewpoints. "When a person is like that, don't they need someone to help them . . . someone to, uh, *hug* them?"

"Hey, don't look at me!"

"Right." Her eyes were calm again. "It was just a thought." The two departed.

Wil watched their fliers disappear over the trees. Around him, broken glass was being vacuumed up, the torn walls removed. Already his hands felt warm and comfortable. He sat in the roadway, at peace. Eventually he would get hungry and go inside.

TWENTY

After supper, Wil sat for a long time in the ruins of his living room. He was directly responsible for very little of the destruction: He had punched bloody holes in one wall and demolished a mirror. The guard autons had let that go on for perhaps fifteen seconds before deciding it was a threat to his safety. Then they bobbled him: The walls near the mirror were cut by a clean, curving line. A smooth depression dipped thirty centimeters below the floor, into the foundation. Even the bobbling had not caused the worst damage. That happened when Yelén and Della cut the bobble out of the house. Apparently they wanted their equipment to have a direct view when it burst. He looked at the wall clock. It was the same day as before; they'd kept him on ice just long enough to get him out of the house.

If Wil's sense of humor had been enabled, he might have smiled. All this supported Yelén's claim that the house was not infested by her equipment. The best the protection autons could do was bobble everything and call for help.

Things were different now. From where he sat, Wil saw several robots foaming a temporary wall. Beside his chair sat a medical auton, about as animated as a garbage can. Somewhere it had hands; they'd been a big help with supper.

190

He watched the reconstruction with interest, even turned on the room lights when night came. This GriefStop was great stuff. Simple drives like hunger weren't affected. He felt as alert and coordinated as usual. He was simply beyond the reach of emotion; yet, strangely, it was easy to imagine how things would affect him without the drug. And that knowledge did make for some weak motivation. For instance, he hoped the Dasguptas would not stop by on their way home. He guessed that explanations would be difficult.

Wil stood and walked to his reading table. The auton glided silently after him. Something smaller floated up from the mantel. He sat down, suddenly guessing that GriefStop had never been a hit on the recreational drug market. There were side effects: Everything moved a little bit slow. Sounds came low-pitched, drawn out. It wasn't enough to panic him (he doubted if anything could do that just now), but reality had a faint edge of waking nightmare. His silent visitors intensified the feeling. . . . Ah well, paranoia was the name of the game.

He turned on his desk lamp, cut the room lights. Somehow the destruction had spared the desk and reading display. The last page of Marta's diary floated in the circle of light. He guessed that rereading that page would be very upsetting to his normal self—so he didn't look at it. Della was right. There ought to be better leisure-time activities. This day would hang his normal self low for a long time to come. He hoped that he wouldn't come back to the diary, to tear at the wounds he'd opened today. Perhaps he should erase it; the inconvenience of coercing another copy from Yelén might be enough to save his normal self.

Wil spoke into the darkness. "House. Delete Marta's diary." The display showed his command and the ideation net associated with "Marta's diary."

"The whole thing?" the house asked.

Wil's hand hovered over the commit. "Unh, no. Wait." Curiosity was a powerful thing with Brierson. He'd just remembered something that could force his normal self to go against all common sense and retrieve another copy. Better check it out now, *then* zap the diary.

When he first received the diary, he'd asked for all references to himself. There had been four. He had seen three: She'd mentioned calling him back from the beach the day of the Peacer rescue. There'd been the fisher she'd named after him. Then, around year thirty-eight, she'd recommended Yelén use his services—even though she'd forgotten his name by then. That was the reference which hurt so much the first time he looked at the document. Wil guessed he could forgive that now; those years would have destroyed the soul of a lesser person, not simply blurred a few memories.

But what was the fourth reference? Wil repeated the context search. Ah. No wonder he had missed it. It appeared about year thirteen, tucked away in one of her essays on the plan. In this one, she wrote on each of the low-techs she remembered, citing strengths and weaknesses, trying to guess how they would react to the plan. In a sense it was a foolish exercise—Marta granted that much more elaborate analysis existed on the Korolev db's—but she hoped her "time of solitude" had given her new insights. Besides (unsaid), she needed to be doing something useful in the years that stretched before her.

≪ Wil Brierson. An important one. I never believed the commercial mythology, much less the novels his son wrote. Yet . . . since we've known him in person, I've concluded he may be almost as sharp as they make him out to be. At least in some ways. If you and I can't figure out who did this to me, he might still be able to.

≪ Brierson has a lot of respect among the low-techs. That and his general competence would be a real help against Steve Fraley and whoever will run the Peacer show. But what if he opposes our plan? That may seem ridiculous; he was born in a civilized era. Yet I'm not sure of the man. One thing about civilization, it allows the most extreme types to find a niche where they can live to their own and others' benefit. Here, we are temporarily beyond civilization; people we could abide before might now be dangerous. Wil is still disoriented; maybe that accounts for his behavior. But he may have a mean, irrational streak under his friendly exterior. I only have one piece of evidence, something I've been a little ashamed to tell you about:

<< You know I was attracted to the guy. Well, he followed me when I stormed out of Don Robinson's show. Now, I wasn't trying to flirt; I was just so mad at Don's sneakiness, I had to open up to someone—and you were in deep connect. We talked for several minutes before I realized that the pats on my shoulder, the hand at my waist, were not brotherly comfort. It was my fault for letting it get that far, but he wouldn't take no for an answer. The guy is big; he actually started knocking me around. If the rest of the evening hadn't begun my great "adventure," the bruises he left on my chest would have had medical attention. You see, Lelya? Mean to beat me when I refused him. Irrational for doing it with Fred just five meters away. I had to suppress the auton's reflexes, or Brierson would have been stunned for a week. Finally, I slapped his face as hard as I could, and threatened him with Fred. He backed off then, and seemed genuinely embarrassed. >>

Wil read the paragraph again and again. It hung in the circle of light from his desk lamp . . . and not one letter changed. He wondered how his normal self would react to Marta's words. Would he be enraged? Or simply crushed that she could say such a lie?

He thought for a long time, vaguely aware of the nightmare edge of the darkness around him. Finally he knew. The reaction would not be rage, would not be hurt. When he could feel again, there would be *triumph:*

The case had cracked. For the first time, he knew he would get Marta's murderer.

TWENTY-ONE

Yelén gave him the promised two days off and even removed the autons from his house. When he walked near a window, he could see something hovering just below the sill. He had no doubt it would come rushing in at the smallest sign of erratic behavior. Wil did his best to give no such sign. He did all his research away from the windows; Yelén might see his return to the diary as a bad method of recuperating.

But now Wil wasn't reading the diary. He was using all the (feeble) automation at his command to *study* it.

When Yelén came around with her list of places to visit and low-techs to talk to, Wil begged off. Forty-eight hours was not enough, he said. He needed to rest, to avoid the case completely.

The tactic bought him a week of uninterrupted quiet—probably enough time to squeeze the last clues from Marta's story; almost enough time to prepare his strategy. The seventh day, Yelén was on the holo again. "No more excuses, Brierson. I've been talking to Della." *The great human-relations expert?* thought Wil. "We don't think you're doing anything to help yourself. Three times the Dasguptas have tried to get you out of the house; you put them off the same way you do me. We think your 'recuperation' is an exercise in self-pity.

"So"—she smiled coldly—"your vacation is over." A light gleamed at the base of his data set. "I just sent you a record of the party Fraley threw yesterday. I got his speech and most of the related conversation. As usual, I think I'm missing nuances. I want you to—"

Wil resisted the impulse to straighten his slumped shoulders; his plan might as well begin now. "Any more evidence of high-tech interference?"

"No. I would scarcely need your help to detect *that*. But—"

Then the rest scarcely matters. But he didn't say it out loud. Not yet. "Okay, Yelén. Consider me back from psych leave."

"Good."

"But before I go after this Fraley thing, I want to talk to you and Della. Together."

"Jesus Christ, Brierson! I need you, but there are limits." She looked at him. "Okay. It'll be a couple of hours. She's beyond Luna, closing down some of my operations." Yelén's holo flicked off.

It was a long two hours. This meeting was supposed to be a surprise. He wouldn't have forced things if he'd known Lu was not immediately available. Wil watched the clock; now he was stuck.

Just short of 150 minutes later, Yelén was back. "Okay, Brierson, how may we humor you?"

A second holo came to life, showing Della Lu. "Are you back at Town Korolev, Della?" Wil asked.

There was no time lag to her reply. "No. I'm at my home, about two hundred klicks above you. Do you really want me on the ground?"

"Uh, no." *You may be in the best possible position.* "Okay, Della, Yelén. I have a quick question. If the answer is no, then I hope you will quickly make it yes. . . . Are you *both* still providing me with heavy security?"

"Sure." "Yes."

That would have to be good enough. He leaned forward and spoke slowly. "There are some things you should know. Most important: Marta knew who murdered her."

Silence. Yelén's impatience was blown away; she simply stared. But when she spoke, her voice was flat, enraged. "You stupid jerk. If she knew, why didn't she tell us? She had forty years to tell us." On the other holo, Della appeared to be swapped out. *Has she already imagined the consequences?*

"Because, Yelén, all through those forty years she was being watched by the murderer, or his autons. And she knew *that*, too."

Again, silence. This time it was Della who spoke. "How do *you* know this, Wil?" The distant look was gone. She was intent, neither accepting nor rejecting his assertions. He wondered if this were her original peace-cop personality looking out at him.

"I don't think Marta herself guessed the truth during the first ten years. When she did, she spent the rest of her life playing a double game with the diary—leaving clues that would not alert the murderer, yet which could be understood later."

Yelén bent forward, her hands clenched. "What clues?"

"I don't want to say just yet."

"Brierson, I lived with that diary for a hundred years. For a hundred years I read it, analyzed it with programs you can't even imagine. And I lived with Marta for almost two hundred years before that. I knew every secret, every thought." Her voice was shaking; he hadn't seen such lethal fury in her since right after the murder. "You opportunistic slime. You say she left thoughts *you* could follow and *I* could not!"

"Yelén!" Della's interruption froze Korolev in midrage. For a moment, both women were silent, staring.

Yelén's hands went limp; she seemed to shrink in on herself. "Of course. I wasn't thinking."

Della nodded, and glanced at Wil. "Perhaps we should spell this out for you." She smiled. "Though I suspect you're way ahead of us. *If* the murderer had access to realtime while Marta was marooned, then there are consequences, some so radical that they caused us to dismiss the possibility.

"The killer did more than meddle with the length of the group jump; he did not even participate in it. That means the sabotage was not a shallow manipulation of the Korolev system; the killer must have deep penetration of the system."

Wil nodded. *And who could have deeper penetration than the owner of the system?*

"And if that is true, then everything that goes through Yelén's db's—including this conversation—may be known to the enemy. It's conceivable that her own weapons might be turned against us. . . . In your place, I'd be a bit edgy, Wil."

"Even granting Brierson's claims, the rest doesn't necessarily follow. The killer could have left an unlisted auton in realtime. That could be what Marta noticed." But the fire was gone from Yelén's voice. She didn't look up from the pinkish marble of her desk.

Wil said softly, "You don't really believe that, do you?"

". . . No. In forty years, Marta could have outsmarted one of those, could have left clues that even *I* would recognize." She looked up at him. "Come on, Inspector. Get it over with. 'If the murderer could get into realtime, then why did she let Marta survive there?' That's the next rhetorical question, isn't it? And the obvious answer—'It's just the sort of irrational thing a jealous lover might do.' So. I admit to being a jealous type. And I surely loved Marta. But no matter what either of you believes, I did not maroon her."

She was on the far side of anger. It was not quite the reaction Wil had expected. It really affected Yelén that her two closest colleagues—"friends" was still too strong a word—might think she had killed Marta. Given her general insensitivity to the perceptions of others, he doubted her performance was an act. Finally he said, "I'm not accusing you, Yelén. . . . You're capable of violence, but you have honor. I trust you." That last was a necessary exaggeration. "I would like some trust in return. Believe me when I say that Marta knew, that she left clues that you would not notice. Hell, she probably did it to protect you. The moment you got suspicious, the murderer would also be alerted. Instead, Marta tried to talk to me. I'm totally disconnected from your system, an inconsequential low-tech. I've had a week to think on the problem, to figure how to get this news to you with minimum risk of an ambush."

"Yet, for all the clues, you don't really know who the killer is."

Wil smiled. "That's right, Della. If I did, it would have been the first thing I said."

"You would have been safer to keep quiet, then, till you had her whole message figured out."

He shook his head. "Unfortunately, Marta could never risk putting solid information in her diary. There's nothing in any of the four cairns that will tell us the killer's name."

"So you've told us this just to raise our blood pressure? If she could communicate all you say, she sure as hell would tell us the enemy's name." Yelén was clearly recovering.

"She did, but not in any of the four cairns. She knew those would be 'inspected' before you ever saw them; only the subtlest clues would escape detection. What I've discovered is that there's a *fifth* cairn that no one, not even the murderer, knew about. That's where she wrote the clear truth."

"Even if you're right, that's fifty thousand years ago now. Whatever she left would be completely destroyed."

Wil put on his most sober expression. "I know that, Yelén, and Marta must have known it could be that long, too. I think she took that into account."

"So you know where it is, Wil?"

"Yes. At least to within a few kilometers. I don't want to say exactly where; I assume we have a silent partner in this conversation."

Della shrugged. "It's conceivable the enemy doesn't have direct bugs. He may have access only when certain tasks are executing."

"In any case, I suggest you keep a close watch on the airspace above all the places Marta visited. The murderer may have some guesses of his own now. We don't want to be scooped."

There was silence as Della and Yelén retreated into their systems. Then: "Okay, Brierson. We're set. We have heavy monitoring of the south shore, the pass Marta used through the Alps, and the whole area around Peacer Lake. I've given Della observer status on my system. She'll be running critical subsystems in parallel. If anybody starts playing games there, she should notice.

"Now. The important thing. Della is bringing in fighters from the Lagrange zones. I have a fleet I've been keeping in stasis; its next lookabout is in three hours. All together that should be enough to face down any opposition when we go treasure hunting. All you have to do is lie low for another three hours. Then tell us the cairn's location and we'll—"

Wil held up a hand. "Yes. Get your guns. But I'm going along."

"What? Okay, okay. You can come along."

"And I don't want to leave till tomorrow morning. I need a few more hours with the diary; some final things to check out."

Yelén opened her mouth, but no sound came. Della was more articulate. "Wil. Surely *you* understand the situation. We're bringing everything out to protect you. We'll be burning a normal year's worth of consumables every hour we stay on station around you. We can't do that for long; yet every minute you keep this secret, you stay at the top of someone's hit list—and we lose what little surprise we might have had. You've *got* to hustle."

"There are things I have to figure first. Tomorrow morning. It's the fastest I can make it. I'm sorry, Della."

Yelén muttered an obscenity and cut her connection. Even Della seemed startled by the abruptness of her departure. She looked back at Wil. "She's still cooperating, but she's mad as hell. . . . Okay. So we wait till tomorrow. But believe me, Wil. An active defense is expensive. Yelén and I are willing to spend most of what we have to get the killer, but waiting till tomorrow cuts the protection per unit time. . . . It would help if you could say how long things might drag out beyond that."

He pretended to think on the question. "We'll have the secret diary by tomorrow afternoon. If things don't blow up by then, I doubt they ever will."

"I'll be going, then." She paused. "You know, Wil, once upon a time I was a government cop. I think I was pretty good at power games. So. Advice from an old pro: Don't get in over your head."

Brierson summoned his most confident, professional look. "Everything will work out, Della."

After Della signed off, Wil went into the kitchen. He started to mix himself a drink, realized he had no business drinking just now, and scarfed some cake instead. *Under all this pressure, it's just one bad habit or another,* he told himself. He wandered back into the living room and looked out. In his era, letting a protected witness parade in front of a window would be insanity. It didn't matter much here, with the weapons and counter-measures the high-techs had.

The afternoon was clear, dry. He could hear dry rustling in the trees. Only a short stretch of road was visible. All the greenery didn't leave much to see. The only nice views were from the second floor. Still, he was getting fond of the place. It was a bit like the lower-class digs he and Virginia had started in.

He leaned out the window, looked straight up. The two autons were floating lower than usual. Farther up, almost lost in the haze, was something *big.* He tried to imagine the forces that must be piled up in the first few hundred klicks above him. He knew the firepower Della and Yelén admitted to. It far exceeded the combined might of all the nations in history; it was probably greater than that of any police service up to the mid-twenty-second. All that force was poised for the protection of one house, one man . . . more precisely, the information in one man's head. All things considered, it wasn't something he took much comfort in.

Wil reviewed the scenarios once more; what could happen in the next twenty-four hours? It would all be over by then, most likely. He was barely conscious of pacing into the kitchen, through the pantry, the laundry, the guest room, and back into the living room. He looked out the window, then repeated the traversal in reverse order. It was a habit that had not been popular with Virginia and the kids: When he was really into a case, he would wander all through the house, cogitating.

Ninety kilos of semiconscious cop lumbering down halls and through doorways was a definite safety hazard. They had threatened to hang a cowbell around his neck.

Something brought Brierson out of the depths. He looked around the laundry, trying to identify the strangeness. Then he realized: He'd been humming, and there was a silly grin on his face. He was back in his element. This was the biggest, most dangerous case of his life. But it was a *case*. And he finally had a handle on it. For the first time since he had been shanghaied, the doubts and dangers were ones he could deal with professionally. His smile widened. Back in the living room, he grabbed his data set and sat down. Just in case they were listening, he should pretend to do some research.

TWENTY-TWO

Yelén was back late that evening. "Kim Tioulang is dead."

Wil's head snapped up. *Is* this *how it begins?* "When? How?"

"Less than ten minutes ago. Three bullets in the head. . . . I'm sending you the details."

"Any evidence who—"

She grimaced, but by now she accepted that what she sent was not immediately part of his memory. "Nothing definite. My security at North Shore has been thin since we switched things around this afternoon. He sneaked out of the Peacer base; not even his own people noticed. It looks like he was trying to board a trans-sea shuttle." The only place that would take him was Town Korolev. "There are no witnesses. In fact, I suspect that no one was on the ground where he was shot. The slugs were dumb exploders, New Mexico five-millimeters." Normally those were pistol-fired, with a max accurate range of thirty meters; who did the killer think he was fooling? "The coincidence is too much to ignore, Brierson. You're right; the enemy must have bugs in my system."

"Yeah." For a second he wasn't listening. He was remembering the North Shore picnic, the withered man that had been Kim Tioulang. He was as tough as anyone Wil had ever met, but his wistfulness about the future had seemed real. The most ancient man in the world . . . and now he was dead. Why? What had he been trying to tell them? He looked up at Yelén. "Since this afternoon, have you noticed anything special with the Peacers? Any evidence of high-tech interference?"

"No. As I said, I can't watch as closely as before. I talked to Phil Genet about it. He hasn't noticed anything with the Peacers, but he says NM radio traffic has changed during the last few hours. I'm looking into that." She paused. For the first time, he saw fear in her face. "These next few hours we could lose it all, Wil. Everything Marta ever hoped for."

"Yes. Or we could nail the enemy cold, and *save* her plan. . . . How are things set for tomorrow?"

His question brought back the normal Yelén. "This delay cost us the advantage of surprise, but it also means we're better prepared. Della has an incredible amount of equipment. I knew her expedition to the Dark Companion made money, but I never imagined she could afford all this. Almost all of it will be in position by tomorrow. She'll land by your place at sunup. It's all your show then."

"You're not coming?"

"No. In fact, I'm out of your inner-security zone. My equipment will handle peripheral issues, but . . . Della and I talked it over. If I—my system—is deeply perverted, the enemy could turn it on you."

"Hmm." He'd been counting on the dual protection; if he'd guessed wrong about one of them, the other would still be there. But if Yelén herself thought she might lose control . . . "Okay. Della seemed in pretty good form this afternoon."

"Yes. I have a theory that under stress the appropriate personality comes to the surface. She's driftiest after she's been by herself for a while. I'm talking to her right now, and she seems okay. With any luck, she'll still be wearing her cop personality tomorrow."

After Yelén signed off, Wil looked at the stuff she was sending over. It grew much faster than he could read it, and there were new developments all the time. Genet was right about the NMs. They were using a new encryption scheme, one that Yelén couldn't break. That in itself was more of an anachronism than polka-dot paint or antigrav volleyballs. Under other circumstances, she would have raided them for it, and diplomacy be damned. . . . Now she was stretched so thin that all she could do was watch.

Tioulang's murder. The high-tech manipulation of Fraley. There was some fundamental aspect of the killer's motivation that Wil didn't understand. If he wanted to destroy the colony, he could have done that long ago. So Wil had concluded that the enemy wanted to rule. Now he wondered. Was the low-techs' survival simply a bargaining chip to the killer?

It was a long night.

Brierson was standing by his window when Della's flier came down. It was still twilight at ground level, but he could see sunlight on the treetops. He grabbed his data set and walked out of the house. His step was brisk, adrenaline-fueled.

"Wait, Wil!" The Dasguptas were on their front porch. He stopped, and they ran down the street toward him. He hoped his guardians weren't trigger-happy.

"Did you know?" Rohan began, and his brother continued. "The Peacer boss was murdered last night. It looks like the NMs did it."

"Where did you hear?" He couldn't imagine Yelén spreading the news.

"The Peacer news service. Is it true, Wil?"

Brierson nodded. "We don't know who did it, though."

"Damn!" Dilip was as upset as Wil had ever seen him. "After all the talk about peaceful competition, I thought the NMs and Peacers had changed their ways. If they start shooting, the rest of us are . . . Look, Wil, back in civilization this couldn't happen. They'd have every police service in Asia down on them. Can—can we count on Yelén to keep these guys out of our way?"

Wil knew that Yelén would die before she'd let the NMs and Peacers fight. But today, dying might not be enough. The Dasguptas saw the tip of a game that extended beyond their knowing—and Wil's. He looked at the brothers, saw unmerited trust in their faces. What could he do? . . . Maybe the truth would help. "We think this is tied up with Marta's murder, Dilip." He jerked a thumb at Della's flier. "That's what I'm checking out now. If there's shooting, I'll bet you see more than low-techs involved. Look. I'll get Yelén to lower her suppressor field; you could bobble up for the next couple of days."

"Our equipment, too."

"Right. In any case, get people spread out and under cover." There was nothing more he could say, and the brothers seemed to know it.

"Okay, Wil," Rohan said quietly. "Luck to us all."

Della's flier was bigger than usual, and there were five pods strapped around its midsection.

But the crew area didn't have the feel of a combat vehicle. It wasn't the lack of control and display panels. When Wil left civilization, those were vanishing items. Even the older models had provided command helmets that allowed the pilot to see the outside world in terms of what was important to the mission. The newer ones didn't need the helmets; the windows themselves were holo panels on artificial reality. But there were no command helmets in Della's flier, and the windows showed the same version of reality that clear glass would. The floor was carpeted. Unwindowed sections of the wall were decorated with Della's strange watercolors.

As he climbed aboard, Wil gestured at the strap-on pods. "Extra guns?"

"No. Those are defensive. There's a tonne of matter/antimatter in each one."

"Ugh." He sat down and strapped in. Defensive—like a flak jacket made of plastique?

Lu pulled more than two g's getting them off the street; no simple elevator rides today. Half a minute passed, and she cut the drive. Up and up and up they fell, Wil's stomach protesting all the way. They topped out around ten thousand meters, where she resumed one g.

It was a beautiful day. The low sun angle put the forested highlands into jagged relief. He couldn't see much of Town Korolev, but Yelén's castle was a shadowed pattern of gold and green. Northwards, clouds hid the lowlands and the sea. To the south, the mountains rose gray above the timberline to snow-topped peaks. The Indonesian Alps were the Rockies writ large.

Lu's eyes were open but unfocused. "Just want to have some maneuvering room." Then she looked at Wil and smiled. "Where to, boss?"

"Della, did you hear what I told the Dasguptas? Yelén should turn off her suppressors. Maybe a few low-techs will bobble out of this era, but she can't just leave everyone exposed."

"Wil, haven't you been reading your mail?"

"Unh, most of it." All night long it had been coming in, faster than he could keep up. He'd read all the red-tag stuff, until falling asleep an hour before dawn.

"We don't know the reason, but it's clear now the enemy may try to kill lots of low-techs. For the last sixty minutes, Yelén's been trying to remove bobble suppression from Australasia. She can't do it."

"Why not? It's her own equipment!" Wil felt stupid the moment he spoke.

"Yes. You could scarcely ask for better proof that her system is perverted, could you?" Her smile widened.

"If she can't turn them off, can you just blow them up?"

"We may decide to try that. But we don't know exactly how her defenses might respond. Besides, the enemy may have his own suppressor system ready to come on the moment Yelén's drops out."

"So no one can bobble up."

"It's a large-volume, low-intensity field, good enough to suppress any low-tech generators. But my bobblers can still self-enclose; my best still have some range."

For a moment, the purpose of this trip was forgotten. There must be some way to protect low-techs. Evacuate them from the suppression zone? That maneuver might put them in even more danger. Fly in high-power bobblers? He abruptly realized that the high-techs must be giving much deeper thought than he could to the problem. The problem he had precipitated. *Face it.* The only way he could contribute now was by succeeding with his mission: to identify the killer. Della's original question was the one he should be answering. *Where to?* "Are we certified free of eavesdroppers?" Lu nodded. "Okay. We start from Peacer Lake."

The flier boosted across the Inland Sea. But Della was not satisfied with the directions. "You don't know the cairn's coordinates?"

"I know what I'm looking for. We'll follow a search pattern."

"But searches could be done faster from orbit."

"Surely there are some sensors that need low, slow platforms?"

"Yes, but—"

"And surely we'd want to be with such sensors to pick up the find immediately?"

"Ah!" She was smiling again, and did not ask him to point out the equipment he referred to.

They flew in silence for several minutes. Wil tried to see evidence of their escort. There was a flier ahead of them. To the right and left of their path, he saw two more. There was an occasional glint from beyond these, as from objects flying distant formation. It wasn't very impressive—until he wondered how far the formation extended.

"Really, Wil. No one else can listen; I'm not even recording. You can 'fess up."

Brierson looked at her questioningly, and Della continued. "It's obvious you saw something in the diary that—for all our deep analysis, and all Yelén's years with Marta—we did not. She was trying to tell us that the murderer was stalking her, and that the Korolev system had been deeply penetrated. . . . But this story about a fifth cairn"—she raised an eyebrow, her expression mischievous—"is ridiculous."

Wil pretended great interest in the ground. "Why 'ridiculous'?"

"In the first place, it's unlikely the killer lived every second of those forty years in realtime. But if he was so interested that Marta felt his presence, and felt the need to write with hidden meanings—then I think it's reasonable he had sensors watching *all* the time. How could Marta sneak away from her camp, build another cairn, and get back—all without tipping him off?

"In the second place, even if she succeeded in fooling the killer, we're still talking about something that happened *fifty thousand* years ago. Do you have any conception how long that is? All recorded history wasn't much over six thousand years. And most of that's been lost. Only an incredible accident could preserve a written record across such a span."

"Yes, Yelén raised the same objection. But—"

"Right. You told her Marta had taken all that into account. I'll give you this, Wil. When you feel like it, you're one of the most convincing people I've ever seen—and I've seen some experts. . . . By the way, I backed you on this. I think Yelén is convinced; she believes Marta was all but superhuman, anyway. I wouldn't be surprised if the killer does, too.

"My point is, *I'm* on to you," Lu continued. Wil put on an expression of polite surprise. "You saw something in the diary that we didn't. But you don't know much more than what you've said—and you have no clues. Hence this wild-goose chase." She waved at the lands beyond the flier. "You hope you've convinced the killer that you will soon know his identity. You've posted us as targets, to flush him out." It was a prospect she appeared to enjoy.

And her theory was uncomfortably close to the truth. He had tried to create a situation where the enemy would be forced to attack him. What he couldn't understand was the activity around the low-techs. How could hurting *them* hide the killer?

Wil shrugged; he hoped that none of this turmoil showed on his face.

Della watched him for a second, her head cocked to one side. "No response? So *I'm* still on the suspect list. If you die and I survive, then the others will be on to me—and together, they outgun me. You're trickier than I thought; maybe gutsier, too."

* * *

The morning passed, slow and tense. Della paid no attention to the view. She was rational enough—and perhaps even brighter than usual. But there was a cockiness in her manner, as if she held reality at a distance, thought it all an immensely interesting game. She was full of theories. It was no surprise that her number one suspect was Juan Chanson. "I know he fired on me. Juan is playing the role of racial protector. He reminds me of the centaur. I think our killer must be like that centaur, Wil. The creature was so trapped by his notion of racial duty that he killed the last survivors. We're seeing the same thing here: murders and preparations for more murders."

Wil's "search pattern" took them slowly outwards from Peacer Lake. Fifty thousand years before, this had been vitrified wasteland. The jacaranda forests had won it back thousands of years since. Though this forest had not existed in Marta's time, it was much like the ones she had traveled. Wil was seeing the heaven side of the world Marta had described. To the northeast, a grayish band stretched along the border of the forest domain. That must be the kudzu web, killing the jungle and preventing invasion. On the jac side, there were occasional silver splotches, web attacks on non-jacs that had sprouted beyond the barrier. The jacarandas themselves were an endless green sea, tinged with a bluish foam of flowers. He knew there were vast webs there, too, but they were *below* the leaf canopy, where the spiders' domesticated caterpillars could take advantage of the leaves without shading them out.

Here and there bright puffs of cloud floated above it all, trailing shadow.

Marta had walked many kilometers before finding a display web. From this altitude, they could see several at once. None was less than thirty meters across. They shimmered in the treetop breezes, their colors shifting between red and electric blue. Somewhere down there was a fossil streambed, the remains of a small river Marta had followed on one of her last expeditions out of Peacer Lake. He remembered what the land looked like then: kilometers of grayness, the water and wind still working to break through the glassy surface. She would have carried whatever food she needed.

Ahead, the forest was splattered with random patches of kudzu. Display webs were scattered everywhere. There was more blue and red and silver than green.

Della supplied an explanation. "Marta's plantings spread outward from her signal line. This is where the new forest meets the old; sort of a jac civil war."

Wil smiled at the metaphor. Apparently the two forests and their spiders were different enough to excite the kudzu reflex. He wondered if the display webs were like animal displays at territory boundaries. The colorful jumble passed slowly below, and they were over normal jacs again.

"We're way beyond Marta's furthest trip in this direction, Wil. You really think anyone's going to believe we're doing a serious search here?"

He pretended to ignore the question. "Follow this line another hundred kilometers, then break and head toward the lake where she got the fishers."

Thirty minutes later they were floating above a patch of brownish green water, more a swamp than a lake. The jacs grew right to the edge; it looked like the kudzu web stretched into the water. Fifty thousand years ago there had been ordinary woodland here.

"What's our defense situation, Della?"

"Cool, cool. Except for the suppressor thing, no enemy action. The NMs and Peacers have buttoned up, but they've stopped shouting accusations. We've discussed the threat with all the high-techs. They've agreed to keep out of the air for the time being, and to isolate their forces. If anyone strikes, we'll know his identity. The bottom line, Wil: I don't think the enemy has been bluffed."

There was no help for it, then. "Exactly which way is north, Della?" Damn this flier: no command helmet, no holos. He felt like the inmate of a rubber room.

Suddenly a red arrow labeled NORTH hovered over the forest. It looked solid, kilometers long; so the windows were holo displays after all. "Okay. Back off eastwards from lake.

Come down to a thousand meters." They slid sideways, nearly in free fall. Most of the lake was still visible. "Give me a ring around the original lake site. Mark it off in degrees." He studied the lake and the blue circle that now surrounded it. "I want to get into the forest about ten klicks from the lake on a bearing of thirty degrees from north." They were close enough to the forest canopy that he could see leaves and flowers rushing by. The cover looked deep and dense. "Are you going to have any problem finding a place to get through?"

"No problem at all." Their forward motion ceased. They were just above the treetops. Abruptly, the flier smashed straight down. For an instant, negative g's hung Wil on his harness. Sounds of destruction were sharp around them.

And then they were through. The spaces beneath were lit by the sunlight that followed them through the hole they had punched in the canopy. Beyond that light, all was dark and greenish. Junk was drifting down all around them. Most of it was insubstantial. The underweb carried centuries of twigs and insect remains, flotsam that had not yet percolated to the surface. It was coming down all at once now, swinging back and forth through the light. Some debris—branches, clusters of flowers—was still in the air, supported by fragments of the web. More than anything else, Wil felt as if they had suddenly plunged into deep water. The flier drifted out of the light. His eyes slowly adapted to the dimness.

"We're there, Wil. Now what?"

"How well can the others monitor us down here?"

"It's complicated. Depends on what we do."

"Okay. I think the cairn is southwest of us, near the bearing we took from the lake. After all this time, there won't be any surface evidence, but I'm hoping you can detect the rocks." *And if you can't, I'll have to think of something else.*

"That should be easy." The flier glided around a tree. They were less than a meter up, moving at barely more than a walking pace. They drifted back and forth across the bearing; the sunlight from the entrance hole was lost behind them. Della's flier was five meters tall, and nearly that wide, yet they had no trouble negotiating the search path. He looked out the windows in wonder. Much of the ground was absolutely smooth, a gray-green down. That was the top of fifty thousand years' accumulation of spider dung, of leaf and chitin fragments. The abyssal ooze of the jac forest.

The forest floor was as Marta described, but much gloomier. He wondered if she had really thought it beautiful, or said so to disguise a melancholy like he felt here.

"I—I've got something, Wil!" There was real surprise on Della's face. "Strong echoes, about thirty meters ahead." As she spoke, the flier sprinted forward, dodging intermediate trees. "Most of the rocks are scattered, but there is a central cluster. It—it could really be a cairn. My Lord, Wil, how could you know?"

Their flier settled on the forest floor, next to the secret that had waited fifty thousand years for them.

TWENTY-THREE

The door slid back. Wil stuck his head into the forest air. And jerked it back even more quickly. *Phew:* take mildew and add a flavoring of shit. He took another breath and tried not to gag. Perhaps it was the abrupt transition that made it seem so awful; the flier's air was full of alpine morning.

They stepped onto the forest floor. Gray-green humus lapped around their ankles. He was careful not to kick it up. There was enough junk in the air already.

Della walked a large circle tangent to their landing point. "I've mapped all the rocks. They're not as big as Marta generally used, and not as well shaped. But backtracking their trajectories . . ." She was quiet for second. ". . . I see they were piled in a pyramid at one time. The core is intact, and I think there's something—not rocks or forest dirt—inside. What do you want to do?"

"How long would a careful dig take—say as good as a twenty-first-century archeologist could do?"

"Two or three hours."

Now that they really had something, they had to protect it —and get themselves off ground zero at the same time. "We could bobble the whole thing," he said.

"That would be awkward to haul around if shooting starts.

Look, Marta never left anything of importance outside the core. That's less than a meter across in this case. We could bobble that and be out of here in just a few minutes."

Wil nodded agreement, and Della continued with scarcely a pause. "Okay, it's done. Now stand back a couple of meters."

Dozens of reflections of Wil and Della suddenly looked up from the forest floor; the ground between them was covered by close-packed bobbles.

She walked back, around the field of mirrors. "Bobbles are hard to miss against the neutrino sky; if the enemy has decent equipment, he noticed this." Sonic booms came from beyond the treetops. "Don't worry. That's friendly."

The new arrivals slipped through the hole Della had made in the canopy. They consisted of one auton and a cloud of robots. The robots settled on the bobbles, rooting and pushing. The top layer came off easily, revealing more bobbles beneath. These were pushed aside to get at still deeper layers. On a small scale, Lu was using the standard open-pit mining technique. In minutes, they were looking into a dark, slumping hole. The bobbles were scattered on all sides, glowing copies of the forest canopy above.

One by one, the robots picked them up and flew away.

"Which one is . . . ?"

"You can't tell, can you? I hope the enemy is similarly mystified. We've supplied him with seventy red herrings." He noticed that not all the bobbles were flown directly out. One had been transferred to the auton, and one to Della's flier.

Della climbed aboard the flier, Wil close behind. "If our friend doesn't start shooting in the next few minutes, he never will. I'm taking all the bobbles to my home. That's a million kilometers out now. From there we can see in all directions, shoot in all directions; no one can get us there." She smashed straight through the forest's roof, kept rising at multiple g's.

Wil sank deep into the acceleration couch. All he could see was sky. He squinted at the sunlight and gasped, "He may not attack at all. He may still think we're bluffing."

She chuckled. "Don't you wish." The sky tilted, and he saw green horizon. "Twenty thousand meters. I'm going to nuke out."

Free fall. The sky was black, except at the blue horizon. They were at least one hundred kilometers up. It was like a video cut: One instant they had been at aircraft altitudes, the next they were in space. Something bright and sunlike glowed beneath them—the detonation that had boosted them out of the atmosphere. He wondered fleetingly why she hadn't nuked out from ground level. A technical reason? Or sentiment?

The sky jerked again, the horizon acquiring a distinct curve. "Hm. I have a low-tech on the net, Wil. She wants to talk to you."

Who? "Hold off on the next nuke. Let me talk to her."

Part of one window went flat. He was looking at someone wearing NM fatigues and a display helmet. The space around the figure was crammed with twenty-first-century communications gear.

"Wil!" The speaker cleared the face panel on her helmet. It was Gail Parker. "Thank God! I've been trying to break out for almost an hour. Look. Fraley has gone nuts. We're going to attack the Peacers. He says they'll wipe us if we don't. He says there's no way the high-techs can prevent it. Is that *true*? What's going on?"

Brierson sat in horrified silence. What was the killer's motive, that he would contrive such a war? "Part of it *is* true, Gail. It looks like someone's trying to wipe the entire colony. This war talk must be part of it. Is there anything you can do to—"

"*Me?*" She glanced over her shoulder, then continued in a lower voice. "God damn it, Wil, I'm at the center of our C and C. Sure. I could sabotage our entire defense system. But if the other side really does attack, then I've murdered my own people!"

"None of us will make it otherwise, Gail. I'll try to talk sense to the Peacers. Do . . . do what you can." *What would I do in her place?* His mind shied away from Gail's choices.

Parker nodded. "I—" The picture smeared into an abstract pattern of colors. A screeching noise rose past audibility.

"Signal jammed," said Lu.

"Della? Can you get through to the Peacers?"

Lu shrugged. "It doesn't matter. Why do you think Parker

215

called just then? She thinks she finally broke out of NM security. In fact, the enemy has taken over their system. Letting her through is part of a distraction."

"Distraction?"

"One we can't ignore; he's going to start 'em killing each other. I see ballistic traffic going both ways across the Inland Sea. . . . Someone's blocking my wideband link to Yelén."

A section of window suddenly showed Yelén's office. Korolev was standing. "Both sides are shooting. I've lost several autons. *Both* sides have high-tech backing, Della." Disbelief was mixed with rage and fear. Tears glinted on her face. "You'll have to do without my help for now; I'm going to divert my forces. I can't let my peo— I can't let these people die."

"It's okay, Yelén. But get the others to help you. You can't trust your system alone."

Korolev sat down shakily. "Right. They've agreed to bring their forces up. I'm starting my diversion now." There was a moment of silence. Yelén stared blankly, swapped out. The silence stretched . . . and Yelén's eyes slowly widened. In horror. "Oh, my God, no!" Her image vanished, and he was looking into empty sky.

Wil flinched, the motion floating him against his restraint harness. "More jamming?"

"No. She just stopped transmitting." There was a faint smile on Della's face. "I guessed this might happen. To shift her forces, she had to run control routines that the enemy could not start—but which he had perverted. He's finally shown himself in a big way: Yelén's forces are coming out for us. What she has in far space is moving to block our exit.

"Another minute and we'll know who we've been fighting all this time. Yelén can't take me alone. The killer is going to have to stand up with his own equipment. . . ." Her smile broadened. "You're going to see some real shooting, Wil."

"I can hardly wait." He tucked his data set in the side of his acc chair.

"Oh, don't expect too much; with the naked eye, this won't be very spectacular." And she was humming!

Please God that this insanity does not affect her performance.

216

The horizon jerked once again. There was no acceleration, no sound. It was like botched special effects from an old-time movie. But now they were better than a thousand kilometers up, the Inland Sea a cloud-dotted puddle. And the Earth was visibly falling away from them; they were moving at dozens of klicks per second.

Surely—even without Yelén—the others could protect the low-techs from a few ballistic missiles? Malicious fate gave him quick answer: Three bright sparks glowed on the southern coast, a third of the way from West End to the Eastern Straits. Wil groaned.

"Those were high air bursts, at Town Korolev," said Della. "If the Dasguptas spread your warning, there may not be too many casualties." There was puzzlement in her voice.

"But where are Chanson and Genet and Blumenthal? Surely—"

"Surely they could prevent this?" Della finished the question. She swapped out a moment. Then: *"Oh . . . wow!"* Her words were almost a sigh, filled with endless wonder and surprise. She was silent a moment more. Then her eyes focused on Wil. "All this time, we were expecting to flush the killer into the open. Right? Well . . . we have a little problem. *All* the high-tech forces have turned on us."

Like a gruesome short story Wil once read: Detective locks self in room with suspects. Detective applies definitive test to suspects. All suspects guilty. . . . Unmarked grave for detective. Happy ending for suspects.

"We are now outgunned, Wil. This is going to be very interesting." The smile was almost gone from her face, replaced by a look of intense concentration. Sudden light and shadow flickered across the cabin. Wil looked up, saw a pattern of point lights glowing, fading in the blackness. "They have a lot of stuff at the Lagrange zones. They're bringing it down on us—while their ground-based stuff comes up. No way we can get to my quarters just now."

And they were back at low altitude, the horizon spread flat around them, the Indonesian Alps drifting by below. His restraint harness stiffened and the flier surged forward at multiple g's, then slammed to the side. Wil's consciousness faded into red dimness. Somewhere he heard Della say, ". . . lose realtime every time I nuke out. Can't afford it now." They were in free fall for almost a second, then more crushing acceleration, then free fall again. Brightness flashed all around them, lighting sea and clouds with extra suns. More acceleration. *Things don't get this exciting when they're going right.*

The horizon jerked, and acceleration reversed. Jerk, jerk. Now each translation of the outside world was accompanied by changed acceleration, the agrav being used in concert with the nukes. Della's words came in broken gasps. "Bastards." Around them the horizon rose, kilometers per second. Acceleration was heavy, spacewards. "They're past my defenders." Jerk. They were lower, hurtling parallel to the vast wall that was the Earth. "They're zeroed on me." Jerk. "Seven direct hits in—" Jerk. Jerk.

Jerk. Free fall again. This last had taken them high over the Pacific. All was blue and ocean clouds below. "We've got about a minute's breather. I regrouped my low forces and nuked into the middle of them. The enemy's breaking through right now." To the west, point suns flashed brighter and brighter. In the sky below, weirdness: five contrails, a dozen. The clouds grew like quick crystal, around threads of fire. Directed energy weapons? "We're the king piece; they're trying to force us out of this era."

Somewhere, Wil found his voice. Even more, it sounded calm. "No way, Della."

"Yeah . . . I didn't come this far to fade." Pause. "Okay. There's another way to protect the king piece. A bit risky, but—"

Wil's chair suddenly came alive. The sides swung inward, bringing his arms across his middle. The footrest moved up, forcing his knees to near chest level. At the same time, the entire assembly rotated sideways, to face a similarly trussed Della Lu. The contraption tightened painfully, squeezing the two of them into a round bundle. And then—

TWENTY-FOUR

There was an instant of falling. The acceleration spiked, then stabilized at one g.

The chair relaxed its grip.

The sunlight was gone. The air was hot, dry. *They were no longer in the flier!* The "one-g field" was the Earth's. They were sitting on the ground.

Della was already on her feet, dismantling part of her chair. "Nice sunset, huh?" She nodded toward the horizon.

Sunset or sunrise. He had no sense of direction, but the heat in the air made him guess they were at the end of a day. The sun was squashed and reddish, its light coming sickly across a level plain. He suddenly felt sick himself. Was that disk reddened by its closeness to the horizon, or was the sun *itself* redder? "Della, just—just how long did we jump?"

She looked up from her rummaging. "About forty-five minutes. If we can live another five, we may be okay." She pulled a meter-long pole from the back of her chair, clipped a strap to it, and slung it over her shoulder. He noticed shiny metal where the bobble had cut the chairs away from Della's flier. That bobble had been scarcely more than a meter wide. No wonder he had been cramped. "We need to get out of sight. Help me drag this stuff over there." She pointed at a knoblike hill a hundred meters off.

They were standing in a shallow crater of dirt and freshly cracked rock. Wil took a chair in each hand and pulled; he backed quickly out of the crater, onto grass. Della motioned him to stop. She grabbed one of the chairs and tipped it over. "Drag it on the smooth side. I don't want them to see a trail." She leaned back against the load, dragging it quickly away across the short grass. Wil followed, pulling his with a one-handed grasp.

"When you've got a minute, I'd like to know what we're up to."

"Sure. Soon as we get these under cover." She turned, took the load on her shoulders, and all but trotted toward the stony hill. It took several minutes to reach it; the hill was larger and farther away than he thought. It rose over the grass and scrub like some ominous guardian. Except for the birds that rattled out as they approached, it seemed lifeless.

The ground around it was bare, grooved. The rock bulged over its base, leaving shallow caves along the perimeter. There was a smell of death. He saw bones in the shadows. Della saw them too. She slid her chair in over the bones and waved for Wil to do the same. "I don't like this, but we've got other hunters to worry about first." Once the equipment was hidden, she scrambled up the rock face to a small cave about four meters up. Wil followed, more awkwardly.

He looked around before sitting beside her. The indentation barely qualified as a cave. Nothing would surprise them from behind, though something had used it for dining; there were more well-gnawed bones. The cave was hidden from most of the sky, yet they had a good view of the ground, almost to the base of the rock.

He sat down, impatient for explanations—and suddenly was struck by the silence. All day the tension had grown, reaching a crescendo of violence these last few minutes. Now every sign of that struggle was gone. One hundred meters away, birds flocked around a stunted tree, their cries and flapping wings clear and tiny in the larger silence. Only a sliver of the sun's disk still glowed at the horizon. By that light, the prairie was reddish gold, broken here and there by the dark scrub. The breeze was a slow thing, still warm from the day. It brought perfume and putrescence, and left the sweat dry on his face.

He looked at Della Lu. Dark hair had fallen across her cheek. She didn't seem to notice. "Della?" he said quietly. "Did we lose?"

"Unh?" She looked at him, awareness coming back to her eyes. "Not yet. Maybe not at all if this works. . . . They were concentrating everything on you and me. The only way we could stay in this era and still survive was to disappear. I brought my whole inner guard toward our flier. We exploded almost all our nukes at the same time, and vanished as thousands of meter-sized bobbles. One of those bobbles contained you and me; seventy of them are from the cairn. They're scattered all over now—Earth surface, Earth orbit, solar orbit. Most of the surface ones were timed to burst minutes after impact."

"So we're lost in the turmoil."

Her smile was a ghost of earlier enthusiasm. "Right. They haven't got us yet: I think we brought it off. Given a few hours they could do a thorough search, but I'm not giving them the time. My midguard has come down, and is giving them plenty of other things to worry about.

"We, here, are totally defenseless, Wil. I don't even have a bobbler. The other side could take us out with a five-millimeter pistol—if only they knew where to do the shooting. I had to destroy my inner guard to get away. What's left is outnumbered two to one. Yet . . . yet I think I can win. Fifty seconds out of every minute, I have tight beam comm with my fleet." She patted the meter-long pole that lay on the ground between them. One end consisted of a ten-centimeter sphere. She had laid the pole so that the ball was at the cave's entrance. Wil looked at it more closely, saw iridescence glow and waver. It was some kind of coherent transmitter. Her own forces knew where they were hidden, and needed to keep only one unit in line of sight for Lu to run the battle.

Della's voice was distant, almost indifferent. "Whoever they are, they know how to pervert systems, but not so much about combat. I've fought through centuries of realtime, with bobblers and suppressors, nukes and lasers. I have programs you just couldn't buy in civilization. Even without me, my system fights smarter than the other side's. . . ." A chuckle. "The high-orbit stuff is dead just now. We're playing 'peek and shoot': 'peek' around the shoulder of the Earth, 'shoot' at anything with its head stuck up. Boys and girls running round and round their home, killing each other. . . . I'm winning, Wil, I really am. But we're burning it all. Poor Yelén. So worried that our systems might not last long enough to reestablish civilization. One afternoon we're destroying all we've accumulated."

"What about the low-techs?" Was there anybody left to fight *for?*

"Their little play-war?" She was silent for fifteen seconds, and when she spoke again seemed even further away. "That ended as soon as it had served the enemy's purpose." Perhaps only Town Korolev had been wiped. Della sat against the rear wall of the cave. Now she leaned her head back and closed her eyes.

Wil studied her face. How different she looked from the creature he had seen on the beach. And when she wasn't talking, there were no weird perspectives, no shifting of personalities. Her face was young and innocent, straight black hair still fallen across her cheek. She might have been asleep, occasional dreams twitching her lips and eyelids. Wil reached to brush the hair back from her face—and stopped. The mind in this body was looking far across space, looking down on Earth from all directions, was commanding one side in the largest battle Wil had ever known. Best to let sleeping generals lie.

He crawled along the side of the cave to the entrance. From here he could see the plains and part of the sky, yet was better hidden than Della.

He looked across the land. If there was any way he could help, it was by protecting Della from local varmints. A few of the birds had returned to the rock. They were the only animal life visible; maybe these bone-littered condos were abandoned property. Surely Della had brought handguns and first-aid gear.

He eyed the smooth shells of the acceleration chairs and wondered if he should ask her about them. But Della was in deep
connect; even during the first attack she had not been concentrating like this. . . . Better to wait till he had a certifiable
emergency. For now he would watch and listen.

Twilight slowly faded; a quarter moon slid down the western
sky. From the track of the sun's setting, he guessed they were
in the Northern Hemisphere, away from the tropics. This must
be Calafia or the savanna that faced that island on the west
coast of North America, Somehow, being oriented made Wil
feel better.

The birds had quieted. There was a buzzing he hoped was
insects. It was getting hard to keep his eyes on the ground.
With the coming of night, the sky show was impossible to
ignore. Aurora stretched from north horizon to south. The pale
curtains were as bright as any he had seen, even from Alaska.
The battle itself danced slowly beyond those curtains. Some of
the lights were close-set sparkles, like a gem visible only when
its facets caught some magic light. The lights brightened and
dimmed, but the cluster as a whole didn't move: that must be
a high-orbit fight, perhaps at a Lagrange zone. For half an hour
at a time, that was the only action visible. Then a fragment of
the near-Earth battle would come above the horizon—the
"peek and shoot" crowd. Those lights cast vivid shadows, each
one starting brilliant white, fading to red over five or ten
seconds.

Though he had no idea who was winning, Wil thought he
could follow some of the action. A near-Earth firefight would
start with ten or twenty detonations across a large part of the
sky. These were followed by more nukes in a smaller and
smaller space, presumably fighting past robots towards a central
auton. Even the laser blasts were visible now, threads of light
coruscating bright or faint depending on how much junk was
in the way. Their paths pointed into the contracting net of
detonations. Sometimes the net shrank to nothing, the enemy
destroyed or in long-term stasis. Other times, there was a bright
flash from the center, or a string of flashes heading outwards.
Escape attempts? In any case, the battle would then cease, or

shift many degrees across the sky. Aurora flared in moon-bright knots on the deserted battlefield.

Even moving hundreds of kilometers per second, it took time for the fighters to cross the sky, time for the nuke blasts to fade through red to auroral memories. It was like fireworks photographed in slow motion.

The land around them was empty but for moving shadows, silent but for the insect buzz and occasional uneasy squawking. Only once did he hear anything caused by the battle. Three threads of directed energy laced across the sky from some fight over the horizon. The shots were very low, actually in the atmosphere. Even as they faded, contrails grew around them. After a minute, Wil heard faint thunder.

An hour passed, then two. Della had not said a word. To him, anyway. Light chased back and forth within the ball of her communications scepter, interference fringes shifting as she resighted the link.

Something started yowling. Wil's eyes swept the plain. Just now his only light was from the aurora: there was no near-Earth firefight going, and the high-orbit action was a dim flickering at the western horizon. . . . Ah, there they were! Gray shapes, a couple of hundred meters out. They were loud for their size —or hunkered close to the ground. The yowling spread, was traded back and forth. Were they fighting? Admiring the light show?

. . . They were getting closer, easier to see. The creatures were almost man-sized but stayed close to the ground. They advanced in stages—trotting forward a few meters, then dropping to the ground, resuming the serenade. The pack stayed spread out, though there were pairs and trios that ran together. It all rang a very unpleasant chord in Wil's memory. He came to his knees and crawled back to Della.

Even before he reached her, she began mumbling. "Don't look out, Wil. I have them worn down . . . but they've guessed we're on the surface. Last hour they've been trying to emp me out, mainly over Asia." She gave something like a chuckle. "Nothing like picking on the wrong continent. But they're shifting now. If I can't stop 'em, there'll be low-altitude nukes strung across North America. Stay down, don't look out."

The yowling was even closer. When bad luck comes, it comes in bunches. Wil took Della by the shoulders, gently shook her. "Are there weapons in the acc chairs?"

Her eyes came open, dazed and wild. "Can't talk! If they emp me—"

Wil scrambled back to the cave entrance. What was she talking about? Nothing but aurora lit the sky. He looked down. She *must* have weapons stored in those chairs. Climbing down would expose him to the sky for a few seconds, but once there he could hide under the overhang and work on the chairs. The nearest of the dogthings was only eighty meters out.

Wil swung onto the rock face, and— Della screamed, a tearing, full-throated shriek of pain. Wil's universe went blinding white, and a wave of heat swept over his back, burning his hands and neck. He vaulted back into the cave, rolled to the rear wall. The only sound was the sudden keening of the dogs.

There was a second flash, a third, fourth, fifth. . . . He was curled around Della now, shielding both their faces from the cave entrance. Each flash seemed less bright; the terrible, silent footsteps marched away from them. But with each flash, Della spasmed against him, her coughs spraying wetness across his shirt.

Finally darkness returned. His scalp tingled, and Della's hair clung to his face when he leaned away from her. A tiny blue spark leaped from his fingers when he touched the wall. Lu was moaning wordlessly; each breath ended in a choked cough. He turned her on her side, made sure she wasn't swallowing her tongue. Her breathing quieted, and the spasms subsided.

"Can you hear me, Della?"

There was a long silence, filled with the mewling of the animals outside. Then her breathing roughened and she mumbled something. Wil brought his ear close to her face. ". . . fooled 'em. They won't come sniffing around here for a while . . . but I'm cut off now . . . comm link wrecked."

Beyond the cave, the whimpering continued, but now there were sounds of movement, too. "We've got local problems, Della. Did you bring handguns?"

She squeezed his hand. "Acc chairs. Opens off my signal . . . or thumbprint . . . sorry."

He eased her head to the ground and moved back to the entrance. The comm scepter didn't glow anymore; the sphere end was too hot to touch. He thought about the gear Della had in her skull and shuddered. It was a miracle she still lived.

Wil looked out. The ground was well lit: the residue of the nuke attack shone overhead, a line of glowing splotches that stretched to the western horizon. Five of the dogthings lay writhing in the near distance. Most of the others had gathered in a close-packed herd. There was much whimpering, much snuffling of the ground, sniffing of the air. The brightness had burned their eyes out. They drifted toward the rock and hunkered beneath its overhang, waiting for the dark time to pass. Most of them would have a long wait.

Nine dogs paced along the edge of the herd, baying querulously. Wil could imagine their meaning: "C'mon, c'mon. What's the matter with you?" Somehow, these nine had been shaded from the sky; they could still see.

Maybe he could still get the guns. Wil picked up the comm scepter. It felt heavy, solid—if nothing else, a morningstar. He slipped over the edge of the rock and slid to ground level.

But not unnoticed: The howling began even before he reached the ground. Three of the sighted ones loped toward him. Wil backed into the overhang that hid the chairs. Without taking his eyes off the approaching dogthings, he reached down and pulled the nearest chair into the open.

Then they were on him, the lead dog diving at his ankles. Wil swung the scepter, and met empty air as the creature twisted away. The next one came in thigh-high—and caught Wil's backswing in the face. Metal crunched into bone. The creature didn't even yelp, just crashed and lay unmoving. The third one backed off, circled. Wil raised the chair on end. It was as seamless as he remembered. There were no buttons, latches. He slammed it hard against the rock face. The rock chipped; the shell was unscratched. He'd have to get it up to the cave for Della to touch.

The chair massed forty kilos, but there were good fingerholds on the rock face. He could do it—if his friends stayed intimidated. He slid the scepter through the restraint harness and pulled the chair onto his shoulder. He was less than two meters up the wall when they charged.

He really should have known better; these were like the near-dogs Marta had met at the West End mines. They were as big as komondors, big enough they needn't take no for an answer. Jaws raked and grabbed at his boots. He fell on his side. This was how they liked it; Wil felt an instant of sheer terror as one of them dived for his gut. He pulled the chair across his body, and the creature veered off. Wil got the next one across its neck with his scepter.

They backed off as Wil scrambled to his feet. Around the side of the rock, the blind ones growled and shouted. The cheerleaders.

So much for the acc chairs. He'd be lucky now to get himself back to the cave.

There was motion at the corner of his eye: He looked up. Unlike dogs, these creatures could climb! The animal picked its way carefully across the rock face, its skinny limbs splayed out in four directions. It was almost to the cave entrance. *Della!* He stepped back from the rock and threw the comm scepter as hard as he could. The ball end caught the creature on its spine, midway between shoulder and haunch. It screamed and fell, the scepter clattering down behind it. The creature lay on its back, its hindquarters limp, the forelegs sweeping in all directions. As Wil darted forward to grab the scepter, one of its clawed fingers raked his arm.

Wil was vaguely aware of shooting pain, of wet spreading down his sleeve. So the cave was not safe. Even if he could get back there, it would be hard to defend; there were several approaches. He risked another glance upwards. There was another cave still higher in the rock. The approach was bordered by sheer walls. He might be able to defend it.

The sighted ones circled inwards. He pushed the chair under the overhang, then ran to the rock face, jumping high. The dog things were close behind—only this time he had a free hand. He swung the scepter past their noses, then crawled upwards another meter. One of the creatures was climbing parallel with him. Its progress was slow, no more agile than a human's. Was it coming after him—*or trying to get to Della?* Wil pretended to ignore it. He paused again to swipe at those who harried him from below. He could hear the climber's claws on stone. It was sidling toward him, fingerhold to fingerhold. Still Wil ignored it. *I'm an easy mark, I'm an easy mark.*

One of the lower dogs bit into his boot. He bent, crushed its skull with the scepter.

He knew the other was less than a meter away now, coming down from above. Without turning his head, Wil jammed the scepter upwards. It hit something soft. For an instant man stared at dogthing, neither enjoying the experience. Its jaws opened in a hissing growl. Its claws were within striking distance of Wil's face, but the scepter was pushing against its chest, forcing it off the cliff. Brierson tucked his head against his arm and pushed harder. For a moment they were motionless, each clinging to the rock. Wil felt his hold giving way. Then something crashed into the dog from above, and its growl became a shriek. Its claws scraped desperately against stone. Resistance abruptly ceased and it fell past him.

But the others were still coming. As he scrambled higher, he glanced up. *Something* was looking down at him from the cave. The face was strangely splotched, but human. Somehow, Della had beaned the dog. He would have shouted thanks, but he was too busy hustling up the wall.

He hoisted himself over the cave's edge, turned, and took a poke at the dog that was coming up right after him. This one was lucky, or Wil was slowing down: It snapped its head around Wil's thrust and grabbed the shaft of the scepter. Then it pulled, dragging Wil half out of the cave, tearing the scepter from his hands. The creature fell down the cliffside, taking several comrades with it.

Wil sat for a moment, gasping. What an incompetent jerk he was. Marta had lasted four decades, alone, in this sort of wilderness. He and Della had been on the ground less than four hours. They had made all sorts of stupid mistakes, now losing their only weapon. More dogthings were gathering below. If he and Della lasted another hour, it would be a miracle.

And they wouldn't last ten minutes if they stayed in this cave. Between gasping breaths, he told Della about the cave further up. She was lying on her stomach, her head turned to one side. The dark on her face was blood. Every few seconds, she coughed, sending a dark spray across the stone. Her voice was soft, the words not completely articulated. "I can't climb anywhere, Wil. Had to belly crawl t'get here."

They were coming up the wall again. For a strange instant, Wil considered the prospect of his own demise. Everyone wonders how he'll check out. In a policeman's case there are obvious scenarios. Never in a million years would he have guessed this one—dying with Della Lu, torn to pieces by creatures that in human history did not exist.

The instant passed and he was moving again, doing what he could. "Then I'll carry you." He took her hands. "Can you grab around my neck?"

"Yeah."

"Okay." He turned, guided her arms over his shoulders. He rose to his knees. She held on, her body stretched along his back. He was fleetingly aware of female curves. She had changed more than her hair since that day at the beach.

He wiped one hand on his pants. The nick on his arm was only oozing, but there was enough blood to make him slippery. "Tell me if you start losing your grip." He crawled out of the cave onto an upward-slanting ledge. Della massed more than the acc chair, but she was doing her best to hang on. He had both hands free.

The ledge ended in a narrow chimney heading straight up. Somewhere behind them, a firefight glowed. It brought no anxiety to his mind, only gratitude. The light showed breaks in the rock. He stepped in one on the left side, then one on the right, practically walking up the slot. He could see the entrance to the upper cave, scarcely two meters ahead.

The dogs had made it to the first cave. He could hear them clicking along the ledge. If this was easy for him, it was easy for them. He looked down, saw three of them racing single file up the slot.

"Hold tight!" He scrambled for the top, had his arms hooked over the entrance the same instant the lead dog got his foot. This time, he felt teeth come straight through the plastic. Wil swung his leg away from the wall, the animal a twisting weight on his foot. Its forelegs clawed at his calf.

Then he had the right angle: The boot slipped from his foot. The dog made a frantic effort to crawl up his leg, its claws raking Wil's flesh. Then it was gone, crashing into its comrades below.

Wil pulled himself into the cave and lay Della on her side. His leg was a multiple agony. He pulled back the pants leg. There was a film of blood spreading from the gashes, but no spurting. He could stop the bleeding if given a moment's peace. He pressed down on the deepest wound, at the same time watching for another assault. It probably didn't matter. His fingernails and teeth weren't in a class with the dogs' claws and fifteen-millimeter canines.

. . . *bad luck comes in bunches.* Wil's nose was finally communicating the stench that hung in the cave. The other one had smelled of death, bones crusted with fragments of desiccated flesh; the smell here was of wet putrefaction. Something big and recently dead lay behind them. And something else *still* lived here: Wil heard metallic clicking.

Wil leaned forward and slipped his remaining boot onto his fist. He continued the motion into a quick turn that brought him up and facing into the cave. The distant firefight lit the cave in ambiguous shades of gray. The dead thing had been a near-dog. It lay like some impressionist holo—parts of the torso shrunken, others bloated. Things moved on the body . . . and in it: Enormous beetles studded the corpse, their round shells showing an occasional metallic highlight. These were the source of the clicking.

Wil scrambled across the litter of old bones. Up close, the smell stuffed the cave with invisible cotton, leaving no room for breathable air. It didn't matter. He had to get a close look at those beetles. He took a shallow breath and brought his head close to one of the largest. Its head was stuck into the corpse, the rear exposed. That armored sphere was almost fifteen centimeters across. Its surface was tessellated by a regular pattern of chitin plates.

He sat back, gasped for air. Was it possible? Marta's beetles were in Asia, fifty thousand years ago. Fifty thousand years. That was enough time for them to get across the land bridge . . . also enough time for them to lose their deadly talent.

He was going to find out: The dogs were yowling again. Louder than before. Not loud enough to cover the sound of claws on stone. Wil thrust his hands into the soft, dead flesh and separated the beetle from its meal. Pain stabbed through a finger as it bit him. He moved his grip back to the armored rear and watched the tiny legs wave, the mandibles click.

He heard the dogs coming along the ledge to the chimney. Still no action from his little friend. Wil tossed the creature from hand to hand, then shook it. A puff of hot gas hissed between his fingers. There was a new smell, acrid and burning.

He took the beetle to the cave entrance and gave it another shake. The hiss got louder, became almost sibilant. The armored shell was almost too hot to touch. He kept the insect excited through another ten seconds. Then he saw a dog at the bottom of the slot. It looked back, then charged up the chimney, three others close behind. Wil gave the beetle one last shake and threw it downwards, into the cliff face just above the lead dog. The explosion was a sharp cracking sound, without a flash. The dog gave a bubbling scream and fell against the others. Only the trailing animal kept its footing—and it retreated from the chimney.

Thank you, Marta! Thank you!

There were two more attacks during the next hour. They were easily beaten back. Wil kept a couple of grenade beetles close to the edge of the cave, at least one near the bursting point. How near the bursting point he didn't know, and in the end he feared the beetles more than the dogs. During the last attack, he blew four dogs off the rock—and got his own ear ripped by a piece of chitinous shrapnel.

After that, they stopped coming. Maybe he had killed all the sighted ones; maybe they had wised up. He could still hear the blind ones, down beneath the overhang. The howling had sounded sinister; now it seemed mournful, frightened.

The space battle had wound down, too. The aurora was as bright as ever, but there were no big firefights. Even isolated flashes were rare. The most spectacular sight was an occasional piece of junk progressing stately across the sky, slowly disintegrating into glowing debris as it fell through the atmosphere.

When the dogs stopped coming, Wil sat beside Della. The emp attack had blown the electronics in her skull. Moving her head caused dizziness and intense pain. Most of the time, she lay silent or softly moaning. Sometimes she was lucid: Though she was totally cut off from her autons, she guessed that her side was winning, that it had slowly ground down the other high-techs. And some of the time she was delirious, or wearing one of her weirder personalities, or both. After a half-hour silence, she coughed into her hand and stared at the new blood splattered on the dried. "I could die now. I could really die." There was wonder in her voice, and fascination. "Nine thousand years I have lived. There aren't many people who could do that." Her eyes focused on Wil. "You couldn't. You're too wrapped up in the people around you. You like them too much."

Wil brushed the hair from her face. When she winced, he moved his hand to her shoulder. "So I'm a pussycat?" he said.

". . . No. A civilized person, who can rise to the occasion. . . . But it takes more than that to live as long as I. You need single-mindedness, the ability to ignore your limitations. Nine thousand years. Even with augmentation, I'm like a flatworm attending the opera. A hundred responses a planarian has? And then what does it do with the rest of the show? When I'm connected, I can remember it all, but where is the original me? . . . I've drifted through everything this mind can be. I've run out of happy endings . . . and sad ones, too." There was a long silence. "I wonder why I'm crying."

"Maybe there's something left to see. What brought you this far?"

"Stubbornness, and . . . I wanted to know . . . what happened. I wanted to see into the Singularity."

He patted her shoulder. "That still may be. Stick around."

She gave a small smile, and her hand fell against him. "Okay. You were always good for me, Mike."

Mike? She *was* delirious.

The lasers and nukes had been gone for hours. The aurora was fading with the morning twilight. Della had not spoken again. The rotting dogthing brought warmth (and by now Wil had no sense of smell whatsoever), but the night was cold, less than ten degrees. Wil had moved her next to the creature and covered her with his jacket and shirt. She no longer coughed or moaned. Her breathing was shallow and rapid. Wil lay beside her, shivering and almost grateful to be covered with dogthing gore, dried blood, and general filth. Behind them, the beetles continued their clicking progress through the corpse.

From the sound of Della's breathing, he doubted she could last many more hours. And after the night, he had a good idea of his own wilderness longevity.

He couldn't really believe that Della's forces had won. If they had, why no rescue? If they hadn't, the enemy might never discover where they were hidden—might never even care. And he would never know who was behind the destruction of the last human settlement.

Twilight brightened towards day. Wil crept to the cave entrance. The aurora was gone, blotted out by the blue of morning. From here he wouldn't see the sunrise, but he knew it hadn't happened yet; there were no shadows. All colors were pastels: the blue in the sky, the pale green of the grassland, the darker green in the trees. For a time nothing moved. Cool, peaceful silence.

On the ground, the dogthings rousted themselves. By twos and threes they walked onto the plain, smelling morning but not able to see it. The sighted ones ran out ahead, then circled back, trying to get the others to hustle. From a safe distance, and in daylight, Wil had to admit they were graceful—even amusing—creatures: Slender and flexible, they could run or belly crawl with equal ease. Their long snouts and narrow eyes gave them a perpetually crafty look. One of the sighted ones glanced up at Will, gave an unconvincing growl. More than anything, they reminded him of the frustrated coyote that had chased a roadrunner bird through two centuries of comic animation.

In the western sky, something glittered, metal in sunlight. Dogthings forgotten, Wil stared up. Nothing but blue now. Fifteen seconds passed. Three black specks hung where he'd seen the light. They didn't move across the sky, but slowly grew. A ripple of sonic booms came across the plain.

The fliers decelerated to a smooth stop a couple of meters above the grass. All three were unmarked, unmanned. Wil considered scrambling to the rear of the cave—but he didn't move. If they looked, they would find. Loser or winner, he was damned if he'd cower.

The three hung for a moment in silent conference. Then the nearest slid, silent and implacable, up the air towards Wil.

TWENTY-FIVE

For whatever it might be worth, Wil's side was the winner. He was released by the medics in less than an hour. His body was whole, but stiff and aching; the medical autons didn't waste their time on finishing touches. There were really serious casualties, and only a part of the medical establishment had survived the fight. The worst cases were simply popped into stasis. Della disappeared into her system, with the autons' assurance that she would be substantially well in forty hours.

Wil tried not to think about the disaster that spread all around them, tried not to think that it was his fault. He had thought the search for the cairn would provoke an attack—but on himself and Della, not on all humanity.

That attack had killed almost half the human race. Wil couldn't bring himself to ask Yelén directly, but he knew anyway: Marta's plan was dead. He had failed in the only way that mattered. And yet he still had a job. He still had a murderer to catch. It was something to work on, a barricade against grief.

Although the price was higher than he had ever wished to pay, the battle had given him the sort of clues he'd hoped. Della's system had retrieved the cairn bobble; its contents would be available in twenty-four hours. And there were other things to look at. It was clear now that the enemy's

235

only power had lain in his perversion of others' systems. But, at every step, they had underestimated that power. After Marta's murder, they thought it was a shallow penetration, the perversion of a bug in the Korolev system. After Wil found the clue in the diary, they thought the enemy had deeper penetration, but still of Korolev's system alone; they guessed the killer might be able to usurp parts of Yelén's forces. And then came the war between the low-techs. It had been a diversion, covering the enemy's final, most massive assault. That assault had been not on Korolev's system alone, but on Genet's and Chanson's and Blumenthal's and Raines'. Every system except Lu's had been taken over, turned to the business of killing Wil and Della.

But Della Lu was very hard to kill. She had fought the other systems to a standstill, then beaten them down. In the chaos of defeat, the original owners climbed out of system-metaphorical bunkers and reclaimed what was left of their property.

Everyone agreed it couldn't happen again. They might even be right. What remained of their computing systems was pitifully simple, not deep enough or connected enough for games of subtle perversion. Everyone agreed on something else: The enemy's skill with systems had been the equal of the best and biggest police services from the high-techs' era.

So. It was a big clue, though small compared to the price of the learning. Related, and at least as significant: Della Lu had been immune to the takeover. Wil put the two together and reached some obvious conclusions. He worked straight through the next twenty-four hours, studying Della's copy of GreenInc —especially the garbled coverage of the late twenty-second. It was tedious work. At one time, the document had been seriously damaged; the reconstruction could never be complete. Facts and dates were jumbled. Whole sections were missing. He could understand why Della didn't use the later coverage. Wil kept at it. He knew what to look for . . . and in the end he found it.

A half-trashed db would not convince a court, but Wil was satisfied: He knew who killed Marta Korolev. He spent an empty, hate-full afternoon trying to figure how to destroy the murderer. What did it matter now? Now that the human race was dead.

That night, Juan Chanson dropped by Wil's new quarters. The man was subdued; he spoke scarcely faster than a normal person. "I've checked for bugs, my boy, but I want to keep this short." Chanson looked nervously around the tiny room that was Wil's share of the refugee dorm. "I noticed something during the battle. I think it can save us all." They talked for more than an hour. And when Chanson left, it was with the promise they would talk again in the morning.

Wil sat thinking for a long time after the other left. *My God, if what Juan says is true . . .* Juan's story made sense; it tied up all the loose ends. He noticed he was shivering: not just his hands, his whole body. It was a combination of joy and fear.

He had to talk to Della about this. It would take planning, deception, and good luck, but if they played their cards exactly right, the settlement still had a chance!

On the third day, the survivors gathered at Castle Korolev, in the stone amphitheater. It was mostly empty now. The aborted war between New Mexico and the Peace had killed more than one hundred low-techs. Wil looked across the theater. How different this was from the last meeting here. Now the low-techs crowded together, leaving long sweeps of bench completely empty. There were few uniforms, and the insignia had been ripped from most of those. Ungovs, NMs, Peacers sat mixed together, hard to tell apart; they all looked beaten. No one sat on the top benches—where you could look down through the castle's jacarandas at the swath of burn and glaze that had been Town Korolev.

Brierson had seen the list of dead. Still, his eyes searched across the crowd, as if he might somehow see the friends—and the enemy—he had lost. Derek Lindemann was gone. Wil was genuinely sorry about that—not so much for the man, but for losing the chance to prove he could face him without rage. Rohan was dead. Cheerful, decent Rohan. The brothers had taken Wil's warning and hidden beneath their farm. Hours passed. The autons left. Rohan went outside to bring down the last of their equipment. When the bombs fell, he was caught in the open.

Dilip had come to the meeting alone. Now he sat with Gail Parker, talking softly.

"I suppose we can begin." Yelén's voice cut across the murmur of the crowd. Only the amplification gave her voice force; her tone was listless. The burden she had carried since Marta died had finally slipped, and crushed her. "For the low-techs, some explanations. You fought a war three days ago. By now, you know you were maneuvered into fighting. It was a cover for someone to grab our high-tech systems and start the larger fight you've seen in near space. . . . Your war killed or maimed half the human race. Our war destroyed about ninety percent of our equipment." She leaned against the podium, her head down. "It's the end of our plan; we have neither the genetic resources nor the equipment to reestablish civilization.

"I don't know about the other high-techs, but I'm not going to bobble out. I have enough resources to support you all for a few years. If I spread it around, what's left of my medical resources should be enough to provide a twentieth-century level of care for many decades. After that . . . well, our life in the wilderness will be better than Marta's, I guess. If we're lucky, we may last a century; Sánchez did, and he had fewer people."

She paused, and seemed to swallow something painful. "And you have another option. I—I've cut the suppressor field. You are all free to bobble out of this era." Her gaze moved reluctantly across the audience, to where Tammy Robinson sat. She sat alone, her face somber. Yelén had released her from stasis at the first opportunity after the battle. So far, Tammy had done nothing to take advantage of the debacle; her sympathy seemed genuine. On the other hand, she had nothing to lose by magnanimity. The wreckage of the Korolev plan was now hers for the taking.

Yelén continued. "I suppose that we really didn't need a meeting for me to say this. But even though what Marta and I hoped for is dead, I still have one goal before we all fade into the wilderness." She straightened, and the old fire came back

238

to her voice. "I want to get the creature that killed Marta and wrecked the settlement! Except for some wounded low-techs, everyone is here this afternoon. . . . Odds are the killer is, too. W. W. Brierson claims he knows who the killer is . . . *and can prove it.*" She looked up at him, her smile a bitter mocking. "What would you do, ladies and gentlemen, confronted by the most famous cop in all civilization—telling you he had suddenly solved the case you had spent a hundred years thinking on? What would you do if that cop refused to reveal the secret except to a meeting of all concerned? . . . I laughed in his face. But then I thought, what more is there to lose? This *is* W. W. Brierson; in the novels, he solves all his cases with a flashy denouement." She bowed in his direction. "Your last case, Inspector. I wish you luck." She walked from the stage.

Wil was already on his feet, walking slowly down the curve of the amphitheater. Someday he would have to read Billy's novels. Had the boy really ended each by a confrontation with a roomful of suspects? In his real life, this was only the third time he had ever seen such a thing. Normally, you identified the criminal, then arrested him. A denouement with a roomful —in this case, an auditoriumful—of suspects meant that you lacked either the knowledge or the power to accomplish an arrest. Any competent criminal realized this, too; the situation was failure in the making.

And sometimes it was the best you could do. Wil was aware of the crowd's absolute silence, of their eyes following him down the steps. Even the high-techs might be given pause by his reputation. For once, he was going to use the hype for all it was worth.

He stepped onto the stage and put his data set on the podium. He was the only person who could see the two clocks on the display. At this instant they read 00:11:32 and 00:24:52; the seconds ticked implacably downwards. He had about five minutes to set things up, else he would have to string the affair along for another twenty. Best to try for the first deadline— even that would require some stalling.

He looked across his audience, caught Juan's eye. None of this would have been possible without him. "For the moment, forget the disaster this has come to. What do we have? Several isolated murders, the manipulation of the governments, and finally the takeover of the high-techs' control systems. The murder of Marta Korolev and the system takeover are totally beyond the abilities of us low-techs. On the other hand, we know the enemy is not supernaturally powerful: He blew years of careful penetration in order to grab the systems. For all the damage he did, he wasn't able to maintain control—and now his perversions have been recognized and repaired." *We hope.*

"So. The enemy is one of the high-techs. One of these seven people." With a sweep of his hand he pointed at the seven. They were all in the first few rows, but with the exception of Blumenthal—who sat at the edge of the low-techs—they were spread out, each an isolated human being.

Della Lu was dressed in something gray and shapeless. Her head injuries had been repaired, but the temporary substitute for her implants was a bulky interface band. She was into her weirdness act. Her eyes roamed randomly around the theater. Her expression flickered through various emotions, none having reasonable connection with the scene around her. Yet without her firepower, Wil knew, Philippe Genet and Monica Raines could not have been persuaded to attend.

Genet sat three rows in front of Della. For all that his attendance was coerced, he seemed to be enjoying himself. He leaned against the edge of the bench behind him, his hands resting across his middle. The smile on his face held the same amused arrogance Wil had seen at the North Shore picnic.

There was no pleasure in Monica Raines' narrow face. She sat with hands tightly clasped, her mouth turned down at one side. Before the meeting, she'd made it clear that things had merely turned out as she had predicted. The human race had zapped itself once again; she had no interest in attending the wake.

Yelén had retreated to the far end of the front bench, as far from the rest of humanity as one could sit. Her face was pale, the previous emotion gone. She watched him intently. For all her mocking, she believed him . . . and revenge was all she had left now.

Wil let the silence stretch through two beats. "For various reasons, several of these seven might want to destroy the settlement. Tunç Blumenthal and Della Lu may not even be human —Juan has warned us often enough about the exterminators. Monica Raines has made no secret of her hostility towards the human race. Tammy Robinson's family has the announced goal of breaking up the colony."

"Wil!" Tammy was on her feet, her eyes wide. "We would never kill to—" She was interrupted by Della Lu's quiet laughter. She looked over her shoulder and saw the wild look on Lu's face. She looked back at Wil, her lips trembling. "Wil, believe me."

Brierson waited for her to sit before he continued; the counts on his display flat were 00:10:11 and 00:23:31. "Evidently, a good *motive* is of no use in identifying the enemy. So let's look at the enemy's actions. Both the Peacer and NM governments were infiltrated. Can they tell us anything about who we're up against?" Wil looked across the low-techs, Peacers and NMs together. He recognized top staff people from both sides. Several shook their heads. Someone shouted, "Fraley must have known!"

The last President of the Republic sat alone. His uniform still bore insignia, but he was slouched forward, his elbows on his knees and his hands propping up his chin. "Mr. President?" Wil said softly.

Fraley looked up without raising his head. Even his hatred for Wil seemed burnt out. "I just don't know, Brierson. All our talks were over the comm. He used a synthetic voice and never sent video. He was with us almost from the beginning. Back then, he said he wanted to protect us from Korolev, said we were the only hope for stability. We got inside data, a few medical goodies. We didn't even see the machines that made the deliveries. Later on, he showed me that someone *else* was backing the Peacers. . . . From there, he owned our souls. If the Peace had high-tech backing, we'd be dead without our own. More and more, I was just his mouthpiece. In the end, he was all through our system." Now Fraley raised his head. There were dark rings around his eyes. When he spoke again, there was a strange intensity in his voice; if his old enemy could forgive him, perhaps he could himself. "I had no choice, Brierson. I thought if I didn't play ball, whoever was behind the Peace would kill us all."

A woman—Gail Parker—shouted, "So you had no choice, and the rest of us followed orders. And—and like good little troopers, we all cut our own throats!"

Wil raised his hand. "It doesn't matter, Gail. By that time, the enemy had complete control of your system. If you hadn't pushed the buttons, they would have been pushed for you." The short count on his display read 00:08:52. A map of the land around Castle Korolev suddenly flashed on the display, together with the words: "WIL: HE IS ARMED. GUNS AS ON MAP. I STILL SAY TO GO FOR IT. I'M READY ON THE MARK . . . 00:08:51."

Wil cleared the screen with a casual motion and continued talking. "It's too much to expect that the enemy would have given away his name. . . . Yet I'm sure Kim Tioulang had figured it out. There was some *particular* person he was trying to avoid when he talked to me at the North Shore picnic; he was trying to get to Town Korolev when he was murdered.

"And that raises an interesting question. Steve Fraley is a smart guy. What would Kim see that Steve would not? Kim went back a long way. He was one of the three planetary Directors of the Peace Authority. He was privy to every secret of that government. . . ." Wil looked at Yelén. "We've concentrated so much on superscientific plots and villains, we've forgotten the Machiavellis who came before us."

"There's no way our enemy could be a low-tech." Yelén's words were an objection, but there was sudden enthusiasm in her eyes.

Wil leaned across the podium. "Perhaps not now . . . but originally?" He pointed at Lu. "Consider Della. She grew up in the early twenty-first, was a top Peace cop. She also lived through most of the twenty-second. And now she's probably the most powerful high-tech of all."

Della had been mumbling to herself. Now her dark eyes came alive. She laughed, as if he had made a joke. "So true.

I was born when people still died of old age. Kim and I fought for the last empire. And we fought dirty. Someone like me would be a tough enemy for the likes of you."

"If it's Della, we're dead," said Yelén. *And revenge is impossible.*

Wil nodded. The count stood at 00:07:43. "Who else fills the requirements? Someone high in the Peacer command structure. Of course, GreenInc shows that none of you high-techs have such a past. So this hypothetical other must have eluded capture during the fall of the Peace, covered his tracks, and lived a new life through the twenty-second. It must have been a disappointing situation for him: the Peace forces straggling back into realtime to be mopped up piecemeal, hope for a new Peace dying."

00:07:10. He wasn't speaking hypothetically anymore. "In the end, our enemy saw there was only one chance for the resurrection of his empire: the Peacer fort that was bobbled in Kampuchea. That was the Authority's best-equipped redoubt. Like the others, it was designed to come back to realtime in about fifty years. But by some grotesque accident, its bobbler had generated an enormously longer stasis. All through the twenty-second it lay a few hundred meters below ground, an unremarkable battle relic. But our enemy had plans for it. Fifty million years: surely no other humans would exist in such a remote era. Here was a golden opportunity to start the Peace over, and with an empty world. So our Peacer accumulated equipment, medical supplies, a zygote bank, and left the civilization he hated."

Genet's lazy smile was broader now, showing teeth. "And who might be so high in the Peace Authority that Tioulang would recognize him?" Juan Chanson seemed to shrink in upon himself.

Wil ignored the byplay. "Kim Tioulang was Peace Director for Asia. There were only two other Directors. The American one was killed when Livermore returned to realtime in 2101. The Director for Eurafrica was—"

"Christian Gerrault," said Yelén. She was on her feet, walking slowly across the floor of the amphitheater, her eyes never leaving Genet. "The fat slug they called the Butcher of Eurafrica. He disappeared. All through the twenty-second his enemies waited around likely bobbles, but he was never found."

Genet looked from Yelén to Wil. "I commend you, Inspector, though if you had taken much longer to discover my identity, I would have had to announce it myself. Except for a few loose ends, my success is now complete. It's important that you understand the situation: Survival is still possible . . . but only on my terms." He glanced at Yelén. "Sit down, woman."

00:05:29. The timing was out of Wil's hands now. He had the terrible feeling this had come too soon.

Gerrault/Genet looked at Yelén, who had stopped her advance but was still standing. "I want you all to understand what I have gone through to achieve this moment. You must not doubt that I will show the disobedient no mercy.

"For fifty years I lived in the pitiful anarchy you call *civilization.* For fifty years I played the game. I lightened my skin. I starved one hundred kilos off my normal body weight. I starved myself of the . . . pleasures . . . that are due a great leader. But I suppose that is what makes me Christian Gerrault, and you sheep. I had goals for which I was willing to sacrifice anything and anyone. My new order might take fifty million years to flower, but there was work to be done all along the way. I heard of the Korolevs and their queer plan to rescue the shanghaied. At first, I thought to destroy them; our plans were so much alike. Then I realized that they could be used. Till near the end, they would be my allies. The important thing was that they lack some critical element of success, something only *I* could supply." He smiled at the still-standing Yelén. "You and Marta had everything planned. You even brought enough med equipment and fertilized human eggs to ensure the colony's survival. . . . Have you ever wondered why those zygotes were nonviable?"

"You?"

Gerrault laughed at the horror in Yelén's face. "Of course. Foolish, naive women. I guaranteed your failure even before you left civilization. It was an expensive operation; I had to buy several companies to guarantee your purchase would be trashed. But it was worth it. . . . You see, *my* supply of zygotes and *my* medical equipment still survive. They are the only such in existence now." He came to his feet and turned to face the main part of his audience. His voice boomed across the theater, and Wil wondered that he had not been recognized before. True, his appearance and accent were very different from the historical Gerrault's. He looked more like a North American than an African, and his body was gaunt to the point of emaciation. But when he talked like this, the soul within shone through all disguise. This was the Christian Gerrault of the historical videos. This was the fat, swaggering Director whose megalomania had dominated two continents and dwarfed any rational self-interest.

"Do you understand? It simply does not matter that you outnumber me, and that Della Lu may outgun me. Even before this regrettable little war, the success of the colony was an unlikely thing. Now you've lost much of the medical equipment the other high-techs brought. Without me, there is no chance of a successful settlement. Without me, every one of you low-techs will be dead within a century." He lowered his voice with dramatic effect. "And with me? Success of the colony is certain. Even before the war, the other high-techs could not have supplied the medical and population support that I can. But be warned. I am not a softhearted pansy like Korolev, or Fraley, or Tioulang. I have never tolerated weakness or disloyalty. You will work for me, and you will work very, very hard. But if you do, most of you will survive."

Gerrault's gaze swept the audience. Wil had never seen such horrified fascination on people's faces. An hour ago they were trying to accept the prospect of slow extinction. Now their lives were saved . . . if they would be slaves. One by one, they turned their eyes from the speaker. They were silent, avoiding even each others' eyes. Gerrault nodded. "Good. Afterwards, I want to see Tioulang's staff. He failed me, but some of you were good men once. There may be a place for you in my plans."

He turned to the high-techs. "Your choice is simple: If you bobble out of this era, I want at least one hundred megayears

245

free of your interference. After that, you may die as quickly or as slowly as you wish. If you stay, you give me your equipment, your systems, and your loyalty. If the human race is to survive, it will be on *my* terms." He looked at Yelén. He was smiling again. "I told you once, slut: *Sit down.*"

Yelén's whole body was rigid, her arms half raised. She stared right through Gerrault. For a moment Wil was afraid she might fight. Then something broke and she sat down. She was still loyal to Marta's dream.

"Good. If you can be sensible, perhaps the rest can." He looked up. "You will deliver system control to me now. And then I'll—"

Della laughed and stood up. "I think not, Director. The rest may be domesticated animals, but not me. And I outgun you." Her smile, even her stance, seemed disconnected from the situation. She might have been discussing some parlor game. In its way, her manner was scarier than Gerrault's sadism; it stopped even the Director for a second.

Then he recovered. "I know you; you're the gutless traitor who betrayed the Peace in 2048. You're the sort who bluffs and blusters but is basically spineless. You must also know *me*. I don't bluff about death. If you oppose me, I'll take my zygotes and med equipment, and leave you all to rot; if you pursue and destroy me, I'll make sure the zygotes die too." His voice was flat, determined.

Della shrugged, still smiling. "No need to puff and spit, Christian dear. You don't understand quite what you're up against. You see, I believe every word you say. *But I just don't care.* I'm going to kill you anyway." She walked away from them. "And the first step is to get myself some maneuvering room."

Gerrault's mouth hung open. He looked at the others. "I'll do it, I really will! It will be the end of the human race." It was almost as if he were seeking their moral support. He had been outmonstered.

Yelén shouted, her voice scarcely recognizable, "Please, Della, I *beg!* Come back!"

But Della Lu had disappeared over the crest of the amphitheater. Gerrault stared after her for only a second. Once she got out of the way, suppressor fields and tremendous firepower would be brought to bear on the theater. Everyone here could be killed—and Della had convincingly demonstrated that that wouldn't bother her. Gerrault sprinted for the floor-level exit. "But I'm not bluffing. I'm not!" He stopped for an instant at the door. "If I survive, I'll return with the zygotes. It is your duty to wait for me." Then he was gone, too.

Wil held his breath through the next seconds, praying for anticlimax. Dark shapes shot skywards, leaving thunder behind. But there was no flash of energy beams, no nukes. There was no shifting of sun in sky as might happen if they were bobbled; the combatants had moved their battle away from the amphitheater.

For the moment they lived. The low-techs huddled in clumps; someone was weeping.

Yelén's head was buried in her arms. Juan's eyes were closed, his lower lip caught between his teeth. The other high-techs were caught in less extreme poses . . . but they were all watching action beyond human eyes.

Wil looked at his display flat. It was counting down the last ninety seconds. The western sky flashed incandescent, two closely spaced pulses. Tunç said, "They both nuked out . . . they're over the Indian Ocean now." His voice was distant, only a small part of his attention devoted to reporting the action to those who could not see. "Phil's got his force massed there. He has a local advantage." There was a ripple of brightness, barely perceptible, like lightning beyond mountains. "Firefight. Phil is trying to punch through Della's near-Earth cordon. . . . He made it." There was a scattered and uncertain cheer from the low-techs. "They're outward bound, under heavy nuke drive. Just boosted past three thousand klicks per second. They'll go through the trailing Lagrange zone." Christian Gerrault had some important baggage to pick up on his way out.

And Wil's display read 00:00:00. He looked at Juan Chanson. The man's eyes were still closed, his face a picture of concentration. A second passed. Two. Suddenly he was grinning and giving a thumbs-up sign. Christian's baggage was no longer available for pickup.

For a moment Wil and Juan grinned stupidly at each other. There was no one else to notice. "Five thousand kps. . . . Strange. Phil has stopped boosting. Della will be on top of him in . . . We've got another firefight. She's chewing him up. . . . He's broken off. He's running again, pulling away from her."

Wil spoke across the monologue. "Tell 'em, Juan."

Chanson nodded, still smiling. Suddenly Tunç stopped talking. A second passed. Then he swore and started laughing. The low-techs stared at Blumenthal; all the high-techs were looking at Chanson.

"Are you *sure*, Juan?" Yelén's voice was unsteady.

"Yes, yes, *yes!* It worked perfectly. We're rid of both of them now. See. They've shifted to long-term tactics. However their fight ends, it will be thousands of years, dozens of parsecs from here." Brierson had a sudden, terrible vision of Della pursuing Gerrault into the depths forever.

Fraley's voice cut across Chanson's. "What in *hell* are you talking about? Gerrault has the med equipment and the zygotes. If he's gone, they're gone—and we're dead!"

"No! It's all right. We, I—" He was dancing from one foot to the other, frustrated by the slowness of spoken language. "Wil! Explain what we did."

Brierson pulled his imagination back to Earth and looked across the low-techs. "Juan managed to separate the med equipment from Gerrault," he said quietly. "It's sitting up there in the trailing Lagrange zone, waiting to be picked up." He glanced at Chanson. "You've transferred control to Yelén?"

"Yes. I really don't have much space capability left."

Wil felt his shoulders slowly relax; relief was beginning to percolate through him. "I've suspected 'Genet' almost from the beginning; he knew it, and he didn't care. But during our war, all the high-tech systems were taken over to fight Della. Juan—or any of the others—can tell you what it was like. They were not completely cut out of their systems; they had just lost

248

control. In any battle, a lot of information is flowing between nodes. In this one, things were especially chaotic. In places, data security failed; irrelevant information leaked across. Part of what passed through Juan's node was the specs on Gerrault's med system. Juan saw what Gerrault had, where it was, and the exact lookabout timings of the bobbles that protected Gerrault's zygotes and inner defenses."

He paused. "This meeting was a setup. I-I'm sorry about keeping you all in the dark. There were only certain times when an attack could succeed—and then only if Gerrault had moved most of his defenses away from the trailing Lagrange."

"Yes," said Juan, his excitement reduced to manageable proportions, "this meeting was necessary, but it was the riskiest part of the whole affair. If we trumped him while he was still here, Gerrault might have done something foolish, deadly. Somehow we had to trick him into running without shooting at us first. So Wil told the story you heard, and we played our two greatest enemies against each other." He looked up at Brierson. "Thanks for trusting me, my boy. We'll never know exactly what drove the Lu creature. Maybe she really was human; maybe all her years alone just turned her mind into something alien. But I knew she couldn't resist if you told her the right lies about the zygote bank; she'll chase Gerrault to the end of space-time to destroy it."

Now there really was cheering. Some of the cheerers were a bit exhausted, perhaps: their future had been bounced around like a volleyball these last few minutes. But now: "Now we can make it!" Yelén shouted. Peacers, Ungovs, NMs were embracing. Dilip and a crowd of low-techs came down to the podium to shake Wil's hand. Even the high-tech reserve was broken. Juan and Tunç were in the middle of the crowd. Tammy and Yelén stood less than a meter apart, grinning at each other. Only Monica Raines had not left her seat; as usual, her smile was turned down at one corner. But Wil thought it was not so much disappointment at their salvation as envy that everyone else could be so happy.

Wil suddenly realized that he could leave it at this. Perhaps the settlement *was* saved. Certainly, if he went ahead with the rest of his plan, the danger to himself could be greater than everything up to now.

It was a thought, never a real choice. He owed some people too much to back down now.

Wil broke from the crowd and returned to the podium. He turned up the amplification. "Yelén. Everybody." The laughter and shouting diminished. Gail Parker jumped on a bench and cried, "Yay, Wili! Speech! Speech! Wili for President!" This provoked even more laughter; Gail always did have a sharp sense of the ridiculous. Wil raised his hands, and the uproar subsided again. "There are still some things we must settle."

Yelén looked at him, her face relaxed yet puzzled. "Sure, Wil. I think we can put a lot of things right, now. But—"

"That's not what I mean, Yelén. I still haven't done what you hired me for. . . . I still haven't produced Marta's murderer."

The talk and laughter guttered to a stop. The loudest sounds were the birds stealing from the spiders beyond the amphitheater. Where the faces didn't show blank surprise, Wil could see the fear returning. "But, Wil," Juan said finally, "we *got* Gerrault. . . ."

"Yes. We got him. There's no fakery in that, nor in the equipment we rescued. But Christian Gerrault did not kill Marta, and he didn't take over the high-tech computer systems. Did you notice that he never admitted to either? He was as much a victim of the takeover as any. Finding the systems saboteur was one of the 'loose ends' he intended to clear up."

Juan waved his hands, his speech coming faster than ever. "Semantics. He explicitly admitted to taking over the low-techs' military systems."

Wil shook his head. "No, Juan. Only the Peacers'. All the time we thought one high-tech was stirring up both sides, when actually Gerrault was behind the Peace and *you* were manipulating the NMs."

The words were spoken and Wil still lived.

The little man swallowed. "Please, my boy, after everything I've done to help, how can you say this? . . . I know! You think only a systems penetrator could know about Gerrault's med

250

equipment." He looked imploringly at Yelén and Tammy. "Tell him. Things like that happen in battle, especially when penetration—"

"Sure," Yelén said. "It may seem a farfetched explanation to someone from your era, Wil, but leak-across can really happen." Tunç and Tammy were nodding agreement.

"It doesn't matter." There was no doubt in Wil's face or voice. "I knew that Juan was Marta's killer before he ever came to me about Gerrault." *But can I convince the rest of you?*

Chanson's hands balled into fists. He backed into a bench and sat down abruptly. "Do I have to take this?" he cried to Yelén.

Korolev set her hand on his shoulder. "Let the *Inspector* have his say." When she looked at Wil, her face had the angry ambivalence he knew so well. Together, Wil and Juan had just saved the colony. But she had known Chanson through decades of their lives; Wil was the low-tech that her Marta had damned and praised. There was no telling how long her patience would last.

Brierson stepped around the podium. "At first, it seemed that almost any high-tech could have marooned Marta: There were bugs in the Korolev system that made it easy to sabotage a single bobbling sequence. With those bugs repaired, Yelén and the others thought their systems were secure. Our war showed how terribly wrong they were. For twelve hours, the enemy had complete control of all the systems—except Della's. . . .

"This told me several things. In my time, it was no trivial thing to grab an entire system. Unless the system were perverted to begin with, it took expert, tedious effort to insert all the traps that would make a grab possible. Whoever did this needed years of visitor status on the high-techs' systems. The enemy never had a chance at Della; she was gone from the Solar System since just after the Singularity."

He looked across his audience. The low-techs hung on every word. It was harder to tell about the others. Tammy wasn't even looking at him. Wil could only imagine the analysis and conversations that were going on in parallel with his words.

"So. An expert, using expert tools, must be behind this. But Yelén's GreenInc shows that none of the high-techs have such a background."

Tunç interrupted, "Which only means the killer rewrote history to protect himself."

"Right. It needn't have been much, just a fact here and there. Over the years, the killer could manage it. Della's db's are the only ones that might contain the truth. I spent a lot of time with them after we were rescued. Unfortunately, her general database for the late twenty-second is badly jumbled— so badly that Della herself didn't use it. But after the battle, I knew what to look for. Eventually I found an opening: Jason Mudge. Mudge was just the religious fanatic we knew, though toward the end of the twenty-second he actually had some disciples. Only one of them had sufficient faith to follow him into stasis. That was Juan Chanson. Juan was a wealthy man, probably Mudge's biggest catch." Wil looked at Chanson. "You gave up a lot to follow a religious dream, Juan. Della's db's show you were head of Penetration and Perversion at USAF, Inc." In Wil's time, USAF had been the largest weapons-maker in North America; it had grown from there. "I don't doubt that when Juan left, he took the latest software his division had invented. We were up against industrial-strength sabotage."

Juan was trembling. He looked up at Yelén. She stared back for a second, then looked at Wil. She wasn't convinced. "Yelén," Wil said, keeping his voice level, "don't you remember? The day Mudge was killed, he claimed Chanson had been a religionist."

Yelén shook her head. That memory was three days gone.

Finally Chanson spoke aloud. "Don't you see how you've deluded yourself, Wil? The evidence is all around you. Why do you think Lu's record of civilization was jumbled? *Because she was never there!* At best those records are secondhand, filled with evidence she would use against me or whoever else was a threat. Wil, please. I may be wrong about the details, but whatever the Lu creature is, she's proved she would sacrifice us all for her schemes. No matter what she's done to you, you must be able to see that."

Monica's laugh was almost a cackle. "What a pretty bind you're in, Brierson. The facts explain either theory perfectly. And Della Lu is chasing off into interstellar space."

Wil pretended to give her comment serious consideration; he needed time to think. Finally he shook his head and continued as calmly as before. "Even if you don't believe me, there are data Juan never thought to alter. Marta's diary, for instance. . . . I know, Yelén, you studied that for a hundred years, and you knew Marta far better than I. But Marta knew she wasn't marooned by simple sabotage. She knew the enemy saw what she left in the cairns, and could destroy any of it. Even worse, if she slipped a message past the enemy, and you understood it, the act of understanding might itself trigger an attack.

"But *I* am a low-tech, outside all this automation. Marta got my attention with the one incident that only she and I could know. Yelén, after the Robinson party . . . I didn't—I *never* tried to take advantage of Marta." He looked into Yelén's face, willing belief there.

When there was no response, he continued. "The last years of her life, Marta played a terrible double game. She told us the story of survival and courage and defeat, and at the same time she left clues she hoped would point me at Juan. They were subtle. She named her fishermonkey friends after people in our settlement. There was *always* a Juan Chanson, a solitary creature that delighted in watching her. Marta's last day alive, she mentioned that he was still out there, watching. She *knew* she was being stalked, and by the real Juan Chanson."

Juan slapped the bench. "God *damn* it, man! You can find any message if the coding scheme is nutty enough."

"Unfortunately, you're right. And if that's all she could do, this might be a stalemate, Juan. But for all her misfortunes, Marta had some good luck, too. One of her fishermonkeys was a freak, bigger and brighter than any fisher we've seen. He followed her around, tried to imitate her cairn-building. It wasn't much, but she had an ally in realtime." He smiled wanly. "She named him W. W. Brierson. He got lots of practice building cairns, always in the same position relative to Peace Lake. In the end, she took him north and left him in a normal forest beyond the glazed zone. I don't know how close you were monitoring, Juan, but you missed what that animal took with him, you missed the cairn he built, where Marta never went."

Juan's eyes darted to Yelén, then back to Wil, but he said nothing.

"You've known about that cairn for four days, ever since I told Yelén. You were willing to show your full power—and kill half the human race—to prevent me from getting it." Wil stepped off the platform and walked slowly toward the little man. "Well, Juan, you didn't succeed. I've seen what Marta had to say when she didn't have to write in parables. Everyone else is free to see it, too. And no matter what conspiracies you blame on Della Lu, I suspect the physical evidence will convince Yelén and her lab autons."

Yelén had backed away from Chanson. Tunç's mouth was compressed into a thin line. *Even without a confession, I may be able to win,* thought Wil.

Juan looked around, then back at Wil. "Please. You're reading this all wrong. I didn't kill Marta. I *want* the settlement to succeed. And I've sacrificed more than any of you to preserve it; if I hadn't, none of us would have survived to fifty megayears. But now that's made me look like the guilty one. I've got to convince you. . . .

"Look. Wil. You're right about Mudge and me; I should never have tried to cover that up. I'm embarrassed I ever believed his chiliastic garbage. But I was young, and my nightmares followed me home from work. I needed to believe in something. I gave up my job, everything, for his promises.

"We came out of stasis in 2295, just before Mudge's numerology said Christ would put on the Big Show. There was nothing but ruins, a civilization destroyed, a race exterminated. Mudge reviewed his mumbo-jumbo and concluded that we had overshot, that Christ had come and gone. The stupid jerk! He just could not accept what we saw around us. Something had visited the Solar System in the mid-twenty-third, but it hadn't been holy. The evidence of alien invasion was everywhere. Mudge had arrived with scarcely more than sackcloth and ashes. I'd brought plenty of equipment. I could do analysis, back up my claims. I had the power to save what humans were still in stasis.

"Yelén, right from then my goal was the same as yours. Even while you high-techs were still in stasis, I was planning for it. The only difference was that I knew about the aliens. But I couldn't convince Mudge of them. In fact, the signs were so subtle, I began to wonder if anyone else would believe me." Chanson came to his feet, his talk speeding up. "Unless we guarded against the invaders, all the goodwill in the world could not resurrect the human race. I *had* to do something. I —I enhanced some of the evidence. I nuked a few ruins. Surely, not even a blind man could ignore that!" He looked at Yelén and Tammy accusingly. "Yet when you returned to realtime, you weren't convinced. You couldn't accept even the clearest evidence. . . . I tried. I tried. Over the next two thousand years I traveled all over the Solar System, discovering the signs of the invasion, emphasizing them so even idiots could not miss them.

"In the end, I had a little success. W. W. Sánchez had the patience to look at the facts, the open-mindedness to believe. We persuaded the rest of you to be a bit more cautious. But the burden of vigilance still rested on me. No one else was willing to put sentries in far solar space. Over the years, I destroyed two alien probes—and still Sánchez was the only one who was convinced." Juan was staring through Wil; he might have been talking to himself. "I really liked Bil Sánchez. I wish he hadn't dropped out; his settlement was just too small to succeed. I visited him there several times. It was a long, idyllic, downhill slide. Bil wanted to do research, but all he had was that punched tape he'd found on Charon. He was obsessed with it; the last time I saw him he even claimed it was a fake." A faintly troubled look passed across Juan's face. "Well, that settlement was too small to survive, anyway."

Yelén's eyes were wide, white showing all around the irises;

her whole body had gone rigid. Chanson could not notice, but sudden death was in the air.

Wil stepped into Yelén's line of sight; his voice was a calm echo of Chanson's distant tone. "What about Marta, Juan?"

"Marta?" Juan almost looked at him. "Marta always had an open mind. She granted the possibility of an alien threat. I think Lu's arrival scared her; the creature was so obviously inhuman. Marta talked to Lu, got access to some of her databases. And then—and then"—tears started in his eyes—"she started asking the db about Mudge." *How much had Marta suspected?* At the time, probably nothing; most of the jumbled references to Mudge had no connection with Chanson. It was tragic bad luck she started so close to Juan's secret. "I should never have lied about my past, but now it was too late. Marta could destroy all I had worked for. The colony would be left defenseless. I had to, I had to—"

"Kill her?" Yelén's voice was a shout.

"*No!*" Juan's head snapped up; the reality around him was not to be ignored. "I could never do that. I *liked* Marta! But I had to . . . quarantine her. I watched to see if she would denounce me. She never did—but then I realized I could never be sure what she might say later. I couldn't let her back.

"Please *listen* to me! I made mistakes; I pushed too hard to make you see the truth. But you must *believe.* The invaders are out there, Yelén. They'll destroy everything you and Marta dreamed of if you don't believe m—" Juan's voice became a scream. He fell heavily, lay with arms and legs twitching.

Two quick steps and Wil was kneeling by his side. Wil looked down at the agonized face; he'd had two days to prepare for this moment, to suppress the killing rage he felt every time he saw Chanson. Korolev had had no such time; he could almost feel her eyes boring death through his back. "What did you do to him, Yelén?"

"I shut him down, cut his comm links." She stepped around Wil, to look down at Chanson. "He'll recover." There was a tight smile on her face; in a way, it was scarier than her rage. "I want time to think of just revenge. I want him to understand it when it comes." Her eyes snapped up to the nearest bystanders. "Get him out of my sight." For once there was no debate; her words might as well have been electric prods. Tunç and three low-techs grabbed Chanson, carried him towards the flier that was drifting down the side of the amphitheater. Wil started after them.

"Brierson! I want to talk to you." The words were abrupt, but there was something strange in Yelén's tone. Wil came back down the steps. Yelén led him around the side of the platform—away from the crowd, which was just beginning to come out of shock. "Wil," she said quietly, "I want—I'd like to see what Marta said." *What Marta said when she wasn't writing for Chanson's eyes.*

Wil swallowed; even winning could be hard. He touched her shoulder. "Marta left the fifth cairn, just like I told Chanson. If we'd found it during the first few thousand years. . . . After fifty thousand, all we could see was that there had been a sheaf of reed paper inside. It was powder. We'll never know for sure what she wanted to tell us. . . . I'm sorry, Yelén."

TWENTY-SIX

I t was snowing. From over the hill came shouts, occasional laughter. They were having a snowball fight.

W. W. Brierson crunched down the hillside to the edge of the pines. Strange that with the world so empty he would still want to be alone. Maybe not so strange. Their dormitory was a crowded place. No doubt there were others who'd left the snowballers, who walked beneath the pines and pretended this was a different time.

He found a big rock, clambered up, and dusted off a place to sit. From here he could see alpine glaciers disappearing into the clouds. Wil tapped at his data set and thought. The human race had another chance. Dilip and a lot of other people really seemed to think he was responsible. Well, he'd solved the case. Without a doubt it was the biggest of his career. Even Billy Brierson had not imagined such a great adventure for his father. And the chief bad guy had been punished. Very definitely, Juan had been punished. . . .

Yelén had honored Marta's notions about mercy; she had made that mercy the punishment itself. Juan was executed by a surfeit of life. He was marooned in realtime, without shelter or tools or friends. Yet his was a different torture than Marta's —and perhaps the more terrible. Juan was left with a medical auton. He was free to live *as long as he wished.*

Juan outlived three autons. He lasted ten thousand years. He kept his purpose for nearly two thousand. Wil shook his head as he surveyed the report. If anyone had known that Chanson was into Penetration and Perversion, he would have been an instant suspect—on grounds of personality alone. Wil had known only one such specialist, his company's resident spook. The man was inhumanly patient and devious, but frightened at the same time. He spent so much time in deep connect, the paranoid necessities of defense systems leaked into his perception of the everyday world. Wil could only imagine the madhouse Penetration and Perversion had become by the late twenty-second. Juan made seven attempts to pervert the auton. One involved twelve hundred years of careful observation, timing the failure of various subsystems, maneuvering the auton into a position where he might take control and get transportation to resources in near space.

Yet Chanson never really had a prayer of success. Yelén had hardwired changes to the auton. Juan had none of the software he had stolen from USAF, Inc, and he was without processor support. His glib tongue and two thousand years of effort were not enough to set him free.

As the centuries passed and he had no luck with the auton, Juan spent more and more time trying to talk to Yelén and the other high-techs who occasionally looked into realtime. He kept a journal many times longer than Marta's; he painted endless prose across the rocklands north of his home territory. None of it looked as interesting as Marta's diary. All Juan could talk of was his great message, the threat he saw in the stars. He went on spouting evidence—though after the first centuries it lost all connection with reality.

After five hundred years, his journal became at first irregular, then a decadely summary, then a dead letter. For three thousand years Juan lived without apparent goal, moving from cave to cave. He wore no clothes, he did no work. The auton protected him from local predators. When he did not hunt or farm, the auton brought him food. If the climate of the Eastern Straits had been less mild he would certainly have died. Yet to Wil it was still a miracle the man survived. Through all that time he had enough determination to keep on living. Della had been right. W. W. Brierson would not have lasted a tenth as long; a few centuries and he would have drifted into suicidal funk.

Juan drifted for three thousand years . . . and then his immortal paranoid soul found a new cause. It wasn't clear exactly what it was. He kept no journal; his conversations with the auton were limited to simple commands and incoherent mumbling. Yelén thought that Juan saw himself as somehow the creator of reality. He moved to the seashore. He built heavy baskets and used them to drag millions of loads of soil inland. The dredged shoreland became a maze of channels. He piled the dirt on a rectangular mound that rose steadily through the centuries. That mound reminded Wil of the earthen pyramids the American Indians had left in Illinois. It had taken hundreds of people working over decades to build those. Juan's was the work of one man over millennia. If the climate had not been exceptionally dry and mild in his era, he could not have kept ahead of simple erosion.

Juan's new vision went beyond monuments. Apparently he thought to create an intelligent race. He persuaded the auton to extend its food gathering, to beach schools of fish in the maze he constructed on the shore. Soon there were thousands of fishermonkeys living beneath his temple/pyramid. Through a perversion of its protection programs, he used the auton as an instrument of force: The best fish went to the monkeys who performed properly. The effect was small, but over centuries the fishers at the East End had a different look. The majority were like the "W. W. Brierson" that had helped Marta. They carried rocks to the base of the pyramid. They sat for hours staring up at it.

The four-thousand-year effort was not enough to bring intelligence to the fishers. Yelén's report showed some tool use. Towards the end, they built a stone skirt around the lower part of the pyramid. But they were never the race of hod carriers that Chanson probably intended. It was Juan who continued to drag endless loads of dirt up to his temple, repairing erosion damage, adding ever-higher towers to the topmost platform. At its greatest, the temple covered a rectangle two hundred meters by one hundred, and the top platform was thirty meters above the plain. Its spires crowded tall and spindly all about, more like termite towers or coral than human architecture. Through those last four thousand years, Juan's daily pattern was unchanged. He worked on his new race. He hauled dirt. Each evening, he walked round and round the intricate stairs of the pyramid, till finally he stood at the top, surveying the temple slaves who gathered on the plain before him.

Wil paged through Yelén's report. She had pictures of Juan during those last centuries. His face was blank of all expression, except at day's end—when he always laughed, three times. His every motion was a patterned thing, a reflex. Juan had become an insect, one whose hive spread through time instead of space.

Juan had found peace. He might have lasted forever if only the world had had the same stability. But the climate of the Eastern Straits entered a period of wet and storminess. The auton was programmed to provide minimum protection. In earlier millennia that would have been enough. But now Juan was inflexible. He would not retreat to the highland caves; he would not even come down from the temple during storms. He forbade the auton to approach it during his nightly services.

Of course, Yelén had pictures of Juan's end. The auton was four klicks from the temple; Juan had long since destroyed all bugs. The wind-driven rain blurred and twisted the auton's view. This was just the latest of a series of storms that were tearing down the pyramid faster than Juan could maintain it. His towers and walls were like a child's sand castle melting in an ocean tide. Juan did not notice. He stood on the slumped platform of his temple and looked out upon the storm. Wil watched the wavery image raise its arms—just as Juan always did at day's end, just before he gave his strange laugh. Lightning struck all around, turning the storm darkness to actinic blue, showing Juan's slaves huddled by the thousands below him. The bolts marched across the fallen temple, striking what was left of the spires . . . striking Juan as he stood, arms still upraised to direct the show.

There was little more to Yelén's report. The fishermonkeys had been given a strong push toward intelligence. It was not enough. Biological evolution has no special tendency toward sapience; it heads blindly for local optima. In the case of the fishers, that was their dominance of the shallow waters. For a few hundred years, the race he'd bred still lived at the Eastern Straits, still brought rocks to line the stub of his pyramid, still watched through the evenings. But that was instinct without reward. In the end, they were as Juan had found them.

Wil cleared the display. He shivered—and not just from the cold. He would never forget Juan's crimes; he would never forget his long dying.

The snow had stopped. There was no more shouting from over the hill. Wil looked in surprise at the sunlight slanting through the trees behind him. He'd spent more than an hour looking at Yelén's report. Only now did he notice the cramps in his legs and the cold seeping up from the rock.

Wil tucked the data set under his arm and slipped off the rock. He still had time to enjoy the snow, the pines. It brought echoes of a winter just ten weeks old in his memory, the last days in Michigan before he'd flown to the coast on the Lindemann case. Only these snowfields were almost at the equator, and this world was in the middle of an ice age.

The tropics had cooled. The jacaranda forests had shifted downslope, to the edge of the Inland Sea. But none of the continental ice sheets had reached further south than latitude forty-five. The snow around the site of Town Korolev was due to the altitude. Yelén figured the glaciers coming off the Indonesian Alps wouldn't get below the four-thousand-meter level. She claimed that, as ice ages go, this one was average.

Wil walked a kilometer through the pines. A week before— as his body counted time—this had been the glazed crater of Town Korolev. So much destruction, and not a sign of it now. He climbed a ridgeline and watched the sunset gleaming red and gold across the white. Something hooted faint against the breeze. Far to the north he could see where the jac forests hugged the sea. It was beautiful, but there were good reasons to leave this era. Some of the best ore fields were under ice now. Why cripple the new civilization when it was weakest? . . . And there was Della. She had lots of valuable equipment. They would give her at least a hundred thousand years to return.

Suddenly Wil felt very bleak. *Hell. I would give her a thousand times a hundred thousand.* But what good would it do? After that night with the dogthings, Wil hoped she had found herself. Without her, he could never have set up the double play against Chanson and Gerrault. A crooked smile came across his face. She had fooled both the killers into defeat. The plan was to force Gerrault to run, to chase him long enough to trick Juan. And it had worked! She had played the old, crazy Della so well. *Too well.* She had never returned. No one knew for sure what had happened; it was even conceivable she had died fighting Gerrault. More likely, some battle reflex had taken over. Even if the mood passed, she might pursue the other for unknown millennia. And if the mood didn't pass . . .

Wil remembered the scarcely human thing she had been when he first saw her. Even with her computer-supported memories and all the other enhancements, that Della seemed very much like what Juan Chanson had become towards the end of his punishment. For all her talk of being tough, Della had nothing on Juan when it came to single-mindedness. How much of her life would she spend on this chase? He was terribly afraid she had volunteered for the same fate that had been forced on Juan.

Wil decided he didn't like the cold at all. He glanced at his data set. It showed the date as 17 March 2100; he still had not reset it. Somewhere in its memory were notes about the stuff Virginia wanted him to bring back from the Coast. How much can happen in ten weeks; one must be flexible in these modern times. He turned away from the sunset and the silence, and headed back for the dormitory. He should be satisfied with this happy ending. The next few years would be tough, but he knew they could make it. Yelén had been friendly towards almost everyone the last few days. In the weeks before, she would never have thought of stopping in the middle of this glacial era just to give them a chance to look around.

The tropical twilight snapped down hard, faded quickly into night. When Wil came over the hill above the dorm, its lighted windows were like something out of a Michigan Christmas.

Sometime early tomorrow morning, when they were snug in their beds, Santa Claus Yelén would bobble them up once more. Her sleigh had certainly had a bumpy landing, popping in and out of realtime over the last sixty thousand years. Wil smiled at the crazy image.

Maybe this time they could stop for keeps.

That night was the last time Wil ever had the dream in blue. In most ways it was like the ones before. He was lying down, all breath exhausted from his lungs. *Goodbye, goodbye.* He cried and cried, but no sounds came. She sat beside him, holding his hand. Her face was Virginia's, and also Marta's. She smiled sadly, a smile that could not deny the truth they both knew. . . . *Goodbye, goodbye.* And then the pattern changed. She leaned toward him, snuggled her face against his cheek, just as Virginia used to do. She never spoke, and he couldn't tell if the thought was only his, or somehow comfort from her. *Someone still lives who has not said goodbye, someone who might like you very much.*

Dearest Wil, goodbye.

Brierson woke with a start, gasping for breath. He swung his feet out of bed and sat for a moment. His tiny room was bright with day, but he couldn't see outside; the window was completely fogged over. It was very quiet; normally he could hear plenty of activity through the plastic walls. He got up and stepped out into the hall; not a soul in sight. There was noise from downstairs, though. That's right: There was a big meeting scheduled first thing this morning. The fact that Yelén was willing to meet the low-techs at the dorm was more evidence that she had changed; she had not even demanded his presence. His sleeping late was a half-conscious test of his freedom. For a while he wanted to be a bystander. Managing the last meeting had been a bit . . . traumatic.

Wil padded down the hallway to the second-floor washroom. For once, he had the place all to himself.

What a *weird* dream. Wil looked at his image in the washstand mirror. There was wetness around his eyes, but he was *smiling.* The dream in blue had always been a choking burden, something he must forcibly ignore. But this time it reassured him, even made him happy. He hummed as he washed up, his mind playing with the dream. Virginia had seemed so real. He could still feel her touch on his cheek. He knew now how much hidden anger he had felt at Virginia; he knew, because suddenly the anger was gone. It had cut deep that Virginia had not come after him. He'd told himself that she always intended to, that she was still gathering her resources when the Singularity overtook her. He hadn't believed the excuse; he'd seen what could happen to a personality over a century. But now—for no reason but a dream—he felt differently. Well, what if Della's explanation of the Singularity was correct? What if technology had transcended the intelligible? What if minds had found immortality by growing forever past the human horizon? Why, then, something that had been Virginia might still exist, might want to comfort him.

Wil suddenly realized he was washing his face for the second time. For a moment, he and his mirror image grinned sheepishly at each other, conspirators realizing the insanity of their scheme. If he wasn't careful, he'd be another Jason Mudge, complete with guardian angels and voices from beyond the grave. Still, Della said there was something like religion hiding at the end of her materialism.

A few minutes later he was walking down the side stairs, past the cafeteria. The voices from within were loud but didn't sound angry. He hesitated, then turned away from the door. It might be fantasy, but he wanted to keep the mood of that dream as long as possible. It had been a long time since he'd started the day feeling so good. For the moment he really believed there was "someone who still lives, who might like you very much."

He walked out of the dorm, into daylight.

The building was surrounded by a perfect disk of white—the snow that had been brought through time with their bobble. The sun burned at the snowdrifts, raising a sublimation fog all around him. Wil walked across the slush, through the brilliant mist. He stopped at the edge of the snow and stared at the almost-jacarandas and less identifiable trees that grew all around. It was already a warm day. He stepped back a pace and enjoyed the cool coming off the snow. Except for the shape of some of the hills, the world was the same as before the battle. The glaciers were tamed again, lurked near faraway peaks. Across a ravine and a few hundred meters up a hillside, there was a separate plume of sublimation fog; the golden towers of Castle Korolev gleamed faint within it.

A shadow passed over him. "Wil!" He looked up as Tammy Robinson dropped out of the sky. She brought her platform to a low hover, just as she had when she came to invite the soot pushers to her father's party. She was even dressed in the same perfect white. She stood there a moment, looking down. "I wanted to see you again . . . before I go." She brought the platform all the way to earth, just beyond his toes. Now she was looking up at him. "Thank you, Wil. Gerrault and Chanson would've got us all if it hadn't been for you. Now I think we can all win." Her smile broadened. "Yelén has given me enough equipment to leave this era."

She was almost too perfect to look at. "You've given up on recruiting?"

"Nope. Yelén says I can come back in a hundred years, and any time after. With Gerrault's equipment and the zygotes, you can really succeed. Another century or two, and there'll be more people here than I could ever imagine. They won't feel beaten the way they do now, and a good many will be bored with civilization. There will be dozens, maybe hundreds, who'll come with me. And they'll be people we won't have to support. That's more than Daddy ever hoped for." She paused a second and then said quietly, "I hope you'll come with me, Wil."

"S-some of us have to stay in realtime, or there'll be no civilization for you to raid, Tammy." He tried to smile.

"I know, I know. But a hundred years from now, when I come back . . . what about then?"

What about then? The Robinsons thought all mysteries could be known to those who watched long enough, waited long enough. But a flatworm could watch forever and still not understand the opera. Aloud: "Who knows how I'll feel in a hundred years, Tammy?" He stopped and just stared at her for a second. "But if I don't come with you . . . and if you make it to the end of time . . . I hope you'll remember me to the Creator."

Tammy flinched, then realized he wasn't mocking her. "Okay. If you stay behind, I will." She put her hands on his shoulders and stood on tiptoe to kiss his lips. "See you later, Wil Brierson."

A few seconds later, Tammy was disappearing over the trees. *The one who still lives, the one who has not said goodbye?* He thought not, but he had a hundred years to decide for sure.

Wil walked along the perimeter of the mist, intrigued by the way heat and cool battled at the edge of the snow. He circled the dorm and found himself staring at the entrance. They were still at it in there. He grinned to himself and started back. What the hell.

He was only partway to the entrance when the doors opened. Only one person stepped out. It was Yelén. She surveyed him without surprise. "Hah. I wondered how long you'd stay out here." As she came toward him, he looked for signs of anger in her pale Slavic face. She caught his eye and smiled lopsidedly. "Don't worry. They didn't kick me out. And I'm not leaving in a huff. It's just that all the dickering is a little dull; they've practically got a commodity exchange going in there, splitting up all the stuff that survived our fighting. . . . Do you have a minute, Wil?"

He nodded and followed her out of the chill, back the way he had come. "Have you thought: No matter how well things go, we'll still need police services? People really respect you. That's ninety percent of what made companies like Michigan State Police and Al's Protection Rackets successful."

Brierson shook his head. "It sounds like the game we were playing before. A lot of the ungovs might want to hire me, but without threats from you, I can't imagine the governments tolerating the competition."

"Hey, I'm not looking for a cat's-paw. The fact is, Fraley and Dasgupta are in there right now, colluding on a common offer for your services."

Wil felt his jaw sag. *Fraley?* After all the years of hatred
. . . "Steve would rather die than disgovern."

"A lot of his people did die," she said quietly. "A lot of the
rest aren't taking orders anymore. Even Fraley has changed a
little. Maybe it's fear, maybe it's guilt. It really shook him to
see how easily one high-tech swindled him and perverted the
Republic—even worse, to learn that Chanson did it just to
have a thirty-second diversion available when he grabbed for
our systems."

Yelén laughed. "My advice is to take the job while they still
think it's tough. After a couple of years, there'll be competition; I bet you won't be able to make a living off your fees."

"Hmm. You think things are going to be that tame?"

"I really do, Wil. The high-tech monsters are dead. The
governments may linger on, but in name only. We lost a lot
in the war—parts of our technology may fall to a nineteenth-
century level—but with Gerrault's zygotes and med equipment, we're better off than before. The problem with the
women has disappeared. They can have the kids they want, but
they won't have to be nonstop baby factories. You should have
seen the meeting. There are lots of serious couples now. Gail
and Dilip asked me to *marry* them! 'For old times' sake.' They
said I had been like the captain of a ship to them. What crazy,
crazy people." She shook her head, but her smile was very
proud. These might be the first low-techs to show gratitude for
what she and Marta had done. "I'll tell you how confident I
am: I'm not forcing anyone to stay in this era. If they have a
bobbler, they can take off. I don't think anyone will. It's a bit
too obvious that if we can't make it now, we never will."

"Monica might."

"That's different. But don't be too sure even with her; she's
been lying to herself for a long time. I'm going to ask her to
stay." Yelén's smile was gentle; two weeks ago she would have
been scornful. With Gerrault and Chanson gone, a great
weight had been lifted from her soul, and Wil could see what
—beyond competence and loyalty—Marta had loved in her.

Yelén looked at her feet. "There's another reason I ducked
out of the meeting early. I wanted to apologize. After I read

Marta's diary, I felt like killing you. But I knew I needed you
—Marta didn't have to tell me that. And the more I depended
on you, the more you saw things I had not . . . the more I hated
you.

"Now I know the truth. I'm ashamed. After working with
you, I should have seen through Marta's trick myself."
Abruptly she stuck out her hand. Brierson grasped it, and they
shook. "Thanks, Wil."

The one who still lives, the one who has not said goodbye?
No. But a friend for the years to come.

Behind her, a flier descended. "Time for me to get back to
the house." She jerked a thumb at Castle Korolev.

, "One last thing," she said. "If things are as slow as I think,
you might want to diversify. . . . Give Della a hand."

"Della's back? H-how long? I mean—"

"She's been in solar space about a thousand years; we were
waiting to find the best time to stop. The chase took one
hundred thousand years. I don't know how much lifetime she
spent." She didn't seem much concerned about the last issue.
"You want to talk to her? I think you could do each other
good."

"Where—"

"She was with me, at the meeting. But you don't have to go
inside. You've been set up, Wil. Each of us—Tammy, me,
Della—wanted to talk to you alone. Say the word, and she'll
be out here."

"Okay. Yes!"

Yelén laughed. He was scarcely aware of her walking to the
flier. He started back to the dorm. Della had made it. However
many years she had lived in the dark, she had not died there.
And even if she was the creature from before, even if she was
like Juan Chanson at his ending, Wil could still try to help. He
couldn't take his eyes off the doorway.

The doors opened. She was wearing a jumpsuit, midnight
black, the same color as her short-cut hair. Her face was expressionless as she came down the steps and walked toward him.
Then she smiled. "Hi, Wil. I'm back . . . to stay."

The one who still lives, the one who has not said goodbye.

AFTERWORD

The author's afterword: that's where he explains what he was trying to say with the previous hundred thousand words, right? Well, I'll try to avoid that. Basically, I have an apology and a prediction.

The apology is for the unrealistically slow rate of technological growth predicted. Part of that is reasonable, I suppose. A general war, like the one I put in 1997, can be used to postpone progress anywhere from ten years to forever. But what about after the recovery? I show artificial intelligence and intelligence amplification proceeding at what I suspect is a snail's pace. Sorry. I needed civilization to last long enough to hang a plot on it.

And of course it seems very unlikely that the Singularity would be a clean vanishing of the human race. (On the other hand, such a vanishing is the timelike analog of the silence we find all across the sky.)

From now to 2000 (and then 2001), the Jason Mudges will be coming out of the woodwork, their predictions steadily more clamorous. It's an ironic accident of the calendar that all this religious interest in transcendental events should be mixed with the objective evidence that we're falling into a technological singularity. So, the prediction: If we don't have that general war, then it's *you,* not Della and Wil, who will understand the Singularity in the only possible way—by living through it.

San Diego
1983–1985

271

ABOUT THE AUTHOR

Vernor Vinge is a three-time Hugo Award winner for the novels A Deepness in the Sky and A Fire Upon the Deep, and for the novella "Fast Times at Fairmont High." He is also a three-time Nebula finalist. He's one of the bestselling authors in the field and has been featured in such venues as Rolling Stone, Wired, The New York Times, Esquire, and on NPR's "Fresh Air."

Highly regarded by scientists, journalists, business leaders—as well as readers—for his concept of the technological singularity, Vinge has spoken all over the world on scientific subjects. For many years a mathematician and computer science professor at San Diego State University, he's now a full-time writer. He lives in San Diego, California.